Sara's Gift: Comes the Crow

Copyright © Carol Stucki, 2011. All rights reserved. No part of this book may be reproduced or transmitted in any form or by any means, electronic or mechanical, including photocopying, recording, or by any information storage and retrieval system, without permission in writing from the publisher.

Bedside Books
An imprint of American Book Publishing
5442 So. 900 East, #146
Salt Lake City, UT 84117-7204
www.american-book.com
Printed in the United States of America on acid-free paper.

Sara's Gift: Comes the Crow

Designed by Brandy Quick, design@american-book.com

Publisher's Note: *This is a work of fiction. Names, characters, places, and incidents either are the product of the author's imagination, or are used fictitiously, and any resemblance to actual persons, living or dead, events, or locales is entirely coincidental.*

ISBN-13: 978-1-58982-793-6
ISBN-10: 1-58982-793-7

Stucki, Carol, Sara's Gift: Comes the Crow

Special Sales

These books are available at special discounts for bulk purchases. Special editions, including personalized covers, excerpts of existing books, and corporate imprints, can be created in large quantities for special needs. For more information e-mail info@american-book.com.

Sara's Gift: Comes the Crow

By Carol Stucki

Dedication

For my dad, "Sonny" Thomas, here's to all your dreams of the Diamond E. Miss you!

Introduction

The big black stallion, lathered and sweating, paced and stomped, kicking the side of the stall and screaming. I had to do something for him, so I opened the stall door. He came at me and reared, striking out with his feet. I held out my hand and cried, "Wakiza!" He settled down and I walked toward him.

As I touched his neck, a jolt of pain ran up my arm, and I gasped but didn't pull away.

"Easy, boy. Easy, Wakiza." He snorted and I felt warmth rising in me. Pain ran up my arms and I closed my eyes and concentrated on the warmth. I slid my hands down Wakiza's side and the pain grew. Wakiza trembled as warmth flowed from my hands into him. He whined and snorted; I pushed more. He dropped to his knees and I let warmth turn to fire. It surged through me into Wakiza. He rolled to his side, but I didn't let up, moving my hand down his stomach and he trembled.

I knelt beside him. I could almost see a twist in my mind, a twist of his insides. I concentrated on turning the fire down to just warmth. I moved my hands over his stomach and pushed in. He whined, but I kept pushing. I felt sweat trickle down my back. I took a deep breath and pushed warmth through the twist until it straightened. Wakiza groaned with relief. I collapsed forward onto his stomach gasping for air. The stallion would be fine, but now they knew.

My name is Sara Stillsen, and I'm fourteen. I have a gift for healing animals, though I'm just discovering how to use this gift. I don't really know when it started; I just know that I can do something to help them. I don't consider what I do to be miraculous. I don't claim to know why I have this gift. The gift allows me to understand an animal's needs, of its pain, a way for me to help it, soothe it, and maybe heal it.

Only one person knows that I have this gift: Uncle Buck, my Cherokee mentor and medicine man who told me I'm to help bring balance between animals and people. Most don't know or they don't acknowledge my gift, at least not yet, and something like this isn't easy to hide when you live on a ranch in a small Texas town. Not even my family knows about my gift.

I guess this gift is why so many unusual things happen to me when it comes to animals.

When did I learn about my gift? I was six years old, and I found some newborn kittens in the barn one morning. One of them wasn't moving; the mother seemed to be pushing it away, so I picked it up and held it in my hands. My dad was calling me, but I knelt there by the grain bin holding the little, limp kitten. I heard my dad's steps behind me, and he leaned over my shoulder to see what I was doing.

"You found Old Tabs' new litter." I turned to show him the lifeless-looking kitten in my hands. He looked at me and gently said, "Dink, don't be sad; not all make it into this world for long."

It was then that I felt it was more than a lump of fluffy black and white fur in my hands. I felt a lump in my throat and tears began to well in my eyes. Warmth began to swell in my chest and spread down my arms into my hands. I saw Old Tabs look up at me, right in the eye. I heard a tiny voice in my head, *"You can help him."* I looked down at the kitten, held it up to my face, and blew on it. There was a tingling in my hands, and they got really warm. The kitten sneezed.

"Well I'll be," said Dad as he reached out a finger to stroke the kitten in my hands. Old Tabs mewed and I set the tiny kitten down in with his brothers and sisters, watching as Old Tabs licked at him as he fed.

"Alright, enough dawdling. We got chores." Dad grabbed my hand and pulled me up to my feet. He looked a little surprised. "Wow, your hands are warm."

That's the first time I actually recall feeling the warmth that way, and I've felt it many times since. My spirit guide, as the Cherokee call it, has helped me learn what I can do and sometimes what I can't do. My spirit guide, Foxy, is currently in physical form and is a wolf hybrid. She's with me everywhere I go, except school. If the school would let her, I'm sure she would be with me there too.

Foxy

I was nine when I got Foxy. Ironic name for a wolf-hybrid, but I didn't name her. Foxy, a three-quarters gray wolf, is part of the family. It took all of my persuasive powers to talk my dad into letting me get her. No, I don't really have persuasive gifts, but I'm a "daddy's girl" and he let me have her, probably against his best judgment.

We were visiting my mother's family in Oklahoma, and my cousin, Jarrett, had a breeding pair of hybrids that happened to have a litter while we were there.

It was lots of fun rolling around with them and running from them. They were mostly black, but Jarrett said they would change color as they grew. Their mother was mostly white with a little grey, and their father was darker and had a mark on his sides that looked like the Nike symbol. They called him Swoop because of it. Swoop was huge at about three feet tall at the shoulder. The mother, Tinka, was just about six inches shorter and slimmer.

The pups looked like huskies except their tails didn't curl over their backs and their eyes weren't blue. Well, all but one. They're born with blue eyes, but they change as they grow.

Christa, Jarrett's wife, is Cherokee Indian and her father, Buck Oowatie, often visited his daughter. I loved to listen to Uncle Buck's stories; most were legends of the Cherokee people, and they fascinated me.

One day when I was playing with the pups, Uncle Buck called to me, "Sara, come sit with me."

"You have a real affinity with animals," he said after I had come beside him.

"Yeah, sorta."

"No sorta about it. You have a gift." He looked down at me.

"How can you tell?" I stammered looking up at him, afraid until I saw warmth in his eyes.

"I have a keen, perceptive spirit," he said. "No one else knows about this gift?"

I shook my head and looked down at my feet. "I thought it was just my imagination," I mumbled.

"No, it is not your imagination. You have been chosen. You have a gift that should be used wisely."

"It's not like I can choose when to use it."

"You may not think you can, but you will learn."

One of the pups trotted over to us, leapt into my lap, put its paws on my shoulders, and licked my face.

"You need this one," said Uncle Buck, pointing to the pup.

"Are you crazy?" I gasped. "A wolf on a ranch? There's no way Dad would let me have one."

"All you have to do is ask." My eyes met Uncle Buck's.

"Are you telling me you see the future and I get a pup?" I asked hopefully.

Uncle Buck shook his head. "I am not a fortune-teller, but I do see that you need a guide, and this pup has been chosen to be your guide," he said, looking me in the eye. He didn't smile, so I knew he wasn't joking.

"How do you know it's this pup?" I challenged, squinting back at him.

"She came to you, didn't she?"

"Uh, yeah. So what?"

"She has blue eyes."

"Jarrett says they're all born with blue eyes," I said skeptically.

"Her litter mates' eyes have already changed. Hers haven't," he said triumphantly.

I stared at him for another minute, frowned, and then pushed the pup down and went to look at the rest of the pups' eyes. It took me a little while because they wouldn't keep still. They had either amber or red-brown eyes, all except one whose eyes were blue. I was still holding that last pup when the blue-eyed one yipped at me. I looked at her and set the other pup down. She jumped on me, pushing me on my back, and I laughed. I rolled and pushed her off me, got up and walked back to the steps, and sat down beside Uncle Buck. The pup followed me, Uncle

Buck grinning knowingly at us.

"So what now?" I asked. "How in the world am I gonna convince Dad to let me have her?"

"Just ask him."

"You don't know my dad!"

"I think I can tell his character. He will let you, if you ask."

"Just like that?"

"Yes, just like that."

"Yeah right!" I said, petting the pup for a little bit. "What's her name?"

"Ask her," he said motioning to the pup. I looked at him skeptically then back down at the pup. I decided to give it a try.

"So, pup, what's your name?" There was no answer; I didn't think there would be. I looked back up at Uncle Buck as if to say, "I told you so."

"You need to listen but not with your ears."

I frowned at him but thought what the heck. I took the pup's head in my hands and looked into her eyes. She looked expectantly back at me. "What shall I call you?"

I almost fell over when I heard the voice. It was tiny but distinctly female. *"I am a Kamali. You may call me Tsula."*

Uncle Buck laughed at me and I looked at him. "Did you hear that?"

"Yes, yes I did."

"What does Tsula mean? And what is a Kamali?" I asked looking at the pup that was patiently looking back at me.

"Tsula means 'fox' and she is a spirit guide."

"Fox, for a wolf? Isn't that like an oxymoron?" I asked. The pup sneezed. Uncle Buck roared with laughter. I laughed, too, but mostly at him.

"Tsula, or fox medicine, brings healing power," he said when he stopped laughing. He pointed at me, "You have this power. The wolf teaches balance, cooperation, and how to communicate. Tsula is both fox and wolf. She will be a powerful guide for you, Sara, so she is not an oxymoron."

"Why are you telling me this?" I asked, unsure of whether I believed him.

"Because you have potential and need to know. You will help bring balance between animals and people."

"Oh, okay," I said.

Then Uncle Buck said, "Now go see what the others are called."

I looked at him questioningly, then I put the pups one by one on my lap and looked into their eyes. I was astonished as they told me their names. Each "voice" I heard in my head was different. There were six pups, two female and four male. Hinto, Ama, Koko, Taima were male; Magena was the other female. I had already found out Tsula's name.

I walked back to sit by Uncle Buck. "What did you learn?" he asked me expectantly.

I pointed to each pup as I told him their names and he told me their meanings. "And this one," I said pushing the last, "is Taima."

"Thunder," said Uncle Buck with a nod.

"Hmm. Guess that fits," said Christa from behind us. I jumped and she laughed at me.

"You scared me!" I cried, turning around.

"Sorry, thought you heard me. So have you named them all for us?"

"Nope, they told us their names," said Uncle Buck matter of factly.

"Really?" asked Christa skeptically.

Uncle Buck nodded his head. "Yes. They speak if you listen."

I could tell Christa didn't quite believe her father; I wasn't sure I believed it myself.

Later that evening, as we relaxed on the front porch, Uncle Buck told us the story of how people were created.

"Before people existed, the creator spat on the ground, and used a stick to mix it into clay."

"Eeew!" said Karrie, Jarrett's youngest sibling. I just nodded, but everyone else chuckled.

"The creator then shaped a brown man and woman from clay, Grandfather Brown and Grandmother Brown. Next, he mixed white dust with the clay, forming a man and a woman so light you could see their veins through their skin. They were known as the 'blues.' Then he used yellow powder mixed with clay to form the ancestors of Asian people. Then he mixed in black dust to form black people. The creator took a liking to these clay images and blew his breath on them. When he blew his breath on the clay, he made them come alive. That was how humans were made."

He continued, looking directly at me. "Healing by breath and by moisture comes from the creator, along with the great spirit. But healers must be humble, kind, and selfless."

There were a few beats of silence before Christa said, "I haven't heard that tale since I was a little girl. Thank you, Father."

"You are quite welcome," said Uncle Buck, smiling at everyone. "Now, who can I bribe to get me some of that cake I saw in the kitchen?"

"Me!" both Karrie and I jumped to our feet. Everyone laughed and Christa said, "I better help." Christa, Mom, and Aunt Gina came to help. Karrie and I carried cake out to the porch and then ran back inside to get more.

As we entered the kitchen, I heard Aunt Gina speaking. "Wonder what Buck meant when he added that last part?"

"You never know with my father," said Christa, putting more cake on plates. A light shiver ran down my spine, but I didn't think anything more of it as we carried more cake out.

Soon everyone had a plate and was eating. That's when I broached the subject of getting a pup. "Dad?" I waited for him to look at me. "Jarrett here says the pups are ready to leave their mother, and I was hoping I could have one."

"What?" asked Dad, totally surprised. My brothers snickered and ducked their heads. "What on earth would you want a wolf pup for?"

"Well, they're so cute and friendly. They're very smart, and they rarely bark." My mind raced down the list of things I wanted to say to convince him.

"No! No way will we have a wolf on ranch land!" said Dad, setting his jaw.

"But Dad!" I pleaded. "I'll keep her close to the house and teach her not to hurt any animals. Jarrett says as long as they aren't hungry a wolf won't hunt."

"Don't go bringing me into this," said Jarrett defensively.

"Wolves are born with instincts to hunt and that can't be changed," said Dad, trying to stand firm. Then he stopped for a minute. "What do you mean her?" He looked at me. "Oh no, you already found the one you want!"

"Yes, sir," I said meekly. "Her name is Tsula."

"Fox! That's a heck of a name for a wolf," laughed Christa.

"Glad you remember some of the language." Uncle Buck smiled at his daughter.

"I remember more than you think, old man." She smiled. "Like how you named the pups."

"Least I could do," said Uncle Buck. He turned to Dad, "Sonny, you gonna let Sara have one or not?"

Dad shook his head. "This just isn't fair. The pup will take off some night and get shot because she's chasing some neighbors' livestock. Then I'll have to answer for it."

"But Uncle Charlie borders most of our property. He wouldn't shoot any animal he knows is ours," said my brother, Grant, trying to help me.

"Not you too!" said Dad, shaking his head.

"No one even runs livestock to the south of us anymore," said Tad, my other brother, also taking up the cause.

"Great! Now I'm out numbered!" Dad leaned back in his chair. "Clive, surely you can understand what they're asking?" Dad looked at Grandpa for help.

"I see your side, but I also don't see what harm one pup can get into, especially if it's raised with working dogs," said Grandpa, trying to be diplomatic. He let a smile flash across his face, which everyone noticed.

Dad dropped his head in defeat. "Dang it!" he sighed. "At least let me take a look at this beast before I get saddled with it!"

"Yeah!" I shouted and jumped up to give Dad a hug. I looked over his shoulder at Uncle Buck and he winked at me.

We went to the backyard to look at the pups. I pointed out each and named them in Cherokee and English. I called Tsula over and picked her up. "See Dad isn't she great!"

"Yeah, guess she is," he said with a smile, rubbing her head. "How come her eyes are still blue? Thought they turned after they got older."

"You've been listening to my breeding talks," said Jarrett. "Must be a throw back from her Husky blood."

"Well that may make it easier for me to explain to our neighbors that she isn't all wolf and not a threat to their livestock," said Dad.

"Might work!" said Grandpa.

"We'll just spoil her, and she won't ever wanna leave," said Mom.

"Let's go back inside," said Christa. "The bugs are starting to eat me out here."

Most of the family made their way inside; Karrie and I stayed to play with the pups. Uncle Buck tapped Karrie on the shoulder. "Will you get an old man a glass of water?"

Karrie leapt to her feet. "Sure thing."

"I didn't get a chance to ask what I need a spirit guide for," I said, looking up at Uncle Buck.

"I didn't get a chance to tell you." He smiled at me. "You will need a guide to help you learn how and when to use your gift. Each animal has its own medicine, which is unique as gifted by the Great Spirit. The wolf is the teacher of medicine, or healing in your case. Tsula will teach you to have balance in your life. You will learn to communicate among many creatures and humans. She will teach you who you are, to have confidence and strength. She will teach you to avoid fighting but to stand your ground when it is right."

"What else do you know about animal powers?"

"We call them totems. I know Tad is a bear; he is strong and protective of family. Grant's totem is the hawk, and he represents union with the Great Spirit and supports growth. You have been blessed that they are near you and will help you as you grow in your gifts and power to heal. Your totem is the black fox; your spirit name is Inola. This totem has strong medicine and healing. Foxes are quick thinkers and very instinctive. You have only a small portion of your power to heal; you will come into more powers the summer you turn fifteen."

A chill ran up my spine at his last remark and I stared at him. The screen door slapped, and Karrie came toward us holding a glass of water. I nodded my head at him and smiled weakly. Then I realized what he just said, looked up at him, and started to speak, but he nodded his head toward Karrie. I got the distinct feeling she wasn't to know about our conversation, so I kept my mouth shut.

Christa was at the door. "Hey you guys, come inside. We're gonna play Nerts!" Tsula yipped at me as Uncle Buck and I headed toward the house. "I'm just going inside. I'll see ya in the morning." I knelt down and looked her in the face, "Don't worry we'll have many years together." She licked my face then ran off to play.

On the way home two days later, we were packed into the Suburban, Tsula and I in the third-row seat. Grant and Tad were in the second row. Grant turned to me, "You still gonna call her Tsula?"

"Yeah, why?"

"If you called her Fox, or let's say Foxy, because it's more girly," he said slyly, "someone might not think she was a wolf but maybe just a dog."

"I like that!" said Dad, looking at me in the rearview mirror.

I looked at Tsula, "Should we call you Foxy?" She gave a growl, which I took to be a yes. "Okay, Foxy it is!"

Joey and Super

Late each spring, we need to brand our cows, which requires separating the calves from their mothers. A good working dog is needed for this task, and we have an Australian shepherd named Joey.

During the branding time, we herd cattle into the arena, and the riders take turns cutting, or moving, the calves away from their mothers and roping them. Another rider keeps the mother back while we brand the calf. Cows can be very protective and aggressive, especially when a calf bawls. One morning, we'd been working for about three hours. Grant was on Opossum, his favorite mare, and Tad was on Super, his gelding. Dad would throw the calf and I'd brand it. Foxy was on strict orders to stay in the barn, as she made the cows nervous.

It was hot, smelly work, and no one gets used to burning cow hair and flesh. I flipped my blonde ponytail over my shoulder and wiped sweat off my face as I waited for the next calf. Grant roped this big calf and was dragging it over where Dad and I were working. The cow didn't like being separated from her calf and charged Tad with her head down like she was going to gore him. Tad yelled and we saw him on Super trying to get out of the way. Joey ran to help and nipped at the cow's heels. The cow kicked and Joey jumped out of harm's way.

As the cow charged Tad again, he smacked her with his rope. This only made the cow mad as she charged him again. Joey once again ran in to help by nipping at the cow's heel. When the cow kicked, she caught Joey's right front leg with her hoof. We watched Joey fly several feet into the air. I dropped the brand I was holding and ran towards Joey; It seemed like it took me forever to reach him.

I dropped to my knees by his side; putting my hand on his shoulder, felt a jolt of pain run up my arm. It knocked the breath out of me, and I almost fell over on him. I sucked in air as Foxy appeared at my side. I felt Joey's pain and I knew how to deal with it. I closed my eyes and concentrated on warmth that bloomed in my chest, moving my hands to Joey's side as he whimpered. The warmth spread from my center down my arms, pushing back the pain and spreading into Joey. He whimpered again and I opened my eyes as he lifted his head to look at me. Relief began to fill his eyes as he lay his head back down with a sigh. Dad hit his knees beside me, and I looked up into his worried face. "Is he alright?"

"I think his leg's broken," I said.

"Okay, let's take a look." He gently pushed me back so he could examine Joey. Dad slid one hand under Joey's injured leg and ran the other down its length. "Yep, it's broken, both bones I'd say. Better get him over to Doc Henderson's." He rocked back on his heels. "Let's put a splint on so he doesn't hurt himself more. One of those foreleg shipping boots might work. Keep him quiet I'll be right back."

When my dad mentioned them, a picture flashed in my head of the shipping boots hanging on the wall, but I didn't think anything of it.

I looked down at Joey and felt his pain when I ran my hand over his shoulder. He whimpered. "It'll be alright. We'll get you over to Doc's and he'll fix you up."

I felt that warm feeling again spreading down my arms. There was a tingling in my hand, and I moved my hand down Joey's leg until it rested just over the break. He whimpered slightly as I felt warmth shoot out of my hand into his leg. I closed my eyes and let it flow.

I was still in that position when Dad yelled from the barn door, "Have you seen those shipping boots?"

I looked up and yelled back, "They're hanging behind the tack room door!" Dad nodded and went back inside.

The next thing I knew, Dad knelt down beside me, dropping supplies on the ground between us. He carefully wrapped Joey's leg with an ACE bandage and was just fastening the horse-shipping boot over it when Tad yelled and we looked up.

Tad had a rope around the old, angry cow's head, and she was chasing him and Super. It was almost comical watching them run. The cow slid to a sudden stop when she passed by her calf. However, Tad and Super didn't stop, and the rope around her horns was attached to Tad's saddle horn. As the rope snapped tight, Super was caught midstride and stumbled to his knees. Tad would have gone right over his head if it weren't for the rope holding his leg down onto the saddle. He got a whiplashing that threw his hat right off his head.

Super scrambled to his feet. Grant, who was still holding the calf by his rope, let it drop and rushed to get his horse between the cow and Tad, afraid the cow would turn on Tad. But she was too concerned about getting to her calf. The calf, now free, ran over to its mom, bawling as it trotted to her.

Dad jumped to his feet and called out to Tad. "You alright?" Tad started to shake his head, then that old cow, still attached to Tad and Super, tugged at her end of the rope; Tad winced at the sudden jerk. Super huffed in a horse version of a wince and took a few steps toward the cow to give the rope some slack.

Grant moved beside Tad and untied the rope from Tad's saddle horn. "Let's get this off before she drags you around more."

Tad rubbed his leg. "Thanks."

He winced as he tried turning his head slowly as he dismounted. Super's head was drooping, and Tad was concerned what that jolt had done to his horse.

Dad looked down at me as I gathered Joey in my arms. "Go help with Super; I can get Joey to the truck," I told my dad, seeing the look of concern on his face.

Dad walked over to Tad and Super. The horse's eyes were getting wider and his nostrils were flaring; he seemed to be struggling to breathe. Tad was unbuckling the cinch to get the saddle off, and Dad caught Tad as he fell back when Super went to his knees.

They scrambled to Super's side. I still had Joey in my arms as I ran to them. Grant ran up, too. Super groaned and lifted his head. Tad pushed Super's head back down as Dad pulled the cinch loose. When the cinch came free, Super groaned again.

Dad tossed off his hat and laid his head against Super's side to listen; we held our breath. When Dad lifted his head, he looked concerned. "I don't think he punctured a lung, but he did get the wind knocked out of him. Mighta cracked a rib or something. Let's get this saddle out from under Super."

The three of them got the saddle off, but Super groaned again. Dad looked up, "Tad stay with Super and keep him down. Let him catch his breath for a minute. Grant come with me and let's see get that rope off that cow and her calf and let the herd out. We've done enough for today."

I laid Joey down beside us and moved by Super's neck. I put my hands on him, and a warm surge along with tingling rushed into him. Foxy nudged my shoulder; I glanced at her over my shoulder and nodded. I could feel Super's pain, but I could also feel it ebbing away. His breathing seemed to be getting easier, and his eyes were getting heavy like he might fall asleep. I leaned down to whisper in his ear. "Super, you're gonna be fine. Just got the wind knocked out of you. I'm sure it will help if you got up." He lifted his head slightly rolled his eye to look at me and snorted.

"What did you say to him?" asked Tad as he looked at me with wonder.

I felt Super begin to gather himself, and he heaved himself over so he was on his belly. Tad and I stood up to get out of the horse's way. Everyone turned to look at us, as Super lurched to his feet. He stood there for a few minutes with his head down, taking slow breaths.

Dad came over, put his hand on Super's chest, and patted him. He smiled as he moved to Super's side and poked at his ribs. Super flattened his ears when Dad touched the spots where the cinch had been. "I think he just bruised his ribs and got the breath knocked out of him. I'd put him up for the night and see how he does in the morning. Might not be able to ride him for a week or two, but I think he'll be fine," my dad said as he straightened up. Tad was the most relieved to hear this and finally smiled.

Tad insisted on leading Super into his stall, although I think he was in more pain now than his horse. They both moved slowly, and I think Super moved slow for Tad. Dad walked along behind watching how Super moved but seemed satisfied.

After Tad and Grant got Super into his stall, Dad turned to me. "Now let's go take Joey to Doc's."

Grant and Tad stayed with Super as Dad and I rode up to the house. Mom greeted us on the walk, her hands on her hips, as she waited for us to get close enough to tell her what was happening. Dad explained what happened and that we were taking Joey to the clinic. He kissed Mom and got back in the truck.

When we got to the clinic, Wendy, the new vet, and Doc met us at the door. Dad carried Joey to the exam room as he explained what had happened.

Doc smiled at the foreleg shipping boot. "Would never have thought to use one of these, Sonny."

Once Wendy removed the wrap, she carefully ran her fingers down each side of Joey's leg. He whimpered when she reached the break. She nodded her head. "Yep, broke both bones, but I'd have bet this break was a few days old. Bones feel like they're starting to knit."

Doc and Dad both looked at her in disbelief. "They were sticking out but not through the skin when Sara and I put the splint on him," said Dad with a frown.

"Here let me take a look," said Doc. He ran his fingers down Joey's leg. "Wendy's right. This feels like a set bone that's started to heal." He shook his head. "I'd like to take an x-ray just to be sure. That's if you don't mind Sonny."

Dad shrugged. "No problem."

Joey laid still for the x-ray. Doc and Wendy took their time reviewing the x-ray, but when they came back, they were smiling. "The leg is perfectly set and already knitting," said Doc, shaking his head. "I'll leave ya'll in good hands. I've a few other patients to check on."

Wendy gathered what she needed for the cast. She worked quickly and before I knew it, the cast was done. "Now it needs to dry for a little while," said Wendy with a smile. Then she left to wash up.

While waiting for Joey's cast to set, I walked toward the kennels at the back. There were only a few occupied. As I walked, I was attracted to a huge, gray, wiry-haired dog. He was lying on his bed with his tongue lolling out and a glazed look on his face. Wendy spotted me staring at the dog. "Don't get too close; he's got a nasty temperament. Being sick isn't setting well with him, but then again, he was kinda mean when he was healthy."

It was hard to believe he was bad because he looked pitiful lying there. "What's wrong with him?"

"He has heartworms and he's in the later stages," replied Wendy with a downtrodden look. "If we had gotten to him sooner, we might have done something for him. As it is, he might not live much longer. His heart is infested and even surgery won't help now."

I started to get that warm feeling in my chest as I looked at the dog through the bars. He looked up at me, and I could see a spark in his eyes. "What kinda dog is he?" I felt those familiar tingles running down my arms into in my hands as I looked at the poor guy.

"He's an Irish Wolfhound." Wendy came over to where I knelt. He lifted his head and growled a little at her. "See what I mean about nasty temperament?" She turned towards the exam rooms but turned back to watch me as I reached my hand into the cage to pet his head. He wagged his tail a little and licked his lips.

"There, there poor guy," I said, my voice a croon. "What's his name?"

"Wolfgang," she said, astonished.

I felt warmth gathering in my chest. As I petted him, warmth radiated through my chest and down my arm. He leaned into my hand, and as I held his head, warmth ran into him through my fingers. The warmth trickled to a stop, and he lifted his head to lick my arm.

I heard Doc say from a few feet behind me, "Well, I'll be. That dog won't let anyone hardly touch him, and here you are like you were old friends." Doc walked over and Wolfgang lifted his head and looked back at them then laid his head on the bedding and gave a big sigh.

"Poor fella," said Wendy, "He's really sick. That medicine isn't doing him much good."

"I know. It's a shame we didn't get him in here sooner," said Doc. "I called Mr. C this morning and told him the bad news."

He turned to Wendy. "He said he couldn't come by until morning and wanted us to wait until he gets here before we put him to sleep." He looked down, his chin almost on his chest, and heaved a big sigh, much like Wolfgang did earlier, only Doc's sigh was full of sadness. He turned and walked down the hall to his office. His shoulders were hunched as he went.

I was still petting Wolfgang when Dad called to me. He saw me and came to see what I was doing.

"Who's this?" asked Dad, pointing at Wolfgang. Before I could answer, he said, "I recognize him now. This is Mr. C's dog. He must be real sick. Last time I saw him, he had me and Grant trapped in our truck waiting for Jack to call him off."

"He has heartworms, and Doc says he's going to put him to sleep." I felt tears begin to sting my eyes and felt Dad's hand on my shoulder as he squeezed it briefly.

I sat there petting Wolfgang for a minute. Wendy walked up. "Joey's ready. Come in here and I'll tell ya what to do for him."

We followed Wendy into the exam room. "Here's Joey's pain meds."

She handed me a small white pouch of pills. "He can have one every eight hours if he needs them. Might wanna give him one for tonight whether he looks like he's in pain or not so everyone can get a good night's sleep."

Doc came in, apparently happier than he had been a few minutes before. "We all fixed up now?"

"Looks like we're gonna be just fine." Dad gestured toward Joey.

"Dink, you ready?"

"Yes, sir," I replied. He scooped up Joey in his arms and we headed out. Doc walked with us and held the door. I turned to him, "Can I come by in the morning to see Wolfgang one more time?"

"Sure, come by about seven when we feed. I'm sure Mr. C won't be here before eight," he replied with a sad look on his face.

"Thanks, I'll be here."

Doc waved as we drove off. "You really wanna come back in the morning just to see that dog?" asked Dad.

"I really like him and don't want him to think he's forgotten. It's the least I can do before he gets put down," I said, looking out the side window.

"If that's what you think you gotta do," said Dad with a shake of his head. Neither of us said anything else on the ride home.

Mom held the door for us as Dad carried Joey in. She had laid a cushion on the floor by the fireplace. "Just put him down there," she said, pointing to the cushion.

Dad gently laid Joey down, and the dog licked his hand. "Gonna be just fine fella," said Dad. Foxy came and laid down right beside him.

"You should see this cool dog Doc has at his clinic. It's an Irish wolfhound, and its name is Wolfgang!" I went into the kitchen looking for something to drink.

"Isn't that Mr. C's dog?" asked Grant from the bar in the kitchen.

"Yeah, that's what they said."

"If it is, you better stay clear of him. He'll take a bite out of you if you get too close. He's one mean bugger," said Grant with a grin.

"He was perfectly nice to me," I said. "When did you meet him?" I asked as I sat down next to Grant.

"I went with Dad a few weeks back to the Big C. That thing wouldn't let us out of the truck until Jack came and called him off. That dog even growled at Jack. I wouldn't wanna be Doc and have to treat that thing," said Grant.

Just to poke fun I said, "That vicious dog let me pet him."

Grant looked at me like I was lying. "No way!"

"You better believe it. I saw it with my own eyes. He was putty in her hands." Dad turned and winked at me as he backed up my story.

I turned back to Grant, "Told ya so!"

He sighed. "I should know better by now that there isn't an animal you can't get near. Figures the meanest, most terrifying dog that is used to hunt cougars would be like a puppy for you."

"What are ya'll talking about?" asked Mom as she came into the kitchen and began dinner.

Dad explained the trip to the Big C where he and Grant had met up with Wolfgang and how that same dog was now at Doc's clinic. "I walked in the doors of the clinic to see the same beast. Sara here was petting the poor thing."

"He's just a big softy," I said.

"Big is right," said Grant. "His back comes at least to my hip, but softy is not a word I'd use to describe him."

"What does Mr. C need a dog like that for?" asked Mom. "Doesn't he have some good coon dogs already?"

"Yeah he has plenty of dogs for hunting coons and such, but this dog is supposed to be able to hunt cougars!" said Grant with a gleam in his eye.

"There've been fresh kills with cougar tracks over at the Gartner place, and Mr. C is getting a posse together to go hunt the culprit before it gets any more livestock," said Dad, sitting down at the bar.

"Won't the coon hounds track just as well?" asked Mom.

"Yeah, but they get torn up with a big cat like that. A wolfhound can stand his ground," explained Grant.

"They may have to do without him," I said, thinking of Wolfgang as Foxy came over put her head on my lap and I reached down to pet her. "He was really sick when we saw him. Doc says they're gonna put him to sleep in the morning after Mr. C gets a last good-bye. I'm gonna go over in the morning to say good-bye, too." There was silence for a few beats. "I'll just go wash up for dinner." I walked out of the kitchen, Foxy trailing behind.

I walked past Tad's room and saw he was lying across his bed with an ice pack on his neck. I stuck my head in his door. "Hey, how's Joey?"

"Fine," I crossed to stand next to his bed. I looked down at him. "How're you doing?"

"I'll live." He grimaced as he sat up and swung his legs over the side of his bed.

"You don't look so good."

He chuckled. "You should see the truck that ran over me."

"At least your wit isn't injured," I said and turned toward the door. "How's Super?"

"He feels better than I do." I could hear the gratitude in his voice as he said, "I'm so glad he got up!"

I nodded in agreement. "I think we're all grateful you both weren't hurt more. I hope Dad sells that old cow. She's always been hard to deal with." Tad tried to nod his head in agreement but winced at the movement. I laughed. "You sure you're alright?"

"I'll live. I'll just suffer like a man!" he replied with a smirk.

We both laughed. "Yeah right! Suffer, just not too loudly!" I walked out of his room and into my own.

The next morning I was up bright and early to go see Wolfgang before they put him to sleep. He was all I could think of all night, even in my dreams. I kept seeing him repeatedly running through a field and up the canyon side chasing something. I could hear other dogs baying but never saw them. I could see Wolfgang as he stopped on the top of a ridge and he turned, looking back toward those following him with his big tongue hanging out. He looked so healthy and lithe. I woke up and saw Foxy looking at me. "I think Wolfgang's gonna be better today." Foxy gave me a "yahwool," which I took for a yes. I hoped it wasn't just a dream.

I dressed hurriedly and helped with breakfast. Tad was still asleep, so we ate without him. Dad asked warily, "You still wanna go see that dog?"

"Yes, sir," I replied. "He needs a friend. I wouldn't want Joey or Foxy to be there all alone."

"I'll take you over so I can update Doc on Super," he said not looking up from his plate of eggs and bacon.

"Did he take a turn for the worse last night?" I asked my voice rising in concern.

"No, no, he's just fine. He was walking around this morning like nothing was wrong. He's sore to the touch but doing well," said Dad with a smug smile before he stuffed more food in his mouth.

"You sound almost disappointed," Mom observed.

"Nope, just glad he's alright," said Dad talking around his food.

"I'm glad, too," said Grant. "We were all scared when he went down."

"Has anyone looked in on Tad?" asked Dad looking around at us.

"He was snoring when I passed his door," I said reaching for the jelly.

"He could use some extra sleep," said Mom.

"Yeah, he'll play this for all it's worth," said Grant with a snort. "I'll be doing his chores for a week at least."

"It'll be pay back for that time when you sprained your knee roping last spring," said Mom with a knowing look at Grant.

"Yeah, you're right," moaned Grant.

We finished up breakfast and I left with Dad to go to Doc's. As we pulled up, Doc came out front to greet us. "Good morning! Glad you came. I've got something to show you, Sara."

"What? What's wrong?" I asked, immediately thinking of Wolfgang as my stomach fell to my feet. Then I saw the twinkle in Doc's eye. "He's better, isn't he?" I asked getting excited.

"Just come see," said Doc with a chuckle.

We walked inside and halfway down the hall I could see Wolfgang standing up in his kennel. He was wagging his tail, and he even gave a low "woof" of greeting. I trotted toward him and he licked my face as I knelt at his door. "You are better!"

"He was like this when I came in this morning. He even ate some food, which he hasn't done in two days," said Doc crossing his arms and watching us with a smile on his face. "Darnedest thing. I thought we would have to put him down."

"I'm so glad you don't!" I said with a big smile. Wolfgang gave another little "woof" and looked at the three of us like he was waiting for something. He barked at me and I got the feeling he wanted to get out of the cage. "Can I take him for a short walk?" I asked letting Wolfgang lick my hand through the cage bars once more.

"Yeah, why don't you do that," said Doc handing me a leash.

I clipped the leash on Wolfgang's collar and led him from his cage. He was very polite as he waited for me to get the door. Doc and Dad just looked at each other as I walked out front.

We were gone for about ten minutes. I didn't wanna wear him out when he'd been so sick just yesterday. When we walked back in and down the hall, we passed by an exam room where Wendy was working. "Can you bring Wolfgang in here?" she called out to me.

As we went into the room, Wendy said, "He needs his medicine and since you have a golden touch, you can help me give it to him. He doesn't like it much and I usually have to muzzle him, which I hate to do."

"Okay," I said, a little surprised. Wendy picked up a syringe and some pills. Wolfgang stood there while Wendy injected him.

She handed me pills and a hot dog. "Make him do some tricks and give him these." I tore the hot dog into little pieces and put pills into two of them. I got Wolfgang's attention with the first then asked him to sit, lie down, shake hands, and turn around, rewarding each with a piece of hot dog. When Dad and Doc came in to watch, I told him to speak and he did, then I asked him to lie down once more.

"She must smell better than we do," Doc said as he smiled at Wendy and me. Doc asked me to get Wolfgang on the table. Doc listened to his chest. With a frown, he asked Wendy to listen.

She shook her head. "What's up?" I asked.

"Seems like his heartworms are gone," he said.

"That's good news, isn't it?" I asked.

They both smiled and Doc said, "Yes, it's excellent considering he was in real bad shape when he got here two days ago."

"I'm gonna get an ultrasound of his chest to see," said Wendy. She turned to me. "Will you help me with this? I don't think he'll lie still for me."

"Sure." I shrugged and walked with Wolfgang, following Wendy to another exam room.

After she was done with the ultrasound, Wendy looked up at me. "You can put him back in his kennel now."

I took my time putting Wolfgang back in his kennel, as I felt he didn't really wanna go back in that cage, but he went in calmly and turned to lick my hand as I closed his door. "Don't be sad. You're gonna be just fine now. You should be able to go home, too. I'll come visit ya, big guy," I told him then turned to walk down to the office where Dad was.

I was approaching the door of Doc's office where I could hear Wendy, Doc, and Dad talking.

"I can't think of another explanation. I've never seen anything like this," said Doc.

I stopped in the hallway and listened. My stomach fell to the floor because I knew they were talking about me.

"That dog was almost blind and could hardly walk without stopping to take a breath every few steps because of his heart. I already told Mr. C that he should come say good-bye today, as he would just continue to suffer unless we put him down."

"I don't know what you're getting at, Ed, and I'm not sure I like what you are implying," said Dad. "Why can't the dog just have gotten better?" Doc started to speak but Dad interrupted, "No, I've heard more than enough." I heard his footsteps as he came out of the office. Dad didn't look pleased, but he smiled at me. "Let's go and leave Doc to his work."

"Bring Joey by in two weeks and we'll check to see how he's healing," said Wendy as we walked out.

We drove home in silence. I could tell Dad didn't wanna talk. He usually didn't like to talk about things that made him uncomfortable, and I knew this made me uncomfortable. I didn't even know myself what I could do or how I did it. So I was perfectly happy to keep quiet.

Candy the Dog

My family was at the Leakey Rodeo, I was unsaddling my horse, May Day, after my last event when my two younger cousins, Nellie and Tim, and their dog, Candy, came by the trailer to see me. I knew they were approaching because Foxy "rawwyled" a warning from the roof of the truck. She likes to be up on top where she can keep an eye on things. Joey "woofed" from his vantage point on the toolbox in the back of the truck. Candy sped by me and jumped into the back of the truck with Joey.

Most dogs aren't on leashes around the rodeo, as they're trained working dogs and keep close to their owners' trucks and trailers. Candy was always near Nellie no matter where she went. So it wasn't surprising to see them together. I looked around May Day to see Nellie and Tim walking toward me. "Hello! Nice to see you two," I said.

"Hey, great ride!" said Nellie.

"We didn't do too bad," I replied, shoving my saddle into the tack area of the trailer.

"I would say second place is pretty good," said Tim leaning against the truck. "Cathy Coulter is really miffed. Said if her horse hadn't been traveling all day she would've won the whole thing."

"She may be right," I said. "As much as her daddy paid for that ex-race horse, she should win all the rodeos."

"I love it when us 'plain old ranch folk' seem to surpass the creamy upper crust of society!" said Nellie in a southern belle accent as we laughed.

"When are you gonna start riding in these things?" I asked Nellie and Tim.

"Dad says Tim can next year," said Nellie.

"What are you gonna ride first?" I asked Tim.

"Think I'll just do calf roping," said Tim. "Grant's been helping me and I'm getting better. Of course I won't catch up to either Grant or Tad for years."

"You will sooner than you think." I said brushing May Day. "We come from good stock. Besides, I've never heard of a Stillsen who couldn't rope anything that walked."

"Yeah that's for sure," said Leena, who had just walked up with Tesa. Leena Baker and Tesa Martin are my two best friends. "You can't walk across a parking lot anymore without Tad or Grant throwing a loop at you."

"Can't blame them for wanting to catch a good filly," said Tim blushing and kicking the ground with his boot toe.

"Forward, aren't we?" I asked Tim winking at Leena, whom I knew he had a crush on.

Joey barked and I looked up to see Matt and Mitch, Tesa's older brothers, and Tad coming toward us with a guy I didn't recognize. Matt is a year older than Mitch, they're both tall, blonde, and full of mischief. Of course, my six-foot, dark-haired, blue-eyed brothers were attractive, too.

Joey barked more as a strange dog came up to the truck. "Shut it," commanded Tad sternly. Candy jumped out of the truck and Joey followed. The two stood there, sniffing at the third dog. Foxy, ignoring them, laid her head back down.

"So who's this?" I said gesturing at the very good-looking stranger. He was tall and broad shouldered, with sandy blonde hair, vivid blue eyes, and a very nice smile that made my heart skip a beat when he looked at me.

"I'm JD," he said, tipping his hat at us girls. "Nice riding tonight," he said to me. Tesa smiled, turned toward me with her back to the boys, and raised her eyebrows with a look that said she appreciated JD's looks as well.

"Thanks. Oh, this is Tesa and Leena," I said with a big smile spreading across my face as I noticed JD only glanced at them.

"Sara, have you seen my new rope?" asked Tad as he rummaged through the back of the truck.

I closed my eyes for a second and thought. I got a picture of it in my head. "It's over here in the tack compartment." I opened my eyes to see JD looking at me.

He smiled at me and asked, "Ya'll going to the dance tonight?"

"I'll be there," said Tesa stepping forward to get his attention.

"So will I," said Leena "Wouldn't miss a chance to hear that new band everyone is talking about."

"Found it!" said Tad. "Let's go find some room to practice." The boys turned to walk away when all heck broke loose.

The sniffing dogs began growling and maneuvering around each other until they were next to May Day and me. The third dog nipped at Candy and chased her under May Day's feet. There was another growl and bark. Then Nellie was yelling for Candy, Tad was yelling at Joey, and I was trying to get the dogs away from May Day. May Day laid his ears back, stamped his feet, and then kicked out. There was a loud yelp as Candy flew through the air and landed on her side with a thud. The third dog got a kick, but he ran off yelping and JD ran after him.

"Enough!" I yelled at May Day, jerking on his lead rope, and he settled down immediately with a snort. Nellie screamed as she knelt beside Candy. I ran over to them and saw Candy's head was bleeding and she was having some kind of spasm. Tad and Matt were right there next to us as soon as my knees hit the ground.

"Here, let me take a look," I said, pushing Nellie out of the way. Tesa grabbed Nellie by the shoulders and pulled her back. Foxy was there by my side and whined as she looked at Candy.

"What should we do?" asked Tad.

"Go find Dr. Pierce," I said. "I saw her over by the refreshment stand earlier." Tad took off with Tim.

I leaned over, gingerly touching Candy's head where it was bleeding. I could feel an indentation in her skull. A feeling of dread followed by a bloom of warmth ran across my chest and down my hand. I ran my hand down Candy's side to see whether she was hurt anywhere else, but I couldn't feel any pain other than from her head. "Get me a towel," I said to no one in particular, but I heard feet behind me moving off.

I was pressing lightly on Candy's head wound when I felt tingling sparks going from my hand into her. A towel was thrust over my shoulder; I grabbed it and pressed it against Candy's head. I looked up into Nellie's tear streaked face. "Is she dead?" asked Nellie in a sob.

"She's alive," I said.

"See, she's still breathing," said Mitch, leaning over us. I looked up at Nellie; she nodded her head at me and turned into Tesa sobbing.

I looked down at Candy, closed my eyes, and willed warmth to flow out of me and into her. It seemed like a long time before I heard running feet coming toward us and Matt say, "Tad's coming and I think he has Wendy with him."

Wendy, Doc Henderson's partner, knelt opposite me. "Let me have a look," she said. I lifted the towel as she bent closer. She ran her hand over the wound, and I heard her low intake of breath. "I need my bag," she said rising to her feet. "Keep the towel on the wound," she turned and took off at a run.

"I'll go with her in case she needs help carrying things," said Mitch, running after her.

I felt warmth again flowing through me as I pressed the towel on Candy's head. No one said a word as we waited. I felt Foxy leaning on my side and after a minute, I felt the warmth slowing. Candy whimpered softly. "She's still with us!" I looked up at Nellie, who smiled but sobbed even more at the news.

Candy struggled against my hands, and Tim was beside me helping push her back down. "Here, let me hold her."

I felt her start to shiver, so I scooped her up, rocked back on my heels, then sat on the ground. Foxy licked Candy's face a few times and Candy stopped shivering. As I wiped at Candy's head, I noticed blood was trickling down her ear onto my shirt. I wiped at the blood and let warmth flow again. After a minute, the bleeding stopped. I was rocking Candy, crooning something to comfort her, when she started licking my face. "Yes, you're gonna be alright. Just got a nasty kick."

Nellie knelt beside me to pet Candy. I looked up to see a ring of smiling, relieved faces around me. Dad and Wendy walked up followed by Uncle Charlie, Nellie, and Tim's dad. Wendy pushed through the crowd, and I looked up into her astonished face as she saw Candy licking at Nellie and me. Foxy slipped away and resumed her perch.

"Wow," said Wendy. "She was out cold, now she seems almost okay."

I could hear the bewilderment in her voice. "She's got a nasty cut here that'll need some stitches." I leaned forward so Wendy could see the jagged cut that was still oozing a little. You could see the bone through the cut.

"Here, let me take her from you," said Uncle Charlie as he bent down and picked up Candy.

"Lay her over here on the truck hood. That way Wendy can work without too much dirt," said Dad, hurrying to wipe off the truck hood.

Uncle Charlie laid Candy on the hood, and Wendy opened her bag and started pulling stuff out. She cleaned Candy's cut then stitched her up. After smearing some antibacterial salve across the stitches, she pronounced, "There, she's good to go! She might be a little woozy for a while. Just keep her quiet tonight. Keep the wound clean and dry as you can." She looked at Uncle Charlie and continued, "I'm sure you can remove the stitches yourself in about ten days. Call me if you think she's acting strangely, as she might still have a concussion."

"Thank you so much, Wendy." Uncle Charlie said. "Let me know what I owe for your services."

"I'll just send you a bill," said Wendy as she packed up her stuff.

"Nellie, Tim, let's get Candy home," Uncle Charlie said. "Thank you again, Wendy. I'm really glad you were here this evening." He gathered up Candy and the three of them walked off.

Dad was wiping off the hood of the truck again when he said to Wendy, "You by chance sticking around for the barbeque and dance? Would be nice to introduce you around some more." Doc Henderson had just hired Wendy, and she was fairly new to the canyon area.

"I'd like that. Thank you, Mr. Stillsen," replied Wendy.

"Please, call me Sonny," said Dad, handing her bag to her.

"Thanks, Sonny. I'll see ya at the barbeque after I clean up a little," said Wendy as she turned to go.

Foxy gave a warning, Joey woofed, and we looked up to see JD coming back toward us. "Hey, JD. What happened?" asked Tad.

JD had his hands in his pockets and a guilty look on his face. "The fuss scared Travis, my dog, and he took off. I had to go see to him, but he's all right. I told him to stay with the truck." He looked at Dad, "I apologize for the fuss. I think my dog started the trouble."

"Well, son," said Dad, "that's real nice of you. You might wanna say something to Charlie or Nellie if you get the chance. It was their dog that got hurt." He saw the look on JD's face and quickly added, "But don't worry, it was my horse that did the actual damage. Charlie isn't one to try to fix blame."

"I'll keep Travis on a tight rein from now on," said JD with a duck of his head.

He turned to go and Tad said, "Hey, where ya going?"

"I better go tie Travis up in my truck before he comes back and causes more trouble," replied JD.

"I'll go with ya," said Tad. "Then we can head over to the barbeque. There're some girls I want you to meet."

As JD, Tad, Matt, and Mitch walked off, JD looked back and I heard him say, "I like the girls you got around here." He said something else, but I didn't catch it.

"Did you hear that?" asked Leena.

"We sure did," said Tesa. "Migh-t-fine in them Wranglers!"

Dad cleared his throat to remind us he was still there, causing Leena to blush and Tesa to giggle. "If you'll get packed up, your Mom and I'll leave after the barbeque."

"Aren't you gonna stay for at least a little bit of the dance? You know how Mom likes to dance," I said.

"I guess we could stay for a bit. Would help to get your mom off my back about being a stick in the mud," said Dad with a grin and wink for us girls.

"Great! I'll be done in five minutes," I said excitedly.

Tesa gave me a once over. "I hope you have something else to wear besides that," she said as she stared at my blood-stained shirt and dusty jeans.

I looked down at myself. "This is my extra shirt."

"Hey, don't worry. You can borrow my extra one," said Tesa.

"You're my hero!" I started to give Tesa a hug.

"Hey, don't get me dirty or you won't be able to wear my extra shirt. I'll have to!" said Tesa, pushing me away.

"Sorry!"

"You're just worried that JD wouldn't give you a second look if you wore that," said Leena, pointing at my shirt.

Dad laughed at us. "Careful girls, don't go getting your hopes up. JD is a senior and a heck of a bull rider, from what I hear."

"You know him?" I asked, wanting to find out more about this hot cowboy.

"JD just won at the State High School Rodeo last week," Tesa said. "JD's father and my dad went to A&M together. They meet up at the Houston Stock Show every year."

"Why didn't ya say so earlier?" asked Leena.

"Yeah, how come you acted like you hadn't met him before?" I asked.

"I haven't seen him in a few years," said Tesa. "It was his dad that we saw every year, but he sure has filled out nicely." She sighed.

"I'll say!"

"Come on over to the trailer when you get done here and get that shirt," Tesa told me. "Come on, Leena, let's give her some room to work."

"See ya in five," I said.

"See ya," said Leena and Tesa in unison. They laughed and pointed at each other as they walked off.

"You all set here?" asked Dad after they left.

"I got it under control," I said, looking at him over May Day's back.

He frowned at me. "What?"

"With all the excitement, I just wanted to be sure you were okay," he said, looking me in the eye.

"I think I can handle a little scuffle and some blood after all this time growing up on a ranch," I said while I brushed May Day.

"Okay, if you're sure you're alright. Wouldn't hurt to take a few minutes," he said, throwing a few things in the back of the truck.

"Honest Dad, I'm perfectly fine. Besides I've two best friends and two big ol' brothers that just love to keep an eye on me," I said sarcastically.

"Yeah, I guess you do." Dad nodded his head. "I'll see ya at the barbeque then." He headed off toward the stands to find Mom.

I finished brushing May Day, packed up the stuff, and was just about to walk off when Foxy "rawled," and I saw Jared Taylor and Pete Wexler coming towards me. The Taylor ranch wasn't far from ours, and I had grown up with Jared. Pete lived at the northern end of the canyon and was Jared's best friend.

"Hey, heard you had some excitement here," said Jared. "Whoa, hope that isn't your blood." He pointed to my shirt as I walked around from standing on the other side of May Day.

"No, it's Candy's, Nellie's dog," I said looking down at myself.

"Hope you're not planning on wearing that to the barbeque," said Pete.

"I'm gonna change. I was just heading over to the Martins' trailer to get a shirt from Tesa."

"Tesa's shirt? Really?" said Jared with a snorting laugh.

"What's wrong with Tesa's shirts?" I asked, facing Jared.

"Might be a little big," said Pete, gesturing across his chest.

"I can't believe you guys." I pushed the both of them in the chest.

"Tesa isn't that big."

"Don't kid yourself. Tesa is lots bigger," said Pete. He cried out as I hit him really hard in the arm.

"You two are so immature!" I stomped off.

"Will we still get a dance tonight?" called Jared.

"Only if you're lucky!" I called, walking faster. I heard them laughing behind me, and I waved over my head, not looking back.

I banged on the Martins' trailer door. Before anyone answered, I opened it and walked in. "Whoa! You look fit to be tied," said Tesa as she looked at me.

"Yeah, those two idiots just get my blood boiling sometimes," I said.

"Which two? Your brothers, or some other pair that are too numerous to name?" asked Leena.

"Jared and Pete!" I said exasperated.

"What'd they do now?" asked Tesa as she pointed to the clean shirt she was lending me.

"They said this would be too big for me." I pointed to the shirt.

"Might be, but you can always tie it in front," said Leena. "I do it when I borrow one from her."

"They can be so crude," I said with a huff.

"Hey, they're boys. Whatcha expect?" said Tesa. "Now take that filthy thing off and put this on. I wanna take another look at JD before anyone else gets a chance to put the moves on him."

I had just finished buttoning up the clean shirt when Leena stood in front of me. "Here let me." She undid the bottom few buttons and tied a square knot in the shirttail.

"Hey, that's not bad," I said, looking in the mirror that hung on the bathroom door.

"Now comb your hair and wipe some of that dirt off your pants and face," said Tesa.

"Yes, ma'am!" I said, giving Tesa a little salute.

I was wiping the dirt off my face when Ellen Martin, Tesa's mom, came in. "Hey girls! How's everyone doing?" she asked cheerfully.

"Just fine Mrs. Martin," said Leena.

"We're good, Mom," said Tesa.

"And how are you missy?" asked Mrs. Martin, peering at me around the corner of the bathroom door.

"Just gotta get a little dirt off to make myself presentable," I said.

"Heard about your little fuss." She said reached over me to grab the bloody shirt I'd let drop to the floor. "I'll just put this in the sink to soak."

"Thanks so much, Mrs. Martin." I pulled my long blonde hair out of my ponytail and ran a brush through it.

"No sweat," she said, running water in the sink. "Us girls gotta look out for each other. Besides, I heard you ran into JD." A smirk spread across her face.

"Ain't he hot?" said Leena with a sigh.

"How'd you hear about that so fast?" asked Tesa.

"Your dad ran into the boys over by the practice arena. Your dad said he might need to play referee if JD said anything else about Sara in front of Tad."

"Great, even covered in gore she gets the guy," said Leena as she slumped down into her seat.

"Don't get your knickers in a twist, sister. He said plenty about all ya'll. I think he's quite impressed with the, how did he put it, 'local female scenery was quite nice on the eyes,'" said Mrs. Martin with a big smile at all of us.

"Really? He said that?" asked Leena, brightening up.

"Really!"

"Wonder who else he's been drooling over," I said skeptically.

"I'm sure Matt and Tad drug him over to say hi to Celeste and Trish," said Tesa.

"Well, of course they did," said Mrs. Martin. "Men have to show off their girlfriends."

"Hope that's all," said Leena.

"Hope he didn't introduce him to Cathy Coulter," I said in a snotty tone.

"Yeah," said Leena and Tesa in unison.

"Good looks and money. Who wouldn't want that?" asked Tesa.

"Some men have better sense and can see beyond the surface," said Mrs. Martin. "Now are ya'll ready yet? I'm hungry." She got up from the table.

"I think I'll do. That's if I pass inspection." I looked at Leena and Tesa.

"You look great," said Leena.

"Should we mess up her hair to level the playing field?" asked Tesa with a mischievous grin.

"Naw," said Leena with an air. "Real men look beyond the surface I'm told." At that, we laughed and left the trailer.

The four of us were on our way to the barbeque when we were joined by Bart Martin, Tesa's dad, and my parents.

We had just sat down at a table when Mom spotted Wendy Pierce. "Hey Wendy, come join us."

"Don't mind if I do."

"I see you got cleaned up," she said, gesturing to me.

"Yeah, Tesa lent me a clean shirt," I said, smiling at Tesa.

"That color brings out your green eyes," said Wendy. "Bet all the boys will be asking you for a dance later."

"Not too many I hope," said Dad.

"Don't worry about Sara," said Mr. Martin. "I think your boys scare most of them off." The adults laughed as I shook my head.

"It's those that get through I worry about," said Mom with a smile at me. "Bart, why don't you tell me about this JD everyone is talking about."

My ears perked up, wanting to hear more about the hot cowboy.

"Well, he's the oldest boy of my college roommate," said Mr. Martin. "He's a senior in high school and ranked in the top ten high school bull riders. He just won at the State High School Rodeo last week. His dad sent him out this way for a few weeks to make the rodeo circuit with us while he tends to some business at home."

Leena and I looked at Tesa. "You've been holding out on us," I said.

"I didn't know he was gonna stay with us. He just showed up today," replied Tesa defensively. "I told you I haven't seen him in a few years."

"Yeah, yeah, I believe that one," said Leena, rolling her eyes.

"It's the truth," said Tesa, looking at us defensively.

"Well, well if it isn't the prettiest girls sittin' with the homeliest guy I know," said a tall sandy blonde stranger that walked up behind Mr. Martin.

Mr. Martin jumped up from his seat. "Jesse Dalton! 'Bout time you showed your ugly mug." The two embraced. "When'd you get here?"

"A little bit ago," said Mr. Dalton. "How are ya, Ellen?" He gave her a hug as she stood to greet him.

"I'm just great," said Mrs. Martin. "Where's Lidia?"

"The missus had to stay and take care of the girls this weekend. They had some kinda cheerleading thing."

"That's too bad, but give her my best and the rest of your brood, too," said Mrs. Martin. She introduced the rest of us then she told Mr. Dalton, "Get yourself some barbeque and come join us."

"I think I'll do that. I'm so hungry I could eat the whole cow."

"I'll go with ya and we can catch up a little," said Mr. Martin. The two walked off to get in line.

"Wow, I can tell where JD gets his good looks," said Leena.

"The whole family is that way," said Mrs. Martin. "Lidia is a former model. The twin girls are beauty queens, and the younger boys aren't bad to look at either."

"Well, sounds like we need to keep the girls away from JD more so than the other way around," said Dad, winking at me.

"Whom do we have to keep off JD?" asked Tad as he, JD, Matt, Mitch, and Grant walked up with plates of food.

"Just all the girls for miles around," said Dad. "Might be givin' you boy's some competition."

"My dad didn't send me here to chase girls," said JD, sitting down next to Tad who sat down across from me. Matt sat on the other side of him. Leena was sitting beside me, and Grant sat down beside her, much to her joy.

"Oh good, he's gonna let us pick up the leftovers after he walks by," said Matt, slapping JD on the back.

"I'll settle for that," said Grant.

"Like you have to settle for leftover's," said Tesa.

"What's that suppose to mean?" asked Grant looking at Tesa.

"Like you don't see all those girls swooning after you, following you around in packs, worshiping the ground you walk on," said Tesa.

"Guess I hadn't noticed packs of girls, but I did notice the swooners. A girl that faints too much ain't a girl I wanna be around. Right JD?" said Tad.

"Yeah, I like a girl that can stand the sight of a little blood," replied JD, and he gave me a wink as I looked up at him. He grunted as Tad elbowed him in the ribs. "What was that for?"

"For drooling," said Tad.

The adults chuckled at the jostling. "My, what I wouldn't give to be young again," said Mom.

"Not me," said Dad. "Had a hard enough time catching you the first time."

"Oh puuleeze," said Grant with a groan, "You guys are making me lose my appetite with that mushy talk."

"Really son," said Dad, looking at Grant, "Like we haven't heard enough out of you carrying on about your girlfriends."

"Ha, got you there big brother," I said. "Besides, there ain't anything that would keep ya from eating." We all laughed.

Mr. Martin and Mr. Dalton came back and sat down. The conversation at the table ranged from the events of the day to the fuss at our trailer. Thinking of JD's dog, I asked "Hey, how's your dog? I could've sworn he got kicked, too."

"If he did, it must have been a glancing blow because he seems fine," said JD. "Thanks for asking."

"You bet. This little girl here is always more concerned about the animals than us humans," said Tad.

"Someone has to worry about the animals," said Wendy. "They do take up a good part of our hearts and lives."

"Yes, ma'am," said Grant, "Why Sara here gives her whole heart to the four-legged kind and leaves little else for the two legged." Everyone laughed.

"I can appreciate that," said JD in a low voice that not many heard. But I did and my heart sped up a few beats. "Maybe you'd like to come with me to check him out?"

Leena elbowed me in the ribs lightly and I said, "Sure we could use a walk after this big meal."

"Great," said JD, smiling at me and moving to get up.

"Where ya'll off to?" asked Mr. Martin.

"Sara wants us to check on JD's dog," said Tad. "She thinks he got kicked, too."

"Let me know if he needs me," said Wendy.

"Will do, ma'am," said JD with a slight nod to Wendy. "Mr. and Mrs. Stillsen, nice to meet you. Mr. and Mrs. Martin, thanks again for letting me stay with you. Dad, I'll see you later?"

"Yeah, I'm gonna stay the night before I head back," said Mr. Dalton.

The adults stayed seated as the young adults left to go check out JD's dog. The boys were walking in front and the girls in the back. We came up to a nice truck with Dalton Construction on the side. A dog popped his head up from the truck bed as we neared. "See, he's fine," said JD as he strode up and began petting Travis.

"See, sis, the dog's fine," said Tad. "You worry too much."

I walked up to the truck bed and looked at Travis. He had a sad look in his eyes. I let him sniff my hand, and he licked at me a little before I put my hand on his head.

"Oh," I said, jerking my hand back as I felt a jolt of pain like and electric shock.

"Did he bite you?" asked JD, moving closer and frowning.

"No, no, I just got a shock." I put my hand back on Travis's head. I was prepared this time and let the jolt of pain run up my arm. "I'm not so sure he's okay."

"Why? What's wrong?" asked JD, worried now.

"Let's see if he'll come to the tailgate here." I gestured to the back of the truck.

"Oh boy, here we go again," said Tad as he let the tailgate down.

"Hey, it's my dog and if he's hurt, I wanna know about it," said JD.

"Sorry man!" said Tad. "Didn't mean nothing bad. Just seems my sis here gets into more than her share of animal problems."

I sat down on the tailgate and called Travis to me. He didn't wanna move. JD called him, "Come on boy. It's alright. She ain't gonna hurt ya."

Travis whimpered and limped over. "Yeah, thought so," I said. "Will one of you go back and get Wendy?"

"We will," said Leena as she and Tesa hurried off toward the tables.

"Got a saddle blanket or something for him to lie on?" I asked.

"Matt, grab that blanket from behind the back seat there," said JD.

Matt handed over the blanket, and JD laid it down on the tailgate. "See if you can get him to lie down," I said. JD patted the blanket and Travis came over to lay down on it. He seemed to be favoring his right side, but it didn't look like his leg.

"It's okay, boy," I said as I ran my hand down his right side. I felt the sore spot as I ran my hand over his shoulder and a shock flew up my arm again. Warmth pushed out through my arm, and I let it flow into Travis.

"Must be his shoulder." I looked up at JD, who clearly looked concerned. "I don't think anything's broken since he ran off after being kicked. Couldn't do that if it was broken." I was trying to reassure JD.

"He didn't seem to be bothered earlier," said JD.

"Sometimes the hurt takes a while to set in," said Tad. "Like not feeling bruises you got until after football practice is over."

JD nodded his head. It wasn't long before we heard several people coming our way. It was starting to get dark, so it was hard to see who was coming.

"Want me to turn on the cargo light there?" asked Matt.

"Yeah," said JD.

The light came on as the crowd walked up. It was everyone from the table except my dad. "I sent your dad to get my bag," said Wendy. "I knew when you sent the girls back for me I would need it."

She walked over to the tailgate, and I got out of the way. "So what seems to be the trouble?"

"Might be his shoulder," said JD. "He ran off from the ruckus so fast and didn't seem to be in any pain when I caught up to him."

"Sometimes it takes a little bit for shock to wear off and pain to set in," said Wendy.

"Told ya," said Tad smugly, but no one paid him any mind.

"Which side?" Wendy asked.

"His right," said JD.

Wendy ran her hand down Travis's right side. He yelped and tried to nip her when she touched his shoulder. "Yeah, it hurts right there," she said. "See if you can get him to lie on his left side," she said to JD.

JD got Travis to lie on his left side. Wendy gently took hold of Travis's right front leg with one hand and ran the other up his shoulder. Travis yelped again as she touched his shoulder. She flexed his leg; he didn't seem to mind that too much.

I saw everyone had gathered around, leaning on the bed of the truck to watch what was happening. Wendy began gently prodding along Travis's shoulder until she found the exact spot it hurt. Travis nipped at her.

"Hey, that's enough," said JD to Travis and reached to hold his head.

"It's just a bruise, but I'm sure it hurts. We can give him a little something to make him more comfortable soon as my bag arrives," said Wendy.

JD let out a sigh. "Man, I really didn't think he got kicked at all."

"Don't kick yourself, son," said Mr. Dalton, smiling reassurance at JD. "He's gonna be fine."

It was only a minute before Dad walked up with Wendy's bag. She quickly filled a syringe with something and injected Travis. You could see the relief in his face. She filled a small pouch with some pills and handed it to JD.

"Give him one of these no more than three times a day if he seems to be in pain tomorrow. He'll probably sleep most of the night. I gave him a muscle relaxer as well as pain killer."

"Thanks, Wendy," said JD gratefully.

"What do we owe you for your services?" said Mr. Dalton. "Better settle up now since I'm from out of town."

Wendy and Mr. Dalton discussed the fee, and I stepped over to pet Travis. JD looked up at me, and I felt a warmth rush up my arm instead of down before I realized it was the drugs that Travis was feeling. I lifted my hand and leaned against the truck.

"Thanks, Sara. If it weren't for you, poor Travis here would be suffering all night," said JD.

"You would have noticed before too long," I said, trying to make him feel less guilty and trying to clear the feeling of the drugs Wendy had given Travis from my head. "Besides, it's all taken care of now."

I smiled up at him and felt my stomach do a little flip as he smiled back at me.

"Okay, shows over," said Matt. "I hear the band warming up, and I can't disappoint the ladies by not being present for every song."

"How will you fit that head through the door to the dance floor?" asked Tesa.

We laughed and Matt grabbed his chest. "Sis, you wound me so!" We just laughed harder.

"Are we sure we've looked over all the animals that might need me before I put my bag up one more time?" asked Wendy.

They looked at me "Why are you looking at me?"

"You seem to be the resident worry wart over animals," said Tad.

"I think it's safe for Wendy to put up her bag."

"I'll join ya'll in the dance hall," she said walking away. "Matt, if you can manage it, save a dance for me." Then she hurried off as the boys gave Matt some ribbing about the new lady vet having a thing for him.

Everyone was heading off and I was right behind them when I noticed JD wasn't with us. I turned back and saw he was still sitting on the tailgate petting Travis who was now sleeping peacefully. "Aren't you coming?" I asked.

"Yeah in a minute," he said "Just wanna make sure he's alright."

"He's fine, the doctor said so. See he's asleep," said Tad "You gonna sit and hold his paw all night or are you gonna come dance with the pretty girls"

"I'm coming," said JD. He got up, looked at Travis one last time, and then joined the rest of us as we walked to the dance hall.

The gang split into partners, danced, switched partners, and danced again. Mom and Dad danced for a little while. "You drive home careful," said Dad to Grant. He winked at us as they waved and left.

I hadn't danced with JD yet because every time he started toward me Jared, Pete, Mitch, or Matt grabbed me and off we went. I swear it was on purpose, but Tesa and Leena said it must be my imagination. I'm sure I caught a glimpse of them smiling over my head at each other when they said that. Then Jason Henley asked me to dance; my heart skipped a beat as he took my hand and we walked out on to the dance floor. I'd known Jason all my life, but this past year he had grown into a really cute guy. He had an average build, blonde hair, soft brown eyes, and a great smile. I was happy to find myself in his arms as we glided around the floor.

"Who's the new guy?" asked Jason.

"That's JD. He's a friend of the Martins. He's gonna stay with them as they hit the rodeos for a few weeks."

"Oh," he said, not looking too pleased at the news. The song we were dancing to ended. Then the *Cotton-Eyed Joe* started up and I found myself in a line of people, with Jason on one side of me and JD on the other. Our line whirled around and I saw Tesa and Leena looking at me between Tad and Grant. They both looked a little disappointed.

The song wound down and a slow one started up. JD didn't let go of my hand but neither did Jason. "Do you mind?" JD asked Jason. "I believe you've already had the pleasure and I haven't."

Jason was speechless but quickly regained some composure as he nodded his head to me. "I'll find you in a minute." He walked to the side of the floor where others were watching.

"Thought I wasn't gonna get a chance to dance with you tonight," said JD looking down at me.

"Whatcha mean?" I asked, hoping he couldn't feel my heart thumping away just under his hand that rested on my back.

"Those friends of yours keep cutting me off when I try to ask for a dance." He nodded his head toward Pete and Jared, who were circling us with their partners. I didn't say anything because I had the same feeling myself; they had been acting funny that way all evening.

"Have you looked in on Travis?" I asked, trying to keep the conversation light.

"Not yet but was thinking it's time I did." He looked down at me. "Would you join me?"

I tripped and he caught me.

"Sorry, thanks, uh, yeah I'd like to go with you," I stammered.

"Let's go," he said.

"Now?" I asked surprised. "The song's not over yet."

He chuckled softly. "After the song then."

"What's so funny?" I asked, looking up at him with a frown since I was still afraid he could feel my heart pounding.

"Just thought you might be as worried as I am about Travis," he said teasingly.

"Oh!" I looked over his shoulder, not knowing what else to say. "Well, Wendy said he was fine and he's probably still asleep," I offered in a pathetic attempt to recover.

The song ended and we were close to the door. JD kept my hand in his as he led me out the door.

He was still holding my hand when we heard Matt call out to us, "Hey where ya going? Band ain't taking a break yet."

"I just wanted to look in on Travis," said JD.

"I'll join ya. It's getting hot in there," Matt said.

JD dropped my hand as Matt moved between us and put an arm around each of our shoulders. We walked over to JD's truck, and Travis was still lying on the blanket on the tailgate right where we last saw him. The moon was shinning down on him and he looked peaceful.

I ran my hand over Travis. I couldn't feel any pain, but I did start to get a little lightheaded. "He's sound asleep." I turned my head to look up at JD, who sat on the tailgate beside Travis.

"See ya big softy, nothing to worry about. Dog's fine. Now let's go back and dance some more," Matt said.

"I think I'll sit out here for a little bit and rest my feet," said JD. He looked at me. "You haven't sat down for quite awhile. Sit here with me."

I was moving over to his other side, away from Travis, when Matt sat down there instead. "Might as well rest my feet, too."

JD shook his head. "Is there some conspiracy to keep me from being with Sara?"

I looked at JD in shock then at Matt as he shook with laughter. "What's so funny?" asked Tad and Grant as they walked up.

"JD here thinks we're all in a conspiracy to keep him away from Sara," laughed Matt. Tad and Grant started laughing, too.

"Well?" I asked looking at the three of them. I was starting to get mad. "Are you?"

"Are we what?" asked Grant.

"Are you trying to keep JD away from me?" I asked, getting madder.

"Actually, sis, it's you we're trying to keep away from JD here," said Tad.

"Yeah, you might hurt his steely demeanor and make him love bulls so he won't ride them anymore 'cause he might hurt them," said Matt, snickering and putting his arm around JD's shoulders.

"What?" asked JD, standing up and shrugging off Matt's arm. "Do you really think I would let anything come between me and bull riding?" He didn't sound too amused.

"What's between you and bull riding?" asked Tesa as she and Leena walked up.

"For some reason, ya'll have been trying to keep JD and me apart tonight." I crossed my arms over my chest. "What I can't figure out is why?"

"Well, for starters, you should share," said Leena, sidling up to me and bumping me with her hip.

"Share?" I asked with exasperation. "You're the ones not sharing. I only got one dance with him, and ya'll act like it was a bad thing."

"What's a bad thing?" asked Pete as he and Jared walked up. Jared put his arms around Leena and me.

"You guys are the worst, ya know that?" I shrugged off Jared's arm and walked off in a huff. Leena and Tesa caught up with me, laughing.

"We were just having some fun," said Tesa. "We saw the sparks flying between you two the minute he walked up to your trailer."

"We hatched this little plan to see how long we could keep ya'll apart," Leena added.

"Were the boys in on this, too?"

"Matt was," said Tesa. "I'm sure he got Tad and Grant in on the deal. Jared and Pete were just acting like themselves."

"Was I really that bad?" I asked, feeling embarrassed.

"Naw, if you were that bad, your dad would have drug you home with him," said Tesa with a chuckle as she put an arm around me.

"Come on, let's go get a drink," said Leena. "The band is on break anyhow."

We were walking up to the refreshment stand when we noticed Jason and Trent Masterson coming toward us. "There you are," said Jason. "Been looking all over for you."

"We just went to check on Travis, JD's dog," I said, almost feeling guilty.

"Yeah the boys are still over there I bet," said Leena, trying to give Jason and Trent a hint to leave, but it didn't work. Trent was one of Jason's best friends. He's tall, brown hair, and has amber eyes. Tesa and Leena both liked Trent.

Jason ignored them and looked straight at me. "Can I buy you a cold drink?"

"Sure. We'll just sit down over here and wait for ya," I said, motioning to some tables.

"I'll be right back." He smiled and strode over to the refreshment counter with Trent.

"Glad I ain't in your shoes," said Leena.

"Me, too," said Tesa.

"What am I gonna do?" I asked. "Or is it just a game that JD is playing, too?"

I looked closely at both of their faces to see if they were joking with me.

"No joke there with JD," said Tesa with a sigh.

"So which one you gonna pick?" asked Leena with raised eyebrows.

"Neither," I said after a beat.

"What?" they said in unison and cracked up laughing at each other.

"Oh you two!" I shook my head.

"Here's your drink," said Jason, setting a cup in front of me.

"Thanks," I said, smiling at him. Over the rim of my cup, I saw JD, Matt, Tad, and Grant coming toward us. I choked a little on the soda.

"You should slow down," said Jason.

"I just got an ice chunk," I said hoarsely. I cleared my throat and smiled at him.

"Hey, saw you ride earlier. Did real good, too," said Jason.

"Thanks," I said and looked down as I felt my cheeks flush.

"Gave Cathy Coulter a run for her money," he said, looking down at his cup.

"You mean gave her daddy's money a run," I said and he laughed.

"What's so funny?" asked Tad as the boys walked up. They sat down around us, and JD sat across from me.

"Was just telling Sara she gave the Coulters a run for their money this afternoon," said Jason as he realized the boys were sitting with us.

"You can buy all the fancy horses you want, but it still takes a good rider to win. Right Grant?" said Tad.

"Yeah, gotta be able to ride," said Grant, taking my cup of soda from me and taking a swig.

"Would it hurt you just once in a while to ask before you grab my drink?"

"Okay, I'll go get us all drinks," said Grant as he handed me my cup and got up. "Anyone gonna help me carry?"

"I'll help ya," said Leena.

The conversation shifted to Matt telling jokes. Everyone was rolling when Grant and Leena came back with drinks. Matt didn't let up until the band started playing again.

"Shall we?" asked Jason, standing and holding his hand out to me.

"Sure," I said taking his hand. "Come on ya'll, let's scoot some boot!"

We went back into the dance hall with the rest of the crowd. I danced with Jason a few times and then Pete cut in. Next Jared took me for a turn. Matt grabbed me after that and I asked him, "Hey, were you really trying to keep me from dancing with JD?"

He roared with laughter, and I thought he was gonna stumble.

Finally, he stopped laughing long enough to say, "Yeah, good joke don't ya think?"

"Yeah, just hilarious!" I said, frowning at him.

"He's gonna be round almost all summer. You two will have plenty of time to get to know each other."

"I'm sure you, Tad, and Grant will just allow that to happen." He laughed and whirled us around.

I danced with JD once more before the dance ended. He didn't say much to me, but he did smile when I looked up at him and he would squeeze my hand. Guess he thought he was butting in, as Jason kept cutting in on everyone who asked me to dance.

The lights came up at the end of the last dance. I happened to be partnered with Jared at the time. He swung me up and over his shoulder, despite my protests. He carried me over to my brothers and asked, "Where would you like this sack of potatoes?"

"Just throw her in the back of my truck," said Grant as they turned to leave. Jared followed them.

"Jared, if you don't put me down I'm gonna barf down your back!" He put me down so fast that I fell on my butt. We laughed as Jared apologized profusely.

"Hey, you alright?" asked Jason offering me his hand.

"I'm fine," I said, taking Jason's hand. When I got to my feet, I pushed Jared. "Doofus here just doesn't mind very well."

"Can I walk you to your truck?" asked Jason. I caught the look on JD's face over Jason's shoulder. He seemed to be interested in my answer, so I said diplomatically as I could, "Maybe another night."

Jason's face dropped a little then he smiled and asked, "Well can I call you?"

"Sure," I replied. I turned to catch up with my brothers as they were walking off. We said good-bye to the Martins and JD. Tad put his arm around me as we walked to the truck. "So, are you mad at me?" he asked.

"What for?"

"Because we tried to keep JD and you from dancing with each other," said Grant gleefully.

"I should be." I looked straight ahead. "But revenge is a dish best served cold!"

"We're gonna have to watch our backs!" said Tad, tickling me.

"Yeah and sleep with one eye open!" said Grant.

We laughed and climbed into the truck. "Glad ya'll respect me for something," I said smugly.

"What we respect is that evil, twisted mind of yours that thinks up the most outrageous pranks!" said Grant.

"Well that's kind of like respect!" I said with a smile.

On the way home I was falling asleep when Tad patted his shoulder, indicating for me to lay my head on it. No one said anything else until we were at home and Tad was waking me up.

Foxy was waiting for me on my bed. "Hey girl, nice of you to wait up for me." I chucked off my boots and let my clothes drop on the floor. I pulled on a big t-shirt and crawled into bed. I was asleep again before my head hit the pillow. I dreamt I was dancing first with Jason, then JD, then Jason again.

Fourth of July Rodeo

I rode May Day down to the highway to get the mail. There was a letter from Uncle Buck addressed to me. I was used to getting a letter from him on occasion, but it had been awhile. He always had some advice about my gift and things I could expect to learn. I read it as I rode back to the house.

Dear Sara,

I know this letter will find you and your family well. If you are to do something more than human, you must have more than human powers. Soon you will be fifteen. You will discover more depth in your power to heal. Learn to let the power flow. You will grow much this summer.

The crow is coming to help you. The crow spirit will point the way to the new friend and is an omen of change. Along with being the guardian of healing, the crow is a messenger. It will bring you courage to enter the darkness of the void, which is the home of all that is not yet in form. Tsula will be with you as you find this power. He who would do great things should not attempt them alone. This is why you need the crow.

Do not let your brother bear be overly protective of you and keep you from the crow. Your brother hawk will see the changes and assist you.

Do not fear this change; embrace it. It will lead you to a better understanding of love, compassion, and all that weaves this world together.

Yours truly,
Uncle Buck

I was amazed and more than a little scared about what it said. I wondered about this new friend and who it would be.

Sandy and Ken Miner were new in the canyon, having moved here the beginning of the summer. Sandy and Ken's parents were the new horse trainers at the Big C Ranch.

Then there was JD.

I guess the crow would tell me soon.

I couldn't even begin to understand what the other things meant, but they would be revealed in their time, as always. A chill ran up my spine as I remembered his prophecy that I'd come into more healing power when I turned fifteen.

At the river's edge, under some trees, I heard a "caw, caw, caw" and knew there must be a crow nearby. The crow! Uncle Buck was right; I had met the friend already. My heart skipped a couple of beats. I stopped and looked for the crow. I heard "caw, caw," and two black feathers floated down as a shadow flitted across the sun.

I jumped off May Day and grabbed the feathers, holding them to my chest, excited. What did my crow have to teach me?

I think the best place to be for the Fourth of July is Rocksprings. They have the rodeo, a big parade the morning of the Fourth, and a great dance with a big band.

This year I was actually going to participate in the rodeo myself, knew a few other competitors, and was looking forward to seeing one really cute bull rider again.

We were competing on Friday evening and if we qualified, we would compete in the finals Saturday night. I was sure the boys would make it in team roping, and Grant would probably make it in calf roping, but I wasn't so sure I'd make the barrel racing or pole bending. The competition in this rodeo was stiff because it was so popular.

Friday we got our things ready and loaded three horses, two dogs, and a cooler full of soda, water, and sandwiches. I crawled in the back seat of the truck with Tad, while Grant rode up front with Dad. Mom would join us later. Joey and Foxy, as usual, were in back.

I spent the trip braiding the two crow feathers I had received from my messenger into a hatband.

"Whatcha making me?" asked Tad.

"It's not for you," I said, not looking up.

"Who's it for?"
"Not sure."
"Then why are you making it?"
"Because I want to."
"Oh, that's a good reason," said Tad, scrunching down in his seat leaning his head back. He was asleep in no time.

I'd just finished the hatband as we drove onto the rodeo grounds. We drove around for a minute before spotting the Martins' trailer and pulled in alongside.

Foxy hopped up onto her perch, the truck roof; Joey was on the toolbox as we unloaded the horses. On our way to register, I walked over to the Martins' truck and JD's dog, Travis, popped his head up. "Hey guy." I petted him. "How's the shoulder?" He woofed at me and licked my hand.

As I stood in line at the office, Tesa noticed that I kept looking around.

"He's over there in line," she pointed, smirking.

"Oh, was I too obvious?" I smiled at Tesa.

"Don't worry," she assured me. "He's been looking for you guys to show up, too."

"Really?" I asked as my stomach did a flip.

She nodded her head. "Yeah, really."

"Wow, I only saw him two weeks ago for the first time. Say how'd ya'll do last week in San Antonio?"

"I didn't place, but Matt and Mitch got third in team roping."

"Great for them, but I'm sorry for you. Anyway, that's a big rodeo to place in."

I looked at her, expecting more, but she hesitated, baiting me. "Do I have to drag it out of you, or shall I go ask JD himself?"

"He got first in his age group!"

"Wow! That's great!"

"Where's that old man of yours?" asked Dad, walking up behind us.

"He's over there with Matt and Mitch, signing up for team roping."

"Better get the boys over there." Dad motioned for the boys and handed me some money. "I expect you can sign up yourself?"

"I think I can manage that." Dad walked off and I asked Tesa, "Are you signed up already?"

"Yeah, I only signed up for barrels."

"I'm gonna give it a try in barrels and poles," I said as we walked to get in line. "Has Cathy Coulter signed up yet?"

"Not yet, but I imagine it won't be long before she shows up."

"Before who shows up?" asked JD, coming up behind us.

"Cathy Coulter," I stammered, turning to look at him.

"I'm afraid I don't know who she is," he said as he smiled at me.

"Uh, she's just some rich girl who rides an expensive race horse and hopes to win," I said.

"We know it takes more than a fast horse," said JD. "It takes a real rider."

"And we have plenty of those," said Matt, coming up behind JD hanging an arm around him. "You signed up yet?"

"Waiting on my turn," I said.

"Well, we'll get out of the way and let you ladies talk," said Matt, pulling JD away.

We were walking out of the office after registering when Cathy Coulter and her father walked in. We nodded to them, but Cathy hardly gave us a glance.

"Competition is on!" said Tesa. We gave each other high fives.

"What's the celebration for?" asked Matt.

"Just getting ready for the competition. Did you draw the short straw today to watch us or what?" I asked, surprised to see him and JD there.

"Yes, ma'am, we're watching," said JD with a mischievous smile. A crow cawed from the trees over head. My heart skipped a beat; JD must be the crow!

"We have some riding to do," said Tesa, taking my arm as she pulled me off toward the trailers. I looked back over my shoulder and saw JD and Matt standing there looking at us.

Grant and Tad were already at the practice arena. Dad, Mr. Martin, and Mitch were at the trailers waiting for us.

"Where's Matt and JD?" asked Mr. Martin.

"We left them outside the office," said Tesa.

Tesa and I got our horses ready and rode over to the practice arena, with Matt and Mitch just behind us. As I rode May Day around to get him stretched out, I heard a horse scream at the far end of the arena. I turned to look for the source and saw a sorrel horse was down but couldn't find the rider

"What happened?" I asked as I rode up next to Tad.

"Rope got caught around the horse's back feet," he said.

I stood up in my stirrups but still couldn't see much because of the crowd. "Who is it?"

"Copper," said Tad with a grim face. We heard the horse whine then a voice say, "Okay, let him up."

The horse got up and Mitch was on the ground beside him, leaning down to check the gelding's back leg. Dad and Mr. Martin were there, too. The crowd dispersed, and I walked forward to see what was happening.

"Looks raw," I heard Dad say.

"Yeah, dang it, not sure we can ride now," said Mitch.

"It doesn't look that bad," said Dad. "Walk him out and see how he does."

Copper walked gingerly but didn't limp. Mr. Martin shook his head as Mitch led the horse out of the arena. I followed behind, as did Tad, Grant, Matt, and Tesa.

I jumped off May Day, tied him to the trailer, and opened our horses' first aid box. I found the jar of "pink medicine" Dad made up that always seemed to work wonders on cuts and scrapes and headed to the Martins' trailer.

"It just isn't going to happen son!" Mr. Martin told Mitch as he started to unsaddle his horse.

"Mitch," I asked timidly, "if you want to try this pink medicine Dad makes up, it might work wonders." I felt my fingers tingling as I walked toward Copper.

"Thanks, Sara, but I'm sure it would only help for awhile."

"How close have you looked at the wound?" I asked. "Did you wash it?"

"No, I haven't done either," said Mitch. He paused in undoing his saddle sighed and smiled at me. "I guess you might be right. Let's take a closer look. I'll get some water." He grabbed a bucket and walked over to a tap under the trees.

I walked up to the big gelding and rubbed my hand on his face, "Hey, how are you Copper?" He nickered softly, nudging me.

I closed my eyes and concentrated, feeling some burning and soreness. I walked down Copper's side and ran my hand down his back leg. He lifted it for me, and I saw the raw flesh where the rope had run across. I set the jar of pink medicine on the ground in front of me so I could hold his foot with both hands. Foxy whined at me and I closed my eyes, gathering the warmth from my chest. It flowed down my arms and into the horse's foot. I felt Copper relax as the warmth ebbed and I opened my eyes. I saw the flesh was still raw but not as red. Mitch came back with a bucket of water.

"What's it look like?" he asked.

"A rope burn," I said, looking up at him.

"Here, clean it off a bit," he smiled at me and I took the sponge and dabbed at Copper's raw flesh. He flinched a little, probably because the water was cold and my hands had been very warm. I rinsed the area a few more times.

"It doesn't look so bad," I said and looked up at Mr. Martin and Mitch.

"No, it sure doesn't," said Mitch.

Dad walked up and looked. "Not bad at all."

"Got a towel?" I asked.

"Right here." Mr. Martin grabbed a towel out of his truck. I dabbed at the rope burn to get it dry.

"Here, let me," said Dad. He dabbed on the pink medicine.

I blew on it and felt Copper flinch a little. "Easy fella, almost done." I let his foot down and straightened up. Copper snorted and stamped his hind foot, put his full weight on it, and looked around at us.

"He seems fine," I said.

"Hmm," said Mr. Martin. "Walk him around for a minute."

I stepped back as Mitch took Copper's reins and walked him from between the trailers down the road and back. "He seems fine!"

"Ride him around a minute," Dad directed.

Mitch mounted, rode Copper down the road, and trotted back to us. He was shaking his head. "He seems fine." A big smile spread across his face as Matt rode up.

"Hey, he's fine!" said Matt. "We can ride!"

"We sure can," said Mitch. "Thanks, Sara."

"It's my pleasure. Now go win a buckle or something!"

Mitch laughed and turned to Matt, "You heard the lady! Let's go win a buckle or something!"

He and Matt were laughing as they rode back toward the practice arena.

"How'd Copper get hurt?" I asked Dad.

"Matt's rope got tangled around Copper's back feet and he fell. Was a good thing Mitch stepped off as Copper went down or it could have been worse."

I walked over to May Day. "I better get a little more warm-up in before they call us over."

Dad held May Day as I got on. "Good luck!" he said and patted me on the leg.

"Thanks!" I looked up at Foxy. I smiled, knowing Copper's injury was worse before I helped him.

I rode around in the arena a few times and spied Mitch and Matt riding. Copper was going along just fine.

I saw Tesa and she waved me over. "Mitch sure is in a good mood," she said, nodding toward the boys.

"Yeah, seems to be."

"Let's hope that Copper doesn't pull up lame later," she said.

"I hope he doesn't. It wouldn't be fair to let Tad and Grant take all the glory for themselves." We laughed.

"Guess we better make our way over to the main arena," I said. "Have you seen Cathy yet?"

"No, I haven't," said Tesa, "and I've been looking." We rode over to the main arena.

They started the barrel racing, and Tesa and I took our turns. She ran the cloverleaf pattern around the barrels and came in sixth. My time put me in fifth. When they called Cathy Coulter, Jack Sampson, Foreman at the Big C ranch, had to hold her horse as he hopped along until they got him into the arena. She made a good run and ended up in fourth place. Out of thirty-five entries in our age group, the top fifteen would make it to the next round.

"How's it going?" JD asked as I watered May Day by our trailer after the race.

"Just fine!" My heart started thumping in my chest. "You ready for your ride?"

"I start getting into my groove about thirty minutes before," he said, leaning against the trailer next to me as I held the bucket for May Day.

"What bull did you draw?"

"Hell on Wheels," he said. "Heard he likes to spin."

"Guess you can handle that or you wouldn't be here."

"I can handle many things," he said with a twinkle in his eye.

May Day sloshed the water in the bucket, splashing it everywhere.

"Hey, stop that!" I said to him. "I guess you're done if you're just playing." I turned to JD and he was chuckling.

"Did he get you wet?" I asked.

"No, he didn't."

"Then what's so funny?"

"The way you talk to your animals," he said. "You act like they really understand you."

"They do and I understand them." I patted May Day's neck.

"Oh, don't get me wrong, I like it myself," he said quickly.

"You like that I understand them or that I talk to them?" I asked looking him in the eye.

"Both!" he said and stood face to face with me. May Day pushed me to the side, away from JD.

"Hey! That wasn't very nice!"

May Day nodded his head up and down as if he was laughing. Foxy "yipped" and I pointed at her. "You don't start either!" She did it again and laid down on the roof.

I turned back to JD who was leaning against the trailer again, arms crossed over his chest, watching me with a big smile on his face. My heart skipped a beat and I took a big breath.

"Well, guess I better get going." I put the bucket in the back of the truck, walked to May Day, and put his bridle back on.

"You gonna watch me ride later?" asked JD.

"Of course," I said without turning around.

"You gonna dance with me later tonight?"

I turned to him and smiled, "If you're not too inundated with girls, I will."

"I'd never be too busy for you," he said and took a step toward me.

"Too busy for what?" asked Tad, who had just ridden up.

"Too busy to dance." I turned to Tad and Grant. "Like last time when ya'll tried not to let us dance together."

"Naw, we wouldn't do that," said Tad, feigning innocence. "Would we brother?"

Tad and Grant laughed.

"No, we aren't gonna do that again," said Grant.

"Good." I got up on May Day. "Then we can all have some fun at the dance tonight."

I beckoned to JD and leaned down as he stood up and came over. "Don't go getting hurt," I said, running my hand down his face. Then I rode off.

"Did you see that?" said Tad. "She just…"

I didn't hear any more as I kicked May Day into a trot and headed to the practice arena.

I had to keep May Day limber for pole bending in about fifteen minutes. I needed to catch my breath and get my pulse down a few notches; I could still feel the heat from JD's face on my fingers. I held my hand to my face and smiled. I rode around the practice arena a few times before heading to the paddock.

From the paddock, I spotted my brothers, mom, and dad in the bleachers. Mom, as always, was taking pictures. Mr. and Mrs. Martin and JD were there too. I saw Tesa walk up and sit with them. I smiled to myself, thinking of what I had done to JD. I'm sure my brothers gave him a ribbing about it. Then they called my number and I forgot about JD.

I raced down the line and wove through the six poles and back to the finish line in a fast enough time to put me in the top fifteen.

I patted May Day on the neck as we rode out of the gate. "Nice ride!" said Cathy as I rode past her.

"Thanks!" I said. "Good luck!"

"Thanks."

Cathy took a big nervous breath and began her ride. She was nearly through when she knocked over the last pole. There was a big "aaawww" from the crowd. She looked disappointed as she came out of the gate.

"Too bad," I said. "You were really cooking there."

She shook her head and looked at me, tears in her eyes. "I just can't seem to get it right!"

"Don't be so hard on yourself."

Her horse was still prancing, and I rode up beside them to see if it would calm him down. "You just got Custer here. It takes time to get the groove going so you're in sync."

She sniffed and looked down. I patted Custer on the neck and he settled some. "You're still in the running for the barrels, so concentrate on that."

"You're right. Thanks!"

"Hey, no problem."

I rode off as I saw her father and Jack Sampson coming toward her.

"Oh baby," said Mr. C. "You almost had it!" He patted her leg and as I rode away, she sobbed something I couldn't and didn't want to hear.

I got back to the trailer as the boys were walking up. "Hey sis, not bad!" said Grant.

"Thanks! It's all in the horse!"

"Yeah, tell that to Cathy!" said Tad. "Her horse didn't knock that pole over."

"Them's the breaks." I got off May Day and unsaddled him. We were done for the night.

I started brushing off May Day when Tad came up behind me.

"That little stunt you did earlier," I turned to look at him as he took a breath, "that just encourages a guy. It's like playing with fire."

He walked off a few steps then turned back to me. "And you don't know what kind of fire you're playing with."

He walked off again and I put my hands on my hips and waited. He turned and looked back at me. "What?"

"Just waiting for your next comment." I started to smile.

"Okay, okay, but please don't do that again."

"I got the message. Thanks."

"For what?"

"For being my big, bear brother."

He stepped over to me and gave me a hug. "Don't grow up too fast."

"Hey, aren't you ready yet?" Grant called.

"Be right there," said Tad as he grabbed Super's reins and mounted up. He winked at me and the boys rode off.

I walked over to the bleachers and found Mom, Mrs. Martin, and Tesa. "Hey, you did great!" said Mom. "Gonna be in the finals tomorrow and in both barrels and poles!"

"Yeah, we did okay."

"Okay," said Mom, "you're too modest."

"Well, there's still a lot of competition," I said.

Dad joined us as the team roping started. Grant roped the horns, called heading, and Tad caught the two back feet of the steer, called heeling. They stretched it out and got a good time. Matt and Mitch were next. They, too, did well. When the competition was over, both our teams had made the top ten. We stayed put and waited for the calf roping to watch Grant.

He caught the calf around the neck, jumped off his horse and threw the calf on its side to tie three of its feet together. He threw his hands in the air signaling time. His time was fast enough to earn him third place.

There were a few events left, but all we cared about was the bull riding.

The intermediate events included bronc and saddle bronc riding. In bull riding, the rider holds on with one hand to a rope tied around the midsection of the bull. The rider must hold on for eight seconds. The rider spurs the bull while he bucks to score points.

When the bull-riding event started, we waited anxiously as riders took their turn. By the time JD was up, no one had stayed on for the full eight seconds.

"Tough stock this year," Dad commented.

We watched JD ride. He made it to the buzzer as we cheered. We hung around for the last few riders and only one of them made the eight seconds. Happy, we made our way out of the stands.

We made it back to the trailers before JD and the boys. I changed my shirt in the trailer, shook my hair out of my ponytail, and checked in the mirror.

Mom broke out sodas and sandwiches. We were eating when the boys showed up. "Hey, there's the champs!" said Mrs. Martin. She gave Mitch and Matt a hug and then JD. I noticed when she gave JD a hug he winced. Dad slapped the boys on the back and Mom gave them hugs, then handed out more soda and sandwiches.

I looked around to see if anyone was listening then I told Tesa what I had done when JD asked me about the dance.

"Oh you didn't!" she said.

"Oh I did," biting my lip, watching for her reaction. She smiled at me and shook her head. She didn't express any of the worry Tad had.

"What?" she asked. "What is it you're not telling me?"

"Well," I hesitated. "Tad told me after I got back from running the poles that I was playing with fire and should watch myself with JD." I looked up at Tesa.

She smiled. "Don't you just love it when they get all protective."

"Yeah, I guess so, but he was really worked up about it."

"So follow his advice. Don't be alone with him and have fun flirting." I nodded.

"What're you two girls conniving now?" asked Matt as he walked over.

"How we're gonna soak your drawers in Icy Hot!" said Tesa.

"Don't go giving away all our secrets!" I said pushing Tesa as we laughed.

"Now that doesn't surprise me," said Matt. "No really, are you working on your list of who you'll dance with tonight?"

"Afraid you might need a partner?"

"Nope, just making sure you aren't trying to save room for me on your list as I'm otherwise booked!"

"I think I heard your hat rip!" said Tesa. "Look out it's gonna blow!"

"Very funny!" he said.

"We better get going," Dad said. "It's a long drive home and we need these animals fed and rested."

"Yeah, Sonny's right," said Mr. Martin. "We better load up and shove off as well."

We loaded up the horses and rest of the equipment. I spotted the hatband I had made and a picture of JD flashed in my mind as I heard Uncle Buck's voice: *"Watch for the crow to point the way to the new friend. The crow is also an omen of change. Along with being the guardian of healing, the crow is a messenger. The crow will bring you courage to enter the dark void, home of all that has not yet formed."*

I stuffed the hatband in my back pocket and closed the truck door.

Dad turned to Grant, Tad, and me. "You guys start home before the dance is over."

"Yes sir!"

We heard the band warming up, and I turned and looked at the guys with my hands on my hips.

"What are you looking at?" asked Grant.

"Well, you cowboys have a feather in your hat. JD doesn't have one. We all know that every good rider has a trademark feather," I said.

"We ain't gonna find a feather this time of night," said Tesa.

"I just happened to have one." I held up the hatband.

"Hey that's nice," said JD, walking over to me and taking it. "I lost my turkey feather at State. I like these black ones. What kind are they?"

"Crow feathers," I said. "Crows are guardians and give courage. See if it fits." I glimpsed Tad's face and he didn't look pleased.

JD took the hatband from me and placed it on his hat. "It fits just right!" he said, smiling at me. "Thank you, Sara."

"You're welcome!" I smiled back at him.

"Now can we go?" asked Mitch.

"We'd better before she thinks up something else," said Grant.

I was talking with Tesa after we made it to the dance floor and pointing out some good-looking guys when Jason, Ken, and Jeremy came up to us.

"We're here! Let the party start!" said Ken.

"Glad we can start now!" said Tesa. "Where's your sister, Sandy?"

"She's around here somewhere with Leena," said Ken.

The band started playing and Jared, whom I hadn't seen yet, grabbed my hand from behind and twirled me around into his arms, steering me to the dance floor.

"Well hello!" I said.

"Gotta get my dances in early!"

I laughed and we danced, traded partners, and danced some more. It was about the fifth song when I got a chance to dance with Jason. When he took my hand, I felt a warm tingle.

"Saw you ride tonight," he said. "You did great!"

"Why didn't you come by the trailer?" I asked.

He blushed. "We didn't wanna get in the way." I smiled, accepting the excuse.

When the song was over, he didn't let go of my hand as we walked back to where the rest of our gang was hanging out. I saw JD, Tad, Grant, Matt, and Mitch had joined the group. Jason immediately dropped my hand and put his hands in his pockets. As the band started up with another song, JD took my hand and we were on the floor before I could say anything.

"Wow, are they playing that keep away game again?" I asked him.

He smiled. "Not if I can help it." My heart skipped a beat. I stumbled, tightened my hand on his right shoulder to catch myself, and noticed he winced.

"You're hurt!" I almost stopped dancing, but JD pulled me along.

"It's nothing." He gave a little shrug and looked over my shoulder.

"But you need some ice or something," I said, getting concerned.

He looked down at me and smiled, "You really care for the injured, don't you?"

"Of course I do. I hate seeing things in pain."

"I'm not in pain."

"No, just when someone hugs you or puts pressure on your shoulder."

"You noticed that, huh?"

"Couldn't miss it. Now you gonna let someone take a look at that shoulder before you injure it worse tomorrow?"

"You gonna look at it, Doc?" He teased.

"I can," I said confidently.

"You gonna heal me too?" he asked with a twinkle in his eye that made a thrill run through me. I wondered if he knew about my gift.

"I know when someone needs real medical attention."

"I could use some attention," he said, looking into my eyes and making my heart pound.

"I think you just need some ice and a wrap," I said, looking away to catch my breath.

"Okay," he chuckled, "let's go get some ice." We walked off the dance floor, and he didn't let go of my hand.

"Where you going?" asked Tad as we passed him.

"Getting some ice," said JD.

I looked at Tad and smiled, but I could tell he wasn't happy with the situation. I followed JD out of the gate and over to our trucks. He held my hand the whole way, but we didn't say a word.

Once at the Martins' truck, he let go of my hand and opened the back door. He pulled out a duffle bag and walked around to the back. I opened the tailgate and he set it down. I walked to the back of our Suburban and opened the back where the ice chest was. I pulled out a baggie Mom always kept there and filled it with ice and water. I turned back to the Martins' truck and saw JD standing by the tailgate undoing his shirt.

"Here let me help." I helped him take his shirt off. My breath caught in my throat as I saw his chest and muscles. He was really built.

Regaining my composure, I looked at his shoulder. Even in the moonlight, I could see the bruising.

"Ohhh ouch!"

"It isn't that bad." He looked at his shoulder then at me.

I put the ice bag on his shoulder. He winced and handed me an ACE bandage. "Sit!" I commanded. He smiled as he sat down.

I was wrapping the ice to his shoulder when I heard someone hurrying toward us. "Hey bro!" I said cheerfully as Tad approached. I kept wrapping JD's shoulder.

"Don't 'hey bro' me!" he said angrily.

"Whoa, what're you all in a huff about?" I asked defensively.

"You know very well!"

"I'm just putting some ice on JD's shoulder!"

"Oh!" said Tad, caught totally off guard. "Sorry, I, I…"

"Look, Tad," said JD calmly. "Sara is just helping me out here." I finished wrapping his shoulder and he stood and faced Tad.

"I'm sorry, JD," said Tad. "Are you okay?"

"Yeah, it's just a strain," said JD. "That bull today was a tough one." He smiled at Tad. "But I don't think it's me you should apologize to. It's your sister you don't trust."

Tad looked at me, thought for a second, then looked at JD. "I trust her. She can't help herself, especially when something is hurt."

I was afraid Tad would start something he didn't wanna, so I quickly said, "We're through here. JD, do you need any aspirin?"

"I took some earlier, so I'm fine. Thank you, Sara," said JD. He reached for his shirt.

"Here, let me help," I said. "Maybe we should have done this over the top of your shirt."

I pushed him to sit as I started to unwrap the ice. I looked at Tad. "You gonna stay and supervise or you gonna dance with your girl? Ya know, before we have to leave."

"I think I can wait a second and walk back with you." He crossed his arms and leaned against the Suburban, facing us.

"Suit yourself."

I unwrapped JD's shoulder then helped him put on his shirt. I didn't realize I was leaning in so close to him when he looked up at me, his mouth just inches from mine. I felt my stomach flip. I smiled and continued, knowing Tad was watching carefully. I was wrapping the ice back onto JD's shoulder over his shirt as Matt walked up.

"What's going on over here?" asked Matt.

"First aid station," said Tad in a flat voice. Matt noticed the tone and gave Tad a close look. He looked at us and noticed JD's shoulder.

"What'd you do?" asked Matt, full of concern.

"Just a strain," said JD. "Nothing to get all worked up about. I wouldn't have even done this if little Miss Nurse hadn't made a big deal out of it."

I started to take offense, but he winked at me, which made my heart race.

"If we're through," said Tad, standing up, "let's get back to the dance."

"You gonna tuck your shirt in?" asked Matt, pointing at JD's shirttail.

"Nope," said JD. "Can't move that way just now."

"Don't even think about it," said Tad as he grabbed me by the arm and pulled me with him.

"Hey, what's the hurry?" I pulled my arm out of his grasp. Tad grabbed my arm again and whirled me around to face him. Before he could say anything, I said, "That's enough. I heard you earlier and I was not doing anything but getting him some ice. You really don't trust me do you?"

I didn't wait for an answer as I turned and hurried back to the dance. The boys followed.

There were lots of "Hey, where'd ya go?" and "There you are," but before I could answer, they saw JD and the focus quickly changed to him. Tesa pulled me aside and I filled her in on how great a chest JD had and how Tad came looking for me.

She confessed. "I saw you leave with JD and I sent Matt out after you." I laughed and squeezed her shoulder. "You aren't mad?" she asked.

"No, I'm not mad at you," I took a breath, "I guess I'm relieved that Matt showed up. Tad wasn't too pleased and I think a fight would have started if anything had happened."

Leena showed up as the band was on a break. "Here's my two best buds!" Instantly, she knew something was out of sorts and demanded details. We sat at a table away from the others and I told her all about it. The band started up again when we were done exchanging stories.

"You gonna dance with the healthy ones or do you only like the wounded?" asked Jason, leaning over my shoulder.

"I do enjoy the healthy!" I said, smiling up at him. He took my hand and we were off to the dance floor. I winked at Tesa and Leena on my way.

I danced with Jason a few times until Grant cut in. We didn't speak at first and I was feeling guilty, not sure why since I hadn't done anything.

"You gonna lecture me too?" I finally asked him.

"Why should I lecture you?" he asked, avoiding my gaze.

"Tad did."

"I'm not Tad."

I gave an exasperated sigh. "So what then?"

"Can't a guy just dance with his sister?"

"Yeah, I guess."

He smiled. "You already seem to know based on the guilty look on your face, so I don't have to say anything."

"I didn't do anything," I said in my own defense.

"Oh, but you did." He looked down at me. "You don't even know it, but you did."

I thought for a second then asked, "What exactly did I do?"

"You and your girlfriends are like flowers to us bees. You don't do anything but just look pretty, smell pretty, and wave in the breeze." He took a breath and looked me right in the eye. "Then there are those that reach out to touch the bee. Some get stung."

I looked over his shoulder and saw JD watching us over the top of some girls' heads, then I saw Jason looking at us with a smile. Grant followed my gaze. "There are some that are experienced and some that are more your speed."

"So I'm supposed to pick the slow one?"

He chuckled. "I can't tell you what to do. You'll pick whatever and I'll be here to keep you from getting too burned."

The song ended. "Thanks for the safety net, but sometimes ya gotta let me take a few steps on my own."

I walked off, leaving him on the floor shaking his head.

We danced a few more rounds with our friends and at the next break, Grant announced it was time to get going. So we said good-bye and the Martins walked out with us back to the trucks. There was a strained silence as we walked.

"JD do you need more ice?" I asked.

"Yeah, I could use a refill," he said.

Tesa helped him unwrap his shoulder and she handed me the bag. I filled it up and Tad took it from me and handed it to Tesa. She was wrapping JD's shoulder again when Grant said, "Okay, see ya'll tomorrow."

My brothers and I were silent except for the radio when Tad turned to me. "So what do you see in JD anyway?"

"Well, for starters, he isn't someone that I grew up with."

"Okay, I get that," said Tad. "What else?"

"He looks me in the eye and not at my chest like most guys."

The boys smiled at each other knowingly. "What else?"

"Other than his looks and manners, I haven't been able to get past the surface stuff because I haven't had two minutes alone with him to find out." I started to get irritated. "He might really be a jerk under those vivid blue eyes, wicked smile, and chiseled features, but I can't tell...."

Grant cut me off. "If you had a few minutes alone, what would you ask him?"

I thought for a moment and leaned forward. "I'd ask him about what it's like at his home. What his brothers and sisters are like. Where did he get his dog? What his toughest bull ride was. Does he have a girlfriend back home? Does he..."

"Okay, okay, we get the idea," my brothers said in unison.

Tad, being the smart alec, replied, "I can answer some of those questions for you."

"I wanna hear him tell me. Just like you don't want me to tell you about your girlfriend, Trish or any other girl."

Tad and Grant looked at each other and shrugged. I sighed and sat back, looking out the window. No one said anything more and I fell asleep. The next thing I knew, we were pulling off the highway onto our road to home.

I was in my room about to shut the door when Tad pushed it back. "I'm really sorry about tonight."

I smiled at him. "I forgave you long ago. But," I looked at him, "you could trust me a little more."

He nodded. "Okay, I'll try harder." He told me goodnight and closed the door.

"Well, Foxy," I sat on my bed taking off my boots, "I think JD is the crow who has come to give me courage to look into the void." She gave me a "rawwwll."

"So you agree!" She sneezed. I laughed and patted her head before I changed into my favorite t-shirt and crawled into bed.

It seemed like I had just fallen asleep when something woke me up. It was just getting light outside and I looked around listening. I only heard the birds and the fan over my head. I lay there for a minute and smiled, remembering my dream. JD was about to kiss me when I woke up. Maybe that's why I woke up, so I wouldn't have to see Tad hit him. I was being ridiculous; Tad wouldn't hit him just for that. Would he?

Then I thought about it being the Fourth of July. There were going to be fireworks tonight!

I got up, pulled on some clothes, and ran down to the barn to feed the horses. When I was done, I ran back to the house and jumped into the shower then made my way into the kitchen where I smelled breakfast. The boys were already there, stuffing eggs and toast into their faces.

"So how was the dance?" asked Mom.

"Great, fine... okay," we answered in unison.

"Thanks for whomever fed already," said Grant.

"I did." Everyone was staring at me. "What? I woke up early and thought it would help out." There were mumbled thanks from the boys.

"Oh Dad, you might wanna offer to tape JD's shoulder for him before he rides today," said Grant. "He pulled it yesterday."

"Oh," said Dad. "He didn't seem hurt last night."

"Well, he was," said Tad. "Had a big bruise on it."

"Did he ice it down?" asked Mom.

"Of course. Sara here insisted he do that," laughed Tad.

Dad looked at me, then the boys, like he knew there was something going unsaid, which there was, but he let it go. "I can certainly help if he wants. Just remind me to stick some tape in the first aid box."

After some chores and lunch, we loaded up and headed for Rocksprings. We arrived at the rodeo grounds and found a spot with some shade and an extra space for the Martins since they weren't there yet. We were unloading the horses when they drove in. My stomach fluttered a little when I saw their truck. I took a deep breath and told myself to cool it.

I was making myself busy brushing May Day but still trying to catch a peek at JD. I kept telling myself I was just concerned about his shoulder.

"Hey, how's it going?" asked Tesa, coming up beside me.

"Great. Hey how's JD's shoulder?"

"He's fine." She pointed her chin over my shoulder. "See for yourself."

I turned to look and saw JD looking at us. He waved with his right arm, the hurt one, and I waved back. "I guess he's okay. Grant asked my Dad if he would tape JD's shoulder."

"That's nice," said Tesa. "I almost forgot your Dad used to ride the rodeo."

"Yeah, it was back when they invented rodeo." We laughed.

JD walked up. "Hey cowgirl, how's the steed?" I looked up into his blue eyes.

"Great. How's the shoulder?" I asked smiling at him.

"I'll live."

"My dad can tape that for you if you'd like. It'll keep you from hurting it worse."

He considered that for a second. "Sounds like a good idea. Where is he?"

"I'll go get him for you."

"I'll just wait in the shade over there." JD pointed to the back of the Martins' truck.

I didn't have to walk too far as Dad was coming towards me.

"Hey," I called to my dad as he approached. "JD would like you to tape his shoulder."

"Okay, I was just on my way to see if you needed anything."

"May Day and I are good."

"Hey JD," I called and he sat up. He'd been lying down in the bed of the Martins' truck.

"Hear you want a tape job," said Dad.

"Yeah, I think it'll keep me from hurting it more."

"Take off your shirt and I'll get the tape" Dad walked to the trailer and pulled out the first aid box. He got the stuff he needed and joined JD at the Martins' truck. JD had taken his shirt off and you could see the bruise across his shoulder.

"I remember those," said Dad.

JD looked up at him. "You used to ride?"

"I rode bulls until I got hurt, so I switched to bareback broncs. They both leave the same marks on the shoulder."

"It's that inside spin that always seems to get me."

"There's a trick I used to do you might try," said Dad as he began taping JD's shoulder. He told him about his trick, and they started swapping stories about rides.

Tesa walked up with her horse, "You gonna come warm up?" she asked.

"I'll be right with ya," I said and turned to get May Day.

"See ya at the practice arena," said Tesa, getting on her horse.

I mounted May Day and walked off toward the arena. Tesa came up next to me as we spotted Cathy Coulter coming into the arena. Her horse was already prancing. "Let's get out of the way," I said.

We went to the paddock to wait our turn. There was a ruckus behind us. We turned to see Cathy hanging on to her horse as he was running in circles, with Jack trying to hold him down. Everyone cleared a wide path for them. Cathy was to run before us, so we got out of the way. She ran a great time but not quite as good as yesterday.

"That set the mark," I said.

Tesa ran next and did great. When it was my turn, I did great, too. After the last contestant ran, Tesa and I looked at each other, cheered, and gave each other high fives. I ended up second and Tesa was third, with Cathy Coulter in fifth. Dad, Mom, and the Martins came to congratulate us.

"Way to go, Dink!" Dad patted my leg. "Let's go over to the trailer and get out of the way."

At the trailer, Jason, Trent, and Ken were waiting to congratulate us. Trent gave me a high five. Jason did likewise, only his hand lingered a little longer. Ken was busy congratulating Tesa, but he waved. Dad got May Day some water as I walked with Jason and Trent to the Suburban where Mom handed out sodas.

"One more run for you tonight," said Mom.

"Yeah, but I'm not so sure I'll do as well in this event."

"Don't go giving up yet!" said Jason.

"I'm just being realistic, but thanks for the vote of confidence."

"Only too willing to oblige a pretty lady."

I blushed and smiled at him. "Why thank you kind sir!" I said in my best southern belle drawl.

"Boy I don't wanna be at the Big C tomorrow or even next week," said Ken as he and Tesa walked over.

"Why is that?" asked Mom.

"Cathy will be whining and complaining about not winning and especially about getting beat again by Sara and Tesa," said Ken.

Tad, Grant, Matt, Mitch, and JD showed up and there were more congratulations. "Now you can afford to buy me a real treat," said Tad, putting his arm around my shoulder.

"When you crack open your pocket to buy me something, I'll be happy to reciprocate," I said, pulling his arm off me.

"I'm shocked! I'm the most generous person with my winnings!"

"We know you spend it all on your hot dates," said Grant, "while I tuck most of mine away for college!"

"Good for you," I said. "Now if ya'll will excuse me, I've another ride to warm up for." I walked back to May Day and Jason followed. I was about to mount up when he grabbed me by the arm and kissed me on the cheek. "For good luck!" he said then squeezed my arm before letting go and walking back to where everyone else was gathered.

I put my hand to my cheek and smiled. I had to shake myself before getting on May Day. I waved at everyone as I rode off toward the practice arena.

I was still flying high when I walked out of the practice arena and to the paddock area. I was daydreaming about kissing Jason on the lips when Dad walked up to me and patted my leg. "You ready?" he asked.

"Yes sir!" I said with a big smile. "We're gonna give it our best!"

"Good! That's what I like to hear."

They called my number and I entered the arena. May Day pranced a few steps and we took off. We did a great run, best time we had ever done in this event. I was really flying high tonight! I ended the night with third in poles.

When I got back to the trailer, the boys were there getting ready for their roping event. I jumped down off May Day into Tad's big hug, then Grant, Dad, and Mom. I got high-fives from Trent, Jason, and Tesa. "Wow what a night!" I said.

I stopped hopping up and down long enough to get May Day some water and grain as Dad unsaddled him and put his halter on. The boys rode off to warm up as we made our way into the stands to watch the other events. Jason sat next to me, and Tesa was on my other side, with Ken next to her. To his dismay, Trent was next to Ken.

The team roping started. Tad and Grant did great again. Mitch missed a loop and had to throw a second, making his and Matt's time slow. The team roping ended up with Tad and Grant taking second place. Grant ended up in second place in calf roping, too. After the last roper, we went to the trailer and greeted some very happy guys.

"Now who's buying?" I asked Tad.

"I guess I can splurge and get you a snow cone," he said, ruffling my hair. I socked him in the arm.

"Well, JD," said Mr. Martin. "You're next! How ya feeling?"

"I'm okay," he said.

"Good luck," I said to JD. "We'll be rooting for ya."

"Thanks!" he said with a smile. He made a face at something over my shoulder, and I turned to see Jason waving at me to join the rest of the guys as they made their way to the stands.

"Remember you owe me a dance tonight!" I said to JD.

He smiled again and his eyes twinkled. "I'll be sure to collect!"

We watched the bull riders, but not many made it to the buzzer. When it was JD's turn, I was on the edge of my seat. Mrs. Martin was worried, too, as she kept twisting the program in her hands. JD made it to the buzzer. He was trying to get off when he got hung up. We stood up and held our breath. A silent prayer went through my mind, but then JD was free and running for the fence.

"I bet he hurt that shoulder again," said Mrs. Martin, gathering her stuff and heading out. Mom followed her out.

"Think we should go too?" asked Tesa looking at me.

"I think they can handle it," I said. "Besides there are two more riders we have to hex." I gave her a wink. The next two riders didn't make it to the buzzer. I jumped to my feet as soon as the last rider fell.

"Alright, that puts JD in good standing. Let's go check the boards." We went down to the area by the concession stand where they posted the results for the events.

"Look, JD got first!" said Trent. We cheered and made our way to the trailers. Dad and Mr. Martin were standing by the back of the Martins' truck, and I could see JD sitting on the tailgate.

"I bet he hurts!" said Ken.

We got closer and I could see Dad rubbing JD's shoulder. I saw a flash of pain cross JD's face. "Your No. 1 big guy!" yelled Trent.

JD's face broke into a big smile. "Way to go!" Dad said.

Mrs. Martin threw her arms around JD. "Oh your dad's gonna be so proud!" She quickly let JD go as he winced. "I'm so sorry! I just got carried away!" She turned to Mr. Martin. "Bart! Did you hear? JD won!"

"I heard honey," said Mr. Martin. "Real proud of you son." He turned to the rest of us. "Real proud of everyone! You did real good tonight!"

"Yaaahooo!" said a happy Grant. "Time to celebrate a little!"

"I better change," I said.

"Me, too," said Tesa, "Grab your clothes and come on in our trailer."

I got a clean shirt out of the Suburban and joined Tesa in her trailer. We changed quickly and I fussed with my hair. I decided to pull the top part back and left the rest down. "Here try a little of this," said Tesa, holding up some perfume.

I took the bottle from her and sniffed. "Oooh, that's nice." I spritzed a little on my neck.

"Ya'll decent in there?" asked Matt.

Tesa opened the door. "All yours," she said as we walked out and let the boys in.

"Jason, Trent, and Ken left to get something to eat. Said they'd meet you inside the dance," Tesa's mom told us.

"I could use a hamburger myself." I turned to Tesa.

"Me, too. See ya at the dance," she said to her mom.

We were off to the concession stand and the dance. "I'm still flying!" I said as we were walking.

"Yeah, heck of a ride," said Tesa.

"Not just from that. Jason kissed me!"

"What? And you're just now telling me?" she asked as she pushed me.

"Don't get all worked up. It was just a peck on the cheek."

"Awww, don't do that to me." She pushed me again. "I thought you got the real thing, not some brotherly kiss."

"Tonight might be the night to get the real thing!"

"Oh ya think!"

"Ya, I think the cheek was just a warm up!" We giggled at that and sat on a bench to eat our burgers. When we were done, we heard the band starting up, so we made our way to the dance. We saw our parents over by the tables and went to join them.

"'Bout time you two showed up," said Mr. Martin.

"We have to make an entrance," said Tesa.

Leena ran up and hugged Tesa and me. "Hey saw you ride! You guys did really great!" She let us go. "So have you seen Cathy Coulter?" she asked in a got-gossip tone.

"No," both Tesa and I said.

"She's soooo mad!" said Leena. "I was walking by the trailers looking for ya'll when I passed by hers and heard her yelling at her dad!"

"That's a spoiled brat for ya," said Mrs. Martin with a sniff.

"Yeah, she was yelling at him for not buying her a good enough horse."

"Ungrateful! That's one of the best horses I've seen," said Dad.

"Sonny, we all know it's not the horse, but the horse and rider that makes a team that wins," said Mr. Martin. "Why our girls here have more riding talent in their little toe than that spoiled brat has in her whole body."

"I feel sorry for Ken and Sandy having to listen to her all the time," I said. "Hey where is Sandy?"

"She was over there with Jeremy earlier," said Leena, pointing to a few tables over. "They're getting too mushy to be around."

"Oh the woes of young love," said Mom.

"Yeah, the chasing and chasing and necking!" said Mr. Martin as he hugged Mrs. Martin.

"Bart, don't start. There are children present," said Mrs. Martin as she slapped at her husband. We laughed as the band started playing. The adults got up to dance, leaving us girls to talk.

I sat down as Jason, Ken, and Trent showed up. "There ya'll are!" said Trent, coming over to us.

"Come dance with me," said Jason, holding out his hand. I took it and stood up, smiling at him. I looked back and saw Ken with Tesa and Trent with Leena. We smiled at each other as we twirled onto the dance floor.

Jason dipped his head down a little toward me. "You smell good!"

"Thanks." I looked up into his soft brown eyes. The first song finished and we kept dancing as another started up. We didn't say much to each other; we just looked at each other now and then and smiled.

One time in the third song, I caught myself looking up into Jason's eyes. I was leaning into him and him into me. His hand moved up my back and he drew me closer. As the song ended he leaned in to kiss me, but at the last second, I got a funny feeling and turned my head. He let me go as I looked up and saw his face.

"Sorry," he whispered to me.

I took in a big breath. "I don't... I, sorry," I stammered and walked off the dance floor. He followed me but didn't say anything. "Man I'm thirsty," I said.

"Let me get you a drink," said Jason as he pulled out a chair for me. "I'll be right back." I watched him walk off toward the concession stand. Tesa and Leena pounced on me.

"Spill it!" said Leena eagerly.

"What?"

"Oh like I can't tell that troubled look on your face!" said Tesa.

"Not much to tell." They stared at me with a frown. I shrugged my shoulders and looked down. "He tried to kiss me, and I looked away at the last second."

"Really?" asked Tesa skeptically. "Not a cheek buzz but on the lips?"

"Wait," said Leena. "What's this about a cheek buzz?"

"Just a warm up I guess you'd call it," I said. "Jason kissed me on the cheek for good luck."

"Why didn't you let him kiss you?" asked Tesa.

"I don't know. It was in the middle of the dance floor. Everyone was watching!" I said, feeling embarrassed.

Then Jason came back. Tesa moved over a chair so Jason could sit by me. "Brought a couple of drinks." Jason set three drinks on the table in front of us.

"Thank you," I said, looking up at him with a big smile and trying to make up for earlier.

"Yes, thank you, Jason," said Tesa, taking a cup.

"I have one already but thanks," said Leena.

Trent and Ken joined us and we talked a little. Tad came up behind me and put his hands on my shoulders. "I've come to claim my brotherly right to a dance!" he said very macholike.

"I didn't know brothers had rights," I looked up at him, "other than the right to be obnoxious."

"That and more!" he said and leaned my chair back so he could look into my face. "Now you gonna join me or should I tell Dad you're ready to go home?"

"Okay, okay," I said. "But you'll have to let me down so I can get up."

"Oh, yeah."

Once on the dance floor, Tad said, "I saw that little spectacle." I said nothing, determined not to rise to his baiting. "I'm not sure I approve of that."

"I didn't do anything."

"You came awful close!" he teased.

I looked at him then I caught a whiff of his breath and frowned. "Have you been drinking?"

"Just a little celebration," he said with a very guilty look on his face. I stared at him for a second then I looked off over his shoulder. Trying not to smirk I said, "Tad, I'm not sure I approve of that." We burst out laughing.

"I won't tell if you don't."

"Deal, only if you don't threaten to beat up Jason or intimidate or lay a hand on him in any way."

He laughed. "Just so we're clear. No telling what I drank and I won't beat on your boyfriend." I looked shocked. "What? I didn't get it right?"

"I'm just shocked to think of Jason as my boyfriend." I frowned, "Do you call them a boyfriend if they haven't even taken you out on a date?"

Tad threw his head back and laughed. "Not sure on the etiquette of that!"

"Thanks, I guess." He chuckled some more. "You're not going to tell Grant to lecture me or beat on Jason are you?"

"Don't think I have to tell him. He saw you same as I did. As for the lecture, that's Grants thing, not mine."

"Doesn't seem that way lately."

"Oh, really!" He smiled.

"Yeah really. He hasn't said much." I looked up at Tad. "Except that he would be there for me if I needed him."

"I'm right here!" said Tad, not to be out done. The song ended and I pushed him. "Yeah, but you're a bit too close! Oh and chew some gum."

I turned and walked back toward the tables. Tad put his arm around me. "I know, I'll give ya some room. But if he does anything wrong, just give me the sign!"

"Thanks, I will, but only if I give you the sign right?"

"Right!" he said and hugged me. "Got any gum?" I dug some out of my pocket and he took a piece and smiled at me. "Now to tease your cute friend!"

He strode over to Leena and bowed and held out his hand. "Would my fair lady care to dance?" She took his hand and they were off to the dance floor.

"Everything alright?" asked Jason as I sat down. He looked concerned, so I put my hand on his. "Everything's fine!"

"Good," he said. "Let's go dance." When the band took a break, we walked back toward the tables and sat down, chatting with everyone. JD and Matt came up.

"Hey champ!" said Trent, looking up at JD. He nodded to all of us, but it looked like he was forcing a smile.

"Hey guys!" said Matt, jumping into the middle. He started telling jokes and had everyone laughing in no time.

I was looking over at JD when Jason elbowed me. "Is there someplace you'd rather be?"

"No, I was just worried about JD. He looks like he's in pain." I turned to look at Jason and could tell this bothered him. "You know me, always caring too much for the injured."

He smiled and took my hand as I smiled back. We listened to more of Matt's jokes and laughed.

When the band started up again, JD leaned over to Jason. "Do you mind if I dance with your girl?" A thrill ran through me, but I wasn't sure if it was because of JD asking me to dance or if it was because JD implied I was Jason's girl.

"I don't mind, but you might wanna ask her."

JD turned to me held out his hand. "Would you like to dance?"

"Sure." I put my hand in JD's and a tingle ran up my arm. He led me to the dance floor and whirled me around and into his arms. I looked up at him; he had a slow smoldering smile on his face and his eyes were dancing.

"How's your shoulder?" I asked.

"Its sore, but that stuff your Dad put on it is great. I'm sure I'll mend."

"Hope so. Got another big rodeo next weekend, don't you?"

"Yeah," he sighed. "The fun never seems to end." I gave him a puzzled look. "What?" he asked.

"I thought you liked the rodeos and bull riding."

"I did, once. Now it seems like this is my dad's thing and not mine anymore."

"Well, you're really good at it."

"I guess, but the thrill is kinda going out of it."

"There's still the challenge though."

"Yeah," he chuckled. "There's the challenge of getting a girl's attention."

"Whose attention are you trying to get? Maybe I can help."

"Yours. I want your attention." He gave me a smile that would brighten the dark and I forgot how to breathe.

"I, I, I don't know what to say," I stammered.

"I can tell," he smiled. "I guess I'm too late though."

"Too late?"

"Yeah, I've seen you dancing with that Jason guy." I blushed and looked away. "I don't mind a little competition," he said, chuckling.

"Well, technically, he hasn't even asked me out on a date, so we aren't going steady or anything."

"That's what I like to hear!" He whirled me around and I laughed.

"You might wanna watch out for my brothers though. They seem to think you'll use me then toss me to the side."

"I've already had a few discussions with them." He looked at me. "But you must have said something to them last night as they've both apologized and said they wouldn't bother me unless I was 'inappropriate.'"

"Huh, they do listen now and then!"

"So what'd you say?"

"I told them that I didn't even know if I really liked you, beyond your good looks, because they never let me alone long enough to even talk to you, ya know, to get to know you."

"You like my looks, huh?" he asked with a smirk.

"Yes I do. It's not like you don't know you're a hunk."

He smiled. "So what do you wanna know about me?"

"When did you get Travis?"

He threw back his head and laughed. I looked at him kinda hurt. "I'm sorry. I'm just surprised that was your first personal question." He shook his head, "But then again, since you have an affinity with animals I shouldn't be surprised."

"Well?"

"Oh, yeah." He cleared his throat. "I got Travis from a friend of my dad's about four years ago."

"Did you name him?"

"Actually Hanna did."

"And is Hanna one of your sisters?"

"Yeah." He made a face. "Hanna and Tana are my younger bratty twin sisters." I laughed and he asked, "What's so funny?"

"I guess all big brothers call their younger sisters brats."

"I guess we do that to scare off players!" We both laughed.

"I hope that doesn't make you a player!"

"I dunno. I like being a player now and then," he said wiggling his eyebrows. We were laughing as the song ended. JD didn't let me go, "Do you mind if we dance again?"

"Not at all," I said, smiling up at him.

The next song started up and it was a fast one, so we didn't have a chance to talk. But we didn't stay on the floor for the next one.

"Whew, I'm hot!" I said, wiping my forehead.

"Yes you are!" he said with a mischievous wink.

I pushed him, "You are a player!" and laughed. We headed back to the tables and I glanced at Jason. He didn't look happy. "I'm gonna get a drink. Anyone want something?" I asked looking around.

Tesa thankfully jumped up to join me. "I could use one."

"Bring me one," said Mitch and Matt.

"Okay, be right back," said Tesa as we headed off to the concession stand. After we got away from the table, she leaned into me. "What're you doing?"

"What do you mean?"

"You know very well. Jason just tried to kiss you and you're off flirting with JD again!"

I grinned. "I know. I don't count being tied to Jason just because he kissed me on the cheek."

"Good point!"

Leena joined us. "What's a good point?"

"Sara here was off flirting and dancing with JD after Jason kissed her earlier!" said Tesa.

"And," I interrupted Tesa, "I was telling Miss Manners here that a kiss on the cheek doesn't automatically make Jason my boyfriend. We haven't even been on a date."

"That's true!" said Leena.

"You don't think so?" asked Tesa.

"Nope!" said Leena. "You must have a date, or several dates, to be going steady."

"Yeah I guess you're right," said Tesa. "Sorry I jumped you about it."

"Hey, I still love you!" I put my arm around her. "What would I do without you guys?" I put my other arm around Leena.

We ran into Grant at the concession stand. "Hey, bro."

"Here's my favorite little sister and her lovely lady friends!"

I ordered some sodas and handed a couple of them to Tesa, as Leena was too busy flirting with Grant.

"Just ask her to dance, please!" I whispered in Grant's ear.

"I was getting to that!" he said. "Come ladies, let us find our way back to the dancing!" We laughed as we followed him back to the tables.

"So what's your plan?" asked Tesa.

"I don't really know," I said. "I guess I could start dancing with everyone and show that I'm not attached to anyone."

"Sounds good," said Tesa with a shrug.

We were at the tables again. "Have a drink!" I said, looking at Matt and Mitch.

As if on script, Matt took a cup. "You still saving me a dance or two?"

"I just happen to have some spare spots on my card," I said with a crooked smile.

"Great," he gulped some of his drink and grabbed my hand. "Let's go."

"Whoa," I gulped some of my drink and set it down as Matt pulled me away. As we danced, I saw Jason sitting at the tables pouting. Trying to avoid him, I went from partner to partner for a while. Jared asked me to dance.

"Hey where you been?" I asked.

"Been flirting and chasing!" he said with a grin. "What'd you do to Jason?"

"Nothing." I looked over Jared's shoulder.

"You did something," he said.

"I guess he got the wrong idea. Or maybe I'm just avoiding going too fast with him."

Jared nodded his head. "I like the second excuse better."

"Will you let him know that?"

"I can try," he said, looking at me. "It would be better coming from you."

"Yeah," I sighed, "I know."

The song ended and we walked back to the tables. I asked Jason to dance and he slowly followed me out to the dance floor.

"You mad at me?" I asked.

"A little."

"I, I, I'm just kinda confused," I stammered. "I guess I don't wanna go too fast. I mean we haven't even gone on a date or anything."

He looked at me seriously. "I'm sorry about that. I guess I didn't think."

"Me either," I said, smiling at him.

We were silent for a minute. "I'm sorry if I'm pushing you," he finally said.

"It just wasn't the right place or time and I'm just as guilty, so don't blame yourself."

"Okay," he said and relaxed. "Would you go out with me sometime?"

I smiled at him. "I will. But next week, I have band camp and rodeos the next few weeks after that."

"I can wait," he smiled. When the song was over, we walked back to the table. He didn't try to hold my hand, and I was a little disappointed.

Then there was a loud bang and flash as the fireworks began to pop overhead.

"Oh, I didn't know it was that late. I better go check on May Day. He doesn't like fireworks!"

I ran the whole way to the trailer, worried May Day would be upset. When I got there, he was wild eyed, and his nostrils were flaring. He stamped his feet as the sky lit up again. "Easy, easy big fella," I patted his neck and he calmed some.

I pulled his head around and was talking to him when Grant, Tad, Matt, and Mitch came up.

"What's wrong?" asked Mitch, out of breath.

"Just came to settle May Day," I said not taking my hand off his nose. "He doesn't like fireworks."

"Is that all?"

"Told you it was probably nothing," said Tad, slapping Matt on the shoulder.

"Why did you start running off when you saw Sara run off?" asked Matt, turning to Tad.

"Cause I thought she might need some help," said Tad.

"Good recovery," said Grant.

"What's that supposed to mean?" I asked, looking back and forth between Grant and Tad.

"I, I, um," stammered Tad.

"You what?"

"I saw you talking to Jason, then you ran off, and Jason just stood there looking after you. I thought he might have said something to upset you," said Tad, shuffling his feet.

I shook my head. "Thanks, but as you can see that's not what happened. Everything is fine."

Tesa and JD came up. "What's wrong?" asked Tesa, "Why did everyone run out?"

"Nothing's wrong," said Grant, "Worrywart Tad here jumped to the wrong conclusion is all."

"We might as well sit and enjoy the fireworks," said Mitch, taking a seat on the tailgate of the truck. The rest of them climbed onto the truck, took a seat, and looked up at the sky. I patted May Day a few more times, and he relaxed even more. I climbed on to the back of the truck, too, and leaned against the cab next to Foxy.

When the fireworks ended, the band started playing *God Bless America* and we sang along.

"Didn't know you could sing too," said JD, turning toward me.

"Don't really think I can," I said, blushing.

"You're too modest," said Tesa. "You have more talents than you're giving yourself credit for." She leaned across me toward JD. "Did you know she was a twirler?"

He looked at me surprised. "No, I didn't hear that."

"Yeah, she's really good!" said Grant sarcastically.

"Wish I could see that in action!" said JD with a big smile. "You never said your sister was a twirler too," said JD to Grant.

"Yeah, she throws that thing around and around. Almost hit me a few times. You'll get a chance to see her in the Old Settler's Parade. She'll probably drop her baton and get stampeded by the band."

JD smiled. "I'll definitely have to be here for that."

"Are you guys done embarrassing me?" I asked.

"Yeah, we're done," said Tad, softly socking me in the shoulder. I jumped out of the back of the truck.

"Come on! Let's get back to the dance!" said Matt. Tesa and the guys got off the truck and started walking off.

"I'm just gonna stay here for a few minutes and make sure May Day is calm," I said. Tad started to stay, but Grant pulled him along and said something to him I couldn't hear. I was relieved they were leaving.

Matt turned back to JD. "Aren't you coming?"

"I need some ice for my shoulder," he said. Matt waved and they walked off.

I opened the ice chest, put some ice and water in a bag, and handed it to JD. "I'm surprised one of my brothers isn't staying with us," I said.

"I'm glad they aren't," said JD. "I like talking to you. So what other talents do you have that I don't know about?"

"Um, hard to know where to start when I don't know what you've been told." I took the wrap JD had in his hand, motioning for him to sit on the tailgate.

"Good point," he said. "Now let's see. You must be smart because I saw you were your eighth-grade valedictorian."

"Where did you see that?" I asked, stopping in mid wrap.

"In your school yearbook," said JD. "The Martins have them on a shelf in their den."

"Oh." I wondered how far back he had gone in the yearbooks. I finished wrapping the ice to his shoulder and sat beside him on the tailgate.

"Well, you know all about me! So my turn." I turned to look at him. "How many brothers and sisters do you have?"

"I told you about my twin sisters, Hanna and Tana," he said. "They're sixteen. Mitch is ten and Mark is seven."

"You have a Mitch, too?"

"Yeah, my middle name is Matthew. My dad and Mr. Martin had a good friend in college named Matthew Mitchell who was killed in car wreck. So they named us boys after him."

"That's nice," I said. After a second, I asked, "Are you as protective of your sisters as my brothers are of me?" I looked up as Foxy came to sit beside me.

He chuckled. "No, guess I don't see the need. They're identical twins and they're in separable. So I don't see them needing much protecting."

Someone set off fireworks close by and May Day spooked and reared.

"Easy boy, it's okay," I grabbed his lead and touched his neck and he immediately calmed. "It's okay, it's just loud. It's okay." May Day was nudging me when JD walked up beside us.

"How do you do that?"

"Do what?" I asked, looking up at him.

"Calm him so fast."

I shrugged. "I guess he just knows my voice and trusts me."

"I think there's more to it than that."

I steeled myself, afraid to look at him. "Why do you think that?"

"Because I've been watching you, around animals especially." He reached out and patted May Day. "With Copper yesterday, you knew exactly what to do."

I looked down, afraid to look at him. He put his hand under my chin and lifted it so I was looking at him in the face. "With Travis, you knew he was in pain. You knew I was in pain."

"It's nothing."

"It's not nothing … you're special." I felt my heart skip a beat as I looked into his warm eyes. He rubbed his hand down my cheek and onto my shoulder. "So don't tell me it's nothing."

Foxy and Joey both woofed, and we turned to see my mom and dad coming toward us. JD took a step back from me and turned toward my parents. "Come to check on the animals, too?" he asked jovially.

"Yeah. May Day sure gets spooked by the fireworks," said Dad. "But seems like all's well here."

"I came out as soon as the fireworks started," I said.

"We were getting tired and thought we would call it a night," said Mom. "You might wanna come with us since you have some packing to do," she said, looking at me.

"Packing?" asked JD.

"Yeah, I'm off to band camp in San Marcos tomorrow."

"Gonna learn some more twirling tricks?" he asked with a big smile.

"Yep! Gonna learn some more tricks to go with our fancy sequined suits."

"Well let me help you load up," he said.

"Could use a hand with this," Dad gestured to the ice chest. JD grabbed the other side, and they hoisted it into the back of the truck.

I opened the back of the trailer and led May Day in first. Dad brought Opossum, and JD handed me the lead for Super.

"Is that it?"

"I guess so." I turned to JD. "Will you let my brothers know I went home with my parents?"

"I sure will," he said with a smile. "Ya'll have a safe trip," he said to my mom and dad as they climbed into the truck. Then to me, "You have fun in San Marcos. Is that camp at Texas State University?"

"Yep, I'll be there all week," I said. "Guess I won't see you until the

Uvalde rodeo, so good luck at Nationals!"

"Thanks, I'll need it!"

I got into the truck and Dad handed me a jar of capsaicin. "Give this to JD. He might need it."

"Okay," I got out and ran over to JD as he was by the Martins' truck.

"JD!" I called. He turned to me and I held out the jar. "Dad says you might need this!"

He reached for the jar and put his hand around mine, not letting go. "I'll need more than this," he said with a crooked smile. On impulse, I rolled up on my toes and kissed him on the cheek. "For luck!" I said and ran back to the truck.

I got in and turned to look back as we drove off. I saw JD waving at us with a big smile on his face.

"Nice boy!" said Mom.

"Yeah, great rider," said Dad. "He'll do well at Nationals next week."

"Hope so," I said.

"Why is that?" asked Mom, turning to look at me.

"Because he's a nice guy, not like those other cocky bull riders around here," I said leaning back.

"Oh, I see," said Mom, smiling at Dad knowingly. We drove out of the rodeo grounds and onto the highway. I watched out the window and saw a shooting star. I made a wish that JD would win.

Some Birthday

Band camp was all about getting up early, eating breakfast, going to band practice, going to baton twirling class, lunch, and more twirling. After the first day, we were sore from walking up and down the hills around campus. The second day was worse. We fell into our beds at night and groaned when the alarm went off in the morning.

On the fourth day, I came back to the room before dinner to find an envelope addressed to me taped to our door. I opened it as I went into my room, sat on my bed, unfolded the paper, and sucked in my breath; it was from JD. *"Wish me luck! I ride tonight in the final round. Wish my nurse was here!"*

"JD, I do wish you luck," I said to myself as I lay back on my bed, dreaming of dancing with him.

"What's taking you so long?" called Lori, my roommate and fellow twirler.

"Coming!"

The rest of camp flew by and before I knew it, I was back home.

Tad put his arm around me as we walked to the truck after unloading my stuff from the bus home. I looked up to see Foxy running down the road toward us.

"Wow, I guess I should have asked her to come," said Tad.

I bent down and hugged her. "Missed you too girl!" She licked my face. I stood up and looked at Tad. "You wanna lick my face too?"

"No thanks!"

I laughed. "So did you draw the short straw and have to come get me?" I asked as we put my stuff in the truck and got in. Foxy jumped in the back.

"No, but I wanted to be the one to tell you," he said with a smug look.

"Tell me what?" I asked as he started the truck.

"JD won at Nationals!"

"Wow! That's great!"

"I know!"

"Is he coming back here?"

"Said he was."

"When did you talk to him?"

"I didn't. Matt called last night and said he had won and would be back Sunday."

I was silent for a while. "So think he'll have time for us now that he's a big shot?"

"I'm sure he wouldn't miss a chance to come see you," he said, almost reluctantly.

"What makes you say that?"

"Because he told Matt to pass a message to you specifically."

"What message?"

"That he expects to see you in sequins soon!" I smiled and kept looking straight ahead.

It was back to routine at home. At band practice on Tuesday, I saw Jason.

"I can't believe you have two guys!" said Lori.

"Two?" I said. "I don't have one!"

"Well, you have two interested in you," she said. I shrugged.

Mr. Wilson was handing out new music for the Old Settler's Parade. Old Settlers is a week of celebration with a parade, horse show, craft fair, and rodeo. He announced we were going to wear white T-shirts and jeans in the parade because it was hot. I turned to Carrie, the lead twirler, "Does that mean we won't be wearing our sequined suits?"

"Why, did you promise someone you would show off your new suit?" she asked with a gleam in her eye.

"No," I said. "Can't twirl in jeans."

"Oh yeah, hadn't thought of that," she said.

"I'll think about what to do. Now let's go practice outside," said Carrie.

We were still practicing when the band let out and Jason came to watch. When we were done, I walked over to him.

"How was camp?" he asked.

"Great!" I said. "Got a real good workout walking up and down the hills there." He gave me a wily smile. "I can see you've toned up!"

I blushed and looked away.

Lori ran up to us. "Hey, you gonna do anything special for your birthday Saturday?"

"Your birthday?" asked Jason.

"Yeah, they come 'round every year about the same time!" I said sarcastically.

"No really!" said Lori. "What're you gonna do?"

"The Uvalde rodeo is this weekend. That's where I'll be!"

"Oh!" said Lori, sounding disappointed. "Sounds fun, I guess."

"Yeah, tons!" I said laughing. "Will you be there?" I asked Jason.

"Guess I need to since it's a special occasion," he said with a grin.

"Okay, but no presents!" I said sternly.

"Not even a little one?" asked Lori.

"Nope, just good friends and dancing is all I need to celebrate."

"Hey Jason, how are ya?" Mom asked as she drove up to get me.

"Doing well, Mrs. Stillsen."

"How's your mother?"

"She's doing fine. I'll tell her you asked about her."

"See ya!" We waved and drove off.

"He's such a nice boy," said Mom as we drove out of town toward home.

"Yeah, he is," I said. We rode home in silence.

It was chores, riding, and twirling for the next three days. But Saturday I woke up with a smile on my face: It was my birthday! I was now officially fifteen and never been kissed. "Yet!" I said to myself.

Foxy padded in, jumped on my bed, and yipped softly at me. "Why thank you for the birthday wish!"

I bounced out of bed and pulled on some clothes and ran with Foxy to the barn to feed the horses. The sun was just coming up and everything glowed. I opened the front door and several horses greeted me with low neighs. I fed them and made sure their water was full.

I went into Andrea's stall and patted her belly. "Looking good mama!" She turned from her feed to look at me and snorted. "Yeah, you're gonna be a great mama."

We had bred her with our champion stud earlier in the year, and I made it my personal goal to take good care of Andrea because I had plans for her foal. I was gonna make a champion horse out of it.

I walked out of her stall and over to May Day. "You ready to win today?" I asked him and he nudged me. "I'll take that as a yes!" I patted him on the forehead, then he turned back to his grain.

After taking care of the horses, I ran back to the house. I was coming in the back door of the screened porch and saw Tad coming out of my room.

"There you are!" he said.

"Miss me?" I asked.

"Most people wanna sleep in on Saturday."

"I'm not most people and this Saturday is a special day!" I said with a big smile.

"I know. We have a rodeo today!" he said.

"Yeah that too!" I pushed him, he grabbed me around the head, and we started to scuffle.

"Hey, keep it down," said Grant. "People are trying to sleep!"

We looked up and laughed, as he was fully dressed. "Like who?" I asked.

"Mom and Dad!" he said.

"I guess your sniffer is broke," said Tad. "Can't you smell the bacon?"

"Oh, yeah, well, I was just on my way to feed," said Grant.

"Don't bother," I said. "I already did!"

"You're not supposed to do that, especially not on your birthday!" said Grant.

"Too late and thanks for noticing!" I walked to my door. "Now if you'll excuse me, I need to get presentable for my court!"

I took a shower and got dressed. I was toweling my hair when there was a knock on the door. "Come in!" I sang.

"Whenever her highness is ready we have a special breakfast waiting!" Grant told me.

"Blueberry pancakes?"

"Yep and more," he said. "So hurry it up!"

"Be right there!" I pulled a comb through my hair and ran down the hall into the kitchen. I saw my family standing around the dining table. In front of them was a brand new saddle!

"Whoa, a new saddle!" I said, my voice rising several octaves. "I can't believe you got me a new saddle!"

"Look here," said Tad, pointing. "Dad put your initials on it!"

"Thanks, Dad!" I threw my arms around him.

"You're quite welcome, Dink!" he said. "Well, you aren't so much a Dink anymore, and you need a bigger saddle."

"I love it!" I gave Mom a hug. "Thanks, Mom!"

She laughed. "Now let's eat before the pancakes get any colder!"

"Aww, blueberry pancakes! My favorite! This is turning into a great day!" We laughed and dug in.

"You gonna ride your new saddle today?" asked Tad.

"Of course! Why wouldn't I?"

"It might be a little slick," said Dad.

"I'm willing to take my chances!

"Well, try it out first to see how it feels before you decide to use it tonight," suggested Dad.

"Okay!" I said. We finished up breakfast and I started to clear dishes.

"Just leave this to me," said Mom. "You go try out your new saddle."

"Thanks, Mom!" I turned and Grant was carrying my saddle out the door. "Wow, that's service!"

"Anything for your highness!" he said and bowed a little.

We went down to the barn, and I got May Day out of his stall. I brushed him off and Dad threw a blanket on, then Grant put on my new saddle.

"Wow, that looks great!" I stood back as Grant tightened the cinch.

"Now, if you will please," said Grant, gesturing for me to get on. I got up and Dad and Grant adjusted the stirrups since they were a little long.

"How's that feel?" asked Dad.

"Feels pretty good." I stood up in the stirrups then sat back down. "Now let's try riding around a little."

I rode May Day over to the arena, trotted a little, and then loped around. I did some rollbacks, stops, and came over to the fence where Dad and Grant were watching.

"You're right, it's a little slick."

"It's up to you," said Dad.

"I wanna take this one so I can show it off!"

"But it might affect your riding," said Grant.

"It might," I said. "But I'm not competing at the same level you are."

"Okay," said Dad. "Let's get loaded. Where's Tad?"

"He's back at the house looking for his lucky shirt!" said Grant.

I had a flash of a blue-striped shirt hanging in Dad's closet. "Hmm, maybe it's in someone else's closet," I said as we walked back to the barn.

Dad went to hook up the trailer, and I checked the supplies in the first aid chest. The spot where Dad kept the capsaicin was empty, and I thought wistfully of JD. I got another jar from the medicine cabinet and put it in the box. Grant and I loaded the chest and other equipment we would need today.

Tad still hadn't shown up by the time we loaded the horses. We drove to the house and went inside. I walked down the hall to Tad's room and saw it was in a shambles. "What on earth!" I said and Tad looked out from his closet.

"I can't find my lucky shirt!" he said, exasperated.

"Have you looked in anyone else's closet to see if it got mixed up?" I asked.

"No, I just had it last week!"

"I'll go look in Grant's and Dad's closet," I turned and walked down the hall. I opened Dad's closet and it was right there.

"Found it!" I yelled, coming back down the hall with Tad's lucky shirt.

"Thank goodness!" he said, relieved.

"Just get dressed will ya?" I walked back to my room and grabbed my extra shirt and pair of jeans. I stopped back at Tad's room to see him buttoning his shirt.

"Need me to find anything else for you?" I asked. "Like your head?"

"No, but thanks!"

"Tad, grab the cooler for me!" said Mom as we walked into the kitchen. I rode with Mom in the Suburban, and Tad jumped into the truck with Dad and Grant.

When we got to Uvalde, my stomach started to flutter. I was looking forward to the day's excitement, but I really think I was excited about seeing JD again.

We pulled onto the rodeo grounds, saw the Martins' rig, and pulled up beside them. "Hey Stillsens! How's it going today?" asked Mr. Martin as we got out.

"Doing fine Bart!" said Dad, shaking his hand. "How was Wyoming?"

"Fun!" said Matt, coming up to us.

"I'll bet," said Tad. "Tell me about it!" Matt, Mitch, Tad, and Grant started exchanging stories.

"Where's Tesa?" I asked.

"She'll be here in a few minutes. She had an errand to run," said Mr. Martin with a sly smile.

"Let's get unloaded," I said loud enough that the boys heard and came to help.

I was tying up May Day when I heard a voice behind me. "So here's the birthday girl!"

My heart skipped a few beats, and my stomach hit my boots. I had to compose myself as I turned to see JD leaning against the trailer.

"And here's the national champ!" I said with a big smile. "Congratulations!"

"Thanks," he said. "Did you get my message at band camp?"

"Sure did," I said. "But you didn't need a nurse!"

"Oh, but I did have a nurse. One who helped me realize I like the challenge more than the thrill," he said and moved closer to me. "I got you something." He grinned as he stuck his hand into his pocket and pulled out a silver necklace.

"I saw this and thought of you. Um, actually, I got it before I knew it was your birthday. I kept it with me for good luck." He stepped closer to me, holding it up. "Now this doesn't mean we're going steady or anything because we haven't even been on a date!" We both laughed.

"Wow, it's beautiful." I stepped closer to him and put my hand under the silver figure of a running horse. It sparkled in the sunlight as it dangled from the silver chain.

"Here, let me help you put it on." He undid the clasp and lifted it around my head. I turned my back to him and he fastened it. He turned me. "Yeah, that looks great!" His hands were still on my shoulders and I looked up into his vivid blue eyes. My heart pounded. He leaned in and kissed me on the lips very briefly.

"Happy birthday."

I opened my eyes and he was smiling down at me with his hands still on my shoulders. I felt a little dizzy and I took a breath.

"Thank you," I said softy.

"There she is!" said Tesa, hopping up and down as she came toward us. JD dropped his hands and stepped back as Tesa bounded up and gave me a big hug. "Happy birthday!"

"Now Tesa," I said, looking sternly at her. "Promise me you didn't get the announcer to announce this to the world like last year!"

"No, I didn't do that!" she said. "But I did do something else!"

"Oh no, now what?" I asked in horror.

"Awww, you aren't gonna be any fun about this are you?" she pouted.

"I'm all about fun," I said. "Just not about public displays and embarrassment."

"I know," she said smiling. "This is more subtle."

"Uggh, can't wait!"

"Now, now," said JD, slapping me on the shoulder. "Can't be that bad to be the center of attention."

"Oh, it can be!" I said and they both laughed at me.

"Any presents so far?" asked Tesa with a huge smile.

"As a matter of fact, yes!" I looked up at JD and smiled. "JD just gave me this necklace."

"Oh really!" said Tesa and bent closer to look. "Hey that's pretty," she turned to JD. "Nice going! Did you get anything else?"

"I did." I walked over to the tack compartment and pulled out my new saddle.

"Wow!" said Tesa. "It turned out great!"

"You knew!"

"Yeah, helped pick it out!" she said smugly.

"You did great!" I gave her a hug. "Thanks!"

"Don't thank me yet!"

I drew back quickly. "Why?" I glared at her.

"Just cause!" she said and walked off laughing.

"That girl worries me!"

"Yeah, but she means well," said JD. "Everyone needs good friends."

"Yeah, I love her to death," I said. "But sometimes…"

JD laughed at me as Tad, Grant, Mitch, and Matt walked up.

"Hey, there's the champ!" said Grant, slapping JD on the back. Tad did the same.

"Yeah, did alright in Wyoming!" said JD.

"Alright?" said Matt. "You cleaned up! You should've seen him. He was stuck like glue to those bulls."

"How many did you have to ride?" asked Tad.

"Four!" said JD. "There were supposed to be five rounds, but so many didn't qualify in the second, they collapsed the rounds to four."

Dad and Mr. Martin joined us. "Congratulations, JD!" said Dad.

"Thank you, sir," said JD. "That trick and secret ingredient really helped!"

"Trick?" asked Tad and Grant.

"Yeah," said JD. "Shift and swivel." JD moved his hips in a way that would make Elvis Presley proud.

"Well, guess that works on bulls," said Mitch and they laughed.

Mom started handing out sandwiches and sodas. We were eating when Tesa slipped away and came back holding a cake with candles and sparklers on it. Everyone started singing *Happy Birthday* to me while Mom took pictures.

"Thanks, but really you shouldn't have!"

"Oh, but we did!" said Matt.

"We?" asked Tesa.

"Well, I sang!" said Matt and we laughed. Mrs. Martin cut the cake and served us.

I had just taken a bite when Jared ran up behind me. "Happy birthday!" he cried, sticking his finger in my cake.

"Aaaawwww, Jared!" I yelled. "That was good cake!"

"Sure is!" he said, licking his finger.

"Have some then!" I shoved my cake at him.

"Thanks!"

"Here, have a clean piece," said Mrs. Martin, handing me another as she laughed.

"Thanks!" I said. Pete, Jeremy, and Jason came up and gave me more birthday wishes, and Mrs. Martin handed out more cake.

After a little while Mr. Martin said, "If we're done celebrating we need to get warmed up."

I put my new saddle on May Day, Tesa and I waved at each other as we rode around the warming arena. I was feeling very giddy.

They called the barrel racers over to the paddock. I rubbed my new necklace as we waited.

"Wanna let me rub that for luck, too?" asked Tesa, watching me.

"Sure!" I said and leaned toward her.

She pushed me back. "I was just kidding!"

"Might be what ya need!"

"I'll let you have all of it today!"

There was a ruckus behind us, and we turned to see Cathy Coulter on the way over. Or should I say Cathy Coulter hanging on as Jack Sampson tried to hold her horse as they pranced by us.

"Let's get back," said Tesa, and we moved back out of the way as we watched them struggle to get the horse into the arena. I felt sorry for them as they had passed second call already. You get three calls and if you don't appear in the arena by the third, you're scratched from the event.

So I rode up beside Cathy and talked to her horse Custer. "Easy big fella, easy now."

Custer bumped into us, and I held May Day next to him. Cathy looked at me, almost in a panic. I smiled at her and patted Custer. He settled down enough that we could walk up to the gate.

"Good luck!" I said to Cathy as Jack led the horse into the arena.

Jack looked at me. "Thanks so much! That horse is too much for her ... and me!"

"He's fine. Just needs a buddy!" I said to Jack. "Ya know, race horses have another horse to escort them to the gate. That's what Custer needs."

"Humph," said Jack. "Never even thought of that. We'll give it a try."

We waited for Cathy to finish. She did very well and came back all smiles.

"Thanks so much!" she said to me as I stood there waiting. Custer sidled up to us.

"No sweat." I walked beside them until they were clear of the paddock area. "Think you can handle it from here?" I asked Cathy then looked at Jack.

"Yeah, we can make it," he said with a grateful look.

"Yeah, thanks," said Cathy.

I got back to the paddock in time to see Tesa ride.

"You did great!" I said as she came out of the gate. I gave her a high five.

"Yeah for once!" she said and laughed. "Hey, you did a good deed there with Cathy."

I shrugged. "Us super heroes gotta come out now and then."

"Oh you!" she said, slapping my back.

When it was my turn, I rubbed the horse necklace JD gave me and smiled to myself. I could hear his voice: *"I kept it with me for good luck."*

"Good luck!" said Tesa. "As if you need it!"

I made a face at her as I entered the arena. I patted May Day, took a big breath, and turned him loose. As we were rounding the second barrel, I slid a little in my saddle and hit the barrel with my leg. I saw the barrel wobbling but kept going. There was a searing pain in my knee, but I was determined to finish.

I kicked May Day and we flew around the last barrel and made it home. We slid to a stop, and I looked down and froze. There was blood on May Day's shoulder. I put my hand on May Day and felt no pain radiating from him. I looked around for my dad. They opened the gate and I walked out.

Tesa was there. "You okay?" she asked, but it seemed like her voice was coming from far away.

I looked down as Doc Henderson walked up with a worried look on his face. "You okay?" he asked, checking May Day over.

I looked at him then Dad was there and looked at the blood on May Day's shoulder. "What the heck?" He patted my leg and I winced. "Sara you're hurt!"

I sucked in air through my teeth. "My knee's on fire!"

"Let's move over out of the way," Dad said as he walked beside me.

Dad looked at my knee again. He poked at the rip in my jeans, and I jerked away and bit my lip. He grabbed the rip and pulled it open more. I groaned and he nodded his head. "You gotta bad cut."

Doc leaned in. "Definitely needs some stitches. Let's get her over to the trailer."

Dad swung up behind me, and I leaned back on him as we rode to the trailer. JD was there and looked up as we approached. I could see the worry on his face.

"What happened?" he asked.

"She hit a barrel and cut her leg," said Dad. "Here, help her down."

I slid down into JD's arms as Dad got off and tied May Day to the trailer.

"Put her over here," said Doc, indicating the tailgate of the truck. Foxy jumped down from her perch to see what was going on. JD set me down, and Dad was right there. JD sat behind me to prop me up as Dad whipped out his pocketknife and cut the leg of my jeans. Foxy lay down beside me and whined. I reached to pet her, and she licked my hand.

"Ohhh!" said Dad. "That's a nasty gash!"

"Here," said Doc, handing Dad some gauze and sterile water to wash off my leg. I winced as it stung, and JD grabbed my hand.

"Yeah, bad gash. Needs stitches!" said Dad. "Let's get you down to the emergency room."

"Can't Doc just stitch me up?" I asked.

"No, no, I'm only licensed for animals, not humans," he said, handing Dad some gauze.

Dad wrapped my knee, but it kept bleeding through. JD carried me to the front of the truck as Doc opened the door. JD slid me onto the seat. He patted my shoulder and wiped a tear that ran down my cheek.

"You'll be fixed up in no time!" he said and winked at me.

I nodded my head. "Thanks!"

I heard Dad tell Foxy and Joey to get down and stay. He got in the truck and we took off. "What about Mom?" I asked.

Dad pointed and there was Mom coming toward us. I scooted over and she got in the truck beside me.

"Wow!" said Mom. "I knew you hit that barrel, but didn't know it was that hard!"

"I think the barrel had a rusty edge!" said Dad, driving faster than he should be through the grounds. "Cut pretty deep."

We got to the emergency room, and Dad carried me inside as Mom parked the truck. A male nurse met us as we came through the doors. He pointed to a gurney and Dad set me down. The nurse started asking a ton of questions as another nurse showed up and wheeled me to a room.

They cut off the gauze wrap, and the gash started to bleed again. They put a pressure bandage on my leg and asked me if I'd rather take off my jeans or let them cut them off. I looked up at Mom then at the nurse. "Can't you just cut them up a little higher?"

The nurse shrugged. "Guess so."

He cut my jeans further up my thigh and wiped off all the blood he could.

"Hey Dr. Bailey!" said Mom, recognizing the man as he walked into my room. He had treated my brothers and me many times before.

"Well, nice to see the Stillsens, but this isn't the way I like to see them. Now what do we have here?"

The nurse rattled off the problem before anyone else could answer.

Dr. Bailey turned to me. "What did you do?"

"Hit a barrel!" I said, gritting my teeth.

"Well, let's get you stitched up. You in much pain?" asked Dr. Bailey

"It feels like my knee's on fire!"

"We'll get you a little something for that!" He wrote something on the chart and walked out.

A nurse came back a minute later and gave me a shot. After a second, I could feel the pain floating away.

The male nurse came back in. "Let's get this boot off." I winced as he pulled off my boot as gently as he could. Mom took it from him and went to sit by Dad.

Dr. Bailey came back in. "Now let's look at this gash." He pulled off the pressure packing and poked at the gash. "Wow, nasty!" He told Rob, the nurse, to get him some stuff then he looked up at my dad, who was now standing beside me.

"Come around here Sonny, let me show you." He poked again as Dad watched. "This is the ligament, and it's cut some here. Now I can stitch that up or you can call in an orthopedist to do it."

"I trust you, Dr. Bailey," said Dad. "Go ahead and stitch it up."

"Will do," said Dr. Bailey as Rob came back with a tray of stuff.

Dr. Bailey filled a syringe with something and looked at me. "Let's get this deadened up so we can clean it up better, then we'll do some fancy whip stitches. Now a little stick."

I winced and Dad held my hand as Dr. Bailey stuck me repeatedly.

Once the area was sufficiently numb, Dr. Bailey cleaned up the wound and began stitching me up. I must have dozed off because next thing I knew Mom was shaking my shoulder.

"Time to get up!"

"Wow," I said, sitting up and feeling dizzy.

"Easy does it," said Rob. "Just sit for a minute while I get you some crutches and your brace."

"Crutches!" I said alarmed, "and a brace!"

"Now honey," said Mom. "You won't be able to walk on that for a few days or you'll rip the ligament even more."

I looked down at my bandaged leg and shook my head. "What a birthday this turned out to be!"

Rob came back and wrapped the brace around my leg. It went from my ankle to high on my thigh. He adjusted the height of the crutches for me. He handed Mom some papers. "This is a prescription for pain, and here is one for an antibiotic. No getting the stitches wet. The external ones will need to come out in about ten days."

"Do I have to go home or can I stay?" I asked my parents as we drove back to the arena.
"You can do whatever you feel like," said Dad.
"I feel like staying at least until the end of the rodeo. I hope I haven't missed all of it!"
We pulled into the grounds and could hear the announcer calling the bull riders to report. "We haven't missed everything!" said Mom.
"Where to?" asked Dad.
"Back to the trailers, please. I wanna check on May Day."
Dad laughed and drove toward our trailer. "Just like you to worry about your horse!"
"Hey, he's my partner!"
"We know," said Mom. "We're just happy you care for your animals. Now take it easy!"
"Yes, ma'am," I said as we got out.
Mom handed me my crutches and I hobbled over to May Day. He turned to me, neighed softly, and bobbed his head at me. "Hey big guy, how are you?" I patted him. I stroked his shoulder that I thought had been cut. Someone had washed the blood off his shoulder.
I was leaning on him, grateful he wasn't hurt, when Foxy came up and nudged me. "Hey girl!" I felt warmth and peacefulness run through me as I stood there.
"You gonna live?" asked Grant, breaking my reverie.
I turned to him and smiled. "Yeah I'll make it!"
"How bad?" he asked, pointing at my knee.
"Cut the ligament some."
"Ouch! How many stitches?"
"Uh, I don't know." I looked over Grant's shoulder. "Hey Mom, how many stitches?"
"About ten on the inside and fifteen on the outside. He did small ones so there wouldn't be a big scar. I'm gonna run to the pharmacy and get these prescriptions filled. Need anything?"
"No, I'm good."
"You need some new jeans," said Grant. "Or are you going for a new look?"
I looked down. "I guess I should change. Will you please grab my

other jeans and shirt out of the Suburban before Mom takes off?"

"Sure." said Grant and he yelled at Mom. He came back in a second with my jeans and shirt. "I'll put them in the trailer for you," He opened the door and set them inside. "Need any help?"

"Probably, but I'd prefer Tesa."

"I'll go find her. Here, let me help you into the trailer first."

"Thanks." I sat down and he walked out and closed the door. I had changed my shirt when there was a knock on the door.

"Who is it?"

"Tesa!"

"Come in!"

"So how are you?"

"I'll live, but first I need to split this seam in my jeans. They won't go up over this wrapping."

"No problem. I'll get my mom to do it. She's right outside."

"You aren't watching JD ride?" I asked as I handed Tesa the jeans.

"He rides last and we can make it over. They're still running the bronc riders, though."

She said, "Be back in a second." I relaxed a minute.

I heard voices outside and Tesa came in.

"Wow that was fast!" I said.

She handed me my jeans and helped me get them on. "Hey just right!"

"Yeah, real sexy," said Tesa looking at me as I stood up. The seam was split up my thigh. "Might even start a new trend."

"Yeah, right!" I rolled my eyes. "Just wait 'til I put this big ol' brace on. Then ask my how sexy it looks."

Tesa helped me put the brace on. When she opened the door for me, Grant was there.

"Here, allow me." He lifted me down to the ground.

"Thanks!" I looked around and saw lots of friendly faces. "Hey ya'll!" Tesa handed me my crutches.

"What did that barrel do to you?" asked Jared.

"Laid my knee wide open and cut my ligament."

"Ouch! You gonna be able to dance tonight?" asked Jared.

"Only if you carry me," I said, laughing.

"I can do that!"

"No way, buddy," said Grant. "I don't want you dropping her on her head and making her worse."

"Okay, well are you going?" asked Jared.

Everyone was looking at me expectantly. "I'm considering it."

"What's to consider?" asked Pete.

"All I can do is sit."

"You can enjoy our company!" said Jared.

"Why are ya'll making such a big deal out of this?" I asked warily.

"Hey, you were the one who said no presents, just dancing with friends," said Jason.

"I'll go for a while."

Grant slapped me on the shoulder. "That's the spirit! If you wanna watch JD ride, we better hurry."

"I can't hurry much of anywhere," I said. "Ya'll go on. I'll wait here."

"Nonsense," said Grant. "We'll carry you." Jared and Grant made a chair with their arms, and they carried me over to the stands.

"This is great!" I said.

"Anything for your highness," said Grant, chuckling. "But just for today!"

"Aww, the fantasy ends at midnight!"

"How's the knee?" Mrs. Martin asked as she joined us in the stands.

"Cut the ligament some, but I'll heal."

We watched as the first bull rider came out of the chute. He didn't make it to the buzzer. The next seven came out and only one made it to the buzzer. Then they announced JD as the national high school champion. He came out of the chute and we held our breath. The buzzer sounded and he stepped off like it was nothing. He waved to the cheering crowd.

"That ought to put him in first!" said Grant. They announced JD's score and he had won.

Then it hit me. "Hey," I said to Grant, "I didn't even ask how did ya'll end up doing?"

"I got first in calf roping. Matt and Mitch took second in team roping, and Tad and I took fourth." He looked over at Tesa. "She got second in barrels and poles." He hesitated and smiled at me.

"And you my fair lady, even with hitting that barrel, got first!"

"What? But I knocked it over!"

"Nope," said Mrs. Martin. "It wobbled but never tipped over!" She handed me my first place belt buckle. "Here's your prize."

"No way!" I said. "I hit that thing too hard."

"Well, believe it!" said Tesa. "The one chance I have and you still beat me!" But she was smiling.

"Wow!" I said, "must be some birthday luck. Thank you, Mrs. Martin, for collecting this for me!"

"Now can we help you down the stands?" Grant asked.

"I think I can handle it now that everyone else has passed," I said, getting up.

I made my way slowly back to the trailers, and Grant and Tesa walked beside me as the others walked ahead.

"You gonna be okay?" Tad asked me.

"Yeah, I'll still be around to make your life miserable!" I said, smiling at him.

"What'd the doctor say?"

"I cut the ligament and will be on these stupid crutches for a week or so."

"Could've been worse," Tad patted my shoulder. "Glad you're okay."

"Hey champ!" said Tad, giving JD a high five as he approached with some of the guys. Several others followed him as I made my way over to the truck and sat down on the tailgate. Foxy came and lay down beside me. I swung my leg up, setting it on the tailgate to rest, and leaned against Foxy.

"You planning on going to the dance?" Dad asked.

"I'd like to, but I don't wanna make the boys leave too early."

"I'm sure they'd accommodate you tonight," said Dad. He called Grant and Tad over. "You two okay with taking your sister to the dance and leaving early if she asks?"

"Yeah, I think we could do that *this* time!" said Grant.

"Yeah, but just tonight!" said Tad, nudging me.

"Okay. When your Mom gets here, we'll take off and leave you to it," said Dad. "Now let's load up."

"You sure you're okay to go to the dance?" JD asked as he watched me hobbling.

"I think I can manage to sit around and talk to my friends."

"I'd be happy to sit with you."

"I'd like that, but I think some of your fans might be disappointed if you didn't dance with them some."

He laughed lightly. "This champion thing might take some getting used to."

"Just don't go getting cocky," I said with a smile.

"I'll try not to! I better go change if we're going to the dance! Can I help you over to the truck again?"

"I think I can make it on my own, but thanks for the offer." He walked off toward the Martins' trailer as I hobbled back to the truck and opened the back door.

Mom drove up with a bag from the pharmacy. "You need one of these now?" she asked, taking the bottle out of the bag and looking at the label. "Wow, this is strong stuff!"

Mom handed me the bottle of pills. "What am I supposed to do with these? They won't fit in my pocket."

"Hmm," said Mom as she turned and walked to the trailer.

She came back and handed me a baggie with a few pills in it. "I'll leave the ice chest in the Suburban with some bags in case you want ice for your knee, and there's a pillow if you wanna use it to prop your leg up."

"Thanks, Mom!" I said. "You're so thoughtful!"

"Well, been dealing with rodeo wounds for a long time now," she said with a wink.

Dad came over. "I guess we're ready to go!"

"Me too!" I said and slid out of the truck. "See ya'll later!" I hobbled to the back of the truck and gave Foxy a pat. "Don't worry, I'm fine." She gave me a "yaawwl" then sniffed. I heard Dad chuckle and I looked at him. "What?"

"I sometimes get the impression you two really can talk to each other!"

"We do!" I said with a smile. I hobbled toward the gang waiting between the Martins' trailer and ours.

"Hey, there's the birthday girl!" said Matt, pointing to me. "Now can we go?"

"Yeah, let's go!" yelled Trent and they moved off toward the dance floor. I looked at Jason, who stayed beside me and shrugged. "I'll be moving at a much slower pace."

"No you won't!" said Grant and Tad, coming up behind me and scooping me up in their "arm chair."

I dropped my crutches and Jason said, "I'll get them."

"Thanks, guys! I was afraid I might not make it there before the dance was over!"

"So did we," said Tad. "We would miss all the fun waiting for you."

"Well, thanks for flexing your muscles for me!"

My brothers carried me up to the door, and Jason handed me my crutches as we went inside. The gang had already staked out some tables. JD pulled out a chair for me and Matt swung another around so I could prop my leg up.

"Anything else you need your highness?" asked Tad.

I laughed. "I could use a cold drink!"

"Your wish is my command," said Tad with a bow. I laughed at him as he walked off. The band started up and many of the gang paired off and hit the floor.

Jason sat down beside me. "So how do you feel now?"

"I'm okay!"

"Not hurting?"

"Nope. My knee is still numb, but I'm thirsty."

"Here comes the cure for that," he said as Tad set a drink in front of me.

"Bless you!" I said to Tad and gulped down half of it.

"Wow I better go get some more!" he said and walked off again.

Jason sat with me for a few songs. Much to my relief, Leena showed up. "What in the world did you do?" she demanded.

"I cut my knee on a barrel!"

"Yeah, but she won anyway!" said Tesa, coming up behind her.

"Wow! How do you do that?" asked Leena.

"Not sure!" JD walked up behind Tesa and Leena. "Must be some special luck one gets on their birthday!"

I smiled at JD as I put my hand to my necklace.

"How long you gonna be on those?" asked Leena as she sat down.

"At least a week. Might not get to march in the Old Settler's Parade."

"What?" asked JD. "I was looking forward to seeing you in sequins!"

I blushed a little. Tad came back with three drinks and set them down in front of me. "Whoa, I don't think I'm that thirsty!"

"Well share then!" said Leena, taking one of the cups. "Thanks, Tad!"

"Don't mention it!" he said and smiled at her.

"Well, folks," I said, putting my leg down and sitting up. "I need to go find a bathroom." Jason jumped up and handed me my crutches as I stood up.

"We'll go with you," said Tesa.

"Yeah, you might fall in if we don't," said Leena.

"Har har!" I hobbled out from the tables and down the side toward the bathrooms.

"So you gonna tell Leena about your present from JD?" asked Tesa.

"JD gave you a present?"

I stopped for a second and held up the necklace. "He gave me this!" I said, smiling.

"Wow, that's pretty!" said Leena. "So how'd he do it?"

"He gave it to me this morning. He told me he saw it, thought of me, and kept it with him for luck."

"Must have gotten it when we were in Wyoming," said Tesa.

"He said he got it before he knew it was my birthday."

"Yeah, well he didn't know about that until I started making plans with my mom last week."

I looked at Tesa then at Leena. "After he helped me put on the necklace, he kissed me."

"What? Oh my gosh! How was it?" they asked me.

"Rather nice!" I smiled. "Made my heart race. But he quoted my words from Rocksprings back to me." I sighed.

"And that was?" asked Leena.

"That this doesn't mean anything since we haven't gone out on a date or anything."

"Whoa, that's, well, that means he likes you!" said Leena.

"Yeah. He likes you and I mean *likes* you!" said Tesa.

"Okay, so he likes me."

We finally arrived at the bathroom. There wasn't a line yet and I was grateful.

"So he likes you," said Leena. "What are you trying to tell us?"

"What am I supposed to do with Jason hovering around me?" I asked. "I like him and all, but I like JD more. I know JD's gonna leave in a few weeks and will probably forget all about me, but I'd like to get to know him while he's around."

"I can help with Jason," said Leena. "I'll ask him to dance, and I'm sure Tesa would help, too."

"Are you okay?" Leena asked me as I came back out of the stall, wincing in pain.

"I'm starting to feel my knee again, but it's not bad."

"My mom said I was to make you take your medicine if you started hurting," said Tesa.

"I don't wanna take it yet. This stuff makes me loopy."

We washed our hands and went back to the tables. I sat down and sighed.

"Hey, why don't you come dance with me?" Leena said to Jason.

He turned to me. "You need me for anything?"

"No, go have fun," I said, waving him off.

I grabbed one of the cups in front of me, leaned back, relaxed, and gulped down some soda. Jared came up and kicked the chair my knee was on by accident, and I winced as the shock ran up my leg.

"Sorry!"

"It's okay," I said as he sat down beside me. "You didn't mean it!" I took a deep breath and let it out slowly, pushing down the pain.

Grant came over with a worried look on his face. "Hey, we can leave any time."

"No, no, I'll be fine." I pushed Jared. "Doofus here kicked the chair, and it jolted me."

Grant frowned. "I said I was sorry!" Jared said defensively.

"I'll let it slide this time!" Grant turned and walked over to a group of girls from Uvalde and asked one of them to dance.

"Don't hang around here just to be nice!" I said to Jared. "Really, go dance!"

He got up. "If you say so." He turned to Tesa. "Wanna dance?"

"Sure," she said and winked at me as they went off.

I leaned back, took another deep breath, and let it out slowly.

"I know that look," said JD, coming over and sitting down beside me. "It says the numb is wearing off, and the pain is like fire."

"It isn't too bad," I said. "Just need to hold still for a little bit."

"Uh huh, then it'll creep up on you and the painkillers won't kick in fast enough." He leaned to face me. "Now be a good girl and take a pill!"

"Yes, nurse!" I said, smiling at him. I fished out a pill, popped it in my mouth, and took a swig of soda. "There, now you'll have to carry me back to the truck in a little while because I don't think I could walk, let alone on crutches, with this stuff in me."

"Be happy to," said JD as he sat back. "So did they tell ya you won after hitting that barrel?"

"Yeah, Grant told me. I'm still shocked."

"Matt said the crowd held their breath as that barrel wobbled back and forth," said JD with a smile.

"I'll have to ask him for a play by play later."

"Scared me when you came riding up with your dad. You were white as a sheet, and there was blood all over your horse."

"Well, thanks for catching me, carrying me, and holding my hand."

"Least I could do for my good luck charm." He winked at me.

"Some luck!"

"Hey, you still won, didn't you?"

"Yeah but at what cost! Now I can't even show you how well I twirl."

"I'll be here for a few weeks, and you'll be all better soon."

"I hope so."

"I know so," he said with a warm smile.

We watched people dancing by us, and I felt the painkiller kick in. In between songs, everyone came by and said hello. JD danced with Leena and Tesa and a few Uvalde girls but always came back to sit beside me. Then the band took a break and all my friends were there chatting away.

"You okay?" asked Grant, sitting next to me leaning in real close.

"Yeah why?"

"Because you look like you're flying high!"

"Maybe because I am. These drugs are great!"

He laughed and patted me on the shoulder. "I better not leave you alone."

"I haven't been alone all night. Someone's always been right here beside me keeping me company." I sighed. "Besides it's kinda nice just to sit and watch."

Grant chuckled as Tad came over. "We need to leave?" he asked.

"She says she's fine," said Grant.

Tad looked at me. "How high are you?"

"I'm feeling no pain," I said, smiling.

"Let us know when it's time to leave. Don't play brave," said Grant.

"Yes sir!" I gave them a salute.

The band started up again and everyone was gone. I thought I was by myself, but JD appeared beside me. "You still okay?"

"Why does everyone keep asking me that?"

"Because we care."

"I just wondered if I looked stupid or was drooling."

"No, you look pretty as usual," said JD with a crooked smile.

"I could use some fresh air. Do you mind coming outside with me?"

"Not at all." He stood up and handed me my crutches and we went out the front door.

"Wow! It's lots cooler out here," I said.

"Let's go sit over there." JD pointed to a picnic table. I sat down and swung my leg up on the bench. JD sat across from me.

"So you got anymore questions you wanna ask me?"

"Let's see, you told me about your family. So tell me about your friends and life in Houston."

He told me about his two best friends, Larry and Seth. He told me how he worked for his dad part time in construction. He wanted to go to Texas A&M and get an engineering degree so someday he could be a partner with his dad in the family business. He told me how his dad usually came with him to the rodeos, but he had a big job that was going wrong and the foreman quit, so his dad had to get the Martins to take him around.

"Did your family get to see you ride at Nationals?"

"Yeah, they flew up for the week. They're planning on coming to Old Settler's, so you can meet them then. Well, the rest of them; you already met my dad."

"That seems like a long time ago already."

"Not to me," he said. "I can still picture when I first saw you."

I frowned. "And when was that exactly?"

He smiled. "You were riding the barrels. Your blonde hair was flying behind you. You match that big palomino gelding you ride."

"How do I match him?"

"All calm on the outside and full of wild power inside," he said, leaning toward me.

"May Day has power. Not sure I'd call it wild."

"Not untamed wild. Just able to run free when he gets the chance." He looked at my necklace and pointed. "That's what I saw when I spotted that necklace: speed, strength, and grace all running free."

I nodded. "I can see that."

"You're about one of a handful of riders I know who can get more out of your horse without spurs or a whip."

"I don't ask for more than they wanna give."

"I like that," he said. He leaned across the table and looked at me closely. Then he kissed me. My heart skipped a beat at the thrill of his warm lips on mine. He pulled back and I opened my eyes. He was smiling at me as he sat back. "Sorry I couldn't help myself."

"Don't be sorry," I said breathlessly. "Never apologize for something that feels right."

"Well then," he leaned over and kissed me again, but this time he put a hand on my cheek and a warm tingle ran across my face and down my spine. He sat back, pulling my hair through this hand. He let it go as he looked over my shoulder.

"Right on cue!" he said, nodding over my shoulder.

I turned to see what he was nodding at and saw Tad and Grant walking toward us. They were smiling, so I was relieved.

"There you are!" said Grant as they walked up.

"Got hot in there!" I said. "JD was telling me about Nationals."

Tad looked back and forth between JD and me, but I couldn't read his face.

"What?" I asked.

"Nothing," said Tad, sitting down beside me. "You look beat."

"I'm getting a little tired."

"Well let's go then," said Tad, getting up.

"Go dance another round or two and by that time I'll have made it back to the Suburban."

"I think you need an escort," said Grant. "I don't think you can make it that far on your own."

"Go dance a few rounds and say good-bye to your girls. Then bring the Suburban around closer and we'll leave."

"Full of drugs and she still makes perfect sense," said Grant. "Come on, Tad, let's go dance a little more. They're fine." Grant walked off and Tad followed him.

"Wow," said JD. "I was expecting more of a confrontation."

I shrugged. "Either they didn't see you kissing me or they took what I said to heart."

"And just what did you say?" asked JD, putting his hand on mine.

I felt my heart skip a beat. I smiled as I looked up at him. "I told Tad that he needed to trust me and you too."

"And if I break that trust?"

"Well, in this small town, they would just drag you out behind the barn and thrash you to within an inch of your life."

"Wow, that's harsh!"

"That's life in a small town."

"I better stay on the good side of everyone then!"

"I don't think you have to worry about that. Staying on the good side, I mean."

"How so?"

"You've already reached fame status."

"Is that all I have to do to be untouchable?"

"Yeah, that little thing!"

He sighed. "You really make me feel good."

"Well, you make me feel pretty good, too."

He squeezed my hand and nodded over my shoulder. "Well fun is about to end for this evening." He got up and came around beside me. "You think you can walk?"

I looked up at him and shook my head. "Not really."

"Then I get to carry you."

"Okay!" I smiled up at him.

Tad came over with Tesa, Leena, Mitch, and Matt. "Grant went to get the Suburban," said Matt.

"Need any help?" asked Tesa.

"Nope." I stood up and JD caught me as I wavered. I patted him on the chest. "JD here has offered to be my trusty steed and carry me, as I can no longer walk. But someone could grab my crutches."

Tad took a breath and grabbed my crutches. The lights of the Suburban flashed across us and Grant honked.

"Well, that's our cue." JD swung me up into his arms. As we walked to the Suburban, I laid my head on JD's shoulder and whispered to him. "I wish you were coming with me. I could use a nice chest like this to lean on during the drive home. You give me courage to look into the darkness of the void."

"I'm not sure what that meant, but I think you'll be out in about two minutes anyway," he said.

We were at the Suburban, and Tesa got the door. I slid into the back seat, and Tad put my crutches in back.

"Hope you had a happy birthday after all," said Tesa.

"Yeah, happy birthday!" said Leena.

"Thanks!"

"Here's a couple of pillows," said Tad, handing them to me across the back seat. JD grabbed one, lifted my leg, and tucked the pillow under it. I flipped the other behind my head and smiled at him.

"All set?" he asked.

"Yeah, thanks."

He squeezed my ankle then shut the door. "Drive safe!" he said to Tad and Grant. We waved and said "bye" as we drove off. I looked out the back window and saw JD put his arms around Leena and Tesa as they headed back into the dance. I leaned back with a sigh and closed my eyes.

"You need any more pain meds?" asked Tad, turning to look at me over the seat.

"Naw, I'm good."

"Is that the pain medicine or the kiss talking?" asked Tad. "And don't try to deny it."

I opened my eyes to look at him. I shrugged and smiled. "Maybe both?"

Grant laughed. "Tad, our little sister is growing up!"

Tad turned around and sighed. "Yeah I know!"

Grant laughed as we drove on. Tad turned on the radio and tuned in a country station he liked. Before we got out of town, I was asleep.

Teaching Leena to Cook

Light fell across my face and I felt a cool hand on my head. I opened my eyes. I could see Mom silhouetted in the hall light.

"You alright?" she asked. It was about three in the morning, and I was lying on my bed fully clothed. Foxy was beside me and whined as she laid her head on my stomach.

"I think so," I said, patting Foxy.

"You were murmuring," said Mom. "Thought you might need some pain medicine."

I sat up and winced. "Yeah, think I do."

"Here," said Mom, handing me a pill and some water.

I took the pill and drank the water. She set the glass on my nightstand. "I don't remember getting home."

Mom laughed softly. "You were totally out of it when Tad carried you in. You wouldn't let me help you get undressed."

"Guess I can get out of these things now." Mom helped me change into my favorite big t-shirt and shorts.

"Where did you get that?" asked Mom, pointing at my necklace.

I held it up so she could see and smiled. "JD gave it to me!"

"He did?" she asked, sitting on the edge of the bed.

"Yeah, he said he saw it while he was at Nationals and thought of me."

"It's very nice."

"He, he also kissed me," I stammered.

Mom laughed. "And Tad didn't make a scene?"

"Nope. He's finally starting to trust me." I yawned and laid back.

She got up pushed my hair out of my face. "I'm glad you have big brothers who care about you."

"Me too!"

She smiled and turned to leave. "Night!"

"Night!"

She closed the door, Foxy crawled up next to me, and I petted her. "Ya know Foxy, this wasn't a bad birthday all in all."

I was standing on a cliff with the wind blowing in my hair. There were dark clouds off to the west that blocked the sun. The lightning flashed and there was JD walking toward me. A crow flew by and JD was standing behind me, pointing over my shoulder. I looked to the east and saw a dark void, but I wasn't afraid. I felt the warmth in my chest and tingles ran down my arms. The lightning flashed again then the thunder boomed. Then more thunder, but it didn't sound right. I couldn't figure out what it was.

There it was again, a knocking. I struggled to open my eyes. It was so bright. I heard Tad's voice, "You gonna get up anytime this afternoon?"

My eyes shot open. "Afternoon? What time is it?"

"It's one thirty!"

"Ugh, my mouth feels like it's full of cotton."

"Here have some water." Tad held out a glass. I sat up and steadied myself; I was dizzy. He sat down on the bed and looked at me concerned. "You okay?"

"I just need to wake up! I've been asleep forever." I took the glass from him and gulped it down.

"You up for some company?"

"Not right now. Why who's here?"

"I meant me," he said, laying across the foot of my bed.

"Oh. Let me make a pit stop first," I swung my legs over the side and steadied myself again. Tad started to help me. "No don't get up. I'll be fine."

I grabbed my crutches that were propped against the chair that was now next to my bed and hobbled to the bathroom. When I came back, Tad was lying on my bed, staring up at the ceiling.

"So what did you wanna talk about?" I asked, sitting down and scooting back so I could roll on my side and face him.

"Well, I wanted to let you know I think JD is a great guy." He was picking at my blanket and not looking at me.

"But?"

"But he's just so, so experienced, and I'm worried he might hurt you."

"Tad, I understand you wanna protect me from the players in the world, but I don't think JD's that kind of guy."

"I think I saw that when I watched him with you last night."

"Oh? How did it seem last night?"

He smiled at me. "You don't remember?"

"Well, I remember most of it, I think."

He smiled. "You don't remember hanging all over him and telling everyone you were gonna run off together?"

"I did not!" I said slapping at him. He laughed as I grabbed a pillow and hit him with it. "You're such a cad!"

"Hey, what's the ruckus?" asked Grant. "This is an invalid's room! Stop that!"

I threw a pillow at Grant. "You should hear what Tad is trying to tell me I did last night."

"What did Tad say you did, and why don't you remember?" asked Grant, looking at me sideways.

"Nevermind. I know I won't get the truth out of either of you!"

Grant laughed and sat down on my bed, too. "So how's the knee today?"

"It hurts some, but I don't want any more of that pain medicine. I might sleep my life away."

"We'll get you some aspirin. But first," said Grant, "tell me about the kiss!"

"What kiss?" I asked with a blank look, but my heart started racing at the thought of kissing JD.

"What kiss?" said Grant with a snort. "Can you believe this act?" He looked at Tad.

"What did I do?" I said innocently.

Grant and Tad, both appearing shocked, looked at each other then at me. "You really don't remember sitting at the picnic table with JD?" asked Grant.

"Um, no, not ringing any bells." I frowned, trying not to smile. I wanted to find out how much they saw before I said anything.

"Man, you must have been more out of it than I thought!" said Tad.

"Why? What happened?" I asked with a concerned look on my face.

"You were outside the dance sitting on a picnic table talking to JD, or should I say he was kissing you when we spotted you," Grant explained.

"Oh!" I said, looking surprised, "Guess I really was out of it." I decided to let them off the hook as they both looked befuddled. "I remember him kissing me twice!"

"You little minx!" said Grant and he hit me with a pillow. I squealed and Tad poked me and I jerked away. "Oh ouch, ouch, ouch!" I said, grabbing for my knee.

"Sorry!" said Grant and Tad. I sucked in air through my teeth and held my breath. I shook my head and closed my eyes. "What did you do?" asked Tad.

Through clenched teeth I said, "I bent my knee a little when you tickled me. Oh man, that hurts!"

"What did you do?" asked Mom coming in.

"We were horsing around," said Tad. "We didn't mean to hurt her."

"It's okay," I said, sucking in more air and letting it out slow. "I did it to myself." I took another breath as they watched me with worried faces. "I just gotta learn not to bend it." I tried to smile. "Please stop staring at me."

"Well, let's get you some medicine," said Mom, reaching for the bottle of pills by my bed.

"No! No, not those," I said. "I don't wanna sleep anymore."

"I could cut one in half," offered Mom. "Seems like you need a dose right now anyway."

"Well, okay," I said and Mom left the room.

"Want some ice or something?" asked Grant.

"Ya know, what I really want," I said sitting up, "is for you to finish telling me about last night. Then I could use some food."

"Uh well," said Tad, "we were looking for you at the dance and we decided to check the truck. That's when we spotted ya'll sitting at the tables outside. I saw JD lean across the table and kiss you." He finished with a smirk.

"Yeah, that seems about right!" I said smugly.

Tad spotted my new necklace. "Hey, where'd you get this?" he asked, reaching for it.

"JD gave it to me!"

"Really? When?" asked Grant, crossing his arms and frowning at me.

"Yesterday morning, just after we got there," I said, looking down at the necklace.

"He said he saw it when he was at finals and it reminded him of me."

"Hmm," said Tad. "He's got good taste."

"I think so, too!" said Mom, coming back in and handing me half a pill and some water.

"You knew about this?" asked Grant, pointing.

"Yeah, she told me last night," said Mom. "You let them be!" she said shaking her finger at them.

"Yes ma'am," they both said with a smile.

She turned to me. "Now missy, do you want something to eat?"

"Yes please!" I said and scooted to the side of the bed to get up.

"I've got you," said Grant as he scooped me up in his arms. "Man, did you gain weight?"

I slapped his chest. "Yep, it's called muscle. I got it at band camp!"

They laughed as we walked down the hall and into the kitchen. Grant set me down on one of the barstools then sat down beside me. Mom placed a sandwich and some milk in front of me. "Thanks, Mom!" I bit into the sandwich.

"I got some great shots from the rodeo last night," said Mom. "You should check them out."

"I will," I said around another bite.

Dad walked in. "Hey, there's my sleepy head! How's the knee?"

"I'm okay," I said around a bite. "As long as I don't bend it, I'm fine."

"Good." He sat down and Mom handed him a glass of ice water.

"Who cleaned up May Day last night?" I asked, looking around at my family.

"I did," said Tad. "He was stomping his feet and didn't like the smell of your blood on him."

"I cleaned off your new saddle, or at least as much of the blood as I could get off," said Grant.

"Well, thank you both," I said, smiling at them.

"I cleaned the rest of the blood off your saddle this morning," said Dad. "I used some oil to darken it so the stains don't show."

"Thanks, Dad," I said. "I'm sure lucky you know what to do."

He nodded as the phone rang. Mom answered and we listened. "She's doing pretty good." Pause. "Yeah, I think that would be a good idea." Pause. "Okay." Pause. "Yeah I'll tell them. Saturday then. Thanks Ellen." She hung up the phone.

"Well?" asked Dad, "What does Ellen have in mind?"

"She asked about Sara. Then asked if it would be alright if Tesa and the boys come for a visit and practice Saturday."

"All right!" said Grant. "Time to get some payback!"

"For what?" asked Dad.

"Uh, um, for them beating us at Uvalde," said Tad quickly.

"Just keep it civil," said Dad, looking at them knowingly.

"Yes, sir!" said Tad and Grant.

"Now I need you boys to help with a few chores." Dad got up and the boys followed him out.

"I need a shower," I said. "How am I supposed to not get my knee wet?"

"Wrap plastic wrap around and tape it," said Mom. "Come on, I'll help you," she said, grabbing the plastic wrap and tape.

"I don't have my crutches."

"I'm sure a little weight on it won't hurt. Besides if you don't use those muscles some, you'll get all weak and lopsided."

"I'm sure glad you're my mom!" I said, slipping off the barstool and limping towards the hall.

"You say the nicest things!" said Mom, ruffling my hair.

After I had a shower and got on some clean clothes, I felt much better. I limped in and sat at Mom's computer. I brought up the pictures from the last few weeks. There were some great shots of everyone. I was staring at a good one of JD. He was smiling and looking at something that wasn't in the picture. Mom came in behind me. "I see you found the pictures."

"Yes, ma'am," I said and pointed at the one of JD. "When was this?"

"Hmm, let's see." She took the mouse from me and clicked a few things. A picture came up on the screen that showed a broader view of the same picture of JD. "This was when we were eating cake," she said, straightening up. I took the mouse and zoomed in to the left of where JD was looking. I saw me sitting and looking over at him. Mom squeezed my shoulder. "He does smile a lot at you."

"There's something about him," I said with a smile.

"Like what?"

"Like he's kind and trustworthy."

She patted my shoulder. "Trust your instincts, but don't go overboard. Remember, he'll only be here a few more weeks."

"I know," I said with a sigh. I took one last look at the other picture Mom had cropped of him and I turned off the computer.

Mom helped me settle on the couch with a book. Foxy came and laid down beside me. I think I read about ten pages before I fell asleep. The phone ringing woke me up. I heard Mom in the kitchen but I couldn't make out what was said. Then she hung up. "Who was that?" I yelled.

Mom came in. "I thought you were asleep."

"The phone woke me. So who was it?"

"That was Leena. She's coming by in a little while."

"Oh that's great!"

Next thing I knew, a car was driving up and Joey was barking. Foxy trotted to the door and wagged her tail. Must be someone we knew because she didn't wag her tail at strangers. "Enough Joey!" I called. He stopped barking but kept a low growl until I heard the car stop at the gate and a door slam.

Joey ran out and then I heard Leena. "Hey Joey how's my boy?" Leena walked up to the door.

"Come on in, Leena!" I called.

"Brought you some cake!" she said, holding out a box.

"Thanks," I said. "That isn't just because I got a bum knee, is it?"

"No silly. It's for your birthday!"

"Two days in a row. I can do that!"

"Who made you one yesterday?"

"Tesa did. Well, she bought one."

"Well, mine is homemade!"

"Hey Leena. Oh cake!" said Grant, peeking in the box that Leena had set on the table. "You make this for me?"

"I made it but not for you! It's for Sara. Kinda belated birthday cake."

"Still, it's cake!" said Grant, walking into the kitchen.

"Thought you couldn't cook?" I said with a smile.

"I can bake really well. Just can't seem to do the dinner thing," said Leena.

"All you need is practice," I said. "Hope you can stay for dinner."

"Love to! I'll call my mom and let her know I'll be home later." She trotted into the kitchen to call her mom.

Tad and Grant came in with sodas and as Grant was about to sit, I asked, "Will you please get me a drink, too? And offer one to Leena while you're in there."

"Sure," said Grant, going back in the kitchen.

"Whatcha reading?" asked Tad.

"A murder mystery," I said and moved around to put my leg on the coffee table so I could face the room.

"Figures," said Tad.

"What's that supposed to mean?"

"You must get your evil prank ideas from somewhere."

"No way, dude, I come up with my pranks all on my own!"

"You thought up sewing my underwear together all by yourself?"

"Yeah. That was a good one!"

"And the whipped cream pillows?"

"That too!"

"Where do you get these ideas?"

"I just think them up!" I said laughing.

Grant and Leena came out of the kitchen laughing. Leena handed me a soda. "Thanks!" I said. "What's so funny?"

"Grant was telling me how you 'didn't remember' last night."

"Oh that! Was rather good!"

"The trick or the kiss?" asked Tad.

"Both!" I said, giving Tad a crooked smile.

"Just don't go making a spectacle of yourself. Nothing worse than a clingy girl."

"Clingy?"

"Yeah, clingy, as in a girl that won't take her hands off a guy. Always has to be holding his hand or touching him or right next to him."

"Oh gag," said Leena. "I'd kick your butt if you did that!"

"Well don't worry," I said. "I don't do clingy."

Mom came in. "Hey Leena!"

"Hi Mrs. Stillsen."

"How's your family?"

"Doing well."

"Good! Why don't you girls come sit at the bar and gossip with me while I make dinner?" said Mom.

"Can I help?" asked Leena, jumping up. "I could use some practice cooking."

"You sure can," said Mom as she walked toward the kitchen.

I got up and Tad looked around. "Where are your crutches?"

"I guess still in my room." Tad started to get up, but I held up my hands. "I can put some weight on my leg. I'm alright. Just sit and relax while us girls stir up some poison for ya hunks!" I winked at him.

"Great!" said Grant. "Now we have to watch our food, too!"

I laughed and limped into the kitchen and sat on a barstool to watch. Mom laid out the fixings for fried chicken, mashed potatoes, green beans, and a salad. There were rolls already rising in a pan beside the stove. Leena was stirring the gravy when Tad and Grant walked into the kitchen and inspected the food.

"Looking good, Mom," said Tad.

"You guys get out of here and let us finish dinner," said Mom. "It's too crowded with you brutes in here."

Tad and Grant went out front to practice tricks with a rope. A few minutes passed when Grant came in and told us to come out and check out what Tad could do with a rope. We went out to the front porch to see. After a minute of seeing the same old thing Tad had always done, I said, "Is that all? I hobbled out here just to see that?"

"It wasn't that bad!" said Mom laughing. "Let's go finish dinner. You boys come wash up."

Mom handed me plates and I was setting the table when I heard Leena. "Oh no I ruined it!"

"What do you mean you ruined it?" asked Mom. "The gravy was perfect."

"Well, it's not anymore!" said Leena. "It's blue!"

"What?" both Mom and I said.

Mom looked at the pan of gravy and laughed. "That Grant!"

"What are we gonna do?" asked Leena.

"Hmm," said Mom. She tasted the gravy. "Tastes fine. Guess we will just serve blue gravy!"

Leena shrugged. "Okay!"

Mom and Leena dished up the food as Dad came in. "Wow, smells great! I'll go wash up."

The boys came in with smirks on their faces. Mom put the gravy in a gravy boat with a lid and set it on the table. No one said a word as we sat down but there were lots of smirks.

"What's so funny?" asked Dad.

"Nothing!" said Grant. "Just happy to have this wonderful meal prepared for us!"

"Uh huh," said Dad. "What did you do?"

"Nothing!" said Grant. "Everything looks great."

"Okay, then say the prayer," said Dad.

Grant said the prayer. Then we started passing the food around. Everyone was quiet and no one wanted to touch the gravy.

"Pass the gravy, would ya Marcy?" asked Dad. Mom passed the gravy with the lid still on to Tad. Tad passed it to me and I passed it to Dad. Dad took the lid off and set it aside. We all watched.

"What the heck?" asked Dad looking up. We burst out laughing. "Who made the gravy?"

"I made the gravy, but it wasn't blue," said Leena.

"Must have been Grant," said Mom, recovering long enough to speak. "Don't worry, it still tastes fine."

Dad tilted his head, poured some on his mashed potatoes, and passed the gravy on. He tasted it and said, "Looks odd but tastes okay. Grant, don't do that again."

"No sir!"

When we were done with the main course, Leena got up. "I'll get dessert!"

"Is it blue, too?" asked Dad with a wink. We laughed.

"No sir, it's Mississippi mud cake!" said Leena. "Best thing you ever tasted." Mom got up to help her serve.

"This is good!" I said when I tasted my piece.

"Oh man, this is heaven!" said Grant.

"Really?" asked Leena, "You really like it?"

"Yes ma'am," said Grant.

"It's awesome," said Tad.

"Wonderful," said Mom.

"Really good," said Dad.

Leena smiled. "Glad ya'll like it."

"Don't tell Tesa, but this is the best birthday cake ever!" I said.

After we finished, the boys did the dishes to make up for their mischief as the rest of us went into the living room.

"You going to band practice Tuesday?" asked Leena.

"I guess I could go and watch," I said. "The boys will be going in for football practice anyway."

"Good, I'd hate for you to miss out on the festivities. You might still get to march at the parade anyway," said Leena.

"I just might," I said, smiling.

Leena looked at the clock. "I better be going."

"Hey, thanks again for the cake it's really great!"

"You're quite welcome. See ya at practice!" She poked her head into the kitchen and I heard her say, "Thanks for the gravy lesson guys!"

They laughed and said good-bye.

I made myself at home on the couch for the next couple days. On Tuesday afternoon, I went with the boys into town. They dropped me off at the band hall and went on to football practice.

"It's true!" said Carrie when she saw me. "Please tell me you'll be getting that off soon!"

"I might still be able to make the parade," I said. "I have to keep it straight to let it heal."

"That doesn't sound reassuring," said Carrie. She looked at Nadine and Lori. "I guess we better practice without her for now."

I started following them out of the band hall when Tesa came running in and saw me. "Hey, JD's outside looking for you!" Then she went to get her saxophone.

My face broke into a big smile. I hadn't seen him since Saturday night when he carried me to the Suburban. I remembered the feel of his kiss. I sighed and hobbled out the door.

"Hey JD!" I called as I spotted him leaning against one of the Martins' trucks.

"Hey, how ya doing?"

"I'm managing to get around. What are you doing here?" I'd finally made it over to where he was standing.

"I decided to ride in with the Martins so I could see you," he said with a smile.

"Well, here I am in all my glory!" I said raising my arms as much as I could without dropping my crutches.

"I'm still waiting for the sequins," he said with a crooked smile and reached to take one of my hands.

"I'm working on that!"

"Hey, you guys gonna come watch?" asked Tesa, running by us and off to the field where everyone was gathering.

"Do you wanna go watch with me?"

"That's why I'm here," he said and dropped my hand so I could use my crutches.

We walked over to the bleachers and sat on the bottom row. The drum major, Christine Carter, blew her whistle and the band got lined up. She whistled to the beat, they started playing, and marching. The twirlers were in front, followed by Christine, then the band.

"They don't sound too bad," I said. "Of course, nothing like the big schools in Houston."

JD laughed. "I don't think I made it to one game last year."

"Where's your school spirit?"

"My school's so big they wouldn't notice if I was there or not."

"Well, you're gonna see your sisters cheer this year, aren't you?"

"I guess my mom will drag me to a few games. Just what I need to do is watch while all those guys drool over them."

"Well, don't act like Tad and it'll be fine," I laughed.

We were silent as the band marched by us. When they'd gone by, JD asked, "Do you remember what you said to me last Saturday when I was carrying you to the Suburban?"

I looked at him and slowly smiled. "I'm pretty sure I do. Why?"

"What did it mean?"

"That I wanted you with me on the ride home."

"Not that part. The part where you said, 'You give me courage to look into the darkness of the void.'"

"Oh that?" I said looking down. "I didn't realize I said that out loud."

"What is this void?"

"The void is what is not yet," I said, looking up at him, "kinda like the future."

He looked at me and his eyes twinkled. "So I give you courage?"

"Yeah, you do."

"Well, how about you give me something then?"

"And what might that be?"

"I'd like you to come with me on a date."

My breath caught in my chest and I smiled really big. "Where would we go?"

"I don't really know. Where do people go on dates around here?"

I laughed. "Sure did your homework on this one." He laughed, too.

"Well there's the movies here in town or the show in Uvalde or dinner in Uvalde or something like that."

"Hmm, well, I think I'd like to take you to Uvalde to dinner and a movie on Friday."

"I'd like that very much. I'll check with my folks to see if it's okay. I'll call you tomorrow and let you know."

"You do that," he said, smiling at me.

The band came around again and stopped in front of us. Carrie, Nadine, and Lori were doing the twirling routine we'd learned at band camp. JD leaned into me and said in my ear, "Can't wait to see you do that."

When they hit the last note of the song, Christine whistled and everyone relaxed. Mr. Wilson clapped and told them they did great.

After they were dismissed, Tesa and Leena bounded over to where we were. "Hey, JD," said Leena. "Nice to see ya here."

"Had to come check out the rest of the ladies."

"Impressed?" asked Tesa with a wry smile.

"There are a few."

Tesa hit him and laughed. "How rude!" JD looked at me and winked.

"Sara, come back next Tuesday without the brace and crutches," said Carrie as she walked up to us.

"That's my plan," I said. "Carrie, Nadine, I don't believe you've met JD."

"Nice to meet you," said Nadine. "What brings you to the canyon?"

"He's staying with us for awhile and hitting some rodeos," said Tesa.

"Will you be here for Old Settler's?" asked Carrie.

"I'll be riding in the rodeo," said JD.

"Well, then I'll see you at the dances," said Nadine, giving JD an inviting look.

"Hey, we should go watch the boys practice," said Tesa, trying to break up the conversation.

"Yeah we should. Sara, you're coming with us," said JD.

"See ya next Tuesday," I said to Nadine, Carrie, and Lori.

"Nice meeting you," said JD and he turned with Leena, Tesa, and me. Leena said she had to get home and left. Tesa, JD, and I got into the front seat, with me in the middle as we drove over to the football field.

The boys were still practicing so we sat on the bleachers to watch.

Tesa and I sat on either side of JD. The guys weren't in full pads, but they had their helmets on. "Look, more showoffs," said Tesa, pointing at the cheerleaders that were off to the side practicing.

We watched as the quarterback let the ball fly down the field; one fast runner caught it right before Ken and Mitch tackled him. The whistles blew and Coach Baker started yelling. "We are not tackling today, men!"

"Poor Bobby," I said. "That had to hurt."

"I think Mitch and Ken enjoyed that," said Tesa.

We saw Bobby get up slowly, shaking his head. Coach Baker blew the whistle and yelled for everyone to line up. They ran some wind sprints then practice was over.

Matt and Mitch ran up into the stands and hugged me. "Sara, so glad you could make it. We were so worried about you."

"Gross! You guys, please get off me!" I cried trying to push them off. JD and Tesa had moved over to get out of the way.

Finally, Matt and Mitch let me go. "Yuck!" I said wiping the sweat from them off my arms and face. I turned to JD. "Thanks for the help!"

"Hey, nothing I could do!" he laughed.

"You could have at least warned me when you saw them!"

"Aw Sara, you don't love me!" said Matt teasingly.

"I love you, Matt, just not your sweat!" We laughed and Matt turned toward where the cheerleaders were handing out lemonade. "Look, Mitch," said Matt. "We're missing out!" They ran off to get some lemonade.

"Anyone got a towel?" I asked.

"Here take mine," said Ken as he walked over to us.

"Thanks! So you gonna like playing with a small-town team?"

"I think I could learn to like this."

"Hey ya'll," said Grant as he came over with Mitch, Jared, and Pete, sitting down and drinking the last of his lemonade. "I think I need more than lemonade."

"Hey, let's go to the drugstore and get a shake," I said.

"We gotta drag the lover boys over there away from their girls," said Mitch. We saw Matt with his girl Celeste and Tad with Trish. The girls were both cheerleaders and busy flirting.

"We do have two vehicles; I think they can find their way over to the drugstore by themselves. You're coming, too, right Ken?"

"Yeah, just let me go change and I'll meet ya over there."

"I'll go tell the lovers about the plan," said Mitch. "Then I'll change and meet ya at the truck."

"That's my cue to go change," said Grant, getting up and walking to the field house.

When we got to the drugstore, I asked JD, "Have you had one of these shakes yet?"

"Haven't had the pleasure."

"Try the chocolate. They're the best," said Tesa.

"What flavor do you like?" he asked me.

"I like strawberry the best."

"I'll have a chocolate monkey," said Grant.

"What is that?" asked JD.

"Chocolate with a banana."

"They can put a banana in strawberry if you like," said Tesa. Mitch ordered chocolate. Then the girl looked at JD. "Guess I'll try the chocolate monkey."

"I'll try one of those, too," said Ken.

We got our shakes and JD carried my shake for me. We sat at a table in the back. Matt, Tad, Celeste, and Trish came in. They got their orders and sat at the table across from us. Celeste stopped and looked at me. "Sara, sorry to hear about your knee. Guess you won't be twirling in the parade."

"I'm still hoping I might."

"Hope you can," she said and her eyes slid from me to JD. She smiled and then turned away slowly and sat next to Matt.

Tesa and I looked at each other across the table and started laughing.

"What's so funny?" asked Mitch.

We shook our heads and didn't answer.

After talking and laughing for awhile, it was time to go home. JD walked me to our Suburban and opened the door. I put my crutches in and turned to face him. No one was paying attention to us. JD put his finger under my chin. "I'll be waiting for that answer." He kissed me lightly. I opened my eyes and he was smiling at me. "Courage for the void."

I smiled back at him. Grant and Tad walked up.

"I'm looking forward to seeing you rope," said Grant.

"I'm looking forward to showing you. I'll have to borrow a horse."

"You can ride May Day," I said. "He's good."

"There you have it," said Tad. "No backing out now!" He and Grant got in the Suburban.

"Wouldn't wanna disappoint," said JD. I scooted back and JD closed the door. "See ya Thursday."

"See ya!" I said. We waved and drove off.

"Hey, there's the athletes!" said Mom from the kitchen. "Can I get you poor tired guys anything?"

"No ma'am," said Grant. "We stopped at the drugstore and had a shake."

"Put your workout clothes in the washer," said Mom. "I don't want them to sit around smelling for days."

"Yes ma'am," they both said, walking off down the hall to their rooms.

"Mom?" I asked, sitting on a barstool in the kitchen.

"Yeah?"

"Would it be alright if I went to the movie in Uvalde with JD this Friday?"

Mom turned to me and smiled. "You mean like a date?"

"Yeah, it's a date."

"I don't see why not. He's a well-mannered young man."

"Who's a well-mannered young man?" asked Dad, coming in the kitchen.

"JD," said Mom. "He wants to take our Sara on a date this Friday."

Dad looked at me. "Where ya going?"

"To the movie in Uvalde."

He thought for a second. "I guess that's alright."

"Thanks, Dad!" I got off my stool and limped down the hall, forgetting my crutches. Foxy jumped on my bed as we got to my room. "Well, girl," I said, sitting down beside her, "this is going to be my first date!"

"Date?" asked Tad, poking his head around the door, "Did I hear you say date?"

"Yep! JD asked me to the movie in Uvalde on Friday."

"I don't know about that," he walked over and stood in front of me with his arms crossed over his chest.

"Mom and Dad already said I could go, so I don't think you can tell me I can't."

"I'll have to be sure to go to the movie in Uvalde too and keep an eye on you."

"No, you won't!"

"Why not?"

"Because you said you would trust me!"

"But you're my baby sister!" he smiled.

"Do you wanna wake up one night sewn into your sheets?" I threatened. "Or your fingers super glued to your face again?"

He laughed. "You wouldn't!"

"Oh, but I would!" I glared at him.

"Okay, okay!" he held up his hands defensively. "I'll leave you alone!"

"Thank you, that's all I ask."

He sat next to me. "I know you might think I'm being too protective, but I know what guys think like. I just don't wanna see you hurt."

"I understand that, Tad." I patted his leg. "But I'd rather get out there in the world now and learn while you and Grant are still around to catch me if I fall."

Tad hugged me to him. "I'll be here for you, but you have to promise me you won't do anything that you shouldn't or don't feel is right."

I smiled. "I promise."

"Okay, I'll try to hold my tongue."

"Thanks."

"If you change your mind and want me to go to Uvalde to the movie, let me know."

"Get out of here!" I said, throwing a sock at him. He laughed as he dodged and ran out of my room.

I lay back on my bed and stared up at my ceiling. Foxy crawled up beside me and laid her head on my stomach. "Ya know girl, this growing thing seems to be harder on my brothers than me."

I waited until eight the next morning before I called the Martins to tell JD I could go on a date with him.

"Hi, Mr. Martin, this is Sara."

"Hey, Sara, Tesa's right here."

"No, no," I said quickly. "It's actually JD I called to talk to."

"Oh, I'll go get him, hang on."
I smiled and my stomach fluttered as I waited.
"Hello?"
"Hey JD. It's Sara."
"Hey Sara!" I could hear the smile in his voice. "I hope you're calling to tell me we're on Friday."
"I am!"
"That's great. Well I guess I should let you know what time I'll pick you up. How long does it take to get to your house from here?"
"Um, about twenty minutes."
"And how long does it take to get to Uvalde from your house?"
"Twenty minutes."
"The movie starts at seven so I should be at your house by five-thirty."
"Okay," I said slowly as I didn't get the math. Five-thirty seemed way too early.
"I'll be taking you to eat, too," he chuckled.
"Oh! That'd be great!"
"Will I see you at football practice tomorrow?"
"I'm planning on it."
"Great. So I'll see ya tomorrow then."
"Okay, bye."
"Bye."
"So what's the plan?" asked Grant from behind me. I jumped as he spoke and dropped the phone. He laughed as he picked up it.
"Uh, well, he's gonna pick me up at five-thirty. We're gonna eat and then go to the movie."
"Sounds like fun," said Grant. He walked off down the hall laughing.

Thursday we pulled up to the football field but didn't see the Martins' truck. Grant and Tad trotted over to the field house, and I limped over toward the bleachers.
"Hey, peg leg!" said Jared, trotting over to me.
"Hey Jared."
"You're getting around better."
"Yeah a little."
"Still think you'll be able to march in the parade next Friday?"
"I hope so. I at least wanna ride in the horse show."

"Well, I'll be rooting for ya. Gotta run!" he said and trotted off.

"Hey! How's the knee today?" Leena asked as I sat on one of the bleachers.

"It's fine as long as I don't bend it."

"You think you'll be able to march next week?"

I laughed. "I need a sign."

"What kind of sign?"

"One that says what my plans are for the next two weeks so I don't have to keep repeating myself."

"I hope you don't have all the details on that sign," said JD coming towards us.

"Why not?" I asked smiling.

He sat down next to me. "Well for starters, it's none of their business."

I snickered. "That may be, but you haven't lived in a small town."

Leena laughed. "Yeah, we have inquiring, nosy minds." She turned to me. "So, are you?"

"I'm gonna try, but I'm really hoping to ride in the horse show."

"Hey, where's Tesa?" I asked after a second.

"She decided to stay home and do some practicing," said JD.

Coach Baker blew the whistle and practice began. A few other people I knew showed up and sat on the bleachers. Then the cheerleaders came and started their practice.

We watched the boys making comments now and then. After about fifteen minutes, Nadine and Christine showed up. Nadine came right up to us and asked, "How's the knee?" but her eyes kept slipping over to JD.

"Doing better," I said. "Christine I don't believe you've met JD yet," I said, trying to be polite as Nadine wasn't.

"JD's been staying with the Martin's, hitting some rodeos." Nadine explained to Christine.

"So you're the champion bull rider everyone's been talking about," said Christine. "Nice to meet you."

JD nodded at Christine, acknowledging her comment.

"You gonna have a seat and watch the practice, or are you just passing through?" I asked Nadine and Christine.

"I guess we could stay a while," said Nadine and she sat down on the other side of JD. JD didn't look very pleased and Leena gave a light snort. I looked at her and she rolled her eyes.

"Did you see that?" asked Leena, pointing to Bobby Garmin as he ran down the field. Trent threw a long pass and Bobby caught it and ran past everyone like lightning.

"Guess Trent's gonna give Sam Wexler a run for the quarterback spot!"

"No way," said Nadine. "Sam's a senior!"

"So?" I asked looking at her. "Just because he's a senior doesn't mean he's better."

Christine laughed. "She's got ya there, Nadine."

"Well, I think Sam's better!" said Nadine with a huff.

"We're lucky to have two good quarterbacks," said Leena.

"Now if we can get a good defensive line," I said, "we might have a good team this year."

"Well, Ken sure seems to add a lot," said Leena. "He and Mitch seem to be pairing up on the corners well."

"Yeah, I can see that," I said nodding. "Wonder if Coach Baker is just trying that for now or if they'll play there during the season."

"Leena, is your dad the coach?" asked JD.

"No, he's my uncle."

"How do you girls know so much about football?"

Leena and I looked at each other and shrugged. "I guess because my brothers have played it all their lives," I said.

"My dad was a coach in Devine before we moved back here," said Leena.

"Not like there's much else to do around here in the fall anyway," I said.

"There are lots better things I can think of to do," said Nadine.

"Like what?" I asked.

"Well there's going to the movie, watching TV, going shopping, and I'd guess some would say horseback riding and swimming," she said.

"Those are all good things," I said, "but can't do many of them on Friday night during the fall when it's dark and cold outside. So what better way to spend your evening than watch guys fighting it out on the field like warriors!"

"Didn't know you were so into contact sports," said JD.

"Hey, I play with animals," I said. "There's lots of contact."

"Well, we better go if we're gonna help decorate the senior float," said Christine.

Nadine got up and looked at JD. "Nice to see you again."

JD nodded at her but didn't say anything. He just patted my leg.

"What a snot!" said Leena once they were out of earshot.

I snickered and JD looked at me. "Glad to see that kind doesn't ruffle you."

"What kind is that?" I asked.

"The kind that thinks they're better than others."

The coaches blew the whistles and ended practice. The boys went over to the cheerleaders to get lemonade. Matt came up the steps first. I pointed at him, "Do not come too close!"

"Aww Sara!" said Matt. "You wound me so!"

"Just keep your distance," I said, still pointing at him. Matt just smiled and sat down. "Wow! That was too easy!"

"I'm too tired to mess with ya tonight," he said, lying back on the bleachers.

"You feel okay?" asked Leena. "You never give up a chance to hassle us."

"It ain't as fun to pick on an invalid," said Matt.

"Is he giving you a hard time?" asked Tad coming up the steps towards us.

"A lot less than usual," I said. "I think he's sick."

"Naw, he's just as tired as I am," said Tad, flopping down on the bleachers. "Coach ran us a lot today."

"I thought you guys were in shape from all that hard labor Dad puts us through."

"Dad doesn't make us run all over on our own two feet," said Tad.

"Hey guys," said Grant, Ken, and Mitch. They plopped down and stretched out.

"Wow," I said, "I may have to drive home."

"No way," said Grant. "You aren't licensed and you have a bad right leg."

"Fine, you stay here until you recover. JD, Leena, and I'll go down to the drugstore, get a shake, and wait."

"Not without me," said Tad.

"Nor me," said Matt.

"You think you can drive?" I asked.

"Yeah, I think I can aim the truck in the right direction," said Grant.

We got up and started out of the bleachers. "Where's your crutches?" asked JD.

"At home," I said. "I've been getting around without them for a few days now." The boys walked ahead of us and I came to the top of the steps.

"Need help?" asked JD from behind me.

"No thanks." I hopped down the steps on one leg.

"Leena, you wanna ride with me?" asked Ken.

"Sure!" said Leena, bounding over to Ken's truck.

"I'll ride with Tad and Grant," said Mitch. "That way Sara can sit by JD."

"Thanks," said JD. He opened the passenger door of the Martins' truck for me.

Matt was already in the truck and as I scooted over next to him, he and gave me a hug. "Ugh, wish you guys had the strength to go change before we left," I said, pushing him away.

"Every girl needs some perfume."

"Your personal musk is not what I care to wear."

"Aw, there you go again hurting my feelings," said Matt as he backed out of the parking spot.

"I'm not sure what you have qualifies as feelings."

"So what are they then?"

"Carnal desires," I said. JD cracked up.

"What are those? And why's that so funny?" asked Matt, looking at JD.

"They're basic physical desires of the flesh!" said JD.

"Well someone pays attention in school," I said.

"And that is funny because?" asked Matt.

"Because you act and don't think," I said. "Just basic instinct, like a caveman."

"I always wanted to club a good-looking woman over the head and drag her off to my cave," said Matt with a wild look in his eye and a big smile on his face.

"I can imagine you doing that." I laughed at him. At the drugstore, we went inside, ordered, and sat down in the back.

"So what shall we make our prize for our little practice tournament on Saturday?" asked Mitch.

"You're gonna have your own practice tournament?" asked Ken.

"Yeah, you're welcome to come join us at our place," said Grant. "You got a horse?"

"I think I can wrestle one up," said Ken. "Leena gonna be there?"

"If she wants to be," said Tad. "Tesa will be."

"Sandy can come, too," I said.

"Is this just team roping or you gonna rope calves, too?" asked Ken.

"Both," said Grant.

"So what should be the prize?" asked Mitch.

"Your dad coming?" asked Tad, looking at Mitch.

"I think so. Why?"

"If your dad ropes, then my dad will rope, and it makes the pot a little sweeter," said Tad.

"You wanna put money up?" asked Grant.

"Why not?" said Tad shrugging. "We each put in five bucks, winners take all."

"You gonna split that over both calf and team roping?" I asked. "What if one guy wins calf roping and a different team wins team roping?"

"Okay, five bucks per event," said Tad.

"Who's gonna keep time?" asked Ken.

"I will," I volunteered. "I can't ride anyway."

"Well, do we have some kind of handicap since Grant is too good at calf roping and you brothers have already been working together and would have an advantage in team roping?" said Ken.

"Why don't you draw names for partners for each of three rounds and score each rider with the team time and lowest time at the end of the three rounds wins?" I said.

"Well smarty, how do you handicap the calf roping?" asked Grant.

"I dunno, tie weights to your arm?" I said. They laughed at that.

"Maybe the Internet has a handicap calculator for calf roping," said Ken. "I'll look tonight and let ya know what I find."

"That man is using his brain," said Tad.

"All this math is giving me a headache," said Matt.

"Let's go," said Mitch. "I'm beat."

We walked out to the street. "See ya tomorrow," said JD, taking my hand.

"I'm looking forward to it," I said with a big smile.

As my brothers and friends were just a few feet from us, JD tapped my nose with his finger. "Until tomorrow then." He smiled and squeezed my hand and stepped back. I reluctantly let his hand go, and he took another step back still facing me.

"Come on," said Tad, pushing me gently. "You're gonna see him tomorrow."

I turned and got into the truck and slid over so Tad could get in. We waved as Ken and Leena drove off. He must be giving her a ride home. We drove off as the Martins and JD headed in the opposite direction.

First Date

It was five o'clock; my stomach was full of butterflies. I was trying to decide what to do with my hair when there was a knock at my door. He couldn't be here already! Wait! I didn't hear Joey bark, and he always barked when someone came by.

"Come in!" I said, breathing again.

"Do you need any help?" asked Mom.

"I can't decide what to do with my hair." I looked up at her in the mirror.

"Why don't you leave it down and curl the ends a little?" She fluffed my long hair with her fingers.

"Yeah, I guess."

Mom picked up the curling iron. "I'll get the back for you." She did the sides, too, and when she was done, I turned to see the sides in the mirror.

"You're not gonna wear your brace?"

"No, if we're going to the movie, I can't sit very well in those seats with it. Besides, I have it wrapped so I can't bend it too much and rip my stitches. They sure have been itching a lot today. And no, it isn't infected."

"Okay, do you need anything else?" she asked with a low laugh.

"How do I look?" I held my arms out and turned side to side.

"You look beautiful."

"Is this shirt alright?" I asked, plucking at the scoop neckline. It was sleeveless white eyelet that buttoned up the front and fit nicely on my figure.

"The shirt looks great. Don't worry, he's seen you before," she put her hands on my shoulders. "And he still asked you out."

"Yeah, you're right." There was another knock at the door. "Come in."

Tad opened the door and looked at me then Mom. "Oh, sorry, wanted to see if she was still trying to pick out a shirt."

"And you thought I needed your advice?"

"I could offer an opinion," he said, walking over to my closet. "Like maybe you should wear this." He pulled out a long sleeve flannel shirt that was actually a hand me down.

Mom and I laughed. "Don't you think that will be a little hot?" asked Mom.

"Hot is not how I want her to look!" said Tad. "I was going for frumpy."

"In that case, Mom, can I borrow your fuzzy slippers?" We laughed.

"Hey, what's going on here?" asked Grant coming in.

"Tad was offering me fashion advice."

Grant looked at the shirt Tad was holding. "No, no, not that!" He walked to my closet and pulled out a long black skirt and black long sleeve turtleneck sweater. "Now this is what you should wear!" he said with a smile.

We burst out laughing. "Yeah right!"

We heard Joey barking. "Sorry guys, but I guess I'll have to wear what I got on!"

"I think he would wait if you care to change," said Grant in a pleading tone.

"Give me those," said Mom, taking the clothes from Tad and Grant. "You go be polite and show JD in. Your father is in the front room so I know you'll behave."

She pushed them out of my room. I started to follow. "Just give it a second. It's always nice to make an entrance."

"Oh, okay." I turned to my dresser. I picked up my lip gloss and put a little more on. I turned back to my mother. "Now can I go?"

She sighed. "Yeah." She gave me a hug and when I let her go, I saw a tear in her eye.

"Mom, don't start that!"

"Nope didn't see anything," she said blinking. "Do you mind if I get a picture of you two?"

"I guess if you have to!" She laughed and we walked down the hall.

Rather I limped and she walked.

We turned the corner of the hall, and I got a thrill when I saw JD standing by the fireplace. He was wearing a light blue shirt that set off his eyes. He smiled at me as I limped the last few feet into the living room. I didn't see anyone else for a second, as I only had eyes for JD.

"Here she is," said Dad, coming over to my side. He put his arm around me and looked at JD. "Now JD, this is my little girl."

"Oh Dad," I said. Tad snickered from across the room, and I glanced over to see him and Grant with their hands over their mouths, trying not to laugh.

"Humor me a minute, will ya?" he asked, looking down at me, "A father has to do these things right." I rolled my eyes and he continued. "I know Sara here can get a little wild."

"What?" He was chuckling and winked at me.

"So don't let her run around and get hurt again." He squeezed me to him as we laughed. "Now, where are you going and when will you be home?"

"We'll be getting a bite to eat then go to the movie. We should be back by ten-thirty or eleven at the latest, depending on when the movie lets out," said JD easily.

Dad nodded his head. "Very good. Go have some fun." I stepped toward JD.

"Wait, wait," said Mom, reaching for her camera.

"I'm sorry," I said to JD, "she always does this."

He smiled and put his arm around me. "I don't mind."

"Okay, turn toward me. That looks good right in front of the fireplace," said Mom.

I smiled and there was a flash. I looked up at JD and there was another flash. JD looked down at me and the flash went off again. "Is that enough?" I pleaded. Mom took one more and I had to blink to clear my eyes.

"Okay, I'm done." She walked over and gave me a hug. She looked at JD and said, "Drive safe."

"Yes ma'am." He took my hand. "Don't worry, I'll keep her safe."

"Let's go before they think of something else," I said, pushing JD.

JD nodded at Grant and Tad as we passed. They were still smiling behind their hands, and their shoulders were jerking as they tried not to laugh. We made it out the door and were walking down the sidewalk to the gate when Foxy ran up to me.

"Hey girl!" I patted her head. I stopped for a second but didn't let go of JD's hand. I put my other hand under Foxy's chin. "I'll see ya later." I let her chin go and she gave me a "yawwwll."

I turned back to JD and he was smiling as he shook his head once to the side. "What?" I asked.

"I just get a kick out of the way you talk to your animals," he said as he opened the gate for me. We walked over to his truck and he opened the passenger side door for me. I turned around to slide in backwards. "Hey, where's your brace?"

"I don't think I can sit comfortably in the seats at the movie with it on. Don't worry, I have it wrapped so I can't bend it enough to rip any stitches."

"Okay," he said, "but if you hurt it again, I'm the one that'll get the blame."

I put my hand on his chest. "I promise not to hurt my knee again."

He laughed at me. "Get in."

I scooted back and he shut the door. I was scooting over and he got in and smiled at me. "Think it's safe to sit so close to me when we're all alone?"

"I'll risk it!" I said, leaning into his shoulder.

"See, that right there's why your dad gave me the warning!"

"You didn't take him seriously, did you?"

"I take all your family seriously," he said and started the truck.

He stopped as we got to the water crossing. "I hope you don't mind, but I've been waiting to do this for too long." He put his hand on my cheek and kissed me on the lips. I felt the warmth spread from my chest down my arms. I put my hand on his shoulder and pulled him closer to me. I felt warm tingling in my fingers, and he kissed me a little harder.

After a minute, he pulled back. I opened my eyes and he took my hand from his shoulder and held it to his face. "Wow, your hand is warm!"

"Oh!" I tried to pull my hand away. The warmth receded up my arm in a flash. He frowned for split second then smiled at me and let my hand go.

He brushed his lips against mine again then sat back and sighed. "We better get going or I won't get this official date in." He gave me a dazzling smile that took my breath away.

I didn't say anything and he tore his eyes away and started the truck across the river. He put his hand on my leg, and I put my hand over his. I saw him smile as I sighed.

"This is beautiful country."

"I like it, but it has a few draw backs being out in the middle of nowhere west Texas."

"Like what?"

"Well, we can't get decent cell phone reception for one."

"You don't know how obnoxious cell phones are." He laughed.

"What's so funny?"

"I was thinking about how addicted my sisters are to their phones, texting, and how they're gonna have a fit being here without reception."

"Well, they'll have to adapt."

He shook his head. "I'm not sure how good they are at adapting. They're spoiled rotten."

"They can't be that bad."

"Yeah, they can. Just you wait and see."

"Okay, I'll let ya know after I meet them if I share your opinion."

We were pulling out on to the highway. "So who gave you directions to find my house?" I asked.

"I followed my senses and they led me right to you."

I laughed. "I'm so sure that's how you found your way."

"Ah, you wound me."

"I'm sure that's not how you found your way," I said pulling out a paper from the visor.

"Dang! Thought I had you going there."

I opened the paper and saw the neat handwriting. "Must be Mr. Martin's directions."

"He drew it for me while I was on the phone with you Wednesday."

"Guess he was in a hurry to get rid of you."

"Hey, they love me!"

"I know they do," I said, pushing him. "Mind if I turn on the radio?"

"Please do."

I turned it on and it was already on the one decent station we could get in the canyon. The song *When I Close My Eyes* by Kenny Chesney was playing. JD sighed. "I feel that way," as Kenny sang the chorus.

I blushed and looked down. "That makes two of us."

He squeezed my leg and looked straight ahead. "So what else is a drawback about living in such beautiful country?"

"Well, the radio reception is poor and we get only a few stations."

"Yeah, I experienced that. What else?"

"The television reception is bad. We can't get cable and Dad won't spring for satellite."

"You mean you don't watch TV?"

"We usually get one or two channels."

"I guess that's why you're so smart. You don't get a mushy brain watching TV. So what do you do to pass the time? Besides your homework."

"I read lots."

"What do you like to read?"

"Fiction mostly. Mainly I just like a good story."

"I can't remember the last book I read."

"What do you do to pass the time while on the road between rodeos?"

"Mostly watch the scenery go by and sleep. Guess I'm a sloth."

"No, just not taking the opportunity to broaden your horizons, as my English teacher would say."

"I'll have to start reading then. What would you recommend for me?"

"Hmm, that's a hard one." I thought for a moment. "Maybe you should try a mystery. Sherlock Holmes maybe."

"Really? Why do ya think I'd like that?"

"Well a mystery because you like games."

"Games?"

"You compete in rodeos don't you? That's a game. Besides you like challenges."

"Okay, why else?"

"Holmes is very down to earth and practical. He isn't awestruck by people with titles. He speaks the truth just as he sees it. You have a lot in common with him."

He smiled. "I have that in common with him?"

"Seems to me you do. That was meant as a compliment."

"I didn't take offense. I've never been described that way."

"How have you been described?"

"Other than bull rider? Champion bull rider, cowboy, or a nice package," he glanced at me as he said the last part. "I don't remember

142

much else."

"Not even from teachers at school?"

"Nope. I go to a very large school. I'm just a face in the crowd or a number on a seating chart."

"You have seating charts? Like assigned seating?"

"No, not many teachers have assigned seating. But if you sit there the first day, you put your name on a chart and that's where you sit the rest of the semester. That's how they take roll."

"Didn't think of that. See, that might be another disadvantage of living in the sticks. Everyone knows you."

"That doesn't seem to be a bad thing."

"No, but you don't get to hide from the gossips or past mistakes. Some people here forgive, but they don't forget."

"I'll keep that in mind." We were entering Uvalde and JD slowed down. "Where would you like to eat?"

"Uh, Sonic sounds good to me."

"Sonic? Really?"

"Yeah, junk food and fast food are my weaknesses."

"I can't argue with that." He smiled.

"Look out!" I said pointing at a large yellow lab that was running out into the road. JD stopped in time but the car to our right didn't, and it hit the dog before it could stop.

Without thinking, I scooted across the seat and was out the door. I limped over to the front of the car and saw the dog lying in front of it. It was moving a little. I felt a strong burst of warmth flow from my chest down my arms and legs. I knelt by the dog and put my hands on it. I felt pain and shock. JD was there beside me and so was the driver of the car.

"Is he still alive?" asked JD.

"Yeah but barely," I said.

"I tried to stop," said the older man who was driving the car that hit the dog.

"I know, we saw," said JD, reassuring the man.

I felt the dog move under my hands, and I held her down with one hand and ran the other over her body to see where she was hurt. I felt mostly broken ribs. There was a sloshy feeling or did I hear that in my head? She must have punctured a lung. I saw a bloody froth coming out of her mouth and decided that was her lung. A wave of warmth coursed through my hands and ran down my fingers into the dog's chest. I bent closer and heard she was breathing. Then she took a bigger breath and whined.

"Shhh, easy girl, you're gonna be all right."

"Ginger!" screamed a little girl as she ran across the street toward us. JD caught her and held her to him as I tended to her dog. She sobbed into his shirt.

A lady came running up. "Lisa, Lisa!" The little girl released JD and grabbed her mother.

"Ginger's dead!" cried the little girl.

"No she's not!" I said.

The lady looked at me. "What can we do for her?"

"She'll need a vet, but she's very lucky," I said. Ginger lifted her head and whined. "Easy now."

Then a sheriff pulled up and turned on his lights. I closed my eyes one more time and pushed another surge of warmth into Ginger. I got dizzy and I opened my eyes. The sheriff surveyed the scene.

"What do you need?" he asked me.

"Got a blanket?"

"Sure do." He went back to his car. "Move this truck please!" he barked as he walked.

JD moved his truck as Lisa and her mother moved in front of the car and out of the way. The sheriff waved traffic around then came back to me with the blanket.

"Lay it right here next to her," I said. "Okay, now let's gently move Ginger here onto the blanket. Support her shoulders and I'll get her hips. I think she has a few broken ribs, and we don't wanna rock her too much or she'll puncture something inside. Okay, on three. Ready one, two, three."

We lifted Ginger onto the blanket and the dog whined again. "You're gonna be fine girl, just fine." I looked up at the lady. "You got a car to take her to the vet?"

"Sure I'll get it. Lisa, come with me."

"I wanna stay with Ginger."

"It's okay, she can help me," I said. The lady nodded and made her way back across the street. "Lisa, come here. Kneel down here and pet her and talk to her."

"What do I say?"

"Just tell her your here and that she's gonna be fine. That's it keep petting her softly."

"Oh, Ginger, you're gonna be fine. You gotta be fine or I'm gonna be in big trouble."

"Why is that?" I asked Lisa.

"Because I left the gate open," she sobbed.

"I don't think you'll get in trouble." I patted her shoulder. "Just remember next time to close it." I smiled at her and she tried to smile back at me through her tears.

The lady was back with her car. The sheriff waved her over next to us.

"Here let me." JD tapped me on the shoulder then motioned for me to move over.

I looked up at him. "She needs to be kept level as possible. You should lift the corners of the blanket."

"Okay." He looked up. "Sheriff, can you help me lift the dog into the car?"

"Of course," he said, kneeling down.

"Lift by the corners of the blanket," I said. "Let me get out of the way." I rocked back and put my hand on the bumper of the car to push myself up. JD grabbed my other hand and helped me. I leaned against the car, as I was very dizzy.

"I'm fine," I said, looking at JD. "Now get Ginger." I gestured at the dog.

"Lisa, you wanna go wait by the car for us?" asked JD. The little girl got up and went to her mom's car.

"Now, sheriff, on three. Ready? One, two, three." They lifted Ginger smoothly and put her in the back of the lady's car.

"Can I ride in the back with her?" asked Lisa, looking at JD.

"Sure, just sit by her head here and put on your seatbelt. Keep petting her. She likes that."

The older man who was driving the car walked up to the lady's front window and handed her a card. "Please allow me to pay the vet bill!" he said. "It's the least I can do."

"Oh, you don't have to do that!"

"Please humor an old man and ease my conscience."

"You are most kind!"

"Just send me the bill and I'll pay it," he said. "If you go to Dr. Morrison, just give him my card and tell him to bill me. We go way back."

"I will. Thank you," said the lady and they drove off.

I was smiling as JD walked up to me. "You okay?" he asked me taking my hands.

"I'm fine." I smiled up at him.

He smiled and squeezed my hands. "Warm again," he said and winked. He turned to the sheriff and asked, "Need us for anything?"

"No, you can go. Not anything to report here," he said and waved us on. He walked up to the older man and patted him on the back. "You too, sir. Just move it along."

I walked with JD to the truck. "Hey you're not limping!" he said.

"Guess I forgot about my knee."

"How is your knee?" he asked. "You were kneeling on the street, ya know."

"I know, but I don't feel any pain." I rubbed my knee and felt the wrap. "It does itch some." JD shook his head once and opened the driver's side door for me. I got in and scooted over. He got in and closed the door.

"Still feel like eating?"

"Yeah, suddenly I'm starving."

"Still want Sonic?"

"A mustard burger sounds great!"

"Mustard, huh?" he asked with a crooked smile.

"Yeah, what's wrong with mustard?"

"Not a thing," he said and chuckled. "I happen to be the only one in my family that likes it."

"Really? Me too!" We laughed.

We drove in silence for a minute. I sighed.

JD looked at me with concern. "Your knee hurting?"

"No, just relaxing!"

He smiled. Seemed like only a minute before we pulled into the Sonic parking lot. JD parked in a spot toward the back. He rolled down the windows and turned off the engine. "Now let's see. You want a mustard burger. Any cheese?"

"American, please."

"Fries? And Coke?"

"Fries but make it a strawberry limeade please." JD chuckled and pressed the call button to order.

"What's so funny?" I asked. He held up a finger for me to wait as the order taker came on.

JD ordered two of the same thing for us. After the guy repeated it back, JD turned to me. "That's what I was laughing at," he said. "We seem to like the same things."

He took my left hand in both of his and then put it down and picked up my right.

"What now?"

"They aren't warm anymore. I mean not like they were before." He looked me straight in the eye and asked, "Why is that?"

I shrugged. I had no clue what to say.

JD took a breath then asked, "So what other junk food do you like?"

I took a breath, thankful he changed the subject. "Chili cheese dogs. They make a good one here."

"Weinerschnitzel makes them better!" he said smiling. "What else?"

"Nachos with lots of jalapenos, but none of that fake cheese. Has to be the real stuff."

"Oh, so you like Mexican food then?"

"Oh yeah. Mom makes some good stuff. She makes the best green chili chicken enchiladas. I'll ask her to make some for us tomorrow."

"That would be nice," he said. "I like Mexican food, too."

"Do you like it better than Italian?"

"Hmm, maybe I do. Haven't thought of it that way. So what other junk food do you like?"

"Potato chips."

"I like those," he nodded.

"Aw, but can you eat a whole bag at one time?"

He laughed at me. "Not you!"

"I make Tad and Grant really mad sometimes because I eat the whole bag in one sitting."

"So do you like popcorn, too?"

"Absolutely! With lots of butter and salt!"

Just then, the carhop appeared with our order. JD turned the key and rolled up the window a little so she could put the tray on it. JD paid and she skated off. He handed me a drink first. I took a sip and then sucked down more, as I was thirstier than I realized. He smiled at me and I put the drink on the dashboard as he handed me a burger and fries.

"Thanks!" I unwrapped the burger and took a bite. "Mmm, this is what I needed."

We ate for a few minutes in silence. Then I looked at the clock on the truck dashboard and asked, "Is this right?"

"Yeah. Looks like we missed the start of the movie. Guess we can't go to the late movie because I promised your dad I'd have you home by ten-thirty or so."

"I'm sorry. It's my fault that we missed the movie."

"Hey, don't be sorry about that. You were helping someone in need. Besides, I'd much rather spend time talking with you than sitting in the dark watching a movie."

"Thank you!"

"For what?"

"For being such a great guy!"

"I'll pass that along to my parents and let them know they raised me right!" said JD with a twinkle in his eye. "Now where can we go so we can sit and talk in peace?"

"The river is my favorite place," I said. "I know a few places where we could look up at the stars."

"Okay, let's go," he said.

Once back on the highway, he turned up the radio and the same Kenny Chesney song we heard on the way down was playing. We laughed. "Guess that's our song," he said.

"Oh I hope not!"

"Why not?"

"Because it's about a guy who lost his girlfriend."

"I just liked the chorus part about how she's always on his mind, even in his dreams."

"Yeah, I like that part."

"So what would be good to have as our song?"

"*Cowboy Take Me Away* by the Dixie Chicks might be alright."

"Yeah that would do."

"But?"

"Well, it says something about sleeping on the hard ground."

"Don't tell me that you don't like camping?"

"Never been."

"What?"

"Nope. Never been camping. Well, not like in the woods with a campfire and sleeping bags on the ground. But I've spent time in a trailer at rodeos."

"I guess that counts for something. But if you've never slept on the ground, how do you know you don't like it?"

"I don't like sleeping on the floor or in the back of a truck."

"Sounds like you're a big softy to me."

"Really, I ride bulls and you call me a softy."

I laughed. "Sorry, didn't mean to hurt your ego."

"My ego is just fine. It's the impression I must be giving you that I'm worried about."

"You impress me more and more all the time."

We turned off the highway at the road to my house. At the river crossing, I said, "Turn there," and pointed to a dirt road that ran down the side of the river.

We drove slowly down the dirt road and came to a rise that overlooked the river. "Stop here," I said.

JD put the truck in park and turned off the engine but left the radio on. "Let's get out and sit on the tail gate," I said.

JD smiled at me and got out. He let me slide down off the seat then pulled me into his arms and kissed me. I wrapped my arms around his neck, kissing him back. I felt warmth bloom in my chest and it radiated down my arms and my fingers tingled.

Then JD lifted his head. I slowly opened my eyes and looked up to see a glow in his that hadn't been there before. He pulled my arms from around his neck and held my hands in his.

"Your hands are warm again!"

"I guess you just make me warm," I said, blushing, and stepped back.

He led me to the back of the truck and let down the tailgate. I sat on the tailgate and he stood in front of me. He had a serious look on his face.

"Your hands were warm after you helped that dog tonight, too."

I stared at him and held my breath. My heart pounded. I didn't know what to say.

"How about I give you my theory and you let me know how close I am?"

"Okay," I whispered.

He took a breath and put both hands around mine. "I think you have a gift, a very special gift." My heart fluttered. "I think you not only have an affinity for animals, you can actually heal them."

My mouth dropped open and my stomach flipped. I heard Uncle

Buck's voice in my head: *"Trust him, Sara. He can only walk and speak the truth. He will guard you."*

"I must have hit pretty close to the mark if you're speechless," he said.

"How'd you figure it out?" I whispered.

"So I'm right?" he asked smiling. I nodded my head.

"Wow!" he said and leaned back a little. "Well, there was what you did for Copper. You calmed May Day and that other barrel racer's horse way too easily. I mostly know what happened with the dog Candy. I know what you did for Travis. Then I saw it in action tonight."

"Oh!" I said scared of what might come next. I looked down not knowing what else to do.

He lifted my chin so I'd look at him. "Sara, I'm not about to go shouting this from the roof tops. You have nothing to fear from me. I can keep this a secret if that's what you want."

I nodded as tears welled up in my eyes.

He hugged me to him. "Don't cry. It'll be fine."

I took a ragged breath. "I'm so glad you're here."

He pushed me back and held my face in his hands. "So why are you crying?" He brushed away a tear that ran down my face.

"Because it's a relief."

"Does anyone else know?"

"Just Uncle Buck. Well, he really isn't an uncle. He's my cousin's father-in-law. He's a full blood Cherokee."

"Ah, that explains a few things." JD pulled me into his chest. I turned my head and wiped the tears from my face. I took a deep breath and let it out slowly. "Just what you wanted in a date!"

"Hey, I knew what I might be getting into when I asked you out."

"And now that you know?"

"You think that since my curiosity is satisfied I'll move on?"

"Something like that."

"Well, you're wrong. I'm drawn to you in a way that I've never been drawn to anything else in my life."

I smiled. "Is that your carnal desire talking?"

He laughed. "That may be part of it I'll admit. But I do feel like I need to be near you."

"Why is that?"

"I just know that when you're in my sight I feel happy and relaxed. When you're not around, I get anxious." He sat beside me on the tailgate holding my hand. "There's a dream I had before I came to stay with the Martins. I've had it twice since I got here."

"What's the dream?"

JD smiled. "I was flying over the land. Part of the land was light and part was very dark. I'd fly in and out of the light and dark. Neither was cold or hot. I remember looking down at myself once and saw black feathers and I realized I was a big black bird. Well, at least I thought I was big until this hawk came up beside me and showed me to this beautiful valley. A river ran the length of the valley. There were deer, raccoons, cows, and horses. It was so peaceful, just flying around."

"Wow! You are the crow!"

"I'm the what?"

"Uncle Buck sent me a letter telling me the crow was coming to help me."

"Help you do what?"

"That may be harder to explain, but first, was there anything else in your dream? You said you had it more than once. Did it change?"

"Yes it did!" he said, looking at me intently. "The second time I spotted a black fox and flew down to investigate. The hawk just watched me carefully. But the next time I had the dream, this big bear came out at me and scared me."

I laughed.

"What?"

"How much do you know about totems and Indian folk lore?" I asked.

"Not much I suppose. I know that totems are usually animals like spirit guardians. Is that what you mean?"

"Yeah. Each animal totem or spirit has special gifts. People have a totem that is represented by these animals. They're actually pretty accurate when you recognize them and match the animal to the person."

"So what's your totem?"

"The black fox."

"What? Oh wow, that's cool. What does the black fox mean?"

"Strong medicine and healing. They're quick thinkers and very instinctive."

"I suppose I'm a crow," he said. "Is that why you gave me the crow feathers? I was so shocked when you handed me that hatband with them on it."

"Yes, that's why. I felt impressed to give them to you."

"What does the crow totem mean?"

"The crow is the guardian of healing. They dispel fear. They're an omen of change and bring messages from the spirit world."

"I'm starting to see why I'm drawn to you so much. So what or who is this bear and hawk in my dream?"

"Think about it for a minute and you'll realize who they are. Think about them in your dream now that you know I'm the fox and you're the crow."

He frowned as he thought then a smile spread across his face as the answer dawned on him. "Whoa, Grant and Tad!" he said surprised.

"Yeah! The hawk is a guardian and very practical. He supports change and growth of the spirit. The bear is strong, wise, and very protective of family."

JD laughed. "Tad's the bear alright!"

"Yeah, sometimes to a fault."

"So what does the horse totem mean?"

"You already know," I looked at him and touched my necklace. "You told me when you gave me this."

"I did?" He paused for a minute then smiled. "Speed, strength, and grace. Or is it freedom?"

"It's all of those things," I said, smiling at him. "Now, do you believe some of what I just told you? Or do you think I'm wacky?"

"I think some of what you say about totem spirit types is true. I can see where they fit."

"But?"

"But I still don't understand why I'm here and why you have this really special gift."

"Well," I said, "I was told that I'd come into more power the summer I turn fifteen."

"I guess that can be scary. So why do you have this gift?"

"I was told it was to help bring balance between animals and people. I'm still trying to find the meaning of that, but I'm just going along with it for now."

"How long have you had this gift?"

"I first remember when I was about six doing something that was similar to what I did today."

"And that was?"

"I found a litter of newborn kittens in the barn. One of them wasn't moving, I picked it up, and my hands got warm. I blew on the kitten's face and he came to life."

"Do your hands always get warm when you heal something?"

"Yeah, it starts here," I pointed to my chest, "and flows out through my arms and hands. Sometimes it's just warm, but sometimes it has tingling shocks that come with it."

JD smiled at me. "So you can't do this to humans, only animals?"

"I've tried a few times with my brothers and a hurt kid at school but never had much affect. I can tell they hurt and where, but I can't seem to help."

"Do you think that might change this summer?"

"I don't think so." I shook my head.

"Would you like to know I think you helped me?"

"You think? When?"

"When we stopped at the river and I kissed you. I felt it again when I kissed you just now."

"What? Wait, I touched your shoulder. I thought you were over that?"

"No, it's been bothering me. Until now that is." He moved his arm around testing his shoulder.

"How did it feel?"

"I'm not sure I can separate the effects of the kiss from the healing." He smiled at me. "But I remember your hand feeling really warm, and it spread down into my shoulder. It tingled some. I felt like I was gonna float away."

"Hmm, maybe that's what I'm supposed to learn."

"What?"

"How to make you fly!"

He laughed and patted my leg. "I think you got that one down." Then he asked, "Do you think you healed yourself?" He pointed to my knee.

"I haven't even felt a twinge since we stopped by that dog. I did feel a surge through my whole body like I've never felt before when I knelt by that dog."

"You wanna take a look and see?"

"I don't think I could get my jeans' leg up high enough to get the wrap off."

"You girls and your tight jeans!" said JD, shaking his head.

"Hey, we only do it to get the attention of you guys!"

"You have my attention." JD turned to me. "Wait, does this still constitute a date if I only did half what I invited you to do?"

"You did buy me my favorite dinner!"

"In that case, since we've been on a date technically, does that mean I can call you my girlfriend?" My heart skipped a beat and my stomach flipped. "I don't mean to push you."

"I, you're not pushing me," I stammered. "But why would you wanna call me that?"

"Because I want you all to myself."

"You've got me," I said, looking up at him. Then he kissed me. I put my arm around his shoulder and he put his other arm around me and we lay back on the truck bed.

A fire started in my chest, and I felt a warm surge run through my arms and legs. JD tried to pull back, but I held him to me and he kissed me harder. I felt tingles all over then JD pushed himself up, ending the kiss.

He was smiling down at me. I still had my hands on his arms.

"You're doing it again!" he said.

"Sorry, does it hurt?"

"No, nothing like that. It feels great. I feel this warmth spreading through me when you kiss me." He brushed a strand of hair from my cheek.

"I think I need to learn to control myself better."

"Why? Don't you trust me?"

"I trust you. I just don't wanna hurt you."

He chuckled. "I'm the one that usually says that to a girl."

"Oh really? So how many girls do you have back in Houston?"

"I don't have any. I've dated here and there but nothing serious. Well, nothing that lasted more than a few months. How about you?"

"I haven't dated anyone."

"You mean this is your first date?"

"Yeah."

"No wonder Tad and Grant were giving me such a hard time. And your mom with the pictures."

"Yeah, my mom and her pictures."

"I bet she has some good ones of you," he said, lightening the mood.

"She has lots of all of us. She even has some of you at the rodeos. I'll show them to you tomorrow."

JD sighed. "Aw, tomorrow."

"What? You not coming?" I asked quickly. Afraid he wouldn't come.

He smiled at me. "I wouldn't miss a chance to see you," he said and kissed me lightly. He traced the side of my face with his finger.

"But?"

He smiled. "But I do have to get you back at a decent hour tonight. It must be ten already."

"Wow, time seems to fly when I'm with you."

JD got off the tailgate and stood in front of me. He put his hands on my legs, leaned in, and kissed me. He put a finger under my chin. "Now we really should go."

He helped me off the tailgate and put it back up. We got into the truck and drove up to the house. Joey was barking and then Dad yelled at him to stop. JD got out of the truck and took my hand as I got out. He got the gate for me. Foxy ran up to us.

"Hey girl!" I rubbed her head. She gave me a "raaawwl" then turned and bounded off around the back of the house.

JD pulled my hand and we walked to the porch. I turned toward him, expecting him to say good-bye here, but he opened the door instead and I gave him a quizzical look.

"I wanna make sure they see I brought you home safe and to explain why we didn't make it to the movie."

"Okay," I said and walked through the door.

Dad put down his book and Mom looked up from some sewing. "You're home early!" said Dad.

"Yes, sir," said JD.

"Was the movie bad?" asked Mom.

"No, ma'am, we didn't make it to the movie," said JD.

"Why, what happened?"

"Someone hit a dog in front of us on the way into town," I said. I pulled JD over to sit on the couch. This would take a little while to explain.

"Uh huh?" said Dad with that "You should continue" look on his face as he watched us sit down.

"We helped this lady and little girl with their dog. I think she'll be alright," I said.

"So you stopped to help a dog you didn't hit. Did you take the dog to the vet?" asked Dad.

"No, sir, the lady did. JD and the sheriff helped put the dog in the lady's car."

"The sheriff?" asked Mom.

"Yes, ma'am," said JD. "We were blocking traffic and he took over the situation."

"What did you two do all this time?" asked Dad.

"We went to Sonic to eat," I said.

Dad laughed at that. "Can't even pass up junk food on a date!"

"I don't mind," said JD. "It's one of my favorites."

"Well, glad you had a good time," said Dad. He implied he gave us permission to leave.

"I'll walk ya to your truck." I stood up and motioned for JD to follow.

Mom looked at me quizzically as I walked JD to the door. I waved a little at her as we walked out the door onto the porch. JD took my hand as we walked to his truck. I heard a trucking coming.

"That must be Grant in Dad's truck," I said, looking up at JD.

"I guess this will be brief then," he said.

"He won't be here for a few minutes yet. You can hear a car coming once they cross the river."

"That's why you had me turn off before the river."

"Yeah," I said. "Do you not approve of my devious ways?"

He kissed me. "I like everything about you."

Then we heard a second truck. "That must be Tad."

"Now I'm in for it!" said JD with a chuckle. "If I leave now…"

"They'll get you twice as bad tomorrow and in front of everyone," I finished for him. "If you stay, you might earn a little respect."

Lights flashed across us and Grant pulled around to the back of the house. He got out and walked up to us, "Hey, you're home early! So how was the movie?"

"We didn't make it to the movie," said JD.

"What happened?"

Lights from the second truck flashed across us. "We might as well wait and tell you both at the same time," I said. "I hate repeating myself."

We waited for Tad to park the truck. "Hey, I was hoping to beat ya'll home and heckle you about the kiss good night!"

"Thanks for the warning!" I said.

"So how was the movie?" asked Tad.

"They didn't make it to the movie, and JD was just about to explain why," said Grant.

"Before you start in, we've already been inside and explained all this to Mom and Dad," I said.

"So what happened?" asked Grant, crossing his arms over his chest in a stance of judgment.

We told them the story of the dog being hit by a car.

"Is that all?" asked Tad.

"Pretty much," I said. "After that we went to Sonic."

"Don't tell me she made you take her there!" said Grant "I'll bet she had that awful mustard burger, too!"

"As a matter of fact, that's one of my favorites," said JD.

"Oh, well, I beg your pardon," said Grant tipping his hat at JD.

JD laughed at them. "You guys better get your rest. Matt and Mitch are gunning for ya tomorrow."

"Yeah, JD's right Tad, we should get our rest. Big day of whomping tomorrow! Bring some swim shorts because we'll probably take a swim to cool off afterward. See ya, JD." Grant turned to leave.

Tad was much slower. "Yeah, I guess we can whomp on them a bit." But he didn't move. So Grant grabbed him from behind. "Come on, let them say good-night." He pulled Tad through the gate.

JD shook his head and chuckled as he turned to face me. "Now I best be getting off to bed. I'll be here roping tomorrow, too."

"I'll have May Day ready for you."

JD put his hand on my cheek and kissed me. "Good-night," he said.

"Night." I turned and walked back to the gate as I heard him singing softly, "When I close my eyes...." I smiled and kept walking.

When I walked into the house, everyone was in the living room. I smiled at them. "Guess I'll say good night. Got a big day of refereeing tomorrow."

"Wait just a minute," said Mom. "Why aren't you limping anymore?"

I looked down and held out my leg. "I guess it doesn't hurt anymore."

"Humph. I'll bet she can't feel it for walking on clouds," said Grant in a low voice. Tad snickered.

Dad raised his eyebrows. "Well as long as it doesn't hurt."

"Well good-night," I said and walked down the hall to my room. I turned on the light, closed my door, and began to sing, "When I close my eyes, you're easy to find..."

I pulled off my jeans and unwrapped my knee. There was a red line with scattered bits of blue stitching poking up. "Wow, that's cool."

I pulled on my big t-shirt and some shorts. I went across the hall to the bathroom and found some tweezers. I put my foot up on the toilet and bent over my knee, humming to myself and plucking out the bits of blue stitches.

"What're you doing?" asked Tad, pushing the door open wider. "Are you pulling out your stitches?"

"No, I'm just taking out the parts that aren't needed anymore."

"Looks like you're taking them out to me!"

"Come here and look!" I pointed at my knee. "The cut is healed!"

Tad walked over and looked. "Wow, just a red scar. What are those?" he asked, pointing at the blue material poking out.

"That's what's left of the stitches. I was pulling that out."

"You're pulling what out?" asked Mom, coming into the bathroom.

"Look Mom," said Tad. "Her cut is all healed!"

Mom came over and looked. "Yeah, it sure is." She touched the red line. "So you're just pulling out the leftovers?"

"Yeah. No big thing," I said.

"Here let me." She took the tweezers from me and plucked the remaining parts out in no time. "There!"

I put my foot down and looked up. Tad was still standing in the doorway. "Can you bend it?" he asked.

I bent my leg slowly. I stopped when it got to about a thirty-degree angle. "Seems a little tight, but it doesn't hurt."

"Don't push it. Just take it easy," said Mom.

"Yes, ma'am," I said, smiling at her. Mom nodded her head and walked out.

I yawned. "Been a big night. I'm gonna turn in." I turned to walk past Tad and he grabbed my arm.

"I'm glad you had a nice time," he said. "Just remember he's leaving after Old Settler's."

"I know." I smiled at him and headed into my room. I closed the door, turned off the light, and crawled into my bed. I sighed as Foxy jumped up on the bed and laid down next to me. I patted her head and fell asleep.

The Practice

I was flying over the canyon and saw the river below. The sun sparkled off the water as it flowed south. I dipped down, touched my wings in the water, soared up again over a field, and saw horses running below me. I dipped toward them and then was among them, running free. I felt the wind in my mane. I heard the thunder of hooves. The thunder pounded.

Wait, that wasn't thunder. I opened my eyes. It was barely light outside. There was another soft knocking then my bedroom door squeaked open and I rolled over to see Tad coming in.

"You awake?"

"I am now. What do you want?"

Tad came and stood over me. "I want the real scoop about last night, but I'll settle for you helping me feed."

"Is that all?" I asked, sitting up. "I'll be right with you if you can give me a minute."

I got dressed and met Tad at the back door then we walked down to the barn. It was getting lighter outside. In the west, the morning star was fading. The birds were chirping, and the crickets were slowly fading out as we walked.

Foxy trotted off to pounce on some poor critter in the bushes. We didn't say a word the whole way there.

Tad slid back the front door, and we were greeted by several soft neighs. I filled the bucket with grain and carried it around, pouring out a portion to each horse as Tad brought them hay.

I went into Andrea's stall. She was very friendly, rubbing up against me. I scratched her ears as I held the bucket of grain for her. She nudged me and I laughed at her. "Here, I'll let you do it yourself." I poured the rest of the grain into her feed trough.

I was coming out of her stall and almost ran into Tad. "You really do talk to them like they understand you."

"Yeah, I think they do understand me. I treat them the way I'd wanna be treated if I were in their place."

"Huh, never thought of it that way," he said and I could see him thinking about something, so I waited until he spoke. "Do you think I treat Super badly?"

"No, I don't. You don't use spurs or a whip. You don't jerk on his mouth like I've seen some do."

"Yeah, heard JD mention to Mr. Martin how he's never seen anyone get as much out of a barrel horse without using spurs or a whip as you do."

"He asked me about that," I said, turning to walk out of the barn. Foxy bounded out ahead of us.

Tad followed along side of me. "What did you tell him?"

"I said that I don't ask more of the horse than they're willing to give. I don't make them do what they don't wanna."

"I can see that. That's kinda what Dad does. He figures out what the horse is good at and then helps them get better at it, like Flaxie. She'll never be a good roping or a cutting horse."

"I think she might make a good cutting horse. She's very attentive as well as fast. You think Dad would let me ride her in the horse show next week?"

"What about May Day?"

"I'll ride him some, but I'd like to see how Flaxie does in the ring. I wanna see if she'll settle down with all that noise and distraction."

"I'm sure Dad would let you do whatever you want," said Tad, grabbing me around the neck.

"I know, I'm the spoiled brat!"

"Ya know we say that to keep you humble."

"I know you do it with love."

"Now you gonna tell me any details from last night?" He asked, teasing me.

"He has a lot more to him than the outside package portrays."

"You mean he isn't a jerk."

"Not at all. He's a perfect gentleman."

"So what did ya'll do between the time you left the doggy scene and returned home?"

"We went to eat then we talked for a long time."

"You sat at the Sonic and talked for hours?"

"No, not for hours. We came back, parked down by the river, and looked at the stars."

"And he kissed you a lot?"

"I wouldn't say a lot."

"And he was a perfect gentleman, you say?"

"Yes, Tad, he was. Now have I satisfied your curiosity enough?"

"I guess I've asked more than I should."

"I wouldn't do anything I wasn't willing to tell the truth about, if that's what you're worried about. Besides, I don't think JD would try anything with me. He knows you would drag him behind the barn and beat on him."

"He does?"

"Yeah, I told him that's how it was living in a small town. You step out of line too much, and the folks make sure you know you did wrong."

"Wow, I think you scared me enough not to try anything with Trish or any other girl from here on out."

"Good, would hate to have your pretty face all messed up because you did something stupid."

He puffed out his chest. "Not gonna happen. I'll always be a perfect gentleman!" I laughed.

When we got back to the house, breakfast was cooking and Dad was at the table reading yesterday's paper. "Morning," I said, coming into the kitchen. Dad looked up from his paper. "You go feed already?"

"Yes, sir!" said Tad, "Drug the delinquent here with me to get her started making up for her slovenly ways this past week."

"When you say it like that, it makes me feel like I'm a slave that's been really lazy," I said.

"Why don't you two save your energy for later?" asked Mom, putting plates of eggs and bacon down in front of us.

"Where's Grant?" I asked.

"Right here!" he said, coming into the kitchen. "What'd I miss?"

"Not a thing," I said.

"Dad, can I ride Flaxie in the horse show next week? Just a couple classes?"

Dad raised his eyebrows and looked at me. "Might not be a bad idea to see how she handles the noise and crowd."

I looked across the table at Tad. He smiled and shook his head.

"You might wanna ride her today and every day for a few hours to get her ready," Dad suggested.

"Will do!" I said cheerfully.

"Dad, you gonna rope with us today?" asked Grant.

"I heard that you're making a pot the winners would collect." Then he smiled. "Would hate to take your hard-earned money."

"Do I hear a challenge?" asked Tad with a smile.

"How do you plan on keeping score?" asked Mom.

"For team roping, Sara came up with the idea that we draw names for each of three rounds, score each rider with the team time, and lowest time at the end of the three rounds wins," said Grant.

"Hmm, that sounds like a nice way to level the playing field," said Dad. "What about calf roping?"

"We haven't figured that one out yet," said Grant.

"How about everyone gets three tries, you take the best time and give it to everyone to replace their worst, then take the average of the three times," said Mom.

"That sounds like a good idea to me," said Grant.

"Man, I gotta start paying attention more in school," said Tad.

"Why's that?" asked Dad.

"Because the women in this family are way smarter!"

"Mom, can you make chicken enchiladas for us tonight?" I asked. "I'm sure the Martins would stay for dinner, too. I'll help."

"You must have read my mind. I was just thinking about doing that," said Mom, getting up from the table. I helped her cleanup before I went to get ready.

I changed into jeans and a t-shirt, pulled on my boots, and pulled my hair back into a ponytail. I made my bed and picked up the clothes off my floor. I sniffed my shirt from last night and it smelled like JD, so I deeply inhaled the scent.

"I've got a sweaty shirt you can have if you want a real man's smell," said Grant as he stuck his head in my door.

"Very funny," I yelled.

Joey started barking and my heart was thrilled at the thought that it might be JD already. I walked out onto the back porch and around to the front of the house and saw a truck and trailer I didn't recognize pulling up.

"Shut it, Joey!" said Grant. Joey sat and growled low in his throat. The truck turned as if to head toward the barn but stopped in the road. The door opened and out stepped Ken.

"Hey Ken!" yelled Grant. "Glad you could make it!"

"Glad to be invited," said Ken, walking toward Grant.

Sandy got out of the truck. "Hey guys!" she said as she walked towards us.

"Should I pull on down to the barn?" asked Ken.

"Yeah, I'll go with you and help you unload," said Grant as he and Ken walked back to the truck.

"Come on inside," I called to Sandy. "We'll wait for the rest to show up before we head over to the arena." We went into the house and got a soda.

It wasn't long before Joey started barking, signaling the Martins had arrived. They brought two trucks; the truck with the trailer pulled around and we waved as they drove on down toward the barn. The second truck stopped, and Tesa, Leena, and Mrs. Martin got out.

"Hey, ya'll come in and get a drink before we get started," I called.

"Hey there, Sara," said Mrs. Martin, coming up the walk. "Where's your mom?"

"I'm right here! Come in and get a drink!"

Mom held the door as Mrs. Martin went inside. Tesa and Leena came up to me. "Hey Sandy! Hey Sara, how was the date?" asked Tesa.

"Good, real good," I said smiling.

"You're gonna give us details, aren't you?" asked Leena.

"I'll tell you as much as I told my brothers," I said.

"Oh man!" said Tesa, pleading, "I want details!"

I laughed at them. "Come in and get a drink." I waved them inside.

We went into the kitchen where Mrs. Martin and my Mom were. They sat at the bar, and I got some sodas for them.

"Did you notice Sara isn't limping?" asked Sandy.

"Yeah, that gash is just a thin red line now, and the stitches had started to dissolve," said Mom.

"I can bend it pretty well but not all the way," I said.

"Wish I was young and healed that fast!" said Mrs. Martin.

"Now tell us about your date!" said Tesa.

"Yes, tell us," said Mrs. Martin. "Haven't been able to get more than a few words out of JD."

I smiled and told them about helping the dog that got hit by a car and that we didn't make it to the movie in time. By the time I was done with the story and answering nosy questions, we heard the guys coming. They filed into the kitchen from the back door.

"Well, we gonna rope or talk?" asked Mr. Martin, taking off his hat and sitting down.

"Does anyone need a drink first?" asked Mom, getting up from the table. She was handing out drinks as JD walked in followed by Tad and Grant. They had grins on their faces, but JD's was the one that made my stomach flip. He nodded at me from across the room and I nodded back.

Mr. Martin turned to JD. "You can go stand by her, son. We know you wanna."

Mrs. Martin slapped at Mr. Martin. "Oh Bart, just leave it be for once."

We laughed, but JD did come over by me. I scooted over on the stool I was sitting on, and he set a hip on the other side. Tingles ran up my arm as he brushed against me.

"Well now, here's what I understand is gonna be the way we do this," said Mr. Martin. "For team roping, we're gonna draw names for three rounds. The team time will be written down for each partner. At the end of the three rounds, the best time takes the pot. Did I get that right, Sara?"

"Yes, sir!"

"Okay, so did anyone figure how to do the calf roping?" asked Mr. Martin.

"Marcy came up with an idea," said Dad. "We let everyone have three tries, take the best time, and give it to everyone to replace his worst time. Average the times and the best one wins."

"That sounds good to me," said Ken.

"All we need is for everyone to sign up by putting their five bucks in the pot for each event. I won't be doing the calf roping, so ya'll don't have to worry about losing twice to me!" said Mr. Martin. We laughed at that. Mom pulled out two mason jars, and everyone dropped money in.

"Is anyone else not participating in an event?" asked Dad.

"None of the girls are planning to compete," I said, looking at Tesa to be sure. She shook her head.

"So Bart, you're the only chicken holding out," said Dad. "You sure you don't wanna teach these young guns a lesson?"

"Well, if you put it that way, how can I refuse?" said Mr. Martin and we cheered. Dad put his money in for calf roping as well.

I leaned over to JD and asked, "You ready for this?"

"I got my lucky feathers and girl. I can't lose," he said, leaning into me. "Knee still good?"

"Yeah." I told him how it was healed.

He smiled and bumped me with his shoulder. "Told ya."

"Hey JD, you gonna put your money up or are you just planning on flirting today?" asked Matt.

"I can do both and still beat you," said JD, getting up and pulling money out of his pocket.

"Ooohh, do I hear a side bet brewing?" asked Matt.

"I can go for that!" said JD. "What do ya wanna bet, Matt?"

Matt's mouth opened and closed like a fish for a few seconds before he smiled. "The loser has to wear a pink shirt both nights at the Old Settler's rodeo!" We burst out laughing.

"Aw now son, you can't think of anything better than that?" asked Mr. Martin.

"How about a flowered shirt for one night?" said Grant.

"Now where ya gonna get a flowered shirt to fit Matt?" asked Tad.

"I did not just hear my best friend doubt me!" said Matt.

"Wait, this is just between Matt and JD right?" asked Mitch. "Maybe the loser should have to shave his head."

"I thought you were the smart one!" said Mr. Martin. "Now that's real incentive!"

JD leaned over to me and asked in a whisper, "Can May Day perform as well as Matt's horse?"

"He might be a little bit better," I said. "Question is can you rope better than Matt?"

"Would you still be seen with me if I didn't have my hair?" asked JD loud enough so everyone one heard.

"Hey, you got a nice hat if you lose, but Matt's the one that should be worried," I said.

"Why's that Miss Sara?"

"Because if you lose, we'll see all those knots on your head."

"Knots?"

"From hitting your big head on the doorways you try to walk through!" Everyone laughed at that.

"Just for that, I accept the bet be that the loser has to shave his head!" said Matt with a defiant smile.

"I accept as well," said JD. "Now so we're clear. This is on the team roping alone and best man wins!"

"Okay!" said Matt. "Let's shake on it!" They shook hands and laughed. Then they rubbed their heads.

"Does it always get this interesting at these practices?" asked Sandy.

"No, they're usually pretty boring," said Tesa.

"Let's get over to the arena and get started," said Dad.

"We'll make up the name slips and bring them over to the arena while ya'll go get saddled up." I looked at Dad. "I told JD he could ride May Day. Can you show him the right bridle to use?"

"Sure thing," said Dad. "Come on, JD. Let's get you set up."

The girls fixed the jars with the names, and I got stopwatches and a flag. Then we headed for the barn.

"Aren't you worried about JD losing his bet?" asked Leena.

I shrugged. "Not really. Besides, it's not a permanent change if he loses. I just can't imagine Matt without that curly blonde hair."

"Yeah. Celeste will have a fit if he loses," said Tesa.

"Nothing a good hat won't cure until it grows back," I said.

We got to the barn and I saw that JD had May Day saddled. The girls walked to the arena as I walked up to JD. I patted May Day and he turned to neigh a soft greeting to me.

"You be good for JD!" I said. He bobbed his head as if saying yes and JD laughed.

"Now all you have to do is talk to him. Go easy on the bit, he reins very well, and when you lean forward, he goes faster. He won't shoot out of the box until you tell him. Give him a good 'ha!' and he'll leap out there. He's been known to bite at the steers and calf if they aren't roped by the time you catch up to them, so watch for that."

"Yes ma'am," said JD. "Any other instructions?"

"Just one!" I grabbed his shirt, pulled him to me, and kissed him quickly. "Have fun!"

He laughed and pinned me between him and May Day. I looked up into his dancing blue eyes. "I had a very nice time last night and would like to do it again."

"I'd like that."

"Would you go with me to the movie tomorrow night in Uvalde?"

"I'm willing to try again."

"Great, pick you up at five-thirty. Now, would you come to dinner with my family when they get here Thursday?"

"Whoa, two commitments at once! Dinner with your family, are you sure?"

"Absolutely," he said, smiling at me.

"I'll be at the horse show all day Thursday, but I guess I can go with you to dinner. Where are you going?"

"Not sure yet. I'll have to let you know. And I'll be at the horse show to watch you win."

"Okay. You better get on May Day and get acquainted before they come drag us away in an embarrassing manner." He laughed and kissed me lightly on the lips then dropped his arms so I could pass.

He got on and May Day turned to look at me. "Pay attention!" I said to May Day. He snorted and JD laughed. "What does that mean?"

"He said the equivalent of 'yes ma'am.' Now go play!" I slapped May Day on the behind, and they started for the arena.

I walked to the arena and climbed the fence to sit by Sandy and Leena. Tesa was playing flag man and had gone to get her horse. The guys were moving around in the arena. Mom and Mrs. Martin, with Joey's help, were herding the steers down the far side of the arena into the pen behind the chute.

"Here," I handed a pad and pen to Leena. "You keep track of the times." I handed one of the two stopwatches to Sandy. "You be the second timer. We'll compare times then take the lower of each time. They probably won't be more than a few tenths off, but just in case one fails, and they do that occasionally, we won't have to disappoint the guys."

We drew names for the first round partners. There were four teams, each took their turn, and we recorded the times. It was going to be a close contest. JD and Ken were keeping up just fine with the boys that had been doing this regularly. Dad and Mr. Martin showed they could hang with the group. There was much jibing and cheering for everyone, and we had a good time. You could feel the tension building between JD and Matt because of their bet.

"Last round!" said Mr. Martin. "Last chance for Matt or JD to back out!"

"No way!" said Matt. "You're gonna need a barber, JD!"

"Why wait for a barber? I saw a pair of horse clippers in the barn!" taunted JD.

"Okay girls, draw for us!" said Matt. Leena drew the names, and the final round started.

"Who won?" yelled Matt at us as soon as we called out the time for the last team.

"It'll take a few minutes to figure it up," said Sandy.

"Hurry it up!"

"In a hurry to lose your locks?" shouted JD at Matt.

"Let's break for lunch!" said Dad. "It'll give the girls a chance to figure up the results."

Leena, Sandy, and I left the boys and Tesa to tend the horses. Mom let the steers out to the pasture. Foxy trotted up behind me nudging my hand as we walked back to the house. I scratched her ear then she bounded off ahead of us.

"She follows you everywhere," said Sandy.

"Yeah, she's my guardian," I said.

We got to the house, went into Dad's office, and got his calculator. I handed it to Leena. She looked at me, shocked. "You wrote down the times; you can read your writing. We'll just witness," I said.

Leena was just finishing the last guys' average time when everyone else got to the house. Matt yelled "well?" as he came down the hall to Dad's office.

"Hold your horses, Matt. We're just finishing up," I said.

Sandy laughed and asked, "Are you that worried?"

"I sure am. I got a head of golden locks at stake here!"

"Okay, just need to list them in order," said Leena. "Oh wow!"

"Who won?" asked Matt. Leena pulled the pad back quickly and held it to her chest.

"Not until we're all in the kitchen!" she said. "Now shoo."

Matt started forward; Mr. Martin came up behind him and pulled him back into the hall, "Now son, give the girls a chance to tell us all at once. Your hounding them is only gonna prolong the waiting."

"But Dad!"

"Ain't gonna hear it, now git!" Mr. Martin pushed Matt down the hall. Matt reluctantly walked back to the kitchen. Mr. Martin turned back to us and asked softly, "So who one?"

"Not gonna tell you either!" said Leena, still holding the pad to her chest. "Shoo!"

Mr. Martin laughed and walked down the hall. We heard him telling everyone that we were almost done. I turned to Leena. "You got the winner of the overall as well as who won between Matt and JD?"

"There's a tie!" she said, looking at the pad.

"For what?" I asked.

"For overall," she said. "How do we break that?"

I shrugged. "Maybe they'll be happy to split the pot. We'll ask them."

"Don't you wanna know who won?" asked Leena.

"I can wait like the rest," I said. "I know it's close."

"Okay," said Leena, standing up and clutching the pad to her chest.

We walked down the hall and as we turned the corner, "They're ready!" called Matt loudly. Everyone turned to look as we walked into the kitchen.

"There's a tie!" I said.

"What?" yelled Matt, "How is that possible?"

I held up my hand. "The tie is not over the bet."

"Aw man, had me going there!"

"So what's the tie for?" asked Tad.

"For the overall pot. We can find a way to break the tie or we can have the two split the pot," I said. Several voices said split. I looked around the room. "Anyone not willing to split the pot?" There was silence. "We'll take that as a no, and we'll split the pot."

"Tell us already!" said Matt.

"Leena?" I said.

Leena stepped forward, looked down at her pad, and took a breath. "Grant and JD!"

"What?" yelled Matt. "Does that mean JD won our bet?"

"Seems that way," said Tad, slapping him on the back. Matt turned to Leena. "Please tell me it isn't true!"

"It was close, real close, but your average was three tenths slower than

JD's," said Leena.

"Way to go champ!" said Grant, slapping JD on the back.

"Right back at ya champ!" They gave each other high-fives and everyone was talking at once.

"Where did you see those clippers, JD?" asked Grant loudly.

JD shrugged. "I was just talking. I didn't really see any."

"Well, there are some in the tack room," said Dad. "Want me to get them for you, JD?"

"I'm supposed to cut his hair off?"

"No way!" said Matt.

"Who would you trust?" asked Mr. Martin. "You're not leaving here with that hair. You made the bet now own up to it!"

"Um, ah, um, Mom?" stammered Matt.

"I'll be glad to help you out son," said Mrs. Martin. "But let's eat lunch first!"

We ate lunch and there was lots of talk and ribbing. When we were done Dad said, "Okay, next event. Let's go!"

We walked down to the barn together and got ready for the calf roping. I went with JD to get May Day out of the stall. May Day gave us a welcoming low neigh. I reached up to put the bridle on, and May Day pushed me back.

"Hey, easy there." May Day bobbed his head and curled his upper lip back. "Yeah laugh it up!"

JD was laughing, too. "Here you do it."

I handed JD the bridle and stood back. May Day went right up to him. JD patted May Day's face and put the bridle on.

"Traitor!" I said to May Day as JD led him out of the stall.

May Day flicked his tail and it caught me in the face. Tad burst out laughing, as he was leading out Super right next to us. Andrea hung her head over her stall and whinnied at me.

"Well at least someone still likes me!" I said and went to pet her.

Everyone was saddled and warming up in the arena. Matt's enthusiasm had waned and it showed. The guys started picking at him, hoping to bait him into a better mood, but it didn't help.

Mom and Mrs. Martin, with some help from Joey, again manned the chute for the calves. Tesa was to be the flagman again. Sandy and I had the stopwatches, and Leena would record the times again.

"Whose up first?" asked Tad.

"Does it matter?" asked Mr. Martin.

"No sir! Why don't you show us how it's done Mr. Martin?"

"Don't mind if I do!" Mr. Martin trotted over to the box. The rest of them cleared the arena.

When he was ready, Mr. Martin nodded his head, and the calf was released. He took off and after three swings, he threw his loop and caught the calf. He flew off the horse as it came to a halt and ran down the rope to grab the calf. He tied it quickly and threw up his hands calling time.

"That will set the standard!" yelled Mr. Martin, puffing out his chest. Tesa undid the calf, and it got up and ran off unharmed.

"I'm next!" said Mitch. He put in a very good time. It was on down the line with each guy. Grant was leading in the first round, with Dad and Mitch close behind. Matt was not doing well at all.

The next round started in the same order as the first. Then the final third round came. Grant was still leading, and it was too close to call yet between Dad, Mitch, and Tad. Matt was still not doing well.

Ken took his turn. He did amazingly and got the best time of the day.

"That ought to shake things up a bit!" said Dad, smiling at Ken.

When everyone had their turn, Leena asked, "Now how are we gonna do this?"

"Let's go back to the house and I'll show you," I said. "Sandy, you gotta come too so we don't get accused of cheating."

Sandy nodded and Tesa called out, "Wait for me!"

Back in Dad's office, I explained how we were to score the calf roping. Leena got to work and had the results ready as everyone came into the house. I waited with Leena, Sandy, and Tesa in Dad's office until we knew they were all in the kitchen.

"Okay now!" said Tesa and she led the way down the hall.

When we stepped into the kitchen, it was quieter than this morning. I went to stand by JD as Leena cleared her throat and everyone got quiet. "In last place," she said and everyone snickered, "with a pitiful showing of his talents is Matt!"

We gave a quiet round of applause. "In seventh place, with a good showing for his age, Mr. Martin!" He laughed and bowed a little and sat down.

"In sixth place, a remarkable showing for a bull rider, JD!" We clapped and JD gave a little bow. I patted him on the shoulder.

"Now the next three places were very close. In fifth place, Tad!" We clapped and he bowed like everyone else before him. "In fourth place, with a remarkable comeback in the third round…"

"Ken!" everyone called and there was a round of applause.

"Third place goes to Mitch!" We clapped and Tad slapped Mitch on the back.

"That leaves the two finalists, Grant and Mr. Stillsen!" said Leena, making a big show.

"Now without further ado." Someone started a drum roll on the counter and Leena smiled, "The winner of the First Annual Midsummer Diamond E Roping Fiesta is," and we laughed, "Grant!"

We were clapping as Grant stood up, and Leena threw her arms around him and gave him a big hug. Grant was surprised at first but hugged her back.

Mom handed the money jar to Sandy. She sashayed across the floor and with a game show girl flourish, posed, gave Grant the jar of money, and kissed him on the cheek from the side. We roared with laughter, and Grant grabbed both Leena and Sandy from each side and bowed. There were some flashes as Mom took pictures.

"Now for one last event!" said Mr. Martin, standing up. "The shearing of the golden fleece!"

We laughed as Matt pouted. Dad put some clippers on the table and we laughed harder. Matt, sucking it up, stood up, walked over to the table, and picked up the clippers. "Well, let's get this over with. The sooner it comes off, the sooner it'll grow back!"

"That's the spirit!" said Mr. Martin, slapping Matt on the back. "Now let's go out on the porch so we don't get hair all over in the Stillsens' kitchen. I don't wanna find hair in my enchiladas later."

I slipped off to my room, grabbed a hand mirror, and met everyone as they filed out to the front porch. Mom was there with a video camera. Dad brought out a barstool for Matt to sit on. Tad had a sheet that he wrapped around Matt as he sat down. Grant brought out an extension cord for Mrs. Martin, as she was given the honor of shearing off Matt's hair.

Mrs. Martin ran her fingers through Matt's hair and asked him, "Any last words for your hair?"

"No ma'am. Let's just get this over with!"

Mrs. Martin turned on the clippers, started at the front of his head, and sheared off a strip down the middle. There were oohs and ahs as the hair fell to the porch. Matt closed his eyes as Mrs. Martin continued to shave his head. When she was done, she turned off the clippers and rubbed his head.

"JD, is this shaved enough?"

JD laughed. "Real nice job, Mrs. M!"

I walked forward and handed Matt the mirror. Matt smiled at me and asked, "Is it that bad?"

"See for yourself," I said, trying not to laugh.

Matt took a deep breath and held up the mirror. He straightened and moved the mirror side to side. Then a big smile spread across his face. "Man, am I handsome or what?"

We burst out laughing and Matt stood up. "Well, now that that's over with, I'm in need of a swim!"

"I'm for that!" said Tad. "Let's go!"

We were filing back into the house when Sandy caught my arm. "I didn't know we were gonna swim. I didn't bring a suit."

"You can borrow one of mine." I said. "Tesa will show you where they are. I'll be right there."

Mom was pulling out stuff to start making enchiladas when I entered the kitchen. "Need some help before I run off to swim?"

"No honey, you go and have fun," said Mrs. Martin. "We can handle this."

I looked at Mom and she nodded. "Go on have fun!"

I knocked on my bedroom door as the girls were in there changing. "Who is it?" called Tesa.

"Me!" I said.

"Okay, you can open the door," said Tesa.

"Is it okay if I wear this one?" asked Sandy, holding up an old one-piece suit of mine.

"Yeah if you want, but there are better ones in there," I said walking over. "Do you want a one or two piece?"

"I usually wear a bikini," she said.

"You're in luck. I've a few to choose from." I laid three on the bed. "Take your pick!"

She picked up a red one that I hadn't worn much. "This is pretty!"

"Then it's yours!" I said. I picked up my favorite green suit and changed into it.

"How come the top is more faded than the bottom?" asked Sandy.

"Probably because I usually wear it riding and have cutoffs on covering the bottoms," I said. "See my wonderful tan lines?" I showed her the lines on my thigh. "This is from wearing tennis shoes with my suits too!" I waved at my white feet.

"I have the same look," said Tesa. "Must be a cowgirl thing."

"Yeah, must be," said Sandy, showing us she had the same lines. We laughed.

"I don't have lines quite like that, but my feet are white," said Leena, not to be left out.

There was a knock on the door. "You girls coming or not?" yelled Tad.

"Be there in a second!" said Tesa.

We hurried getting changed. I threw a t-shirt at Sandy. "Might wanna start out with this on over," I said.

We pulled on a t-shirt over our suits, shoved our feet into sneakers, and hurried down the hall. The guys had cutoffs and t-shirts on. Matt looked funny, as his scalp was whiter than his face, but he was smiling. We piled into the truck, most of us in the back. JD pulled me up into the back, and I sat on the side next to him.

"You're gonna love this!" I said to JD. I looked at Ken and Sandy. "You too!"

"Why's that?" asked Ken.

"We have this rope that you can swing on over this whirlpool. When you drop into it, the whirlpool sucks you down then pops you up just downstream. It's really fun!" said Tad.

"What makes the whirlpool stay there?" asked JD. "I thought they came and went."

"There's a spring-fed lake that drains into the river where we're going. A big tree sits just north on the edge where the river bends in, just right where the lake drains into the river, and it makes a whirlpool," said Tad.

"The spring lake water is really cold!" I said. "It's quite a shock but feels great. The river is usually a lot warmer, and there's a place to swim in it just below the whirlpool."

JD caught me as the truck bounced over a rut in the road. His hand on my back was warm, and it sent tingles up my back. I looked down at his legs. They were muscled and tan but not as dark as his arms. He, like the rest of us, spent most of our time in jeans.

We came to a gate and Matt jumped out and opened it. "We should leave him," said Tad as we drove through.

"Hasn't he been tortured enough for one day?" I asked.

"Never!" said Tad. "Makes us strong to suffer!" He puffed out his chest.

Right on cue, as Matt neared the back of the truck, Grant sped off a little ways. We laughed and Matt yelled, "Very funny guys!"

Grant stopped the truck and Matt trotted up, but as he got near again, Grant sped off. Matt threw his hands in the air and looked up at the sky. "Just what did I do to deserve this?" he shouted.

Grant backed up and Matt climbed in, grumbling as we laughed.

We drove up to the river and piled out. You could see the big tree Tad had described and the sunny river beyond. Everyone was stripping off their shirts and throwing them into the truck. When I pulled my shirt off, I saw JD looking at me. A slow smile spread across his face, and I felt a warmth stir in my core.

A shirt hit JD from the side. "Come on you two!" said Grant. "Time for that later!"

We laughed and walked over to join those jumping into the river. There were screams and shouts as they plunged in. Although I didn't limp, I still couldn't run. So everyone was in the water but Sandy, JD, and I.

"Whatcha waiting for?" called Ken to Sandy. "It's not that cold here."

She shrugged her shoulders and jumped in. "Wa, wa, whoa, that's cold!" she said and we laughed.

"Come over here," said Tesa a little farther out. "It's much warmer." Sandy swam over to her and relaxed.

The boys climbed out, grabbed the rope, and started swinging out and back over the river. You could see the big whirlpool, and Tad was the first to drop into it. A second later, he popped up downstream about ten feet away.

Matt did a Tarzan yell and dropped in. "Sounded like a wounded gorilla to me!" yelled Tad.

I pushed JD. "Gotta try it!" He nodded and jumped in and swam over to where the rope swing was.

Grant was next then Mitch then JD. I jumped in and swam over to the tree along with Sandy, Tesa, and Leena. We took turns. Then Sandy grabbed the rope and climbed up higher than we usually did. We watched as she swung out and back then out again. As she swung out, she let go and did a back flip into the water.

"Wow!" we said as she came up smiling.

"Where did you learn to do that?" asked Tad.

"Gymnastics!" she said, swimming back to the tree.

"She's just showing off!" said Ken. "She's been in the state finals for gymnastics the past two years."

"Yeah, but way out here, I might not get to train anymore," said Sandy.

"There's a gymnastics club in Uvalde," said Tesa. "Might wanna check it out!"

"I'll do that! Thanks," said Sandy with a smile.

I swam over to the bank and got out to sit on the edge. JD swam over. "You okay?" he asked.

"Yeah, need to work out this knee some I guess. It's stiff and feels funny kicking."

JD got out and sat beside me. He patted my leg. "Maybe you need some more of your own medicine," he said so only I could hear.

I looked at him and smiled. "Yeah, like I'm gonna try here in front of everyone."

Grant splashed us. "What are you two whispering about over there?"

"He was giving me tips on how to get my knee back in shape!" I said.

"Swimming's good therapy," said Grant and he pulled me into the water. I grabbed JD and pulled him in with me. The boys started a cannonball contest jumping off the bank. Sandy got up and started doing flips into the water. We clapped as she did her tricks.

After we had tired ourselves out, we laid on the bank for a while. "You better put a hat on Matt," said Tesa. "Your head's getting sunburned."

"Great, now it'll peel and I'll really look ghoulish!" said Matt.

"I'm starved," said Tad. "Let's go see if dinner's ready!"

As we girls pulled on our t-shirts, Matt wrapped his around his head and looked like an Arabian prince with his blue eyes and big smile.

"That's an improvement," said Mitch, "Might wanna try that look for a while."

Matt looked at his reflection in the back window of the truck. He fussed with the headdress and turned to us. "I do look rather dashing!"

"Yeah, just let me make one adjustment for you," said Tad. Tad reached over and turned the headdress around so the flap was over Matt's face. "Now that's better!"

Matt didn't move the headdress but flipped the flap over his head. "Some friends I have! They even kick me when I'm down."

"Poor baby," said Tesa, "Thought you were tough enough to take what you dish out."

We pulled up to the house and JD jumped down and reached up for me. I smiled down into his face as he lifted me out of the back of the truck. He put his arm around me as we walked toward the house.

"You ask if you could go to the movie with me tomorrow?"

"Uh no, haven't had the chance. I will right now." I told the girls I'd be with them in a minute. I nodded to JD and went to find my dad.

He and Mr. Martin were in his office. They looked up as I stopped in the doorway.

"What's up?" asked Dad.

"Would it be alright if I went to the movie with JD tomorrow night?" I asked.

"Gonna try it one more time?" asked Mr. Martin.

"Yes sir," I said. I looked at Dad. He smiled.

"Fine by me if it's okay with your mother."

I smiled. "Thanks, Dad!" and went to the kitchen.

"How was the swim?" asked Mom as I came over to her.

"Great! Sandy did flips off the rope swing into the whirlpool!"

"Wow! Is she a gymnast?" asked Mrs. Martin.

"Apparently so. Ken said she was in the state finals the last two years."

"Well, hidden talents all around us!"

I turned to Mom. "Is it okay if I go with JD to the movie tomorrow night?"

"Gonna try it again?" she asked, smiling at me. I nodded. "Did you clear it with your father yet?"

"Yes ma'am. He said it was okay with him if it was alright with you."

"Well then, by all means," said Mom.

I gave her a hug. "Thanks Mom!" She laughed and I bounced down the hall to my room. I was about to knock on my door when JD came out of the bathroom. He looked at me and smiled.

"Well?" he asked.

"I can go," I said with a big smile.

He walked up to me. "Think we'll make it this time?"

I shrugged. "Ya never know what's gonna happen with me around."

"I'm willing to take that chance!"

Grant's door down the hall opened then shut quickly. JD smiled and kissed me lightly. "Can't wait!" Then he turned and walked into Tad's room.

I knocked on my door. "Come in!" I heard and went in.

"Where've you been?" asked Leena.

"Asking permission to go on another date with JD," I said, bouncing on my bed.

"Where ya going on your second date?" asked Leena.

"We're going to the movie," I said.

"I hope it works out better for ya this time," said Sandy.

"I thought the first date was pretty good."

"He must be some kisser!" said Tesa.

"Yeah, he is." I sighed.

They laughed at me. I ignored them and started combing my hair. We heard the boys walking down the hall. Leena looked at me. "Mind if we go ahead?"

"Not at all," I said. "I'll be right there!"

They left and I finished dressing. I found everyone in the front yard; the boys were practicing rope tricks. Sandy asked Grant to show her how to do a trick, and Grant was only too happy to oblige.

Leena, getting a little jealous, walked over to join Grant and Sandy. She didn't quite make it as Matt roped her. Leena was laughing and telling Matt to let her go. Tesa came to her defense, but Tad roped her. The boys pulled them over to a tree and ran around it tying them to the tree.

We were laughing and pointing when Dad and Mr. Martin came out to see what the commotion was. Dad laughed and shook his head. "Boys, let the girls go."

They let Tesa and Leena loose. Tesa turned to Tad and Matt. "I wouldn't wanna be in your shoes!" and she gave them a devilish look.

"Uh oh!" said Matt. "I'm in for it now!"

Tad laughed at Matt. "At least I don't live with her. I can sleep well tonight."

"Oh really?" I said to Tad and gave him my evil eye. "You of all people should know that we amigos stick together!"

Grant and Matt burst out laughing as Tad looked kinda scared for a second. "You better learn to sleep with one eye open!" said Grant.

"Dinner!" called Mom from the door. We laughed as we filed into the kitchen. It was buffet style, so we filled our plates.

"Let's go out onto the front porch," I said to JD. We walked out to the front porch and sat on the swing. Everyone else followed, dragging chairs up.

"How do you like it?" I asked JD after he had a few bites.

"Really good!" he said. "I've had some Mexican food in my day, but these are the best chicken enchiladas I've ever had!"

"Be sure to tell my mom that," I said. "I tell her all the time but she doesn't believe me."

Matt spoke up. "So JD, where you two going tomorrow night?"

"To the movie in Uvalde," said JD. "Thought I'd take a page from Tad and spend my winnings on my girl."

"Gonna make it there this time?" asked Grant with a grin.

"Gonna give it another shot," said JD smiling.

"What happened the first time?" asked Ken. They turned to look at him like he was from another planet. "What? I haven't heard?" he said defensively.

Tesa told the story and filled in Ken. "Oh, is that all!" said Ken. JD and I chuckled and exchanged a look.

When everyone was done eating, we meandered back to the barn to load up. While the Martins were loading up their horses, I took JD by the hand and pulled him over to Andrea's stall. "This is Andrea and my work in progress!" Andrea came up to us and gave a light "hu hu hu." I rubbed her face.

"What do you mean by work in progress?" asked JD.

"She's carrying the next-generation champion," I said. "Should be here after Christmas."

JD smiled. "And you're gonna train it up to do what?"

"First we gotta find out what he's good at. Then improve on it."

"He? You already know the gender?"

"I don't know, but I'm hoping," I looked at JD.

Matt walked up. "There you are! We're loaded up and ready to leave."

"Be right there," said JD.

Matt smiled and walked back the way he came. JD turned to me. "I'll be here at five-thirty tomorrow." Then he kissed me.

"I'll be ready," I said. JD stepped back then turned and walked out of the stall. He winked at me as he latched the stall door. I smiled and leaned back on Andrea's shoulder. She nudged me. I patted her cheek. There was a "yawwl" and I looked up to see Foxy staring down at me from the loft.

"There you are," said Tad. "What ya been doing?"

"I was showing JD my new champion in the making."

"Well, come say good-bye, everyone's leaving."

I followed Tad out of the barn and we waved as the Martins drove off followed by Ken and Sandy.

"Fun day," said Tad as we watched them drive off. I nodded and turned to go back into the barn. "Where you going?"

"I need to ride for a while."

"Why?" asked Tad following me.

"I wanna ride Flaxie for a while, like Dad said."

"Oh," said Tad. "I'll help you saddle her."

I got Flaxie out of her stall and was brushing her off when Tad brought over my saddle. He threw it across her back and started doing up the cinch. I walked around to the other side and rubbed the fender. It was darker than it used to be. You could make out the bloodstain if you looked for it.

I walked back around as Tad was finishing up.

"Need a boost?"

"Naw, my right leg is the bad one. I can get this." I mounted up and Flaxie raised her head. I patted her and she relaxed. "See ya in a little while," I said and rode out of the barn.

I rode out to the big pasture to the south. The sun was getting lower on my right. I urged Flaxie into a trot then we began to lope. Before I knew it, we were running across the field, the wind in my hair. I felt elated and free.

Prep for the Show

I got up early the next day and decided to ride. It was peaceful, with the birds chirping as I walked to the barn. Foxy was exploring the bushes.

I decided to try and run a little to test out my knee. I jogged a few paces and felt okay, so I kept jogging. I had to stop just short of the barn as my knee started to hurt.

As I entered the barn, I was greeted by neighs. I went into the tack room and got a bridle. May Day nodded his head at me. I patted him as I walked up. "Not this morning, big guy. Gonna ride Flaxie a little." I went to Flaxie's stall and she greeted me.

As we entered the arena, the sun was just cresting the eastern wall of the canyon and peeking over the top. She was snorting, feeling a little frisky, so I rode her until she settled into a nice, slow, rocking chair pace. I looked up and saw Dad sitting on the fence. He waved. I came around and stopped.

"You're up early!" he said.

"Gotta make up for some down time." I patted Flaxie on the neck.

"What classes did you have in mind for her?"

"Thought I'd start with equitation." I hesitated. "Can I ride two different horses in reining?"

Dad laughed. "I don't think you can enter two horses, but I'll take a look at the rules."

"Thanks." I turned Flaxie back to our workout. I got her to do flying lead changes. She was smooth and fast. Next, we worked on sliding stops. She had a soft mouth and stopped easily. Then we did some roll backs and spins. She wasn't very good at those but seemed to catch on fast. I patted her on the neck as I ended the last set of rollbacks.

"Looking good, sis!" yelled Grant. I looked up to see him and Tad leaning on the fence. I walked over to them and patted Flaxie, getting her to settle down.

"You gonna ride her in the show?" asked Grant.

"Yep, just asked Dad if I could enter two horses in reining. Whatcha ya think?"

"Whoa."

"Trying to impress anyone?" asked Tad.

"Just trying to determine what this girl has," I said.

"Good luck then," said Grant.

"Thanks." I turned and walked Flaxie around to cool her down.

The rest of the day I spent in my room, lying across my bed, reading a book I had read several times before. I fell asleep and dreamt a familiar dream.

I was standing on a cliff, the wind blowing in my hair, and dark clouds off to the west were blocking out the sun. Lightning struck and there was JD walking toward me. A crow flew by and JD was standing behind me, pointing over my shoulder. I looked to the east and saw a dark void, but I wasn't afraid. I felt warmth in my chest as the lightning flashed then thunder boomed.

I turned toward a bright light that was coming at me. As it got closer, I could see it was Uncle Buck dressed in Indian garb and carrying a big spear decorated with eagle feathers riding a magnificent, gleaming, blue-black stallion. They stopped in front of me and Uncle Buck leaned towards me. As I stepped closer to him, I sucked in wetness.

I jerked upright and a washcloth fell from my face. I looked at the door and heard snickering.

"You better run!" I shouted. Quietly, I slid off my bed, holding the wet washcloth in my hand. I went out my back door, down to Grant's room, and through to the hall. I could see Grant and Tad standing to the side of my door, peeking inside, trying to see me. I took aim, hurled the washcloth at the back of Grant's head, and ran back through his room.

"What the...?" I heard him yell and then feet running down the hall as I rounded the corner onto the back porch, ran down to Tad's room, cut inside, and hid behind his door.

As the boys ran past, I tiptoed into their bathroom, grabbed the shaving cream, and then tiptoed back to wait by Tad's back door.

"Where'd she go?" I heard Grant say.

"Don't know," said Tad. "Where's Foxy? She's always close to where Sara is."

"She's on Sara's bed," said Grant.

"Then she's close," said Tad.

I heard them moving around but couldn't see anything. Tad crept down the back porch, and I saw him through the crack in the door. I turned my head and made a small noise. Tad quickly turned toward his door. I held my breath and got ready to strike.

He slowly crept into his room, looking around. He looked under his bed, and as he stood up, I leaped out from behind the door and squirted shaving cream up the side of his face.

"Oh you didn't!" cried Tad, lunging for me.

I spun around and ran right into Grant, who pinned me. "Oh but she did!"

I laughed and as my hand was pinned in just the right position, I squirted Grant's chin and neck with shaving cream. He laughed, pulled me close, and rubbed his chin on my face. I was laughing so hard I could hardly push him back. Tad came over and rubbed shaving cream in my hair. I squirted more upward, not sure what or if I hit anything.

I stumbled back and we landed on Tad's bed.

"Now you're gonna pay!" shouted Tad.

We wrestled around some more; they were tickling me and trying to get the shaving cream from me. Finally, Tad pried it from my fingers. Grant had me pinned and Tad aimed for my face. He pressed the top, but it just fizzled. We burst out laughing and they let me go.

"What's going on in here?" asked Mom from the door.

"Just horsing around," said Grant, wiping shaving cream from his face. I sat up laughing and felt my head. There was shaving cream in my hair.

"Sara, you better get moving if you're gonna be ready by five-thirty," said Mom.

"What time is it?" I asked, suddenly sober.

"It's a quarter to five," she said.

"Oh, I gotta hurry!" I ran out of the room to the bathroom across the hall.

Tad yelled after me. "Hey, what about my bed?"

"You started it, you clean it up!" I yelled back and jumped in the shower.

I came out of the bathroom and stuck my head into Tad's. He was putting clean sheets on his bed. "Need help?" I asked.

"Naw, you go get gussied up. I can handle this!"

"Don't say I didn't offer!" I walked off to my room.

I was just finishing braiding the front part of my hair when I heard Joey start barking. I glanced at the clock beside my bed and saw it was five twenty-eight; JD was on time. There was a knock on my door.

"Come in!" I said standing up.

Grant poked his head in. "JD's here!"

I walked over to Grant and patted his face. "Hmm, maybe you should use a different shaving cream." I laughed and dodged his poking finger.

Grant followed me down the hall. I was trying to walk just far enough ahead of him so he couldn't poke me in the ribs. I rushed into the living room where I knew it would be safe from Grant. JD was sitting on the couch talking to Dad. He stood up and smiled at me.

"There she is!" said Dad.

"We'll be back by ten-thirty at the latest," said JD as I walked over to him.

"Try to make it to the movie this time!" said Grant. "It's pretty good."

"We'll do that," said JD, taking my hand.

"Drive safe," said Dad.

"Yes, sir," said JD. "I'll bring her home safe." He smiled at me. "Ready?"

"Ready!" I said.

JD turned to Mom and nodded. "Night, Mrs. Stillsen."

"Have a good time!" she said.

We walked outside and down the walkway. JD got the gate and I looked around. "Wait!"

"What's wrong?" asked JD.

Foxy bounded around the corner of the house. "There she is! Couldn't leave without telling her good-bye." I ruffled her head, and she gave me a "rrruuwwl."

"I'll be back soon."

Foxy bounded off and I turned back to JD. He was smiling at me. "Now we can go," I said.

JD opened the passenger side door for me and I got in and scooted over to be in the middle as he came around the driver's side. As we were driving off, I asked, "Why did you get the passenger door for me? I can get in your side."

"Just doesn't seem right," he said with a crooked smile.

"Why not?" I asked frowning.

"Seems presumptive. Besides looks better for the folks, like I'm a gentleman."

"I see." I pushed his shoulder.

JD reached over and turned up the radio. We laughed, as the song playing was *When I Close My Eyes*.

"Definitely our song," said JD. I nodded.

"Well, what did you do today?" he asked.

"I pined away for you all day. Counted the passing of every minute," I said with a southern belle drawl.

JD laughed and shook his head. "You say what a guy wants to hear."

"I sense a but."

"But you twist it with the way you say it. Keeps it real. So what did you really do all day?"

"I rode Flaxie this morning. Then I read for a while. Got into a shaving cream fight with my brothers." I sighed. "The usual."

JD was chuckling. "Who won?"

"They did I'm afraid, but I got my licks in. It's not fair when it's two brutes against little ol' me!"

"I've heard some stories, and I don't think you aren't without your wiles."

"My wiles? Wow! Don't think I've heard a cowboy use that term except in the movies."

"Like it?"

"Yeah. It's attractive to know someone with a decent vocabulary and who can ride a horse."

"I better brush up. Gotta keep you attracted."

"You don't have to worry about that at all."

We pulled onto the highway and turned toward Uvalde. It seemed like no time at all before we were on the outskirts of town. "Keep your fingers crossed," said JD.

"Why?"

"Not sure we could live it down if I couldn't get you to the movie twice in a row." We laughed.

JD pulled up next to an Italian restaurant. We were seated at a booth and JD sat next to me. "What's good here?" he asked.

"I like everything I've tried."

JD looked over the menu then closed it. "Think I'll get the ravioli. You?"

"The manicotti."

The waitress came over and JD ordered for both of us. We were laughing when we recounted Matt getting his hair sheared off.

"Well, well, what's so funny?" said Cathy Coulter, coming over to our table. I could see Yvette Sampson and Kaylene Carter behind her. They waved a little.

I stopped laughing. "Hello, Cathy. Have you met JD?"

"Don't believe so," she said and put on her best smile, filling her eyes with JD.

"JD, this is Cathy Coulter, Yvette Sampson, and Kaylene Carter. JD is staying with…"

"I know who he is," said Cathy in her best flirting voice. "I just haven't had the chance to meet him." She turned to JD. "Congratulations on your national championship."

"Thanks," said JD. The waitress came up with our meals. "If ya'll will excuse us," JD smiled at the girls, "our dinner has arrived."

"Well, see ya at the horse show then," said Cathy and she turned to her groupies. "Come on girls, let's leave them to eat." Yvette and Kaylene waved as they followed Cathy while she tromped off.

The waitress set down our meals and JD laughed. "That was like a sample of my sisters."

"I'm sure they aren't that bad."

"You're too kind to them."

"You don't know Cathy!"

"I know her type."

"What type is that?"

"The type that thinks because they have money they can get anything they want or their daddy will get it for them. They're royal pains in the backside."

"You got Cathy pegged. We used to be good friends."

"Really? When was that?"

"A few years ago, before she got her big head."

"Ah, I understand now."

"Yeah, she went over to the dark side," I laughed.

We finished our dinner then went to the theater. "Whew!" he said with a grin. "We're even early."

"Don't relax yet because we haven't made it inside," I said with a mischievous grin.

"Oh ye of little faith," said JD, putting his arm around me.

"I have faith. Faith that we'll eventually make it to a movie," I teased.

He put his hand on my cheek. "That's what I like about you. Always willing to try." Then he kissed me. The warmth in my chest flared up, and I concentrated on containing it. I backed it down to a simmer and didn't let it spread into my arms.

JD lifted my hand to his face. "Am I losing my touch?"

"No. I held it back. I wanted to see if I could control it."

"Guess it worked." He ran his finger down my nose and with a twinkle in his eye, "We'll practice more later."

After getting our tickets, JD stopped at the concession stand. "Let's see, popcorn with extra butter and salt."

"You got it!" I liked the way he remembered.

He ordered and handed me a large drink. We approached the ticket taker and JD stopped. He looked around. "What are you looking for?" I asked.

"Just seeing if any stray or injured animals were around."

I laughed and pushed him. "Oh you!"

He handed over our tickets and walked down the hall to the theater. We found some seats high up in the middle. Hardly anyone was there, but it was still early.

JD was telling me about what he had done earlier that day when in walked Trent, Jason, and Jeremy. Trent waved at us then Jeremy looked up and waved. I waved back. Jason didn't even look up. They sat several rows in front of us.

JD leaned over and whispered to me, "Someone isn't happy you're with me."

I smiled at him. "I am."

JD smiled at me as the lights dimmed and the previews started. We munched on the popcorn and watched the movie. We kept hitting each other's hands reaching for more popcorn. After most of the popcorn was gone, JD put the bucket on the seat next to him, then he took my hand and laced his fingers with mine. A tingling sensation ran up my arm, and I leaned into him a little.

When the movie got to the sad part, I blinked back tears, and JD squeezed my hand. I didn't dare look at him, as I knew I'd cry.

When the movie was over, we made our way down the steps. JD held my hand as he led the way. I glanced back to see Jason, Trent, and Jeremy still in their seats watching us leave.

We were almost back to the truck when JD said, "We actually did it." I smiled up at him. "Now I don't feel like I've shorted you on an official date."

I stopped walking and asked, "Is there some bet you had that you might be referring to?"

JD pulled me to face him. "What are you talking about?"

"Just checking to see if there was some criteria you had to fulfill for a bet."

JD pulled me close and looked into my eyes. "The only criteria is mine." He kissed me. "The only bet I've made all summer is with Matt yesterday." Then he kissed me again. "Now do you have any more doubts?"

I took a deep breath. "If I did, would you kiss me some more?"

He laughed. "I would even if you didn't. Now let's go practice control."

"Sounds interesting."

He opened the truck door on the driver's side and I got in then he did, too. "Not worried about pretenses here I see."

"Different class of folks here." He backed out of the parking spot and drove out onto the street. We were driving down the highway enjoying the radio. JD looked at the clock. "Good we'll have time."

"Time for what?"

"Practice!" he said, giving me a dazzling smile that made my heart flutter.

"What did you have in mind?"

"You'll see."

We pulled off the highway at the turnoff to my house. When we got to the river crossing, he turned to the right like Friday night. He parked on the rise overlooking the river, smiled at me as he opened the door, and helped me out. He went to the back of the truck and pulled me over to sit on the tailgate. Then he stood in front of me.

He put both hands on my face and kissed me. His hands moved down to my shoulders, and I wrapped my arms around his waist. The warmth burst in my chest and ran down my arms into my hands and fingers. He pulled me to him. I was lost in a surge of warmth. The world began to spin. The warmth turned to a hot fire that was almost painful. I pushed JD back. He released me immediately with a look of concern on his face.

"What's wrong?"

"I suddenly got really hot. Are you okay?"

"I feel great!" he smiled, reaching for my hand. "WOW! Hot."

"It would have been worse if I hadn't pushed you back. Is this what you had in mind?"

"Sort of," he stepped closer again. "Tell me how it felt."

I took a deep breath. "First it was warm and it spread down my arms, then it turned to fire. That's when I pushed you back."

He hugged me to him. "When you held back earlier, what did you do?"

"I concentrated on containing it so it didn't spread to start with."

His eyes sparkled. "I like being the catalyst." He looked down at me.

"I like being with you but not if I'm gonna hurt you."

"That's why you need to learn to control it."

"When did you get this idea I needed to learn this?"

"Friday night I dreamt this big black horse was in pain. You were healing it. Then it started kicking like it was dying. I came up behind you. Your skin was on fire, and I pulled you back away from the horse. Then I woke up. After I thought about the dream, I got the feeling if you hadn't gotten so hot, the horse wouldn't have died. I got the feeling I was supposed to help you with that. Especially since I'm only one of two who knows what you can do."

"But I don't know any big black horses."

"You didn't know that dog Friday either."

I took a deep breath and sighed. "JD, how am I gonna learn to do this?"

"Practice. Now let's try without the kissing. Put your hands on my chest and see if you can make them warm."

I did as he asked. He smiled down at me, and I closed my eyes and concentrated. Warmth flared and I concentrated on slowing it. I allowed it slowly to push down my arms to my hands.

"Now look at me but don't stop."

I opened my eyes slowly and looked up into his. A surge rippled through me. "Concentrate!" he said.

I concentrated on slowing the flow and it became a trickle. "That's good."

I dropped my hands and cut off the warmth. I looked up at JD and he was smiling. "Not bad. Let's try a little more. Don't worry. You can heal me if you accidentally hurt me." He smiled, but I didn't.

"Ya know, in *my* dream, you're standing behind me."

He had a big smile on his face. "You're dreaming about me?"

I told him about my recurring dream of standing on a cliff and a storm coming from the west. "Wow. Now the void is the future?"

"Yeah, I think so. That which is not yet with form. That's what I was told."

"Okay, so I'm behind you?"

"Yeah."

"Let's try it." He pulled me in front of him and put his arms around me. I leaned back into him and felt tingles run up my back. He spoke softly in my ear, "Okay, concentrate and see what you can do."

I felt inside and urged the warmth to start, letting it grow and flow slowly into my hands. I held my hands up, looked at my fingers, and let it get warmer. "That's it, slowly," whispered JD in my ear.

As I opened up the flow, it got hot and my arms started to tingle. "Steady." I took a breath. "That's it, breathe." I swallowed and let the tingles gather. "Keep breathing."

I allowed the tingles to run down my arms and my fingers itched. "Okay now, back it off slowly." I closed my eyes and drew it back. "You're doing it." I pulled it back more and pushed it into my middle, squashing it into a ball in my chest. "Now, let it out again, slowly."

I was breathing harder, and I let it slowly flow down into my hands. "Now pull it back again." My arms trembled and he squeezed me. I felt him against me, and my back got warmer. "Don't think of me; concentrate on the warmth."

My arms trembled and I sucked in a breath. A flash popped in my head of a hawk flying over water. I dropped my arms and the warmth disappeared.

"What happened?"

"Grant's coming."

"How do you know?" We heard a truck coming up the road from the highway. We were far enough up the road that he wouldn't see us. We watched as the truck came into view and slowed to cross the river. It was one of our trucks all right, but I couldn't tell who was in it in the dark.

JD turned me in his arms. "How'd you know?"

"I got this flash in my head of a hawk flying over water."

"And the hawk is Grant. Do you get these flashes often?"

"Only when someone loses something."

"You have another gift?" I nodded. He pulled me into a hug. "You're full of surprises."

"How does that work?"

"When someone tells me they're looking for something, I get a picture in my head of where it is. Usually it's stuff like a shirt, a shoe, or keys."

"That's handy."

"Yeah, my brothers ask me where stuff is all the time."

"They know about this?"

"No, they don't think anything of it. I try to give them clues sometimes to see if they can find things on their own."

"Could you do this with something that isn't lost?"

"Whatcha ya mean?" I asked, looking at him.

"Like if I asked you where my state trophy buckle was. Could you describe where you see it?"

There was a flash in my mind then I smiled at him, "Ya mean the one that's in a drawer next to some red polka dotted underwear?"

He laughed and nodded his head. "They were a gag gift! The buckle is in my room at home in Houston."

"Oh wow. I thought distance may be the problem."

"What problem?"

"I've tried to find those lost kids from the milk cartons a few times. But nothing ever came to me."

"Maybe you have to have something of the person near you."

"Like how near?" I asked, leaning into him.

He put his arm around me, leaned me back, and kissed me. I put my arms around him. A flutter of warmth sprang up in my chest, and I pushed it back down. He looked into my eyes and kissed me. "Does this close work?"

"Always," I said breathlessly.

"Good. Now let's get you home before someone comes looking." We got off the tailgate, and JD lifted it back into place. We drove across the river and up to the house. Foxy greeted us as we got out.

JD took my hand as we walked through the gate and up to the front porch. We stopped to the side of the door where no one from inside could see us. He kissed me softly. "Will you be at practice on Tuesday?"

"I'll be at band practice. I'm gonna try to twirl."

"See ya there then." He kissed me again, squeezed my hand, and turned to walk back to his truck. I leaned against the porch post as I watched him walk away.

Dad and I looked at the clock as I walked inside: ten-thirty on the dot. "Right on time!" said Dad.

"How was the movie?" asked Grant from the couch, "or did you not make it again?"

"The movie was good," I said.

Grant leaned toward me. "So tell me a few things about the movie."

"Why? You need proof I was there?"

"Grant, let it be. If she said she went, I believe her," said Dad.

"Yes, sir."

I walked over to Dad and kissed him on the cheek. "Thanks!"

"For what?"

"For keeping my obnoxious, overly protective brothers off my back."

"De nada!" I smiled at him and walked down the hall.

I saw Mom in her sewing room, and I walked in behind her. She was looking at pictures she had taken during the past few years. "Hey! I'm home."

She whirled around in her chair to face me. "How was the movie?"

"It was good. Dinner was good, too."

"Where'd ya go?"

"Luigi's."

"Oh that's nice."

"It was nice right up to the point when Cathy Coulter came over. You should have been there, Mom. JD brushed her off like it was no big thing. She walked off in a huff." Mom and I laughed. "JD said his sisters act the way Cathy does, and I should watch out for them when they come down this week."

"I'm sure he sees them differently than others, like your brothers see you differently than other boys. If they turn out to be spoiled rotten, kill them with kindness."

I smiled. "Thanks. I'll try that the next time I see Cathy. I'm gonna turn in now. Night!"

I walked down the hall and past Tad's room. I saw him lying on his bed reading a book.

"Are you sick?" I asked dramatically.

"What are you talking about?" he asked, looking at me like I was crazy.

"You're reading!" I pointed to the book in his hand.

"Yeah thought I might 'broaden my horizons' like Mrs. Potter is always saying."

I laughed. "So whatcha reading?" I grabbed the book out of his hands and stepped back.

"Hey!" cried Tad, grabbing at me.

I looked at the front of the book. "This is my book!"

"Well, it's a good book, now give it back. I was just at the good part."

I handed it back to him, smiling. "I can't believe you're reading."

"I was bored and thought I'd read. Now will ya leave me alone?"

"Okay, okay I'm going." I got halfway across the room when I turned back. "Aren't you even gonna ask me about my date?"

"Oh." He put down the book and smiled. "Make it to the movie this time?"

"Yes, we made it to the movie. Thank you for asking."

He shrugged, "Okay, night!" I cocked my head to the side and walked out. That was a first. My overly protective brother didn't want details.

I went into my room without turning on the light and closed the door. I changed and fell across my bed. Foxy came in and jumped up beside me. I petted her head and closed my eyes. Images of JD flashed before me.

The lightning flashed, the thunder boomed. I turned toward a bright light that was coming at me. As it got closer, I could see it was Uncle Buck dressed in Indian garb and carrying a big spear decorated with eagle feathers. He was riding a magnificent stallion whose color was a gleaming blue black. They stopped in front of me, and Uncle Buck leaned toward me: *"You have found the source of your gift. It will burn you out if you do not take care. You cannot control it yet. You need to go slowly. Remember, you are just learning about your gift. Do not abuse it or flaunt it or it will be taken from you. A healer is humble, kind, and selfless."* Then he turned and rode off.

I opened my eyes and it was morning. I lay there and listened to the birds. They sounded cheerful. I got up and pulled on some jeans and t-shirt. I smelled breakfast, so I went into the kitchen and found Mom putting biscuits in the oven. I sat at the table. Dad came in followed by Grant.

"Hey Sunshine, about time you got up," said Grant. I looked up at the clock; it was six-thirty.

"Yeah, six-thirty is really late!" I said sarcastically.

Tad came in and sat down. His eyes were red. "There's the other ray of sunshine," said Grant.

"Bite me!"

"Mister growly bear today," said Grant.

"Didn't sleep well?" asked Mom, putting a jug of juice on the table.

"Stayed up too late reading." There was dead silence.

"Did you say reading?" asked Dad. I poured myself some juice.

"Yeah, one of Sara's stupid mystery things," said Tad, pouring juice for himself.

"I think I felt the ground shift!" said Grant and we laughed.

Mom put food on the table and we dug in. After breakfast, I went to the barn, got Flaxie, and worked her in the arena like I did the morning before. Then I got May Day out and put him through the same paces. I was walking May Day around cooling him off when Dad came over to the fence. "Gonna ride into town to talk to the horse show committee. Wanna come with me?"

"Sure! Do I have time to get cleaned up?"

"If you hurry."

I put May Day up and Dad drove us to the house. I jumped in the shower, got dressed, pulled my wet hair into a ponytail, and found Dad in the kitchen reading the paper. "I'm ready."

Dad looked up and folded his paper. "Okay, let's go." He told Mom we were leaving.

We pulled into the courthouse, got out, and walked up the steps into the building. We entered the door that said "Old Settler's Horse Show and Rodeo Committee."

"Hello Gladys!" Dad greeted Gladys White, the mayor's wife and chairman of the Old Settler's Committee.

"What can I do for you, Sonny? Hello, Sara," said Gladys cheerfully.

"Got a question for you about a horse show event," said Dad. "Actually, it's Sara's question. I'll let her ask."

I swallowed, suddenly nervous. "I was wondering if there's any rule that prevents entering more than one horse in the reining class."

"You mean one rider and two different horses?" asked Gladys.

"Yes, ma'am."

"Hmm, I don't remember the rules saying that you couldn't in an event like that. Let me check." She walked back to a desk, opened a pamphlet, and flipped through it. She read and came back to the counter. "Doesn't seem to be any rule against it. So what two horses are you gonna ride in reining?"

"May Day and Flaxie," I said.

"Sounds interesting. Did you wanna sign up today?"

"Yes, ma'am," said Dad. Gladys handed us the class registration forms and we filled them out. Dad paid the entry fees and we left.

"That was easy," I said as we got back in the truck.

"Yeah. I expected a little more fuss, but I'm not holding my breath. Someone might make a fuss at the show when you're called in the second time."

"Well, we'll handle it if and when it happens!" I said in a falsetto male voice. He laughed at me recognizing his own words.

"I need to run in here and get a few things," said Dad as we pulled into Varnell's Feed and Lumber. I saw the Henleys' truck outside and wondered if Jason was inside and if he would even acknowledge me. Dad went to the back as I meandered through the aisles.

I turned the corner of the aisle with hammers and saws and almost ran into Jason, who was squatted down looking at hammers.

"Hello!" I said. Jason stood. His face was blank.

"Can't even manage a hello?" I asked.

"Hello," he said in a flat tone.

"Okay, guess you aren't talking to me anymore." I moved past him on down the aisle.

"Wait!" said Jason. I stopped and turned. "I'm sorry. I just, well I thought we might have had something between us then I see you with Mr. Champion. It made me mad."

I took a step toward him and smiled. "Jason, don't be mad at me. I still wanna be your friend."

"I do to," he said, looking down.

"Okay then," I said. "How've you been?"

"I'm doing okay."

"Football going alright?"

"Yeah. You've seen us at practice."

"Do you think Trent will beat out Sam for starting quarterback this year?"

Jason seemed to relax. He smiled. "He sure is giving Sam a run for it."

"We're lucky to have two good quarterbacks, regardless of who starts."

"Yeah, we are. And with Bobby and his speed, we should do well this year. Ken moving in helps a lot, too. He and Mitch are a dynamic duo."

"I hear Rocksprings has a good team this year."

Jason snickered. "They say that every year."

Dad called me from the front of the store. "Gotta run. Nice talking to you again!"

"Yeah, see ya!" said Jason.

When we got home, I practiced my twirling. I still couldn't quite bend my knee all the way, but I thought I could manage to march in the parade. I still had to convince Carrie Wilds, as she was lead twirler. I'd give it my best shot at practice.

The next day I rode Flaxie and May Day. I thought Flaxie would do well in reining. I wondered if she would do well in pole bending because she was so fast at her flying lead changes. I'd wait to see how she managed with the crowds at the horse show before I decided.

I was brushing May Day after our ride when Dad came up to me. "Would you show Big Joe in the halter class?" he asked.

"I thought Grant was gonna do that."

"I think Big Joe would look better with you showing him. Would show some folks that are coming to look at him for breeding that he's gentle enough for a young girl to handle."

"I'll have to work with him. Guess I better get started."

"That's my girl!"

Big Joe greeted me as I walked up to his stall. "Hey big fella, how ya doing?" He nudged my hand and looked for the treats I usually offered him. I happened to have some sugar cubes in my pocket, so I gave them to him. He bobbed his head as he chewed. "Like that do ya?"

I entered his stall, snapped on the lead rope, and led him out. I brushed him all over. His coat was a beautiful rich red with black stockings and one white foot. He was the most perfectly proportioned quarter horse I had seen. He was what I hoped Andrea's foal would someday be.

After brushing him, I took him into the arena and made him stand and square up his feet. You do this in a show so the horse's conformation stands out. We trotted some and I backed him up. He was very gentle, smart, and knew just what to do. Satisfied, I led him back to his stall.

I was unsnapping his lead when Grant walked over. "Looks like you got the job I see."

"Guess so."

"Let's hope these breeders take notice. Would do some good for our ranch if they decide to use Big Joe here."

I patted Big Joe. "We'll give it our best then, won't we Joe?" He bobbed his head as if in agreement.

Grant laughed. "Come on, let's go get ready for practice."

"Wow, is it that time already?"

"Yeah, Mom will have dinner ready by the time we get to the house."

"Shoot, I wanted to shower before we went."

"Why? You're just gonna get sweaty again twirling."

"Well, I won't start out smelling like a horse."

He laughed at me. "Let me guess, JD will be there?"

"He said he would."

"Let's hurry so you can shower. Can't have you disappointing the local hero!"

I rushed through dinner and a shower. I jumped in the truck with Grant and Tad and off we went to practice. They dropped me at the band hall and took off for the football field.

"Hey Sara!" called Leena. "Gonna show Carrie you can march?"

"Yep. I hope she has changed her mind about wearing our new suits, too," I said.

"Now's your chance. Here she comes."

I turned to see Carrie, Nadine, and Lori coming out of the band hall. "Sara! Glad you're here," said Nadine. "Where's that hunky JD?"

"I don't know. Why?"

"Just wondering."

"So, Sara," said Carrie. "I see you're no longer in a brace. Looks like you can walk well enough but can you march?"

"Why don't we go see?" I said cheerfully.

Carrie smiled. "After you." She made a flourishing wave toward the practice field.

I nodded my head and led the way. Carrie had us line up and run through the routine. I kept up fine. I didn't notice that JD had shown up and was sitting on the bleachers. We kept twirling until Nadine dropped her baton.

"Okay, I've seen enough!" shouted Carrie. We stopped and came over to her. "I think you're healing well, so let's wait for the band and march with them. If you can keep up then you can march with us Friday."

"Yes!" I said and Carrie laughed.

"Nadine!" said Carrie, trying to get her attention. "What are you looking at?" We turned to look and JD waved at me. I waved back. Meanwhile, the band began to gather on the field.

Christine blew her whistle and the band members lined up. She blew the whistle again and they started playing. She blew the whistle four times and we started marching. My knee was tight but didn't hurt.

I made it around the field without any problems. Christine blew the whistle twice and we stopped. When the song ended, she gave the command to stand at ease. Mr. Wilson addressed the band. He told us to be at the band hall fully dressed at four o'clock on Friday. Then he dismissed us.

"So Carrie, what's your verdict?"

She turned to me. "I believe you're fit to march."

"Oh thank you!" I said. "Do we get to wear our new sequined suits?"

"I think we should!" said Lori.

"I definitely think we should!" said Nadine, stealing looks at the bleachers.

"In that case, it's unanimous," said Carrie. "We'll wear our sequin suits." We cheered.

"Is there anything else or can we be dismissed?" asked Nadine.

"Oh go on!" said Carrie. "You aren't paying attention anyway!" We started to turn away.

"Um Sara?"

"Yeah?" I turned back to Carrie as the others walked off.

"You might wanna wrap your knee on Friday. The parade route is a lot longer than just around this field. I noticed you aren't quite one hundred percent. I'd hate to see you drop out in the middle of the parade."

"Good advice. I'll do that."

When I turned to go say hello to JD, I saw Nadine flirting, or at least trying to flirt with him. JD saw me over her shoulder and I smiled. I sat down on the bottom bench of the bleachers and waited.

"You really won state and nationals for bull riding?" asked Nadine.

"Yeah I did. Now if you'll excuse me, there's someone I wanna talk to."

I didn't turn around to look as JD came and sat beside me. I heard Nadine give a "humph!" I tried to hold in a laugh as she stomped down the bleachers and off toward the band hall.

"She's relentless!" said JD in my ear. Then he kissed me on the cheek. "You looked really good out there twirling. How was the rest of your day?"

"Never better!" I said. "I got my job back as a twirler. I get to ride both May Day and Flaxie in the same reining class. I get to show my dad's prize stud in the open halter class! And to top it all off, I get to see you!" I bumped his shoulder. "So how was your day?"

"Not nearly as exciting," said JD.

"Hey, JD," called Tesa, who was standing next to Leena. "You guys gonna go watch the end of the football practice with us?"

JD looked at me and I nodded. "Yeah!" yelled JD. He stood up, held his hand out to me, and pulled me to my feet. We walked hand in hand over to Tesa and Leena.

"Well?" asked Tesa, "Is Carrie letting you march Friday?"

"Yes! And we're gonna wear our new sequined suits!"

"Aw and all we get to wear are white t-shirts and jeans," Leena said sarcastically.

We laughed and got into the Martins' truck. I got in by JD, while Leena and Tesa were in the back seat. Tesa leaned over the seat. "I heard Cathy Coulter was gonna ride one of the new horses that the Miners have been working on for her in the show."

"Good, just ups the excitement of beating her at yet another horse event," I said.

"Sara, is it true you're gonna ride two different horses in the reining class?" asked Tesa.

"How'd you hear about that already?"

"Gladys was telling everyone about it when we went to sign up," said Tesa. "So besides May Day, who you gonna ride?"

"Flaxie."

"Sure hope you don't beat me twice in one class," said Tesa.

"I'll be happy to finish the pattern with Flaxie. She's still kinda skittish. She would make a heck of a pole bending horse. Her flying lead changes are fantastic and she's fast."

"At least I can hold my own with the barrels," said Tesa.

"I don't know, you might be way ahead of me anymore. May Day seemed to like roping," I said, leaning on JD.

"I just got lucky!" said JD.

"Some luck. You showed up the guys who do it regularly," said Tesa.

"How's Matt getting along without his hair?" asked Leena. "Has Celeste seen him yet?"

"I think today at practice will be the first time Matt has seen her," said Tesa.

"He hasn't taken a hat off since Friday night except when your mom makes him at meals," said JD.

"This ought to be good," said Leena.

We got to the football field and sat on the bleachers. The guys were still running plays. We saw Celeste practicing with the cheerleaders on the sidelines.

"Did you play football at your school?" I asked JD.

"Only in junior high," he said. "I'm too small and not fast enough for my high school."

"So besides fending off relentless girls, is rodeo the only sport you do?" I asked.

"The fending is pretty much a full-time sport," he said. "I just get to rodeo once in a while." We laughed.

There was a loud crack, and we turned our attention to the field. There were two guys lying sprawled out on their backs. Coach Baker and Coach Carter ran over to them.

"Who's that?" I asked. I looked at the rest of the guys on the field. I saw Grant, Matt, and Mitch. I kept looking and sighed as I saw Tad.

After a few minutes, we saw one of the guys get up. He took off his helmet, and we saw it was Ken. He was shaking his head. "Bet that rung his bell good!" said JD.

I nodded, trying to see who the other guy was. They sat him up and I saw a helmet put on the ground but still couldn't see who it was because the coaches were in the way. The player stood up, and I saw it was Jared. Coach Baker blew the whistle and announced practice was over.

Grant and Tad trotted over to the cheerleaders and got a cup of lemonade. Tad lingered to talk to Trish as Grant came up the steps. Mitch and Ken got some lemonade and came to sit by us, too. I saw Matt and he had a bandana tied over his head. He made it over to the cheerleaders and they handed him a cup.

"Watch this!" said Grant pointing. We turned to see Celeste talking to Matt. She was pointing at his head. Matt shook his head and stepped back from her. Bobby Garmin walked up behind Matt snatched the bandana off his head and ran. Matt didn't even try to chase him. He turned back around, and Celeste started laughing at him.

"This isn't gonna be good," said Tesa.

Matt said something, and Celeste got mad and said something back. She stomped off, and Matt stood there for a second then he came over to the bleachers. We turned and acted like we hadn't seen. Matt walked up the steps and came toward us.

"Hey Matt!" said Leena, trying to be nonchalant. He flopped down on the bench. "Bad practice?"

Tad walked up the steps and came over. "Hey everybody," he said. "Matt, Celeste is really upset. You should go apologize."

"What for? She said I looked ridiculous," said Matt.

"I think she was referring to the bandana," said Tad.

"Well, I'm not gonna talk to her," said Matt.

"Gosh, you're acting like you're five," said Tesa. "Thought we were raised better than that." Matt just shrugged.

Ken was rubbing his neck. "Hey Ken, you want a neck rub?" asked Leena.

"Naw, I'll be alright," said Ken.

"No really, let me rub it for you. I know this trick my dad showed me. It will help," said Leena.

"Can't you take a hint?" said Mitch. "The lady can't wait to get her hands on you!" We laughed and Ken went and sat down in front of Leena. She rubbed his neck and shoulders.

Jared came up and sat down. He was moving slowly. "You alright?" I asked.

"I want the license of that truck!"

"He's sitting right here!" said Tesa, patting Ken on the shoulder.

"Leena, I'm next!" said Jared.

I scooted over. "Here let me help." Jared leaned up to let me behind him. I put my hands on his shoulders and rubbed. My fingers tingled a little as I massaged his neck.

JD leaned over and whispered, "Warm?" I shook my head no. He motioned for me to try. I concentrated but really couldn't feel anything start. I tried to picture being by the river and calling the warmth, but it didn't work.

"Okay, me next," said Tad, pushing Jared aside.

"Hey, that was rude!" I said.

"Yeah but I'm bigger," said Tad.

"You're not hurt." I pushed Tad away. "You okay Jared?"

"I feel some better. Thanks."

"Let me look at your eyes," said Tesa. Jared looked at her. "Yep there's nothing there!"

"If we're done fawning over the invalids, let's go get a shake!" said Grant.

"Come on, Jared, I'll buy ya a shake," said Ken.

We gathered at the drug store, ordered shakes, and sat in the back talking.

"Sara, heard you were gonna ride two horses in one class," said Mitch.

"Yeah, gonna try out Flaxie," I said.

"She better not beat me twice in one class!" said Tesa.

"Hey, you get your share!"

"You gonna ride in the show, Grant?" asked Mitch.

"Nope. I'm leaving all the hard work to Sara. She even gets to show Big Joe this year in the open halter class."

"I get to show the Big C stud in that class," said Ken.

"Really? Which one?" I asked.

"His name's Midnight Fury," said Ken. "He's this big, black beast."

"Did you say he was black?" asked JD.

"Yeah. He's so black he almost looks bluish." said Ken. JD and I exchanged a look.

"I get to show Copper's daddy, King Coin," said Tesa.

"Do I hear a bet coming?" asked Tad.

"Between who?" asked Ken. "And for what? I'm not about to bet my hair."

We laughed, but Matt just pouted. "Hey bro, lighten up. Your head doesn't look like a cue ball!" said Mitch.

"That's not what Celeste thinks," muttered Matt.

"If all she liked you for was your golden locks, then she's really shallow," said Leena.

"Yeah, she's shallow!" said Matt. "She doesn't deserve me!"

"That's the spirit!" said Tad.

"Well guys, it's getting late and we have to get up early tomorrow," said Grant.

We got up and wandered out of the drugstore. The guys were getting into the trucks.

"Jared, you okay to drive?" I asked as he walked by.

"Yeah, my hard head is fine!" he said, "See ya at the show." He waved, got into his truck, and drove off.

"Isn't he too young to drive?" asked JD.

"Legally yes," I said. "But this is a small town, and we get away with a few things like that."

JD put his hands on my hips. "What can I get away with?" he asked, smiling down at me.

"Lots of things. You're famous remember?" I said, smiling back at him.

"I don't wanna think about what a temptation that makes. I better let you get home." He kissed me briefly. "And for luck." He kissed me again.

"I got luck right here!" I touched the horse necklace he'd given me. He smiled at me and I started leaning into him again, but Grant honked the horn.

"I'll see ya at the show!" said JD and he let me go. I turned away and got in the truck. He waved as we drove off.

The Show

I was riding bareback on a big black horse across a green pasture. The wind was blowing in my face. There were dark clouds overhead. Lightning flashed, so I bent closer to the horse and he sped up.

The thunder boomed. We rode down by a river. The horse slowed as we splashed into the water. We crossed the river, and the horse stopped and reared. I looked up and saw Uncle Buck standing on a rise above us.

I slid off the horse and walked over to Uncle Buck. *"Our first teacher is our own heart. You are on your way. You already possess everything you need to become great,"* he said and vanished.

I woke with a start and Foxy whined at me. I patted her head. I saw it was just getting light outside. I got up and started for the bathroom.

Grant's door opened as I crossed the hall. "You better not have already fed. That's my job today."

"I just got up. I'll leave the hard work to you strong types." I laughed and went into the bathroom, showered, and went back to my room.

I combed out my hair, braided it, and wrapped the braid into a bun at the base of my neck. I laid out two shirts, one medium blue and one teal. I pulled on some dark jeans, my boots, and a t-shirt. I turned back to look at the shirts when Mom came in. "Need some help?"

"I can't decide what shirt to wear." I gestured to the shirts on the bed.

"Wear the teal one," she said. "And your black hat."

"Okay, thanks!"

"Come get some breakfast."

I followed Mom down the hall to the kitchen. Everyone else was already eating. "There's my girl!" said Dad. "Ready for today?"

"Yes, sir!" Mom put a plate of eggs in front of me. "Thanks!"

"You ready to win a few more ribbons showgirl?" asked Tad.

"Yes and I plan on winning two in one event. Let's see you do that!" They laughed at me.

After breakfast, we loaded up the horses and equipment. We had bathed Big Joe, Flaxie, and May Day the day before, so all we had to do was remove their blankets and brush them down when we got to the show.

We arrived at the arena a little after seven. There was plenty of activity.

"I'll go get you registered and pick up your numbers," said Mom after we parked.

"I'll go with you," said Tad.

We unloaded the horses. Flaxie was very nervous, so we tied her next to May Day. I went into the trailer to change into my dressy show shirt while Dad and Grant brushed the horses.

I came out of the trailer as Mom came up with my numbers. "I wrote the names on the back so you won't forget what number is for what horse."

"Okay, pin Big Joe's number on me please. He's first."

I saw the Big C rig pull in and park. Mr. Miner walked a big, beautiful black stallion down the ramp. My breath caught in my throat as I recognized the horse from my dream. The necklace at my throat tingled. The stud's coat shone blue in the sun. He stomped and looked around proudly.

"Whatcha gawking at?" asked Grant. He followed my line of sight and gawked, too.

"He's gorgeous," I said. The horse reared as Mr. Miner tried to tie him to the trailer. Mr. Miner spoke to him and he settled down. I turned around as I heard someone approaching.

"You look great," said JD, walking up. "I almost didn't recognize you." He turned to my mom. "Morning Mrs. Stillsen."

"Good morning, JD," she said. "Your folks coming in tomorrow?"

"Actually, they got in last night," said JD. "They're around here somewhere. I'll have to introduce you to my mother."

"That's a nice surprise," said Mom. "Be sure to bring your mother 'round. I'll probably be taking pictures from the stands or somewhere there about."

"Did you see the Big C stud?" I asked, pointing behind JD. He turned to look. I watched JD's face, and I saw that he recognized the horse, too. He snapped his head back to me, and I nodded a little before he said anything.

"Yeah, beautiful blue-black color," said Mom. "I hope that comes out in pictures."

Dad and Mr. Martin walked over. "Did ya see the Big C stud?"

"Yes, sir, we all did." I said.

"Do you know who's gonna show him?" asked Dad.

"Ken said he was," said Grant.

Dad nodded. "He sure is nice to look at."

"You pay that much money, you should have something that nice to look at," said Mr. Martin.

"We'll see how he handles in the ring," said Grant. "He was rearing up earlier."

"We're here to show how gentle our boy is along with his good looks," said Dad. "We should get to it. They're almost done with the junior halter class."

"Just need my hat." I stepped into the trailer and got my hat out of its box.

JD stepped in behind me. "Mind if I join you for a second?"

"Not at all," I said, turning to face him. He took my hat and set it on the counter, pulled me to him, and kissed me. He raised his head, and I looked into his eyes. He was worried about something.

"What's wrong?"

"That horse," he said. "He's the one from my dream."

"I've had a few dreams about him myself."

"Are they like mine?"

"One was, but the others aren't. I was riding him in my dream last night."

"You aren't worried?" he asked, holding my face in his hands and looking into my eyes.

I smiled at him. "No, they're just dreams. They aren't exactly predictions."

He relaxed. "I was worried when I saw the horse that you might be scared."

"Nope," I said. "Nothing to be scared of when you're with me." He smiled and kissed me lightly. I put on my hat and we left the trailer.

JD left with the rest as I walked over to Dad who was holding Big Joe. He was glistening in the sun. His eyes were bright and curious and he gave me a low "hu hu hu."

I patted him on the face. "You ready big guy?" He nudged me and I laughed.

Dad walked with me over to the paddock. Tesa and Mr. Martin were there with their stud, King Coin. He was shining like a new penny with his copper-colored coat. We turned as Ken came over with the black horse.

The horse was bobbing his head, very alert to everything around him. Ken stopped him just to the side.

I saw Erin Wilson with her mare Miss Dolly and waved. She smiled and waved back. Then we were called to enter the arena.

"Remember to keep Big Joe's attention," said Dad.

"Yes, sir." I smiled at him, and he patted Big Joe as we entered the arena.

We walked our horses around once and then the ring steward signaled for us to line up in the middle. Tesa lined up beside me. This part took a long time. The judge walked around each horse. My job was to keep the horse between the judge and myself. I was just a prop or showgirl, as Tad had dubbed me.

When everyone had a chance to do their "thing," the announcer asked us to turn our backs to the judge so he could see our numbers. The judge walked up and down the line twice before he made his decision. The announcer began, "In the open halter competition, in first place, number fifty-one, Midnight Fury from Big C Ranch." There was lots of applause.

"In second place, number twenty-five, Big Joe from Diamond E Ranch." There was more applause, and I trotted Big Joe over to collect our prize.

"In third place, number twenty-nine, King Coin from Rocking A Ranch." There was more applause, and I heard Matt whistle.

I was almost out of the gate when I saw the big black stallion rear suddenly. He almost pulled the lead out of Ken's hands. Ken spoke to him and he settled. He was still talking to him when I approached.

"Need some help?" I asked.

Ken looked up. "He's okay now."

I walked closer and the black horse pricked his ears toward me. Then he stepped toward me. Ken came with the stud as he walked right up and nudged me. I patted him on the face. He gave me a soft "hu hu hu" like he knew me.

I left my hand on him and looked up at Ken, who was looking at me dumbfounded. I smiled. "Hey what can I say? Guys love me!" I laughed. Ken recovered some and smiled.

Mr. Miner came over and stopped beside us. "Well I'll be!" He put his hands on his hips. "Midnight acts like he knows you."

"I'm as shocked as you are." I stepped back from Midnight. He stepped forward and nudged me again.

"You need to go to your trailer," I said to Midnight. He nodded his head and turned to walk away. Ken just followed along. Midnight looked back at me, snorted, then walked on. I stood there watching them walk off. Mr. Miner shook his head, tipped his hat at me, and turned to follow them.

"What was that about?" asked Grant, coming up to me.

"I'm not sure," I said. "Midnight saw me and came right up, practically dragging Ken along. Midnight acted like he knew me." I shook my head and turned to lead Big Joe to our trailer. Grant took Big Joe from me and tied him to the trailer.

JD came over. "Hey!" I said smiling at him.

"You looked so good out there!"

"Thanks! Hope it was good enough to get Dad some points with a breeder."

"I think they were impressed," said Dad. "I'll be talking with them later."

We heard a ruckus and turned to see the Big C horse rearing. I started toward them and Dad grabbed my shoulder. "Where do you think you're going?"

"He came right up to me earlier. I think I can help calm him," I said.

Dad nodded. "I'll go with you."

We walked over to the Big C trailer. Midnight was really fighting them. I stepped forward and called out, "Midnight!" The horse stopped immediately and looked at me. He snorted and tried to walk toward me.

Ken and Mr. Miner grabbed his halter, and I stepped forward to keep Midnight from dragging them. I spoke to him as I walked up. "Easy there, big fella." I patted him on the face and he nudged me. "What's all the ruckus for? They just wanna take you home."

Midnight nickered softly. I patted him and smiled. I took hold of his lead rope, and Mr. Miner and Ken let go. I pulled Midnight after me and we walked around. I looked up at Dad; he had his arms crossed over his chest, and his eyebrows were raised in surprise. Grant was next to him shaking his head. JD was there, too, smiling at me.

I turned around to Mr. Miner. "Should I see if I can get him in the trailer for you?"

"Yes please!" he said, gesturing toward the ramp.

I walked him up the ramp and patted his face. I took the tie chain and attached it to his halter. He nudged me again. "You gonna be good now and go home?" He gave me a "hu hu hu" then snorted.

I heard a distinctly male voice in my head. *"I am Wakiza."* I felt my necklace tingle. "I do know you," I whispered. He nodded and I took a deep breath.

"Okay, you be good, Wakiza." I patted his neck and walked back out. Ken closed the ramp behind me. The men were standing there, watching. Dad looked relieved.

"Thank you, horse charmer!" said Mr. Miner, giving me a hug. "I've never seen a horse take to someone so readily."

"Glad I could help," I said. "Let me know if you need me to come mesmerize him some more."

They laughed. "I should buy you a cold drink!" said Mr. Miner.

"I could use one," I said.

"Would you take a raincheck? I don't know how long Midnight will like being in there," said Mr. Miner, pointing to the trailer. "We'll be back later."

"Sure thing," I said.

"Thanks again," said Ken. "I owe you twice now." They got into their truck and drove off.

"Well, time to get ready for your next class," said Dad. We went back to the trailer.

I put on my chaps; they were chocolate brown on the inside and tan on the outside with long fringe. Dad had made them for me last spring.

"Need any help?" asked JD.

"I think my grooms are about done." I gestured to Dad and Grant.

"All ready with horse number one," said Dad, patting May Day on the behind. "Soon as the class is over, I'll meet you back here to change horses. You ready to warm up a little?"

"Yes, sir," I said.

"I'm sure JD can give you a boost," said Dad.

Then Grant chimed in. "She needs a boost because she can't get on with those chaps on."

"I'll be happy to help out," said JD.

"We'll go on over to the stands then," said Dad. He patted me on the shoulder. "Good luck!" They walked off, leaving me alone with JD.

I turned to JD and he was smiling at me with a different look on his face. "What?" I asked.

"You look so much older with your hair up, and that color shirt really makes your eyes stand out. I thought they were green, but now they match your shirt."

He stepped closer to me and put his hands on my hips. "You constantly surprise me."

I looked up at him, and he turned his head to kiss me. I felt the warmth in me stir, but I pushed it back. He lifted his head, and I opened my eyes. He gave me a crooked smile.

"Now what're you thinking?" I asked.

"Will you come with me and my family to dinner tonight?"

My heart sped up at the thought of meeting his family. "I forgot all about that. I'll ask my Dad after this class. I really better get going."

He laughed and kissed me again. "Nothing for you to be nervous about, trust me."

"I'll try to remember that when they're giving me the once over," I said. "Now, if you'll be so kind as to give me a boost?" I turned to May Day, JD gave me a boost up, and I settled into the saddle.

JD patted me on the leg. "You have all the luck you need. Now go show them who's best." He stepped back and I nodded to him and trotted off toward the practice area.

We watched the twelve-and-under class get their ribbons. I clapped, as Tim Stillsen got second place. As they exited the arena, I called out, "Hey Tim, way to go!" He waved and rode on by as the rest of the class was coming out behind him.

When the arena was clear, they called for our class to enter. Tesa went first, and I followed her in. I put on my straight face and relaxed.

As we turned the corner, I saw Erin Wilson on her bay gelding, then a few others I knew from neighboring towns. Last to enter was Cathy Coulter. She had on a red hat, red blouse, and brown chaps, and it looked great on her flashy sorrel horse. I caught Mom and Dad's eye as I passed the stands and nodded.

We were given the commands to trot, lope, walk, and then reverse direction. We trotted and loped again. We were asked to walk. Then they started calling out numbers for the contestants to line up in the middle of the arena.

Tesa was already there when I was called over. I saw Cathy and a few others I knew in the line. They dismissed the rest. I glanced at the stands and saw JD. He was sitting with the Martins, and I recognized JD's father. I saw a gorgeous woman sitting next to Mr. Dalton. That must be his mother I thought. I saw two similar blonde-haired girls sitting in front of Mr. Dalton. I smiled to myself. Those must be JD's sisters. Oh, this was going to be fun. They were dressed very nicely. I reminded myself to refrain from making judgments until I actually met them.

The judge came down the line and asked each of us to back our horses. He walked behind the line to get our numbers, and the results were handed in. My heart was pounding as the announcer began. "The results of the thirteen-to-eighteen-year-old western pleasure class are in. In first place, number twenty-two, Prairie's May Day ridden by Sara Stillsen." I heard applause as I rode forward to collect my ribbon.

"Next," the announcer said, "in second place, number fifteen, Flying Destiny ridden by Cathy Coulter." More applause. "In third place, number twenty-six, True Heart ridden by Tesa Martin." Applause. "In fourth place, number twelve, Rocky Road ridden by Erin Wilson."

I was out of the arena by now and didn't pay attention to who else placed.

"Way to go cuz!" yelled Tim. I waved at him as I rode by.

"Nice shirt!" said Cathy Coulter in a snotty tone.

I turned to her. "Hey Cathy. Beautiful horse."

"He's new. Daddy had the Miners work him up for me," she said.

"Good for you."

Dad and Grant were walking up as I got to the trailer. "Way to go!" said Grant. "You sure made everyone sit up and take notice."

"I did?" I asked, getting off May Day.

"Yeah, I think all the Daltons were impressed," said Dad, reaching to undo my saddle.

"Did you meet them?" I asked. "What are they like?"

"They're very nice," said Dad.

"The girls are really nice," said Grant with a smile. "Here, let me change your number."

"I guess that means the girls are pretty," I said to Dad. He chuckled.

Dad put my saddle on Flaxie. I patted May Day. "You did great. Now it's the rookie's turn." May Day turned to look at me. "Don't worry. I'll be back for you soon."

"All set," said Dad. I walked around and Grant held Flaxie as Dad gave me a boost up. Flaxie stiffened up, and I patted her on the neck to calm her.

"I better go warm up to see if I can get her over this a little," I said.

"I'll walk over and make sure you don't get into any trouble," said Dad. I nodded and rode toward the practice arena.

After a turn around the arena, I pulled Flaxie up to a slow lope. She had a great rocking-chair-type gait that was a real pleasure to ride. I rounded the far end and looked up to see Dad, JD, and Grant standing at the fence watching me.

"She gonna be alright?" asked Dad.

"She's settling down some," I said. "Guess we'll find out how well when we get in the arena."

"We better get over there," said Grant.

I nodded and turned to go out of the gate. Flaxie seemed to be calming down, yet she was very alert as her ears were pointed forward. When we got to the paddock Dad came over to me. "You just do your best. Don't expect too much."

"Yes, sir," I said. "I'm not expecting miracles out of this rookie." I patted Flaxie on the neck.

"Fair enough," said Dad. He and Grant walked off.

JD walked up and put his hand on my leg. "You look great, no matter what you ride," he said, smiling up at me.

"You say the nicest things!" I said and touched his nose.

"Should I cross my fingers?"

"Nope, just gonna cruise on this one. Save your luck for later. I might need it when I meet your family."

"You already met my dad. My mother and sisters sure took notice of you in that last class. Congratulations by the way."

"Thank you," I said. They started calling my group into the arena. "I have a break after this class, so if you want I can meet them then."

"That's the spirit. Now go show them how it's done." I smiled at him and rode over to the gate.

I waited until Tesa and Erin had gone in before I entered. Cathy came riding up behind me. I patted Flaxie as she startled a little, pulled up, and let Cathy ride past.

I took a deep breath and began to think calming thoughts. I was concentrating on soothing Flaxie, and she seemed to settle down more. She looked at the people behind the fence and snorted. Then the announcer asked us to trot. Flaxie trotted along fine. Then we loped. Her rocking chair lope was heavenly, and I smiled as I passed the stands.

When we were lined up in the middle, the steward asked us one by one to ride a short pattern. Flaxie did very well. Then the judge sent the results up to the announcer. Tesa was beside me. I glanced at her and smiled. She smiled back.

The announcer said, "The results are in for the thirteen-to-eighteen-year-old western equitation class. In first place, number twenty-six, True Heart ridden by Tesa Martin."

Tesa's mouth dropped open and I laughed. There was applause and I heard Matt whistle. I told her, "Yes, you won. Now go get your ribbon!" She smiled big and rode over to accept her first-place ribbon.

The announcer said, "In second place, number fifteen, Flying Destiny ridden by Cathy Coulter." There was applause as Cathy went to accept her ribbon.

Next the announcer said, "In third place, number twenty-three, Flaxie's Depth Chick ridden by Sara Stillsen." I heard whistles and applause.

Back at the trailer, Dad walked up, "You did real good."

"Thanks, Dad!" I said, hugging him.

Then JD was there congratulating me. "Now let me introduce you," he said.

Dad took Flaxie's reins from me. "I'll take care of her."

JD and I walked up to his family. "Sara, this is my mother, Lidia." I turned to see a tall, tanned lady with hair the color of honey that fell in waves just past her shoulders. She had a beautiful, bright-white smile and sparking blue eyes. There was a classic grace about her.

I held out my hand and she took it. "Nice to meet you, Mrs. Dalton."

"Nice to meet the one JD has talked so much about," she said with a genuine smile. She didn't let go of my hand as she continued, "You look so great out there riding."

"Thank you. We try our best," I said.

She let my hand go as JD turned me to his dad. "You remember my dad, Jesse."

"Mr. Dalton, nice to see you again," I said, taking his outstretched hand.

He pulled me into a hug. "You're just about the prettiest thing." He looked at JD. "You sure know how to pick them son." He laughed and let me go.

I looked at JD and he was blushing a little but smiling very big. He turned to his twin sisters. I got the feeling they had been giving me the once over. "This is Hanna and Tana."

I turned my gaze to the twins. They were tall like their mother with lithe bodies and straight, light blonde hair that reached to their waist. There was an alertness about them, as if they were watching for something.

I held out my hand and Hanna took it and smiled at me. "Hi, I'm Hanna." I looked into her eyes. They were the same color as their mother's. In Hanna's, I could see the left one had a little gold fleck in the blue.

"Hello, Hanna," I said, smiling back at her.

I turned to Tana and held out my hand to her. She took my hand and smiled. "Hi." I looked into her eyes, and there was no gold fleck like in Hanna's. Except for that, they were identical in every way, although they didn't have on matching clothes.

"Hello, Tana," I said.

JD gestured to two boys. "This is Mitch," he said, putting his hand on a tall, thin boy's shoulder as he stepped forward. He had the same coloring as JD, but his eyes weren't as blue. Mitch looked at me then looked down shyly. "Aren't you gonna shake hands or say hello?" asked JD.

Mitch walked a step toward me with his head down and held out his hand. "Nice to meet you, Mitch," I said as I took his hand.

He looked up at me briefly and I smiled. His eyes got wide. "Your eyes match your shirt!"

We laughed. "Why, thank you for noticing, Mitch." He blushed big time and turned away quickly.

JD, still shaking his head, said, "Okay Mark, your turn." A blonde boy with the bluest eyes came right up to me, holding out his hand.

"Nice to meet you, Sara," said Mark very seriously. Then he lightened up and asked, "Can I pet your horse?"

"You sure can," I said. "Wanna ride one later?"

A smile broke out on his face, and it was like he radiated sunshine. "Really, can I?"

JD rubbed his head. "Of course, but you have to wait until Sara is through showing them today."

"Okay," said Mark then he turned to his mom and dad. "Did you hear that? Sara's gonna let me ride her horse!"

We laughed and Dad walked up. "Now that everyone has been properly introduced, let's go get a cold drink."

"Ya'll go ahead. I wanna take these chaps off," I said.

JD stayed with me as the rest walked off, but Mark came running back. I held up my hands for him to stop. "Whoa there buddy. Don't run up too fast and startle the brown one okay?" Mark nodded.

"Now walk up slowly and hold out your hand and you can pet her." I watched as he walked slowly up to Flaxie, and she bent her head to him and sniffed his hand. He patted her on the head. He had a huge smile on his face, and JD and I laughed at him.

I put my chaps in the trailer and as I turned to go out the door, I ran right into JD. He took off my hat, pulled me into his arms, and kissed me. I wrapped my arms around his neck and rolled up on my toes. My heart pounded and the warmth in me flared up and ran down into my hands.

"I'm so lucky." He smiled, took my hand, and put it on his face. "Nice and warm!"

I heard Mark, "Hey stop that." He was giggling. We looked and Flaxie was nibbling at his hair.

"We better go or they'll wonder what's happened to us," said JD. He handed me my hat, and I set it on the counter. We stepped out of the trailer and JD took my hand. "Come on Mark."

Mark caught site of Foxy on the roof of the truck. "Is that a wolf?"

"That's Foxy," I said. Foxy jumped down and came over to us. I ruffled her head.

Mark held out his hand, and Foxy rubbed up against him. He scratched her behind the ear. "She likes me!"

"You're very special." I said, "Foxy doesn't come up to just anyone."

He patted Foxy; she licked his face then turned and jumped back up on the roof. "Does she always stay up there?" asked Mark.

"Most of the time," I said. "She likes to watch what's going on." Mark nodded and we turned to go. Mark took my other hand as we walked.

"Do you have horses at home?" I asked.

"Yeah, but they aren't as pretty as yours," said Mark. "None of them are mine."

"Oh, whose are they?"

"One is Dad's, one is JD's, and Hanna and Tana both have one," said Mark. "Mitch might get one soon." Then Mark sighed. "Guess I'll have to wait until next year."

"You get to ride Smitty when I'm gone," said JD.

"Yeah, but I want my own horse," said Mark.

"I can sympathize with that," I said.

"What's sympa...sympat ...?"

"Sympathize," I said. "It means I understand how you feel."

"Oh," said Mark. "Would you tell my dad I need a horse of my own?"

JD and I laughed. JD said, "Mark, I'll help you ask Dad later, okay?"

"Do you really mean it?"

JD held up his hand. "I promise."

"Yippee!" yelled Mark and he ran on ahead of us.

"Wow, didn't know it was that easy to make him happy," said JD.

We walked toward the concession stand and saw our families, plus Mr. and Mrs. Martin, sitting at some tables in the shade. I followed JD over and sat down. The twins were on the other side of our parents. I could see them checking out the guys. There were plenty of them checking the girls out, too.

Tad, Matt, Mitch Martin, and Tesa came up. "Hey winner!" I said to Tesa as she came and sat down beside me. She was beaming. The guys stopped at the other end of the table where the girls were.

"So whatcha think?" asked Tesa in a low voice, nodding toward JD's sisters.

I shrugged my shoulders. "They seem okay. I've only just met them."

"What's your next class?" asked Tesa in conversational tone.

"Reining this afternoon," I said. "Then I'm done."

"You still gonna ride both May Day and Flaxie?" asked Tesa. "I hear the Coulters are going to the judge to object."

Mr. Dalton asked, "Did I hear you say you're gonna ride two horses in the reining class this afternoon?"

"Yes, sir," I said.

"How do you manage that?" asked Mrs. Dalton.

"With some very helpful hands," I said, smiling at my Dad.

"I'll help!" said Mark.

"I'm sure you would, too," said Mr. Dalton. "But we'll just stay back out of the way until they're done, okay?" He said that last part to Mark, who nodded.

"I don't know about anyone else, but I'm getting hungry," I said.

"Let's run down to the Old Timer and get some lunch!" said Mrs. Martin. There were nods of agreement all around.

As everyone was getting up, I said to Dad, "I'm not so sure we should leave Flaxie without someone around. I think I should stay here."

JD was standing behind me. "I'll stay with you. We can grab a hamburger here."

Dad cocked his head to the side. "Suit yourself." Mom called to him, and they left with the rest.

JD turned to me. "How about that hamburger?"

I smiled up at him. "Yes please! I'm starving."

"Didn't you have breakfast?" he asked.

"Yeah, but that was hours ago. Besides, when I'm nervous, I get hungry."

He laughed and led me over to the concession counter and ordered some burgers. We sat down nearby to wait for our order. Trent, Jason, and Jeremy came up. "Hey there, Sara, JD!" said Trent.

"Hey Trent!" I said, smiling at him then nodding at the rest. "Jason, Jeremy. How's it going?"

"Doing fine," said Trent. "But you're doing really good. Beat the Coulters again!"

I smiled. "Just wait for the fireworks this afternoon!"

"Oh yeah," said Jason. "Heard you're gonna ride two horses in one class."

"Can't wait to see the look on Cathy Coulter's face when you beat her twice!" said Jeremy.

"Thanks for the vote of confidence," I said, "but I'm not sure I'll beat her twice."

They laughed. "Yeah, but it's the thought," said Trent. "We'll be cheering for ya."

"Thanks," I said. "Hey, has anyone seen Jared today?"

"He was lying in bed with ice on his neck when we went by his house earlier," said Jeremy. "He'll live. He won't miss the dance Friday for sure."

Our hamburgers were done, and I got up with JD to collect them. "Well, see ya'll later!" I turned to JD. "Mind if we eat at the truck?"

He smiled. "I was just about to suggest that." We carried our burgers to the truck. Big Joe, Flaxie, and May Day greeted us with low neighs. I patted them as JD put down the tailgate. I walked over and sat by him. The truck was parked in the shade of some big oak trees, so it wasn't hot.

"So tell me," said JD. "What do you have to be nervous about?"

I swallowed my bite. "Well, first there's meeting your family, and then there's competing on two different horses!"

JD smiled at me. "I don't think you have anything to worry about with my family. My dad was impressed with you when he met you earlier this summer. My mom is obviously impressed. She's never said much to any of my other girlfriends before. My sisters, well, they're hard to read. Mitch is spellbound, and as for Mark, you're his hero already."

I smiled at him. "We'll see after dinner tonight." I stopped and looked at JD. "Oh my gosh! I forgot to ask." He laughed at me. "See I'm totally losing it."

"Sara, relax. I'm sure it'll work out."

"Yeah, but Dad hates surprises and last-minute plans," I said worriedly.

"Hey, worse case, I'll stay behind with you and let them go off on their own."

"You don't have to do that. They're your family. You haven't seen them in a while."

"I'll see them everyday starting next week." His smile lessened as he looked at me. "I won't get to see you every day. So I'd rather stay with you."

"I'd like that, too."

"So I've been meaning to ask you something," said JD in a lighter tone.

"What?"

"At football practice, when you were rubbing Jared's neck, could you really not help him or did you not wanna try in front of everyone?"

"Oh that," I said and took a breath. "I tried. I told you it's never worked on humans. Well, before you that is."

"Why do you think that is?"

"I guess that's not what my gift is for," I said. I leaned back on my hands and looked up at the tree leaves. "I was told I was to bring balance between animals and humans. I guess I'm supposed to help animals not humans, kinda tip the scale the other way."

"I remember you telling me that," said JD nodding. "What doesn't make sense is that you could help me and yourself."

I looked at him. "You and I are just special animals!" We laughed and Foxy gave a "raawwll." "See, she agrees!"

JD leaned toward me and put his face in my neck, "Umm I could bite this!" I laughed and pushed him back. Then my family drove up.

"Alright break it up," said Tad as he got out. "We've got work to do!"

"We?" I asked. "You haven't been around all morning!"

"Well, I'm here to take charge and get this outfit straightened up. We've got some winning to do!" said Tad, putting his hands on his hips.

"And what are your orders, sir?" asked Dad, walking up next to Tad.

"Uh, well, we should get the first horse saddled," said Tad, gaining confidence as he spoke, "And warmed up!"

"Okay," said Grant. "We'll let *you* saddle the first one!" He patted Tad on the shoulder and we laughed.

Tad dropped his head to his chest and shook it. "What'd I open my mouth for?" he mumbled to himself. He went over to the tack compartment, opened the door, and looked back at me. "Which one are you riding first?"

"May Day," said Dad. "But I think we have time to warm up Flaxie first. She needs it most."

"Okay," said Tad, grabbing Flaxie's bridle.

"Guess I better get ready, too!" I got off the tailgate and went to put on my chaps.

"Your horse is ready!" said Tad, holding Flaxie's reins.

"Just need my hat and to change this number," I said and grabbed them both out of the trailer. I walked over to Flaxie's side. "Could you pin this number over the one I have on?" I said, handing it to JD. He pinned the number twenty-two over the twenty-three. He patted my back and I turned to him again.

"Now, can you give me a boost?" I asked, smiling at JD. He stepped over and boosted me up while Tad held Flaxie. She pranced a little in place, I patted her, and spoke, "Easy girl."

Dad walked up and the boys stepped back. "You be sure to mind her head. Don't let her get going too fast; take it slow so the judge can see."

"Yes, sir," I said. "But we're just gonna warm up."

"I know that, but the boys will be helping you change later, not me," said Dad.

"Oh," I looked at Tad and Grant. "When did you decide that?"

"At lunch," said Dad. "Now go warm up. She needs to be ridden to settle her down again."

I nodded at JD and the boys and then rode toward the arena. I had the distinct feeling more had gone on at lunch.

Satisfied Flaxie had warmed up enough, I looked for Tesa. I wanted to ask her what happened at lunch. She was over by the fence talking to her dad, who was standing next to Dad, the boys, and JD.

As I got close to them, Grant said, "Hey, let's go get setup on May Day." He turned and started walking back to the trailer.

"Grant, what happened at lunch?" I asked, getting off Flaxie.

"Whatcha mean?" he asked, not looking at me.

"Dad said you guys decided at lunch to help me instead of him."

Grant shrugged as he pulled the saddle off Flaxie. "That was about it!" he said and walked around to put the saddle on May Day.

"Okay." I had the feeling that something else went on. I tried another tact. "So how do you like JD's sisters?"

"They're pretty," said Grant, tightening the cinch, "but kinda shallow."

I laughed. "JD says that, too."

Grant turned to me. "They're all coming over for dinner tonight."

"Oh really?" I asked. Finally, someone was telling me what happened!

"Yeah, when Mom heard they wanted to go into town for dinner, she insisted they come over and eat with us. That's why she isn't here yet, had to stop and get some stuff at the store."

"The Martins coming, too?" I asked.

"Yep!" said Grant and then he looked at me. "You ready to get on?" I stepped over and Grant boosted me up. He patted me on the leg. "I'll be waiting with Flaxie over by the paddock. There's only one horse between May Day and Flaxie."

"Do you think the Coulters are going to raise a stink about this?" I asked Grant.

"I'm sure they will."

"Okay," I swallowed. Now I had a ton of butterflies in my stomach.

"Now, go show 'em how it's done!" said Grant winking at me.

I smiled and turned May Day to ride back to the warmup area. I rode him a little to get him stretched out, spotted JD sitting on the fence, and rode over. He smiled as I rode up. "I didn't get a chance to wish you luck," said JD.

I smiled. "I have lots of luck right here." I patted my chest. My necklace was under my shirt, but I felt it there and it comforted me.

"Then let me help calm your nerves," he said with a twinkle in his eye.

I laughed. "That doesn't calm anything." I leaned toward him. May Day sidestepped right next to the fence as if on cue, and JD leaned over and kissed me briefly. May Day stepped back, and I heard the announcer calling all contestants to the paddock. "Well, that's my class!" With one last look at JD, I rode off.

I trotted up to the paddock area where the rest of the contestants were gathered. I rode up next to Tesa. "You ready for this?" I asked.

She took a deep breath. "I'm as ready as I can be!" She looked really nervous.

"Hey, what's to be nervous about?" I asked. "These are our friends and neighbors. We've done this a hundred times already." I sounded more sure than I felt, and I hoped Tesa didn't notice.

I was the second horse to ride; Tesa was between me on May Day and me on Flaxie.

We watched the first rider. When he came out, they called my number. "Good luck!" said Tesa.

"Thanks!" I said. I took a deep breath, straightened my shoulders, and rode through the gate into the arena. I walked to the starting position and stopped. The judge nodded at me, and I began the pattern. We did the circles and lead changes perfectly, the spins with grace, and the rollbacks with a flourish. When I came to the sliding stop, it was like slow motion. We slid and then we backed up. I let May Day stand for a second as I lowered the reins, indicating I was done. I heard applause break out and smiled as I wheeled May Day around and loped over to the gate. My heart was singing.

They opened the gate and I rode by Tesa, giving her a high five. "Good luck!" She looked nervous. "Just breathe!"

She took a deep breath nodded at me and entered the gate.

"Hey!" yelled Grant. I rode over to him and Tad. Tad helped me off. I held May Day as Tad undid my saddle. He quickly walked around, put it on Flaxie, and did up the cinch in no time.

"Okay, ready?" he looked at me and took May Day's reins.

"Oh, take off this number, will ya?" I asked, turning my back to him.

Tad undid the number twenty-two and left twenty-three. "There!" he said.

"Okay, just need a boost," I said. Grant boosted me up and I settled into the saddle. "You gonna wait here with May Day?" I asked Tad.

"Yeah, just in case you need him again," he said.

"Why did I decide to do this?" I asked.

"Because you can!" said Grant and he patted my leg. "Now go show 'em how."

I nodded at him and took a big breath. I turned around to see Tesa just finishing up her pattern. The applause broke out, and she smiled as she came out of the gate. She gave me a high five. "Go show 'em again!" she said and rode on past.

I patted Flaxie and nodded to the gate handler to let me in. I stopped and looked up at the judge, waiting for him to signal he was ready. He had a surprised look on his face, said something to the ring steward who said something back to him, then nodded to me.

I took a breath and urged Flaxie to start. We flew through the pattern. She was smooth, and I was exhilarated as we did each task. At the final sliding stop, I barely pulled back and she slid gracefully. We backed up to the right spot, let her settle, and lowered the reins, showing we were done. The judge stood up and I heard applause. I let out a breath that I had been holding and smiled as I rode back to the gate.

I patted Flaxie as we passed through the gate. "Nice ride!" said Cathy as I looked up. "Too bad it won't count!"

"We'll see," I smiled. "Have a good ride," I said and rode over to where Tad and Grant were standing with May Day.

"Well, that should place high!" said Grant.

"I'm sure the Coulters will be objecting soon," I said.

"Don't go borrowing trouble!" said Dad walking over. "You did real good!"

"Thanks, but I can't take all the credit. You trained her."

"Takes more than a good horse to win," he said, "you know that." I nodded. Flaxie pranced a little, and I patted her neck.

"Let's go over there out of the way," said Dad. I got off Flaxie, stood with Dad and my brothers, and watched the other riders. There were twelve in the class, but it didn't take long before they were done.

There was a long pause as we waited for the results. The announcer came on, "Will Sara Stillsen please report to the arena on foot?"

My stomach dropped to my feet. I looked at Dad. "I'll go with you." I handed Flaxie's reins to Tad.

Waiting in the arena were the judge, the ring steward, Gladys White, and Mr. Coulter.

Gladys White began, "Mr. Coulter has made on official protest over Sara riding two horses in one event." She raised her hand before anyone could speak. "I have reviewed the rule book, and there's no rule against a rider entering twice into an individual event." She cleared her throat. "However, there's an appeal process that Mr. Coulter has elected to use. The final decision rests with our judge. Each of you will have one minute to plead your side." She turned to Mr. Coulter. "Mr. Coulter, you may precede."

Mr. Coulter cleared his throat. "I protest on the fact that the rules do not specifically allow the entering of a contestant in an event more than once. I say the intent of the rules was only to allow one contestant per event regardless if they use different horses." Then he gave a slight bow indicating he was done.

"Mr. Stillsen," said Gladys. "Your statement."

Dad turned to me and I nodded. "Thank you, Mrs. White, but I'll speak for myself as this was my idea." I looked at the judge and Mr. Coulter. "While I understand what you are saying Mr. Coulter, I do not believe either of us can know the intent of what the writers of the rules meant, as we were not there when they were written." I took a breath. "Therefore, I state that because the rules do not specifically deny the entering of a contestant with more than one horse in a single event, there's no intent to prevent this from occurring. I say what I did was perfectly legitimate according to the rules as they're written." I took a breath and continued, "I do thank you all for listening to me and allowing me to compete in such a manner."

"Well said," said Gladys with a smile. She turned to the judge. "Judge, your ruling?"

He had his arms crossed over his chest and looked down in thought for a moment. Then he looked up and spoke, "I did read through the rules, and I saw that they neither specifically allow nor deny the entry of one rider on multiple horses in a single event. I don't know the intent of the writers of the rules. So, based on what the rules currently state, I rule that the contestant is legitimately allowed to enter more than one horse in a single event as long as all requirements of the event are met."

I turned to Dad and smiled big. He patted me on the back. I looked at Mr. Coulter, and he was red in the face. "This won't be the last you hear from me about this Gladys!" He stomped off.

The judge shook his head and stepped toward me. "I did enjoy seeing you ride today. You have real talent."

"Thank you, sir!" I nodded to him.

Dad had his arm around me as we walked away. "Whew!" I said as we got a few steps away.

"Wasn't that bad!" he said. "You stated your case very well. Maybe you should be a lawyer!"

"No way! Too many rules!" We laughed.

We walked out of the gate and over to Tad and Grant. Tesa was there, too. "Well?" they asked.

"Mr. Coulter made his appeal," said Dad. He slapped me on the shoulder. "But Sara here made a very convincing argument, and the judge ruled that she could ride two horses in one event!"

They cheered. I was smiling and feeling very relieved when the announcer came back on. "Will all riders and their horses for the senior reining class please return to the arena!"

I looked at Dad in alarm. "What? I can't ride them both."

"Relax!" he said. "They didn't say you had to ride them. Just appear. Now get on one and lead the other."

"Oh okay," I said, unsure what to do still.

"Here get on May Day," said Grant. Dad helped me up on May Day's bare back. Tad handed me Flaxie's reins. I turned May Day around and led Flaxie into the arena. Tad had pinned my other number to her blanket so all the numbers were represented.

We rode into the arena and lined up. Tesa was on one side of me. We looked up at the stands and I could see the Daltons and Martins there. Mom was taking pictures as usual. She smiled and waved at me and I smiled back.

The announcer began. "In senior reining in first place, number twenty-two, Prairie's May Day ridden by Sara Stillsen." There were cheers and applause. Tesa took Flaxie's reins from me. I gathered my ribbon and came back to the line.

"In second place, number twenty-six, True Heart ridden by Tesa

Martin." There was a round of applause and Matt whistled.

"In third place, number twenty-three, Flaxie's Depth Chick ridden by Sara Stillsen!" I led Flaxie over, collected our third place ribbon, and as we were riding toward the gate, I heard the announcer.

"In fourth place, number fifteen, Flying Destiny ridden by Cathy Coulter." There was some applause but not as much as before.

I rode out of the gate. Dad, Grant, Tad, and Tesa were there, smiling. "Awesome day, isn't it?" I said and they laughed.

"You're my hero!" said Tesa. "You beat Cathy twice!"

"Yeah, we beat her three times!" I said pointing at Tesa.

"Let's go celebrate!" said Tad.

"See ya in a little bit!" I said to Tesa. She rode off, Tad took Flaxie's reins from me, and we walked toward the trailer.

When we got close to the trailer, Mark came running up beside me. "Hey Sara!" he said excitedly. "You won twice!"

I laughed. "Yeah, kinda!"

"Can I ride with you now?" asked Mark, practically jumping up and down.

"Sure can!" I saw JD walking toward us. "Can you give Mark a boost up here with me?"

He smiled. "Sure, come around here buddy." JD led Mark around to my left side.

I slid back and patted May Day in front of me. "Right here so he can drive!"

"Sara, you don't drive a horse," said Mark. "You ride them!"

"Oh," I laughed, "I'm so glad you're here to help me out. I've been doing it wrong!"

JD lifted Mark up in front of me. "It's okay," said Mark. "You've been doing pretty well on your own." JD and I laughed.

"You got the reins?" I asked Mark. He nodded. "Let's take a turn or two around the practice arena," I said and urged May Day forward.

We were walking off when Mark kicked May Day and he started trotting. I put my arms around Mark as he was bouncing off to one side. "Push your heels down and lean back some," I said.

I felt Mark shift and he stopped bouncing so much. "Hey, that works!" he said.

"You're a natural!" I said.

We got to the practice arena, and he turned May Day to go around. "Can we lope now?" asked Mark.

"Do you know how to ask him?" I asked Mark. He shook his head. "Here's what you do. You turn his head a little into the fence and kick with your outside leg. That's this one," I said as I patted his right leg. "I'll be holding on to you. Whenever you're ready."

He nodded his head then we were off at a gentle lope. "Squeeze with your knees a little," I said, as he was bouncing again. He stopped bouncing some. "Lean back a little." He did and stopped bouncing entirely.

"Hey, this is fun!" said Mark. "I normally don't ride without a saddle."

"This is better than a saddle," I said. "You can feel the horse's muscles under you. Feel the power?"

Mark nodded. We rounded the far end, and I saw JD and his sisters at the fence watching us. I waved as we got near. "You wanna go around again?" I asked Mark.

"Yes please!" he said and turned May Day to go along the fence. He waved at JD and his sisters as we rode by. They smiled and waved back. We rounded the far end and came back toward the fence where JD and his sisters were. I saw Grant and Tad walking up behind them.

"Okay, let's stop," I said to Mark.

"Aw, do we have to?"

"Yeah for now," I said. "You can ride some more when we get to our ranch."

"Really?"

"Yeah really! So let's ride up and stop right there." I pointed to the fence. "When I say three, you pull back firmly." He nodded. "One, two, three!" Mark pulled back and May Day slid to a stop.

"Wow, that's cool!"

I patted him on the shoulder. "You're pretty good." I said as we walked over to the fence.

"Wow, Mark, you're good!" said JD, smiling at him.

"Sara did all the work!"

"No sir!" I said, "You're the one with the reins!"

"Yeah, I steered," said Mark.

We laughed. "You ready to go bud?" asked JD.

"Sara said I could ride some more when we get to her ranch!" said Mark.

"I'm sure you can," said JD. He came around the fence and held up his hands to Mark. "Now let me trade with you."

"Aw, alright," said Mark disappointed. JD lifted him down. Mark turned to him. "You sure you know how to ride him?"

JD laughed. "Yep. Sara let me rope off him, and that's why Matt doesn't have any hair!"

The girls burst out laughing. "Is that why?"

"Yeah," said Tad. "JD and Matt made a bet and JD won!"

"You mean you would've shaved your head if you lost?" asked Hanna in disbelief.

"I sure would've," said JD. "I never go back on my word!" Then he turned to me. "Can I ride with you, ma'am?"

"Sure, but you gotta get in back," I said and scooted up. JD swung up behind me. "You wanna take a turn around or shall we go back to the trailer?" I asked urging May Day to walk.

He took my hat off and said into my ear. "I'd ride all the way home like this, but I'll settle for once around."

I laughed. "Hang on, cowboy." I urged May Day into a slow lope. Neither JD nor I bounced. I took a mental note that he rode very well. We slowed to a walk at the far end.

"So we're having dinner at your house," said JD.

"You sound disappointed," I said.

"A little," he said. "I was looking forward to bringing you home and parking by the river for a while so we could be alone."

"I think we can still be alone for a little while," I said smiling.

"That's what I wanted to hear." He kissed my cheek.

We were walking back to the trailer when we crossed paths with Ken and Sandy. "Hey Sara!" said Ken. "JD!"

"Hey guys!" I said.

"Boy you sure put it to Cathy today!" said Ken with a big smile.

"I'm sorry if it causes you any trouble at home," I said.

Sandy and Ken laughed. "I'm not!" they both said and laughed.

"You're welcome to join us for some celebrating tonight at our ranch. My mom invited the Martins and JD's family. I'm sure there'll be plenty if you and your parents wanna sneak away for a bit."

"That's real nice of you," said Ken. He looked at Sandy. She nodded. "We'll just check with our folks."

"We'll look for ya!"

"What time do ya eat?"

"Probably around eight."

"Okay, see ya," said Ken and Sandy as they walked off to find their parents.

"You're always so generous," said JD. squeezing me.

"I can't let them suffer because of me!"

We rode up to the trailer. "There they are!" said Mom. "Come on, I've got dinner to fix!"

"Sorry," I said and JD slipped off and reached up for me. I slid down into his arms and he let me go.

He took the reins from me. "I'll see he gets loaded. You go get those chaps off." He handed me my hat.

"Thanks!"

I quickly pulled off my chaps and put them in the trailer along with my hat. I shut the door and JD was there. "Mind if I ride with you?"

"Absolutely not," I said. "Where's your family?"

"They're loading up over there," said JD pointing to a cream-colored Cadillac Escalade I saw his sisters getting into.

"Where's Dad?" I asked.

"Coming up now," said Grant, pointing over my shoulder. We turned to see Dad and two men walking toward our trailer. The men waved at us and walked off. Dad came over to us, smiling big.

"Well?" asked Grant.

"They not only wanna use Big Joe for breeding, they want me to train four of their horses," said Dad.

"All right!" said Grant and I at the same time.

Dad turned to me and put his hand on my shoulder. "Thank you for showing off for me."

"Least I could do! After all I'm just a showgirl!"

We got in our truck. I was in the back between Grant and JD. Tad was riding with the Martins.

"Oh Mom," I leaned over the seat, "I invited the Miners to join us too."

"That's nice of you," said Mom. "I sure wouldn't wanna be anywhere near the Big C or the Coulters tonight!"

"I think I've just made an enemy for life!" I said.

"Don't make a habit of it," said Dad.

"No sir!" I said. "One enemy is enough!"

At the ranch, Mom got out at the house. Grant helped her with the groceries then we drove on to the barn. We put up the horses and fed them.

"You coming up to the house?" asked Dad.

"I wanna talk to Andrea," I said. "We'll walk back in a few minutes." He nodded got in his truck and drove up to the house.

JD turned me to him, pulled me into his arms, and kissed me deeply. I felt warmth blooming in my chest, but I suppressed it. JD pulled back and reached behind my neck to my hair. "May I?" he asked. I shrugged.

He pulled the pins from my hair and handed them to me. He undid my braid and ran his hands through my hair to loosen it. "That's much better," he said. He cupped my face and kissed me again. I wrapped my arms around his neck and pulled him against me. He kissed me harder.

I felt the warmth bloom and spread slowly down my arms into my fingers. I sighed as JD moved from my lips to kiss my ear and neck. "I can't get enough of you," he whispered huskily in my ear. Then he pulled back and smiled at me. His eyes were smoldering and my knees shook a little. He took my hands, held them to his face, and sighed. "We better go," he said.

"Okay," I said not moving. He kissed me lightly again. He put his arm around me and we walked out of the barn.

We laughed as Foxy bounded past us. "She's always near you, isn't she?"

"Except when I'm at school."

"She's a good friend to have."

"The best," I said. "She doesn't try to borrow my clothes or steal my boyfriends!"

We were nearing the house when Mark came running toward us. "Can we ride now?"

"We need to let them finish eating their dinner first." I said. "Then we can ride. I've a horse you can ride all by yourself."

"Really?" asked Mark. I nodded and he turned and ran back to the house. Foxy bounded alongside him.

"You sure know how to please us Dalton boys," said JD.

"It's my pleasure," I said, smiling at him.

The Martins hadn't arrived yet. They were gonna pull their trailer and horses here rather than go all the way home, then come all the way to our house. So, only the Daltons were there.

"Hey!" we said as we came in. Hanna and Tana looked bored sitting on the couch in the living room. Mark was sitting at the bar next to his dad, who was talking to my dad. Mrs. Dalton was in the kitchen talking to Mom as she prepared dinner. I didn't see Grant or Mitch.

"You girls want a soda?" I asked as JD and I walked by them.

"Sure," said Hanna and Tana in unison. They followed us into the kitchen. I got some sodas and handed them around. "Where're the boys?"

Dad nodded toward the back. "Grant and Mitch went out back a minute ago."

"Well, if ya'll will excuse me, I'd like to change out of this shirt." I looked at Hanna and Tana. "Ya'll are welcome to come with me if you'd like." They shrugged and followed me down the hall to my room.

I closed the door behind us and walked over to close my back door when Foxy pushed her way in. She walked over, jumped up on the bed, and lay down. "Is she a wolf?" asked Hanna, pointing at Foxy.

"She's part wolf," I said. "Hanna, this is Foxy."

"How'd you know I'm Hanna?" she asked. The twins had changed shirts and I wondered why.

I smiled at her. "I'm observant." I looked at Tana. "Tana, this is Foxy."

They sat on the bed and petted Foxy for a minute then Foxy got up went to the door and scratched. I let her out. "Don't take it personal," I said. "She probably hears the boys out back."

I went to my closet to get something else to wear.

"So how long have you been smooching with my brother?" asked Hanna.

"Well, let's see," I said from my closet. "He first kissed me at the Uvalde rodeo and that was two weeks ago." I pulled on a shirt and walked over to my dresser.

"Has JD told you about his girlfriend back home?" asked Tana. I looked into the mirror and saw her smiling at her sister. I got the feeling this was a test.

"He hasn't mentioned anyone," I said like it was no big deal. I trusted that JD had told me the truth about not having a girlfriend back in Houston. I picked up a brush and ran it through my hair. I turned to them. "I'm sure JD has lots of girlfriends. He's a very good-looking guy."

The twins exchanged a glance. They obviously didn't like that this didn't upset me. So they tried again. "Well, he finds a summer romance each year," said Tana.

"Yeah," said Hanna. "I'm sure Sara's used to having guys show up for the summer then leave."

"Oh yeah," I said sarcastically. "That happens all the time here in the middle of nowhere."

They looked at me and smiled a little, but I could tell they were shocked. I pulled some of my hair to the side so it was out of my face. I turned back to the girls. "So whatcha think of the guys around here?" I asked, turning the tables on them.

Hanna smiled. "Your brothers are pretty cute."

"Yeah, Tad is yummy," said Tana.

"Do they have girlfriends?" they asked in stereo.

"Tad has a girl, but Grant doesn't have anyone he dates steady." The girls looked at each other and smiled; I got a funny feeling that they had a plan for my brothers. I'd have to warn the boys, but then again, let them fend for themselves. That's what I asked them to let me do.

"Ya wanna go see what the boys are doing?" I asked them with a smile.

They nodded and we walked out onto the porch. We could see the boys out front trying rope tricks. Grant was showing Mitch how to do something. "Ah, their favorite pastime," I said. "Don't get too close because they might head and heel you."

The girls laughed and we walked out onto the lawn. JD was sitting on a chair on the front porch, so I went over beside him. He pulled me down onto his lap.

"Have they raked you over the coals yet?" asked JD, nodding toward his sisters.

"Nope," I said. "But I think they're disappointed that I didn't fall for the story about your girlfriend back home." JD threw his head back and laughed. "That's not all. They tried to tell me you have lots of summer flings." JD laughed some more.

"And I suppose you just smiled sweetly at them?"

"I was nice. I said you probably do have lots of girlfriends because you're so good looking." He snickered at that. "I also think they're a little surprised that I can tell them apart so easily."

JD looked shocked. "How do you do that? I can't tell them apart most of the time."

"Really?" I asked. "I guess you don't look at your sisters like others do."

"You have some other gift you aren't telling me about?"

"Nope. I'm just observant."

"So what did you observe?"

"That Hanna has a gold fleck in her left eye and Tana doesn't."

"Really?" he said. "Huh!" A smile spread across his face. "Now I can tell them apart, and they won't make me feel bad anymore."

I patted his leg. "Glad I could help."

We heard a truck coming. "That's the Martins!" I said.

"How can you tell?" he asked.

"Because the bump gate didn't slam yet," I said. "When you're pulling a trailer, someone has to hold it open when you go through.

I cocked my head and listened. "I do believe the Miners are right behind them."

The Martins truck crested the rise and they pulled around. They stopped and Tesa and Mrs. Martin got out. The rest of them drove on down the road to the barn.

Mark ran out of the house. He spotted me. "Can we go ride yet?" he asked eagerly.

"Sure," I said and Mark cheered. The guys looked over. "We're gonna go ride a little. Anyone wanna come?" They shook their heads.

"Hey Sara!" said Mrs. Martin. "Congratulations! I brought you this!" She pulled a bottle of sparkling cider out of her bag.

"Thanks, Mrs. Martin, but Tesa and I both are celebrating!"

"We got enough for everyone," said Tesa.

"Good, 'cause I invited the Miners," I said. "I think that's them!" I pointed to the truck coming up the road. Joey started barking at the strange truck. "Shut it, Joey!" It was the Miners, but with the sun glinting off the windshield, I couldn't tell who was in the truck.

The truck stopped by the gate and all four doors opened and out stepped Mr. and Mrs. Miner along with Sandy and Ken.

"Hey folks!" said Dad, coming out of the house. "Glad you could join us!"

"We're really glad we could, too," said Mrs. Miner.

"I'll bet," said Mrs. Martin. They exchanged greetings, and Mom called for Dad to bring them in the house.

I looked at Sandy, Tesa, and Ken. "JD and I are taking Mark for a short ride before dinner. Anyone is welcome to join us."

Ken looked over my shoulder at the guys and Dalton twins and said, "I'll stay here."

"Me too," said Tesa as she made a face that said, "I'll just keep an eye on him with those girls!" I laughed.

"Go make sure they don't get headed and heeled!" I said and Sandy laughed.

Mark was already halfway down the road with Foxy bounding by his side. JD took my hand as we went through the gate. We didn't say anything for a few minutes, enjoying each other's company.

The Martins had unloaded True Heart and King Coin. Tad put each in an empty stall and fed them.

"Matt, Mitch!" yelled Mark, running up to them. "Sara's gonna let me ride!"

They laughed at him. "Is that so? Need any help?" asked Matt as we walked up behind Mark.

"Naw," I said. "Ya'll go on up to the house and get something cold to drink. We'll let Mark get his ride."

"Why don't you introduce Mark to Andrea?" I asked JD. "I'll get her bridle."

Andrea was hanging her head over the stall door and Mark was patting her face. She neighed softly at me as I approached. "Hey girl," I said. "You ready for some exercise?" She gave me a "hu hu."

Mark turned to look at me his eyes wide. "She talks to you?"

"She sure does," I said. "All the animals talk if you listen." I put the bridle on Andrea and opened the door to lead her out.

"JD, did you know Sara talked to animals?" asked Mark.

"Sure did," said JD. "Pretty cool, huh?"

"Way cool!"

I led Andrea to the tack room and tied her to the rail there. I got two brushes out and handed one to Mark. "Okay, you have to help brush her off."

"Okay," he said cheerfully and started brushing Andrea. He actually did a good job.

"You seem to have done this before," I said.

"Yeah," said Mark, "it's one of the things the girls let me do at home."

"Oh really?" asked JD as he leaned against the wall. "What else do the girls let you do?"

"They let me clean their hooves sometimes," said Mark working away. I was on the other side brushing. I looked up at JD and our eyes met and we smiled.

"Anything else?"

"They let me clean out the water trough last week," said Mark.

"What do they let you do in return for this work?"

Mark shrugged. "They let me ride with them sometimes."

I bit my lip to keep from laughing and ducked my head behind Andrea so Mark wouldn't see. I took a deep breath and controlled myself. "Done brushing?"

"Yes, ma'am!" said Mark as he ran around Andrea and handed me the brush.

"Let's get a saddle." Mark followed me into the tack room and I pulled down my old saddle. "Grab that blanket please." Mark grabbed it and followed me back out. He went right over and put it on Andrea. I lifted the saddle on to her back and tightened the cinch

"Need help up?" JD asked Mark.

"Naw, I can pull myself up." Mark reached up, grabbed the saddle skirt and pulled himself up. He stuck his knee into the stirrup, pulled himself up more, then put his foot in the stirrup and swung his leg over and settled into the saddle.

"Okay, let's go." I handed him the reins.

"Where do I go?" asked Mark.

I pointed out the front of the barn. "Out to the arena."

Mark nodded and turned Andrea to walk out of the barn. He had a big smile on this face as he turned back to look at us. He walked into the arena, and I shut the gate behind him.

"Can I trot now?" asked Mark. JD and I climbed up and sat on the fence to watch.

"Sure can. Remember push your heels down," I called to him. He urged Andrea to a trot and bounced a little then settled down into the saddle. He trotted around once.

"How do I lope again?"

"Turn her head to the fence a little and kick with your leg nearest the fence. Squeeze with your knees."

He nodded and started loping by himself. He had the biggest smile on his face. I laughed. JD took my hand. "You know I feel that same way when I'm with you?"

"What do ya mean?" I asked watching Mark.

"Pure joy!" said JD. "It just bursts out all over."

I leaned into his shoulder and he smiled at me. Mark slowed to a walk in front of us. "Can I go the other way now?"

"Sure," I said. "Just walk around once and let her catch her breath."

"She's kinda fat!" said Mark, "You should ride her more."

"She's fat because she's gonna have a baby," I said.

"Really?" asked Mark, stopping in front of us.

"Yes, really. This winter, probably after Christmas."

"Wow, wish I could come see."

"Maybe you can," said JD. "I'm sure Sara would invite us back to visit."

"Really? You would?"

"You're always welcome to come visit."

"Yahoo!" said Mark and started again around the arena.

"Now you've done it," said JD. "I'll have to bring him out here every school holiday."

"Is that so terrible?" I asked, looking at him.

"Only that I'd have to bring him with me when I come," he said and kissed me.

Mark rode by and we watched. He made me feel happy just watching him. He radiated pure joy. Mark rode around a few times then he came over and said, "I think she's getting tired."

"Okay, walk her around three more times to cool her off," I said. Mark nodded and walked around.

"You're so great with him," said JD. "He can be a handful."

"He just needs some place to burn off all that energy. I was that way, too."

"Was?" asked JD with a grin.

"Okay, still am."

He laughed and we climbed off the fence. The sun was just reaching the horizon as JD helped Mark off and unsaddled Andrea. I led her down to her stall, patted her, and took off the bridle.

"Thank you girl!" She nudged me. "Yes, you did really good." I scratched her ears and she bobbed her head. "Yeah, you like that!" I patted her again walked out and closed her door.

"What'd she say?" asked Mark.

"She said she likes you. Now let's go see if dinner's ready!"

"Yeah, we better get some before Matt and Mitch eat it all. They eat lots!" said Mark, heading for the door.

JD pulled me into his arms and kissed me. I kept my eyes closed when he pulled back. I smiled and slowly opened my eyes.

"What are you thinking?" he asked.

"How much I enjoy it when you kiss me." JD pulled me along beside him. "I don't even mind that you have all those other girlfriends."

"What?" JD stopped walking. "I told you…"

"Gotcha!"

"That's so not funny!"

"Oh come on. You know I trust you. I trust you more than I trust myself actually."

"Don't tell me that," he said, shaking his head.

"Why not?"

"Because it puts thoughts in my head. Thoughts I shouldn't be having." We walked on in silence. I wasn't sorry I put thoughts into JD's head. I should be, but I wasn't. I was happy to know that I had an effect on him.

The sun started to dip below the horizon, and the light was turning everything gold and pink. I breathed in the scent of sage and fresh air.

"We should walk down by the river after dinner," I said. "We can see the fireflies."

"Fireflies? Wow! I haven't seen those in years."

We neared the house and heard everyone inside talking. We walked in and saw they were already eating. I smelled chicken enchiladas.

"Don't worry there's plenty!" said Mom. "Grab a plate!"

We filled our plates and stood at the bar to eat, as all the seats were taken.

"We should watch the video of Matt getting scalped," I said to JD.

He laughed. "He'd kill us."

"He'll get over it," I said.

"What are you two conspiring about?" asked Mr. Martin from across the room.

"Just recounting the last time we were gathered here!" I said and winked at Mr. Martin. "We seem to have it on tape!"

"Oh no you don't!" said Matt, standing up and pointing at me.

"Too late!" said Tad, coming in with the videocamera. Matt scrambled from behind the table as he ran to get Tad. Tad was already at the TV, and Mitch and Grant blocked his way.

"Ya'll gotta come see this!" yelled Tad.

We gathered in the living room to watch. Tad started the tape and Matt came into view. He was covered in a sheet, and Mrs. Martin was waving the clippers.

"You had nice hair!" said Hanna.

"I know," said Matt. He gave a theatrical sniff and pretended to wipe his eyes with his shirt. We laughed at him. We looked at the screen and laughed at him some more. The locks dropped to the ground as the clippers stroked over his head until he was bald. Mrs. Martin kissed Matt's head and he stood up.

Then the tape cut to another scene. It was of me asleep on my bed.

"What's this?" I asked. A washcloth flew by and hit me in the face. Everyone laughed. *"You better run!"* I said on tape, jumped off the bed, and ran off camera.

Then the camera showed me running down the hall. You could hear lots of commotion; I was yelling and the boys were yelling then the camera showed Grant and Tad holding me down. There was shaving cream everywhere. Tad aimed the shaving cream at my face and it fizzled. We laughed. Then the tape cut off.

"And you wonder why you hear all those stories about *my* wiles," I said to JD.

He put his arm around me. "You poor thing! I can see how mean they are to you," he said sarcastically.

"Oh please!" I pushed him away. "All you brothers are the same. You just like to hear your sisters squeal!"

I walked back into the kitchen and JD followed. Mom came in behind us. I turned to her. "Just how many of those kinda tapes do you have?"

"A few," said Mom and she smiled. "I've gotta capture what I can."

"Yeah, you've got our lives covered!" I looked up at JD. "You should see the pictures Mom takes at the rodeos. There are several of you riding bulls."

"I'd like to see those."

"Sara knows where they are."

"Come on, let's go look at pictures," I said, pulling JD after me. We walked into Mom's sewing room, and I sat at the computer. JD pulled up a chair. I opened the picture file and started back at the beginning of the summer. We ran through several shots, laughing at some and telling each other about some. I stopped at one of JD riding a bull in Rocksprings.

"That's Hell on Wheels!" said JD. The bull was stretched out with its hind legs in the air. JD's left arm was up, and his chaps were flying. We clicked through a few more, and there was one of me turning around a barrel. May Day was digging into the dirt with his front feet. I was smiling slightly.

"Look how you enjoy that," said JD.

There were a few of the boys roping. There were pictures of the Uvalde rodeo.

"I haven't loaded the pictures from today yet," said Mom. I turned to see her leaning on the doorframe. "I'll print the ones of you, JD. That one in Rocksprings would make a nice one to frame."

"Thank you, Mrs. Stillsen, that would be great."

We heard Mr. Martin calling everyone into the dining room. We got up and went to see what was going on. They'd opened the sparkling cider, and Mrs. Martin and Mrs. Dalton were passing out glasses. When we all had one, Mr. Martin spoke. "It isn't often we get to gather in the good company of friends to celebrate. Tonight we toast to all our champions and winners past and present!"

"Here, here!" We all raised a glass and drank.

"Who all is a past champion?" asked Mr. Miner.

"Well, Sonny here was a past bronc riding champion. He rode bulls but couldn't cut that so had to settle on horses," said Mr. Martin, chiding Dad. "He snagged Marcy here who was Miss Rodeo Oklahoma. How far back was that?"

He laughed as Mom waved her finger at him. "I myself was half a team roping pair back in my day." He slapped Mr. Dalton on the back. "And Jesse here was a pretty good bull rider and roper, too."

"Pretty good?" said Mr. Dalton, "I won more than you did!" They laughed.

"Well, I'm honored to be in such company!" said Mr. Miner as he raised his glass one more time. We drank again.

"Any one for seeing some fireflies?" I asked.

"Fireflies?" asked Hanna and Tana. "Sure!"

All the kids went outside and down by the river. JD held my hand, and we fell back from the rest. Foxy walked beside me, but when she heard Mark laughing, she bounded off after him. I led JD over to a big tree stump, and we sat down.

"Ah there they are," said JD, watching the little yellow lights flash on and off around us.

"When I was little, I used to think they were fairies like Tinkerbell."

JD chuckled. "And did you catch them in jars?"

"Oh no!" I said. "They'd die and I wouldn't get my wish!"

JD reached out and caught one. He cupped it in his hands. "Now what do I do?"

"You whisper your wish into your hands so the fairy can hear but no one else," I said. "Then you let it go."

I watched as JD whispered into his hand. He looked at me and let the firefly go. It flew up and away. "Wanna know what I wished for?"

"Oh no, you can't tell or it won't come true."

"It might!" he said and kissed me.

Mark called out, "Hey Sara, I caught one!"

"Good," I said. "Now you can make a wish!"

"I can? How?"

"You cup it in your hands," said JD. "Like this" and he held hands so Mark could see. "Then you whisper into your hands so only the firefly can hear. When you're done, you let it go."

Mark whispered into his hands, let the firefly go, and laughed. "Wanna know what I wished for?"

"No, no you can't tell anyone or it won't come true."

"Oh!" said Mark and he covered his mouth. He turned and yelled at Hanna and Tana. "Hey, you guys. You can make a wish if you catch one."

We laughed as he told Hanna and Tana how to make a wish. Tad and Matt caught fireflies for the girls.

"What do you think they're wishing for?" I asked, nodding at JD's sisters.

"Probably a new phone or new clothes," said JD. "Mark asked for a horse of his own." He turned to me. "What would you wish for?"

I looked up at the stars and they twinkled. "I don't know. I feel like I have everything I could want right now."

"You really do like the simple things in life."

"Don't get me wrong. I do like new clothes now and then. There was a piercing whistle. "That's my dad," I said. "Your folks must be ready to leave."

The whistle came again. I heard Grant answer, whistling twice to signal that he'd heard.

"Can you do that, too?" asked JD.

"Can't everyone?"

"I can with my fingers."

I laughed. "If you're rounding up around here, you don't wanna stick your fingers in your mouth to whistle."

"Oh yeah," said JD as we were walking back to the house. "Show me!" I took a deep breath and I whistled loud.

"Wow!" said JD. "That's pretty good." Foxy ran up to me and yipped.

"It's okay, girl," I patted her. "I was just showing JD I could whistle loud." She gave me a "warrrll" then bounded off.

We walked by a tree at the back of the house that had a big limb that bent low to the ground.

"This is my favorite place to come read or think," I said. "Foxy lays here sometimes, too."

JD stopped and looked up at the stars. "Nice view."

"It's amazing," I said looking up.

When I looked back down, he was staring at me. He kissed me lightly then pulled me on up the hill. "I'll see you tomorrow, right?" asked JD.

"I'll be in the parade," I said.

"I'll say my goodnight then." JD pulled me to him, put his hand on my cheek, and kissed me. I wrapped my arms around him. A fire raced up my spine and down to my fingers. They tingled as I ran my hand across his shoulder. He released me and shivered.

"I felt that!" he smiled. We walked through the back gate and into the house.

"The rest are right behind us," said JD as his dad looked up expectantly when we walked in.

Mark ran in. "We caught fireflies and made wishes on them!"

"Really?" asked Mrs. Dalton. "What did you wish for?"

"We can't tell," said Mark, "or the wish won't come true!" We laughed as the rest came in.

"Where's Dad?" asked Matt as he looked around.

"He went to load up the horses," said Mrs. Martin. "That should be him pulling up."

We heard a truck pulling up and walked out to the front porch. We said our good-byes and waved as everyone got into their trucks and drove off.

I helped Mom with the last few dishes. When we were done, I hugged her.

"Good night!" I said.

"Night!" she said. "Oh Sara, there's a letter for you on the hall table."

I saw it was from Uncle Buck, and my heart gave a small trill. I walked to my room, fell across the bed, and tore it open. Foxy jumped on my bed as I read.

Dear Sara,

You should have met Wakiza by now. Wakiza means "Desperate Warrior." The necklace you have been given is connected to him. He represents your strength and freedom of spirit. You have a choice to continue or not. No one else can do this for you.

Things will keep changing but not as rapidly now. Do not let yourself be overwhelmed by all the new feelings you have. The Provider does not give more than one can handle. You are stretching and growing into yourself. Be patient.

Do not fret over your family learning about your gifts. They have great love for you and will always protect you. Draw from them and lean on them.

Know that your father already suspects your gifts. Do not hide them from him. Let him come to you with this knowledge. He needs to discover this for himself to be a true believer in the powers of the spirit. He, like your brothers, will shelter you, but do not let him hold you back from your path.

Have courage; your path is bright.

Sincerely,
Uncle Buck

I lay there awhile, wondering what lay in store for me. I got up changed into my favorite sleeping shirt and shorts. I turned off the light and crawled into my bed. I was probably asleep before my head hit the pillow.

Old Settler's

Old Settler's official kickoff was the parade down Main Street. I had been looking forward to this for so long, I couldn't believe it was here. The mayor and Gladys White led the parade in their horse-drawn carriage. There were several floats then the band.

I kept looking for my family and JD in the crowd but hadn't seen them yet. As we got to the park in the middle of town, I heard Dad whistle and saw him standing with Mom, waving. I smiled as I marched on by and then saw JD and his family waving a few feet away. I nodded at him and an easy peacefulness settled over me. I felt free as we pranced and twirled our way down the rest of the route.

In no time, we came to the edge of town and the parade was over. Mr. Wilson told us how proud he was as we cheered and started back to the band hall. Some caught rides on the floats that were going back to the park.

Tesa yelled at me, "Sara, come on!" I saw her on the sophomore float, ran over, and jumped on the back with her and Leena.

"Whew!" I said, "Glad that's over with."

Leena laughed. "Heard about your adventures the past two days!" she said.

"Yeah, where've you been?" I asked.

"Babysitting!" she said. "I went with my parents to see my sister and her new baby in San Antonio."

"That's great! How was the baby?"

"She's a darling angel. I can't believe I'm an aunt!"

"Yeah, you're so old!" said Tesa.

At the park, we jumped off the float and walked the few blocks to the band hall. Tesa and Leena went inside to put away their instruments. While I was waiting outside, I pulled my hair out of its bun and was bending over shaking out my hair when I heard a very warm familiar voice. "That's what I like to see!"

I straightened up, flipping my hair back, and smiled at JD. He was sitting in one of the Martins trucks.

"What is it you see that you like?" I asked walking over to him.

"Flying blonde hair, sparkling sequins, generous green eyes in a beautiful face."

"You do go on so!" I said in a southern belle drawl. We laughed as Tesa and Leena ran out of the band hall.

"Hey, JD, whatcha doing here?" asked Tesa.

"I've been given the pleasure of picking up you girls," said JD.

"Well, let's go!" said Tesa and we piled into the truck.

"Can you drop me at my house?" asked Leena, "It's on the way. I wanna change, and I'll meet you guys later."

"Your wish is my command," said JD. He patted my leg as we drove down the road towards Leena's, dropped her off, and headed to the rodeo grounds.

"You guys looked great marching," said JD to break the silence.

"Kinda disappointing after the big bands you're used to, huh?" said Tesa.

"I never paid much attention to the band back home."

"No band geeks for you?" I asked.

"I think I've been missing out!" We laughed as we turned into the rodeo grounds and parked next to the Martins' trailer. Our trailer was on the other side.

"Where is everyone?" I asked.

"Probably still on their way from the parade," said Tesa. "Come on, let's get out of these geek clothes." She looked at me. "Well, I look like a geek, you look…"

"Like a showgirl!" I said, finishing her sentence.

"Yeah," she said laughing. "Get your stuff and come change with me."

I looked at JD. "Be right back!"

"Don't change on my account!"

"I'm sure I'd raise a few eyebrows running the barrels in this getup!"

I waved at JD as I trotted across to the Martins' trailer; he was leaning against our truck, petting Foxy. I knocked and Tesa let me in. She was already in her jeans and was tucking in her shirt. Tesa helped me with my zipper, and I shrugged out of the suit.

"Last few days with JD," she said. "How do you feel about that?"

"I knew this day would come soon and that he can't come back very often to visit. He might get tired of it, even if he could. It's not like he fell off the earth or anything. I've no ties on him and certainly don't expect him to not see anyone else when he's back in Houston. I think we'll go our separate ways. I'll miss him, but I'm not gonna cry over him leaving. That won't change anything."

Tesa put her hands on her hips. "How long have you been practicing that speech?"

I chuckled, "About three days now. How's it sound?"

"The question is how much of it do you believe?"

I took a deep breath. "I just wanna enjoy while he's here and not worry about tomorrow."

"That sounds more like you," she said. "Now let's go have some fun!"

I grabbed my clothes and followed Tesa out.

I ran over to put my stuff in my trailer. I was just turning around when JD stepped in.

"I can't wait any more." He kissed me. A feeling of elation ran through me. The flame within me flew down my arms, and I caught it just enough so it only simmered in my fingers.

I pulled back and sucked in a breath. "Wow!" I said, trying to suppress the heat.

JD took my hands. "Yeah, wow! These are hot!"

"Careful, I might catch you on fire!"

"I'll risk it!"

"I got another letter from Uncle Buck," I said as I pulled it out of my pocket and handed it to JD.

"You want me to read this?"

"Yeah, you can help me with something."

JD sat down, read it quickly, and looked up at me. "I can't tell you what choice to make or how to help your dad accept your gift."

I smiled at him. "The question I have for you is about this necklace you gave me."

"What about it?"

"Where did you get it?"

"When I was in Wyoming at national finals. I told you that when I gave it to you."

"Who did you buy it from?"

"Oh that," he smiled remembering. "There were some Indians on the sidewalk selling jewelry. One of them beckoned to me as we were walking by, so I stopped and looked at what she had laid out on the blanket beside her. That's when I spotted the necklace. Huh, now that I think about it, she told me it would provide a special connection for someone." He shook his head. "And here I thought it was just for luck."

"It has brought us both luck and a connection." JD smiled at me as someone banged on the side of the trailer.

I pushed open the door. "What?"

"Come on!" said Tesa. "Everyone's going to get burgers."

"Okay, okay," I said and we went with the rest to eat.

After we ate, it was back to our usual rodeo routine. We watched the grand entry as the contestants filed through.

Tesa and I were in the practice arena riding side by side when Cathy Coulter sped by us on her horse.

"Don't worry, I've got your back," said Tesa.

We laughed and watched as Cathy rounded the far end and sped around again. Jack Sampson was there on another horse waiting to escort her. He waved at us as we passed by on our way out.

We stopped back by the trailer as the boys were mounting to go warm up. Hanna and Tana were both by Tad. I could hear them giggling. Grant rode by and rolled his eyes.

Grant turned back to yell at Tad, "Oh brother dear, any time you can pry yourself loose, I would like to warm up."

"Be right there," said Tad. "Excuse me, ladies, I have to go." He mounted up, and the girls waved as he rode off.

"That's trouble brewing," I said to Tesa.

"Whatda ya mean?"

"Tad likes one of them; at least I think it's one, but he still likes Trish."

"Oh, I see," said Tesa. "Well, let's just stay back and enjoy the fireworks."

JD walked up. "You getting down?"

I smiled, got off, and Tesa rode over to her trailer. May Day nudged at JD and he laughed. "Hey nice to see ya, too," he said to May Day, pushing him aside. He smiled at me. "I wanted to ask you something before we get too busy."

"Oh?"

"Will you go out with me Sunday night?"

I smiled at him. "I thought you were leaving Sunday."

"I convinced my dad to stick around another day."

I smiled. "In that case, I'd like that a lot."

"Shall we try dinner and a movie again?"

"Sounds good."

"Hey, JD," said my dad, walking up to us. "Ready for tonight?"

"Yes, sir," he said. "One more time into the spinner!"

Dad turned to me. "I got something for you."

He walked to the trailer and came back with some shin guards. "Thought you might wanna start using these."

"Thanks!"

"Good idea," said JD. "Can't have those pretty legs getting banged up again."

"Here, I'll help you put them on," said Dad as he strapped them on.

"They're kinda big," I said, holding out my leg. "Do you really think this is necessary?"

"Humor me, will ya?" asked Dad.

"Okay," I said sighing.

"Now you better get over to the paddock."

"Yes, sir," I said, getting on May Day.

JD patted the shin guard on my leg. "They don't look so bad."

"I feel kinda stupid wearing these."

"He means well," said JD. "He was pretty shaken when you hit that barrel."

"I know."

"Hey, I don't wanna miss dancing with you, so please wear them for me."

I smiled at him. "Just for you then." I leaned over and kissed him.

"That's my girl!"

I turned and trotted over to the paddock. They were setting the barrels up.

Tesa rode up beside me. She had on shin guards, too. We looked at each other and laughed.

"Don't think you'll be needing those after all," said Dad walking up to us.
"Why not?"
"Look," he said, pointing at the barrels. There were red padded bumpers around the tops.

The announcer came on. "We would like to give a heartfelt thanks to the Big C Ranch for providing the new bumpers around our barrels. These will protect our young ladies from getting banged up should they have the misfortune of hitting a barrel tonight."

"That's awesome!" I said ripping off the shin guards and handing them to my dad. "Not that I'm not grateful, but I feel freer without them."

He laughed and took them from me. "Will you take mine, too?" asked Tesa.

"Sure." He laughed.

Tesa was right before me and set the best time for the night. She came out and we high-fived. "Your turn!" she said.

I nodded at her, took a deep breath, and patted May Day as we walked into the arena. I was the one who needed calming.

I took a breath, and May Day pranced a few steps. I turned him loose, and we flew around the barrels. I smiled the whole way back to the finish line. I didn't care how we did; I was glad to feel the freedom of running again.

Tesa high-fived me as I came out. "Back in the groove!" she cheered.

"Yeah, that felt good," I said. We passed Cathy being escorted by Jack Sampson. "Cathy, thank your father for the bumpers!" I shouted. She smiled and nodded slightly at me; Jack Sampson smiled really big and nodded at us.

"Guess she's still mad at me," I said to Tesa.

"Well, no loss," said Tesa.

We rode back to the trailers, got off, and I got May Day some water. Mark came up to us with JD behind him. "Sara!" yelled Mark. "You ran so fast!"

"Yeah, we did," I said, patting May Day.

"Feel good?" asked JD.

I smiled ear to ear and sighed. "Yeah, feels real good!"

"Whatcha gonna ride next?" asked Mark.

"Pole bending," I said. "Then we get to watch the boy's rope and after them, JD rides!"

"Then we get to dance!" said JD, his eyes twinkling.

"Then we dance," I said softly, looking at JD.

"Aw ya'll aren't gonna kiss now are ya?" whined Mark.

"It's nice kissing pretty girls."

"Yuck," said Mark. "I'm going back to sit with Mom." Mark strode off as we laughed.

"It's very nice kissing pretty girls," said JD as he stepped closer and kissed me.

Tesa yelled at me, "Hey, you better get ready for poles!"

"Coming!" I said as JD followed me to May Day and helped me get on.

"Go have fun!" he said, patting my leg. I smiled at him and trotted off to catch up with Tesa.

We rode around the practice arena a few times then made our way to the paddock. We took our turns. I was before Tesa this time. I ran really well. Tesa turned in a time just a few tenths of a second behind mine.

We were very happy with ourselves as we rode back to the trailers. Dad was there to help me unsaddle May Day.

"Did real good tonight," he said.

"Not done yet," I said. "One more night!"

We walked to the stands and watched the boys. JD was there with his family. I sat behind him and next to Tesa.

Grant was up first in calf roping and turned in a great time. After everyone was done, he was sitting in second place overall. The final round tomorrow night would determine the winner.

We watched the team roping. Matt and Mitch were up first and did great. Then Tad and Grant had a turn. Hanna and Tana giggled as they pointed at Tad; Tesa and I exchanged a look. Tad and Grant ended up just a smidge slower than Matt and Mitch.

I slapped JD on the back. "Your turn!"

He stood up and smiled. "Guess I better get to it!"

"We'll be rooting for ya." I touched my necklace as he smiled.

His dad pushed him on. "Come on boy! We gotta get in the groove!"

We watched the bareback bronc riders, then the saddle broncs, and finally the bull riding started. The first three riders didn't make it to the buzzer, but the next two finished with good scores. Then it was JD's turn. I watched him as if he was in slow motion, slow and graceful as the bull bucked and turned.

JD stuck to him like glue. It seemed like forever before the buzzer signaled the end of eight seconds. JD stepped off and waved as we stood, shouted, and clapped.

"Hey, did you notice other riders have black feathers in their hats now?" asked Tesa.

"No, I didn't." I looked at the cowboys around the chutes. Sure enough, there were several with black feathers in their hats instead the traditional turkey feathers others wore.

"You gonna change before the dance?" asked Tesa.

I looked down at my shirt that May Day had lovingly snorted on and nodded. "Yeah, I'll come with ya."

As we made our way out of the stands, Leena caught up with us. "Hey guys! You did real good tonight!"

"Thanks!"

"Where've you been?" Tesa asked her.

Leena blushed a little. "Hanging with Ken."

"Oh yeah? Grant too much for you?" I asked teasingly.

"Aw, he's always been out of my league," said Leena.

"Come on, we gotta change. Grab your stuff and meet us over there," Tesa said, pointing at their trailer.

I trotted over, grabbed my clean shirt out of the trailer, and then headed to the Martins. I knocked and Leena let me in. Tesa was primping in the mirror as I pulled off my dirty shirt and picked up the red one I had brought.

"Wow," said Leena. "Not gonna miss you tonight!" She smiled her approval as I pulled on the red shirt.

Tesa leaned around the corner of the bathroom to look. "Very nice! Want some lipstick to go with that?"

"Naw, I'm good."

"She doesn't want JD to have to keep wiping it off his face," said Leena.

I blushed as they laughed then I sighed. "What's the heavy sigh for?" asked Tesa.

"Just thinking how good life is right now."

"Not worried about JD leaving yet?" asked Leena.

"You should hear her speech," teased Tesa. "Go ahead, tell her."

Leena looked at me expectantly. "Let's hear it." I put on a serious face and recited it for her. Leena laughed at me. "Now tell me how you really feel," she said.

"I'm just gonna enjoy the time we have while he's here."

"Ya know he talked his dad into staying one more day, don't you?" asked Tesa.

"Yeah, he asked me out again on Sunday. One last date!" I sighed and smiled. "Then we," I pointed to the three of us, "get to go back to school!"

"That's the spirit!" said Leena as we laughed, walking out of the trailer just as JD and the boys were walking up.

"Hey, champs!" said Leena.

"Hey, cowgirls!" said Grant. "Ready for some dancing?"

"You bet!" said Tesa.

I smiled at JD. "Absolutely."

After the boys changed, we went to the dance hall. JD held my hand on the way over and pulled me right onto the floor. As we waltzed around the dance floor, I was lost in his blue eyes and was in heaven. The song ended and JD walked me over to where our friends had gathered. Mr. Dalton was there.

"Mind if I dance with your girl?" he asked JD.

"Not at all," he said, "but you better ask her. She's the independent type."

I smiled at them as Mr. Dalton turned to me and held out his hand. "Would you care to dance?"

I put my hand in his. "I would, thank you!"

We were on the dance floor on the far side away from the others when Mr. Dalton said, "I hope you're not gonna break my boy's heart when we leave."

I looked up at him and saw compassion in his eyes. "Lord knows my brothers tried their hardest to keep us apart, but our heart is our first teacher. I followed my heart and JD followed his. It was meant for JD and me to meet, even if it was just for a while."

He smiled down at me. "Dang if you aren't as smart as you are pretty." He laughed as I blushed. "So tell me, you gonna win the barrels and poles tomorrow night, too?"

"I'm gonna try!" I said smiling. "But Tesa is giving me a run for it."

He laughed. "Yeah, those Martins are a competitive bunch." We whirled around. "So you worried about the Coulter girl at all?"

"Cathy? Naw, she's never been much of a rider. Her dad buys her everything she wants, including push-button horses."

"Hmm, guess us daddies can't help ourselves when it comes to our little girls"

"Well, 'us girls' want our daddies attention and approval more than things."

Mr. Dalton nodded. "I can see you've got your daddy's attention and approval."

I smiled at him as the song ended. He escorted me back to the others. Jared grabbed me and off we went before I could protest.

"Yes, Jared, I'd love to dance!" I said sarcastically.

"You're quite welcome," he said laughing. "Oh don't get all in a twist. I wanted to be sure I got one dance with you tonight."

I laughed at him. "I could never stay mad at you."

"Because I'm so loveable?"

"Yes, Jared, because you're so loveable." We laughed again. When the song was over, JD whirled me out onto the floor.

"So what did you and my father talk about?" he asked.

I looked up at him and decided it wasn't the time to tell him what he really said. "He asked me if I was gonna win at barrels and poles tomorrow. I told him I was gonna try."

"Is that all?"

"He also asked if I was worried about the Coulters. I told him she was a spoiled daddy's girl but not much of a rider."

We whirled around for a minute then JD pulled me closer and whispered in my ear. "What else aren't you telling me?"

I pulled back smiling up at him. "How do you know there's more?"

"Because you're a terrible liar." He laughed at me.

"I didn't lie!"

"You just didn't tell me everything." He laughed again. "I'm not mad." He sighed, pulled me to him, and said in my ear, "I just wanna know what's on your mind."

I swallowed and looked over his shoulder. "He's worried I'll break your heart," I whispered.

JD laughed and hugged me to him. I sensed I had nothing to be afraid of and relief flooded through me. We smiled at each other and didn't say anything else.

The song ended and Dad took my hand. "Might I claim a dance?"

"Of course!" I said and we were off around the floor.

"Before I forget to ask you later, is it alright if I go with JD to dinner and movie on Sunday?"

Dad looked down at me. "You're not going to get broken hearted when he says good-bye, are you?"

"Why does everyone keep asking me that?"

"Probably because it's a small town and we're nosy." He chuckled. "But mostly because we care. Now who is everyone?"

"Tesa, Leena, and Mr. Dalton," I said.

"Jesse?" asked Dad surprised.

"Yeah, just a minute ago."

Dad laughed and squeezed my hand. "He's just a father who cares."

We danced for a minute. "You haven't answered my question yet."

"Oh that," Dad said. "I suppose you should go."

"Thanks, Dad!"

"Now tell me what is going on with Tad."

"Oh well, he thinks he likes Hanna, though I'm not sure he knows which one she is, but he still likes Trish too."

Dad looked down at me. "And you can tell the twins apart?"

"Yeah, can't you?"

"No, smarty, I can't. Jesse was complaining he can't half the time either. So tell me how are they different?"

"Hanna has a gold fleck in her right eye and Tana doesn't."

Dad chuckled. "I should tell Jesse that."

"Yeah, you should," I laughed. "Even JD hadn't noticed."

"And you didn't share this with Tad?"

"No way!" I said. "I told him to stay out of my love life, so I'm staying out of his."

Dad laughed and whirled me around as the song ended. He left me with my friends and took Mom for a spin. JD came up to me. "I need a drink. You want one?"

"I do," I said and followed him out to the concession stand.

"So what did you and your dad talk about so seriously?" asked JD, scooting closer to face me.

"I asked him if I could go with you Sunday. He said yes by the way, but it seems the theme for the night is us being broken hearted when we part."

"Who else has been asking you about that?"

"Tesa, Leena, then your dad, and now my dad."

"So what should we do?"

"Just enjoy each other's company while were together." I looked in his twinkling blue eyes.

"I will!" he said and kissed me.

The band took a break and people came out of the dance hall. The gang all joined us.

After a little bit, the band started up again and we went back inside and danced. I started with JD, danced with Mitch, and then it was back and forth between JD and other guys I knew. I was back in JD's arms again.

"I feel like a yo-yo," I said.

"Your fans want you," said JD.

"I just wanna be alone with you for a while."

JD led me off the dance floor. Mom and Dad hadn't left yet, so we went to sit on the back of our truck. I sighed as we sat down. JD pulled me to him and kissed me lightly. I put my arms around him, and he kissed me harder. My heart pounded, and the warmth in me simmered. He pulled back and as I slowly opened my eyes to look into his, I saw a tenderness and sincerity.

"Your eyes," he said, "I could get lost in them."

"I get lost in yours often."

He smiled slowly, kissed me tenderly, and hugged me to him. "I'm really trying to resist running off with you right now."

I laughed. "Where would we go?"

"I don't know," he said, rocking me. "Mexico?"

"You speak Spanish?"

"I can get by," he said. "Can you?"

"I do alright with the migrant workers that come by to work."

"Mexico it is then. We'll get a shanty on the beach and fish for our food."

"No horses?"

"Animals would come from miles around to be near you." We laughed.

Mom and Dad walked up. "Having a good time?" asked Dad.

"Yes, sir," I said. "You leaving already?" We slid off the tailgate.

"Already?" asked Mom "It's almost midnight."

"Wow, time has flown," I said. "We'll help you load the horses."

When we got the horses loaded, they waved and drove off. I turned to JD. "Let's go dance a little more," he said and took my hand.

We walked back to the dance. When we got to the floor, the band started playing *When I Close My Eyes*.

"They're playing our song," said JD.

"Let's not waste it." He held me close as we danced. When the song ended, he hugged me and we walked over to the gang.

"Have you seen Tad?" asked Grant.

"He was walking by the trailers with Hanna and Tana a little while ago."

"What?" asked Grant? He looked at JD. "And you didn't say anything to him?"

"Nope, it was none of my business. Don't you trust your brother?"

Grant frowned and patted JD on the shoulder. "You're a better man than I am JD, but I'm more afraid of what your sisters might do to Tad."

About three dances later, Tad showed up by himself; his hair was messy and his shirt wasn't buttoned right. Grant grabbed him and dragged him back outside. JD followed my gaze.

"Just don't think about it," he said to me.

"What do you think happened?" I asked.

"I don't know and don't want to know," said JD. Then his sisters came in. They were talking and laughing with each other and looking around.

"See nothing to worry about," said JD.

The lights came up as the band announced they were going to play one more song. JD looked at me. "I've really had enough for tonight," I said.

He nodded. "Let's go see where the rest of our crew is."

We walked out to our trucks; JD and I leaned against the Suburban and waited for the others. We were looking at the stars when Grant and

Tad walked up. Tad was smiling, but Grant didn't look happy. Over their shoulders, I could see Tesa, Matt, and Mitch. Trailing behind them were Hanna and Tana.

"Well, this will be a fun ride home," I said to JD.

"Been a heck of a night," said Matt. "Guess we should shove off so we can come back and do it again tomorrow!" He got into the driver's seat; the twins waved and got in behind Matt.

JD turned to me kissed me quickly. "See ya tomorrow!"

"I'll be here!" I said and got in the back seat of the Suburban. Grant drove off as soon as I shut the door. I sat back and watched out the window until we were well outside of town. No one had said a word for a good five minutes.

"Well, are we not on speaking terms?" I asked.

"Nothing to say," said Grant in a flat tone.

Tad snorted. "You had plenty to say earlier."

"You made a fool of yourself," said Grant.

"I had a good time," said Tad. "I was only showing the girls a good time."

"Yeah and now you've hurt Trish; she doesn't deserve you," said Grant.

"Oh, I didn't think about Trish," he said regretfully.

"Yeah, you didn't think!"

No one spoke for a long time. When we were crossing the river, Tad asked, "Do you think Trish will forgive me?"

Grant looked at Tad then back at me. "I'm not so sure it would be any time soon," said Grant.

Tad looked at me. "I tried to warn you before," I said. "Our first teacher is our own heart. Obviously you didn't follow yours."

"Where did you hear that?" asked Grant.

"Uncle Buck," I said.

"Hmm, good advice."

As we drove up to the house, Foxy bounded over to me and I rubbed her head. She looked at Tad and sneezed. I was closing my back door when Tad pushed on it.

"Can I talk to you?" he asked.

"Sure."

He came in, sat on my bed, and I sat down beside him. Foxy put her head on my lap and I petted her, waiting for Tad to speak.

"I really screwed up," he said. I didn't say anything. After a second he continued. "I don't know what I should do."

"Well, at least apologize to Trish. You owe her that much."

Tad looked at me. "But you don't even know what I did."

"No, I don't know all that happened. I don't want to know. I do know you hurt Trish." Tad nodded. I put my arm around him. "You'll survive this. The important thing is you realize and admit your mistake then you don't go do it again."

Tad just sat there.

"That was a hint for you to get up and leave," I said.

He stood up and I hugged him. "I'll be right here," I said.

"Thanks," he said as he walked out and closed the door.

I changed, crawled into bed, and Foxy put her head on my stomach.

"What are we gonna do with these boys?" She sniffed. "Yeah, that's what I think."

I was lying on a beach with the waves whooshing in as a soft breeze wafted across me. There was splashing; I rolled to my side and held my hand to shade my eyes. I saw JD riding toward me on a dun-colored horse. He had on a straw hat, cutoffs, no shirt or shoes, and his bronzed muscles rippled as he jumped off the horse. He held his hand out to me as he gave me a dazzling smile. I reached up and took his hand; he pulled me up into his arms and opened his mouth to speak…

"You getting up?" asked Grant, leaning in my door.

I rolled over and blinked. It was bright; the sun was already up. I had actually slept in.

"Well?"

"Yeah, what time is it?"

"About eight."

"Why didn't anyone wake me up earlier?" I asked, sitting up.

Grant shrugged. "Not much needed to be done." He was standing at the foot of my bed now, looking like he had something on his mind.

"Well, spit it out," I said.

"Spit what out?"

"Whatever's on your mind."

"Oh, well, uh, I haven't told Mom or Dad what Tad did last night. I'm not sure how to tell them before they hear it from someone else."

"And you want me to help you out?" I asked. "I don't exactly know what happened, and I'm not sure I wanna know."

"Well, maybe I should tell you so you can help us all," said Grant, sitting on my bed. I kept quiet while he gathered his thoughts.

"I warned Tad when Hanna and Tana both started flirting with him. He didn't listen; he just kept flirting back. Last night, well you saw him hanging on both of them at once." Grant shook his head and sighed. "He got in an argument with Trish. She was sitting in her car when I walked by at a break at the dance. I stopped and talked to her."

Grant looked at me and pointed his finger. "She told me she caught Tad making out with both of the girls!"

Grant was really worked up and breathing hard now. I was stunned but didn't know what to say.

"I went to look for him, that's when I saw you on the dance floor and asked if you'd seen Tad."

Grant clenched and unclenched his jaws. "Then he shows up all messy and his shirt's buttoned all wrong!" Grant took a couple of breaths then he stood up and paced. "I drug him outside, yelled at him, and pointed to his shirt. All he did was smile! He just smiled at me like it was no big thing!"

He turned to me with his hands on his hips. "What should we do?"

"We?" I said pointing to myself. I shook my head and waved my finger. "Oh no, not we. We should stay out of this. We already said enough last night."

Grant stared at me, annoyed. "We need to tell Mom and Dad before someone else does."

"What would you tell them?" I asked, resigned to the fact that they should hear about some of this.

"At least that he was making a fool of himself with the twins," said Grant.

I nodded. "I guess that would be wise. However, I don't think they need to hear the other details, except maybe that Tad argued with Trish and hurt her feelings."

"Okay, I guess we can leave the details out. I don't want Tad getting into more trouble."

"Have you seen or talked to Tad this morning?"

"When I got up, he wasn't in his room. His bed was made and the horses had been fed, but I haven't seen him yet."

"Trucks all here?"

"Yeah, why?"

"I talked to him last night after we got home."

"You did?"

I nodded. "He felt really bad about hurting Trish. I told him he at least owed her an apology. I wondered if he'd driven into town to go apologize."

"Wonder where he is?" said Grant.

"My guess would be down by the river bend, skipping rocks."

Grant chuckled and nodded. "Yeah, he's probably there licking his wounds."

"Okay, so you tell Dad and I'll tell Mom. Deal?"

"Deal." He turned and walked from the room.

I got dressed and wandered down the hall to find Mom. She was loading pictures from the past week onto her computer. She looked up as I walked in.

"Hey Sunshine, 'bout time you got up. There's biscuits and gravy if you want."

"Thanks, I'll get some in a minute."

"What's up? I can hear it in your tone."

"It's not me, it's Tad." I sat down. "He did something last night that I think you should know about before you hear it from the local gossip chain."

"Oh?"

I looked down and took a breath, "He was cavorting around with the Dalton twins last night and upset Trish."

"I see," said Mom. "Is that all?"

"Well, there's more. I really don't know all the facts, so let's just leave it at that. Grant and I did talk to Tad last night on the way home about what went on and then I talked to Tad alone before we went to bed. He felt really bad about hurting Trish and acting like a jerk."

"Hmm, guess that's why we haven't seen Tad this morning," said Mom. She sighed and looked at me. "Growing up is all about learning what and what not to do, you just gotta use your head."

"I think in this case he should have followed his heart," I said. "He really does care for Trish. Whether she'll forgive him," I shrugged. "Well, it would take me some time."

Mom smiled. "You guys are growing up so fast!"

I nodded and smiled. I looked down at my hands thinking. "What else is going on in that head?" she asked.

I looked up at her. "I was just thinking that no one asked what the Dalton girls felt about all this, let alone their accountability for their part in it."

"Why do you say that?"

"Well, when they were here the other day, they were asking me if Tad and Grant had girlfriends. I said that Tad did, but Grant didn't. It's like," I sighed, "it seems looking back on it that they planned this."

I looked up at Mom and she was shocked.

"I don't mean to try to shift blame. I know it takes two, or in this case three, but I just can't help feeling that they stirred this up on purpose."

"Whoa," said Mom, sitting back. "What did JD have to say about this?"

"I haven't discussed it with him. He's said all along that his sisters were a handful."

Mom laughed and shook her head. "Oh the drama of our small-town life." She sighed. "Has anyone spoken to your dad?"

"Grant is going to," I said. "What do you think will happen now?"

"Well, I guess the best thing to do is wait to see what Tad does," said Mom. "I'll speak with your father, but that's what I think we should do."

"I'm gonna get some breakfast." I stood up and looked over Mom's shoulder at a picture on her computer screen. It was of Foxy sitting on the roof of the truck with the sunset behind her.

"Mom, that's beautiful. Can I have a big print of that?"

"I was thinking of entering that one in a photo contest coming up, so I'll get a really big print." She smiled at me.

"Thanks! That would be nice." I went into the kitchen and got some breakfast. I was finishing eating when I saw Foxy run across the lawn, jump the fence, and run off down toward the river. I got up and went to investigate.

I walked across the yard and down the slope. I heard angry voices coming from the river. As I got closer, I could tell it was Grant and Tad.

As I cleared the trees at the bottom of the slope, Tad and Grant looked up at me; both had angry looks on their faces.

Tad was wearing the same clothes he had on last night. He must have stayed up all night. Boy, this must really be bothering him. The boys waited until I got closer before anyone said anything.

"So what's going on?" I asked, trying to be neutral.

"Ask him!" said Tad, pointing at Grant.

I looked at Grant; he shook his head. I looked back at Tad.

"Did you get any sleep last night?" I asked Tad.

He shook his head. "No, I've been up all night thinking about what you said."

"Did you come to any conclusion?"

"Just that I'm sorry I hurt Trish," he said, looking down with a pained look on his face.

I looked down for a moment then back at Grant. He shrugged and I looked at Tad. "Do you get the feeling that you might have been manipulated?"

"What?" said Grant and Tad in unison. They had the same shocked look on their faces.

"Explain," said Grant, crossing his arms over his chest.

"Well, remember when the Daltons came home with us after the horse show?"

"Yeah," they said.

"Well, when the girls and I went into my room, they asked me if either of you had a girlfriend. I told them that Tad did, but Grant didn't."

"So?" said Grant.

"So, that coupled with the few things JD has told me about his sisters and what Tesa has said, I get the feeling that they might have stirred things up on purpose."

"Aaaaawwwww! No way!" said Tad, throwing his hands in the air.

"It's just a theory," I said. "I thought that there might be another side to this."

I heard Mom calling, "Sara! Sara!"

"I better go see what she wants." I turned and ran back toward the house.

"Coming!" I yelled when I was half way up the slope and ran into the back of the house.

As the screen door slammed behind me, Mom yelled, "Phone's for you."

I trotted to the hallway and picked up the phone. "Hello?"

"Hey Sara, how's my sunshine?" asked JD.

My heart sang and my stomach flipped a few times. "I'm doing great. To what do I owe this pleasure?"

JD chuckled. "I know I said I wasn't going to get involved in this, but I'm afraid I have to. Seems my sisters have some stake in last night's activities."

"Thought so."

He chuckled. "Nothing gets past you does it?"

"Oh a lot does, but please continue."

"Well, they'll be leaving shortly, so that end will be tied up. But I need Trish's number so they can apologize."

I laughed. "This *is* a soap opera; let me get that number for you." I flipped through the phone book and found Trish's number. "You have a pencil and paper?"

"I do."

"Okay, here it is." I read off the phone number.

"Got it," he said. "Now the family will be by to pay a visit on their way out of town."

"Wait, are you leaving, too?" I asked, terrified to hear the answer.

"No, no! I'm staying. I have to ride tonight." Relief flooded through me, and I thought I might slide to the floor. "Besides, we still have a date."

"Oh," I took a breath. "You scared me there for a minute."

He chuckled. "I couldn't leave without a proper good-bye."

I smiled. "Good. Uh so, when shall we expect you?"

"Around eleven I think."

"Okay, I'll warn the folks."

"You do that." There was a pause. "We might need to take my brothers and go find something else to do for a little bit."

"Not a problem. We've plenty to explore or rope around here."

He laughed. "Always the hostess. See ya later."

"Okay, bye."

"Sara?" called Mom.

"Yes, ma'am?" I walked down the hall.

"What was that all about?" she asked.

I explained to her what JD had said and how they were coming by to apologize. "Oh, guess I better get some refreshments ready," she said, getting up from her chair.

"Mom, they're coming to apologize then to leave. This isn't gonna be very sociable."

"Well, doesn't hurt us to be hospitable," she said, smiling as she passed me. "A cold drink is the least I can do."

I smiled and turned to follow her. "I'll go tell Tad and Grant they're coming. Tad needs to shower. He stayed up all night worrying over this."

"He did?" asked Mom, turning to me. "How do you know?"

"He's got on the same clothes as yesterday, there're dark circles under his eyes, and his bed is made."

"Oh! Well, where is he?"

"I was down by the river breaking up an argument between Grant and Tad when you called me to the phone. I'll just go back and tell them, and I better let Dad know, too."

"Leave your father to me," she said and turned to walk out the front door.

I ran out the back and down to the river and found Tad and Grant skipping rocks. They turned as they heard me run up.

"You're partially off the hook," I said to Tad.

"What? How?" asked Tad.

"Seems two blondes confessed, or something like that," I said. "JD called to say that they're on their way out of town, but first they're stopping by here to apologize."

"They're leaving?"

"JD's staying and I think his dad is, too, but the rest are leaving," I said. Tad hung his head.

"What's wrong now?" I asked.

"I can't believe I fell for it," he said.

"Yeah, well neither can we," said Grant, patting him on the shoulder. "But we're here with ya."

"Uh Tad," he looked up at me. "You might wanna shower and change before they get here." He nodded.

I decided I didn't want to be around when the twins arrived, so I headed for the barn. Foxy bounded ahead of me on the way. Several horses greeted me as I entered the barn. I walked over to Andrea's stall;

she nudged me, I patted her, and walked into her stall. I put my head to her belly hoping to hear something like a heartbeat. I heard some swooshing.

"Hear something good?" asked Dad.

I turned to look at him. "Shouldn't you be able to hear a heartbeat?"

"I'm sure if you have a stethoscope you could hear a lot," he said. I patted Andrea and Dad walked toward me. "I wanted to get your take on what happened last night."

"Oh no, I'm staying out of this," I said. "I'm not about to take sides."

"No one is asking you to take sides. I'm just asking for your opinion."

"Oh well, I'm not sure I know much."

"Tell me what you do know."

"I know that Tad was flirting with both the Dalton twins. I did see him with his arms around both of them. I know Grant isn't happy about Tad hurting Trish with the way he acted, and I do know that both Hanna and Tana knew that Tad had a girlfriend because I told them he did."

"And that's all?"

"Yes, sir. That's all I know for a fact."

He laughed. "But you suspected something about the twins to start with?"

"I, um, I didn't think too much about it until this morning. I, uh, wasn't paying attention to Tad last night."

Dad smiled at me. "I could see that." We heard a vehicle coming then another one following it. "Well, guess we better go see what's what." He turned to go. "Aren't you coming?"

"I'd rather not. Send JD and his brothers down here, and we'll stay out of the way."

"Okay," said Dad with a somber face.

He walked off and I leaned on Andrea. "Oh why do we humans do this to ourselves?" Andrea turned to look at me and snorted. "I agree!" I decided to get a brush and give Andrea some attention while I waited.

I was brushing Andrea when I heard, "Sara, Sara!" I smiled as I walked over to the stall door. "Hey Mark!" I leaned over the door to watch him run up the aisle.

Mark stopped at the door. "Can I ride her?"

"Sure can!" I said opening the door as JD and Mitch walked in. "Hey, you two wanna ride?" I asked.

"Um, yeah," said Mitch with a shy smile.

"Okay, let's get you a horse!" I said to Mitch as I walked toward them. I looked at JD and he was smiling. "What can I get for you?" I asked him.

"Oh, I'll just take this," he grabbed me, dipped me over, and kissed me. I laughed as he stood me up again.

Mark came out of the tack room holding a bridle. "Is this the one for Andrea?" he asked.

I looked at it. "Yes, that's it," I said. "Can you put it on by yourself?"

"You bet," said Mark and he walked over to Andrea's stall.

"I'll go see he does it right," said JD.

I turned to Mitch. "How about you ride May Day?"

"Don't you have to ride him in the rodeo tonight?" asked Mitch as we walked into the tack room.

"Yeah, but he can handle a little extra exercise." I got his bridle and handed it to Mitch. "I'm sure you know how to do this."

He smiled at me. "Yeah I do." Then he went over to May Day's stall.

We got the horses brushed and saddled. Mark and Mitch rode into the arena as JD and I sat on the bench in front of the barn to watch.

"Wonder what's going on up at the house," said JD.

I looked at him. "Thought you wanted to stay out of it."

"I just wonder if this will make your parents think differently about me," he said.

"I doubt it. My dad is one to judge each person by his own merits and actions. He already thinks a lot of you, and my mom always looks beyond the surface of any situation. She understands we all make mistakes in learning how to live our lives."

He smiled at me and took my hand. "I guess that's why you're with this very understanding family. You should remember that when they realize what you can do."

I smiled at JD and we watched his brothers ride around the arena. It wasn't long before Grant came driving down in a truck, stopped, and got out.

"Well?" I asked, "Is the detente over?"

"The what?" asked Grant with a puzzled look.

"I gotta get you guys to read more." I shook my head. "The meeting? Is it over?"

"Oh that, yeah," said Grant. "The meeting's over. They're ready to leave, and I came to get the boys."

"So everything turned out okay?" asked JD.

"I guess as well as can be expected," said Grant. "I think they stirred up more than they intended." He sighed. "I think Tad got the worst end of it, but he'll get over it."

"Well, let's get the boys." I stood up and I called the boys over.

"Aw, do we have to go?" whined Mark.

"Sorry kid," said JD. "It's a long ride back home, and you need to leave now."

"Can't I stay with you and Dad?" asked Mark.

"Mom already told you no," said JD. Mark nodded and reluctantly got off Andrea. He led her over to the tack room, and Grant unsaddled her.

"Why don't you walk her back to her stall and say good-bye?" I said to Mark handing him the reins. Mark nodded, smiled weakly, and then led Andrea down the aisle with Foxy trotting behind them.

JD had unsaddled May Day, and Mitch was leading him to his stall. "Thanks for letting me ride today," said Mitch, stopping beside me.

"You're welcome," I said, smiling at him.

"Can I come back and see the foal when it's born?" asked Mitch.

"You sure can," I said. "I'll let you know as soon as it happens."

Mitch smiled and led May Day on to his stall. We got in the truck and rode up to the house.

Dad and Mr. Dalton were on the front porch talking. "Hello, Mr. Dalton," I said as we walked up.

He smiled at us. "Ready to win tonight?"

"I'm gonna give it my best try," I said.

He smiled and we walked on into the house. The girls were on the couch looking bored. I heard Mom and Mrs. Dalton laughing down the hall.

"Anyone want a drink?" I asked. The girls shook their heads, so I went into the kitchen. JD and Grant followed. We got sodas and were opening them when Mom and Mrs. Dalton came in.

Mrs. Dalton was holding some pictures. She looked at JD, "Marcy got some great shots of you riding, JD. She was kind enough to print me a few and I have a CD of more."

JD smiled, "Let's see what you picked out." He held out his hand and took the pictures; one was of him riding in Rocksprings. There were a few others of him roping on May Day. He looked up at Mom, "You really should consider selling these at the rodeos."

"I'm just a hack," said Mom.

"No, really, you should," said Mrs. Dalton. "These are better than most I've seen at the rodeos."

"Well I might someday," said Mom.

Mrs. Dalton came over to me. "You should consider modeling. You have an inner glow that really comes through in pictures. I could recommend a good agent."

"I don't know what to say," I looked at Mom over Mrs. Dalton's shoulder. She was smiling at me.

"We'll call you if we think we might want to pursue that," said Mom.

"You do that," said Mrs. Dalton. "You are special and don't let anyone ever tell you you're not." She hugged me. "Good luck tonight."

"Thank you."

"We better get on the road," said Mrs. Dalton, turning to the rest of them. We followed them out to their Escalade.

Mark gave me a hug before he got in. "I'll see ya after Christmas," I said. He smiled and got in. All but JD and Mr. Dalton were leaving. We waved as they drove off.

"How about some lunch?" asked Mom as we turned to go back into the house.

"Where's Tad?" I asked Grant as I walked down the hall, but Tad wasn't in his room. I guessed he must be down by the river again. I turned around to go back to the kitchen and ran into JD.

"Oh, sorry," I said.

"I'm not," he said and pulled me to him. "Looking for something?"

"Just wondering where Tad was," I smiled up at him.

"He might want to be alone for a little while," said JD. I nodded and he hugged me to him. "Come on, let's get some lunch. Got to keep up your strength."

"Oh, for what?" I asked as we walked back down the hall.

"To win tonight!"

"We'll see," I said. JD laughed as we entered the kitchen.

I helped Mom make sandwiches. We sat and ate minus Tad. Mr. Dalton and Dad were exchanging stories about work stuff. Dad used to work as a civil engineer for Uvalde County, so he and Mr. Dalton had lots in common. Tad still hadn't shown up after we finished, so I wrapped up a sandwich and told Mom I was going to go find him. She nodded at me.

"Want me to come?" asked JD.

"Naw, I won't be long," I said. "Just wanna see that he eats something."

"Okay, I'll be here," he said. I smiled and went to go find Tad.

I headed out the back and down to the river. Sure enough, Tad was sitting on some rocks throwing pebbles into the river.

"Hungry?" I asked as I approached.

He turned to look at me. "Not really," he said.

I sat down beside him. "You should try anyway." I held the sandwich in front of him.

He took it from me. "Thanks," he said around a mouthful.

I rubbed his back. "It's gonna be alright ya know."

He snorted. "I still can't believe I let myself get into this mess."

"You were mesmerized by two very pretty faces. Ones with experience."

"And I was giving you advice earlier this summer," he said meekly.

"We all make mistakes," I said. "It's what you learn from them that counts." He nodded. "You should come take a nap. You still have to ride tonight."

He sighed. "Yeah I'm beat." He got up and followed me back to the house. We went in the back and down the back porch. I stopped at my room and saw JD lying across my bed, looking at a sketchbook I hadn't touched in a long time.

He looked up as I walked in. "Hope you don't mind," he said.

I shrugged and sat down beside him. "I haven't drawn in a long while," I said.

"You're pretty good," he said looking at my drawings. He stopped at one of a horse running. "When did you do this?"

I pointed to a date in the corner of the picture. It was over six months ago. He looked at me incredulously.

"What?" I asked. "It's just some horse."

"This is my horse. See this?" He pointed to a mark on the horse's flank.

"Yeah?"

"That's the Smith-Gilman brand," he said. It looked like an open parenthesis with a bar connected to an "s." "That's where I bought Smitty."

I looked closer at the picture. It wasn't in color. It was the horse from my dream last night.

"What color is he?" I asked.

"Dun. Why?"

"I had a dream and he was in it," I said.

"When?" asked JD smiling.

"Last night."

"Tell me," he said. I told him about being on the beach and him riding this horse up to me. He laughed. "Mexico, here we come!"

"Shhh!" I said. "They won't let us alone if they think we might run off."

We laughed and looked at other pictures I had drawn. There were various animals and a few of Foxy. "You have so many talents," he said.

"I've learned to develop the few I have."

"So pretty and so humble," he said.

"What's going on in here?" asked Grant walking in.

"Sara is showing me her drawings," said JD. "Bet you haven't seen these." He turned the sketchbook so Grant could see.

"No, I haven't," said Grant as he took the sketchbook and sat down on my bed. He flipped through the pages. "These are really good."

"Thanks!" I said. I looked over at the clock. "Gosh! Look at the time. I better get ready."

Grant and JD stood up. "We better leave her alone or it will take forever," said Grant. They walked out; I grabbed my clothes and went to the bathroom to take a shower.

I hummed to myself as I got ready. I looked in on Tad and he was sound asleep. I woke him and put a Coke in front of him. "Here, drink this!" I said. "It'll help wake you up."

"Thanks," he said groggily and sat up.

I walked back into the kitchen and found Mom packing up her camera. "So you gonna start a business selling rodeo pictures?" I asked.

She laughed. "I think they were just being polite."

"I don't. I think you should try. You'd have fun."

"I'll think about it," she said.

We loaded up the Suburban. Dad, Grant, and JD pulled up with the trailer.

Grant rode with Dad, Tad rode with Mom, and JD and I rode with Mr. Dalton.

JD got out and held the gate for Mom and the truck and trailer. As we waited, Mr. Dalton said, "Got a great place out here. Real pretty and quiet."

"I like it," I said. "Even without the cell phones and cable, we do alright."

Mr. Dalton laughed. "Wish I could move out here and turn off cell phones for a while."

"The ranch to the south of us is for sale. Cell phones don't work out here."

"Careful, you might have Daltons as neighbors," he said.

"I think that would be great!"

"Even with the trouble my girls have caused?" he asked.

I laughed. "They didn't do much harm."

We pulled onto the rodeo grounds and parked between the Martins and our trailer. Tesa waved at me as I got out.

"What's up?" I asked.

"How did the apologies go?"

"Good, I guess."

"What did they say?"

"I don't know. I wasn't there."

"What?"

"I didn't want to be around, so I was at the barn with JD and his brothers."

"Wanna know how it came out at my house?"

"Not really, but I know you're dying to tell someone."

She told me how she overheard the twins talking about how they had hooked Tad and were about to reel him in. They said it was too easy to wrap these country boys around their fingers. That's when she interrupted them. Matt overheard them arguing and then everyone else in the house was in on it.

"Oh is that all?" I said.

"I'm glad they're gone."

"Well" I said, "it doesn't pay to mess with our brothers."

We heard the announcer calling everyone to get ready for the grand entry. "We better get ready," I said.

We were trotting around the practice arena when Cathy Coulter passed. She ran by, turned, and ran past again. "I hope she wins and will let it be for once," I said.

"What?" said Tesa shocked.

"I'm tired of her showing off," I said. "I think if she won, she might get it out of her system some."

"I think it would only make it worse," said Tesa. "She would hold it over our heads all the time."

"Yeah, you might be right." I sighed.

We rode over to the paddock and waited for them to start the barrel racing. Cathy came up, escorted by Jack Sampson. He nodded at us, but Cathy ignored us.

One of the rodeo clowns walked behind us and honked his horn. Cathy's horse reared, jerking the reins away from Jack. Cathy tried to calm him, but he reared again dumping her on the ground and taking off.

Jack was helping Cathy, so I took off to catch Custer, Cathy's horse. Tesa was right behind me. I pointed for her to circle to the right so we could herd him toward the practice arena away from the highway.

Custer, not about to stop for anything, ran flat out into the practice arena and up to the fence. He reared at the fence, pawing at it, catching his shoe on the wire, and falling to the side. He was struggling to get up and whinnying in panic.

I slid to a stop on May Day, jumped off, and walked slowly toward Custer.

"Easy, Custer, easy."

He was kicking and screaming. He got more tangled in the fence.

"Hey, Custer! Enough!"

He stopped and snorted. I stepped up quickly and grabbed his head. A surge of warmth ran down my arms into him.

"Easy guy, you're okay. It's okay. Easy." He struggled a little as I pushed more warmth into him. He settled some.

Tesa rode up. "We need some wire cutters." She spun around and rode off.

As several people ran up, Custer struggled again. "Stay back." I said.

Dad and Doc came up. "He's tangled in the fence," I said.

Dad nodded and Doc came up beside me. Custer struggled again. "Easy fella, easy," I said. Then to Doc, "I think we need to keep everyone back because it's only making him panic more."

We could see the whites of Custer's eyes, and he was breathing hard. Tesa came back with some cutters and her dad riding behind her.

Mr. Martin came over with the wire cutters, but Custer wouldn't let anyone near his feet. There was a wire wrapped around one of his legs, and it was cutting into the flesh.

"I'll get my bag. We'll have to tranquilize him," Doc said.

Custer struggled again. "Easy big fella, easy does it," I could feel his panic and pain.

I took a deep breath, concentrated, and pushed the panic and pain back. I could feel the heat rising in me, and I concentrated on tamping it down. I couldn't lose control.

It seemed like a long time before Doc came back. He filled a syringe, knelt down, and injected Custer in the neck. I felt the rush of the tranquilizer run through Custer. He relaxed and I got dizzy. I raised my hands and Dad steadied me.

He caught my hand, and his eyes went wide. "You're on fire," he whispered. I smiled slightly, nodded, and turned back to Custer. He was breathing better now, and his eyes weren't rolling around anymore.

I pulled my hand from Dad's and patted Custer. "We should cut him loose now," said Doc.

I stood up and Dad steadied me. JD was standing right behind him with an expectant look on his face. We moved back as Doc and Mr. Martin cut Custer loose from the fence. I stepped forward again as the wire around Custer's front leg came loose and blood spurted out. It splashed across me, and I grabbed the cut before Doc.

A surge of fire ran down my arm into my hand; blood dripped between my fingers then stopped. Doc handed me some gauze and I put it over the cut and pressed down. When they pulled the fence out of the way, Custer tried to get up. Dad held him down as Doc came around to check the rest of Custer over.

"I'm gonna need to stitch that cut on his foreleg," said Doc. "But other than that, he seems okay."

"Shall we let him up?" asked Dad.

"Let's just let him lay there," said Doc. He looked up at the crowd. "Can I get a flashlight?"

It wasn't a minute before a flashlight was handed over, and Mr. Martin held it as Doc inspected the wound in Custer's leg. I assisted Doc as he stitched up Custer with a few deft moves.

When he was snipping the thread, Jack Sampson came up. "How is he?" he asked.

"He's gonna be fine," said Doc. "Got himself tangled in the fence here, and we're just finishing stitching him up. I had to give him a tranquilizer before he would let us cut him loose."

"Thank goodness," said Jack.

"How's Cathy?" I asked.

"She might have broken her arm," he said. "Mr. C is taking her into Uvalde."

"We'll help you get Custer up and into your trailer," said Mr. Martin.

"I appreciate that," said Jack.

Doc wrapped up Custer's leg then nodded to Dad to let him up. Custer just lay there. I walked forward and rubbed my hands on his neck.

"Time to get up!" I said and a burst of tingles ran down my arms into Custer. He snorted and I patted him. He rolled to his belly and shook his head and then he heaved himself to his feet.

Jack caught his reins and patted him on the face. "Easy there, fella," he said. We stepped back as Custer wavered a little. Then Jack slowly led him away.

Doc and Mr. Martin followed. I started to follow when Dad caught my shoulder. "You've done enough," he said.

Tad came over with May Day and handed me his reins. "They pushed you and Tesa to the end. You might still make it if you wanna ride."

I took the reins. I had blood all over my hands and shirt. I looked at Dad and he smiled. "You can if you want."

I looked at JD and he smiled. "I guess I can still try."

I wiped my hands on my already bloody shirt and got on May Day. "Ready boy?" He snorted. "I'll take that as a yes."

I smiled at Dad and JD and trotted over to the paddock.

They were just calling Tesa in and she did great. She came out and started to give me a high five, but she stopped when she saw my hand. I laughed. "I'll take a raincheck," she said. "But good luck."

I rode into the arena. May Day pranced a few steps. "Okay boy, one last time," and we took off. We flew around the barrels.

As we rode out of the arena, I gave a big yahoo as we heard our time, the best we had done. Tesa rode with me over to the trailers. Dad and Mr. Dalton were there talking.

"I hope that isn't your blood," said Mr. Dalton as we rode up.

"No, sir, it's a horse's," I said.

Mom came over all worried. "My gosh what did you do?"

"I'm fine Mom. I helped Cathy's horse." I got off and Dad took the reins from me.

He shook his head. "Darnedest thing, Marcy. He was all tangled in the fence. She was the only one he would let near."

"Let's get you cleaned up," she said. "You were causing quite a stir with your bloody shirt. I had flashes of Uvalde running through my head as I watched you ride."

JD walked up behind me. "You won again, too," he said.

I wheeled around to look at him. "What?"

"You heard me," he said. "You won!"

I started to hug him, but he held up his hands. "Mind if I wait until you change?"

We laughed. "Uh, no." I looked down at myself. "That might be a good idea."

I went into the trailer and Mom followed. I took off my shirt, and Mom handed me a washcloth. I looked in the mirror. I had blood splatters on my face, neck, and arms.

"I look like I've sacrificed something. No wonder people are talking."

I scrubbed at my face and neck. I was just finishing buttoning my clean shirt when there was a knock on the door.

"Who is it?" asked Mom.

"If you're gonna ride poles, you better get going," said Dad through the door.

"Be there in a second." I tucked in my shirt and ran out the door.

Dad held the reins for me and I jumped on May Day. "Just relax and have fun."

"Yes, sir," I said and smiled at him.

I trotted off to the paddock. Tesa was there. "You look much better," she said.

"Why didn't someone tell me I looked like I had sacrificed a chicken or something?"

Tesa laughed. "Hey, nothing gets in the way of rodeo."

"Yeah," I sighed. "Poor Cathy."

"Hope she's okay," said Tesa. "I didn't want her out of the competition that way."

They started the poles and I ran and did well. Tesa was right after me and she took first; I came in third.

"We did good tonight," I said to her as we rode back to the trailers. We passed the boys on the way and wished them luck.

Dad was there to help me unsaddle May Day. He turned to me. "When you were helping Custer and I grabbed your hand, why was it so hot?" I saw movement over his shoulder and JD standing there. He turned away but didn't go far.

I heard Uncle Buck's voice in my head: *"Your father already suspects your gifts. Do not hide it from him. Let him come to you with this knowledge. He needs to discover this for himself to be a true believer in the powers of the spirit."* I smiled at Dad. "It's what I can do."

Dad frowned at me. "What is it exactly?"

"I don't know exactly. I know I can help animals." I bit my lip waiting for him to say something.

"Humph! And the Big C stud the other day?"

"That was different. He seemed to know me. Kinda like Foxy picked me out when she was a puppy."

"She picked you out?" asked Dad. I nodded. "And those things Doc keeps asking me about?"

"Yes, Dad, those things, too."

"How long?"

"I was about six when I first noticed." I took a breath. "This summer has been the most ever."

He just stared at me. Then he hugged me to him. "Why didn't you say anything?"

"I didn't know what to say." Tears ran down my face. "I wasn't even sure it was real."

Then he held me back from him. "Don't cry. You're still my little girl." I nodded. "Who else knows?" he asked.

"JD figured it out." I looked at him over Dad's shoulder.

Dad turned to look at JD and motioned him over. Dad gave him a hug and then he looked back at me. I could see tears in his eyes. He patted me on the shoulder and walked away.

I started to follow, but JD pulled me back. "Give him some time to process it."

He turned me and pulled me to him, stroked my head, and I took a deep breath. I pushed back and smiled up at him.

"Thanks for being here."

"You're very welcome," he said, smiling down at me.

He wiped the tears from my face and kissed me. "Let's go watch your brothers beat the Martins."

We walked over to the stands and sat by his father, Mrs. Martin, Tesa, and Mom.

We watched Grant take first in calf roping. The team roping was next. Matt and Mitch took second overall, and Grant and Tad took third.

JD and Mr. Dalton left to get ready for JD's bull riding. "Good luck," I said to JD.

He winked at me. "I got plenty of that!" He followed his dad down the stands.

We were watching the bronc riders when the boys came and sat with us. "Where's Dad?" asked Grant.

"Haven't seen him since he helped me after pole bending," I said.

Then Dad came and sat by Mom as we watched the rest of the bronc riders. Mom got up to get closer as the bull riding started. She wanted to get some shots of JD.

We watched the first five riders; only two made it to the buzzer. Then it was JD's turn. I touched my necklace and said a silent prayer. We watched as the bull came out of the chute and started to spin. JD hung in and when the bull lurched back the other way, JD stuck right to his back.

Dad yelled "yeah!" when the buzzer sounded and JD jumped off; we stood and clapped.

Dad and the boys went to congratulate JD, but I stayed. "I wanna stay and hex the other riders," I explained.

Tesa and Mrs. Martin laughed and stayed with me and watched the rest ride. Only two others made the buzzer. We made our way down the stands to go see the scores.

Mr. Dalton was there waiting. "JD did it again!" he said. "Wahoo!" He grabbed me up and swung me around.

"Hey, old man," said JD, "Put my girl down!" Mr. Dalton put me down and grabbed up JD in a hug.

"I liked it better when you were squeezing her," JD protested.

We laughed and Mr. Dalton patted us on the backs. "I couldn't be prouder or happier than right now!" he said. "Now let's go get a cold drink."

"I'll go change first," said JD. "I smell like bulls."

"We'll wait for you by the concession stand," said Mr. Dalton. JD winked at me and went to change.

We were enjoying a drink when JD came to join us. He had on his black hat and a blue shirt with a slightly shiny stripe in it that set off his eyes. He smiled at me, and my stomach did a flip. Matt, who had been sitting beside me, got up and let JD have his chair.

"Well son," said Mr. Dalton. "Nice way to wrap up a great run."

"Can't argue with that," said JD, taking my hand.

"How's that horse you helped out earlier?" asked Mr. Dalton.

"I think he's fine."

"What set him off?" asked Mr. Martin.

"The clowns walked behind us and honked their horn," said Tesa. "Spooked Custer, so he reared and Cathy fell off. He took off and we went to catch him."

"He just ran into the fence?" asked Mr. Martin.

"He reared and pawed at it. He got his foot hung and fell over. He kept kicking and got all tangled," I said. "I jumped off to try to quiet him. That's when everyone else showed up."

"So how'd you get that blood all over you?" asked Mr. Dalton.

"When we cut him loose from the wire, it let off the pressure on a cut that spurted all over," said Dad. "Sara just grabbed it before Doc did."

"Looked like you sacrificed something," said Tesa. "Is that the secret to your winning?"

"That's so not funny," I said as they all laughed.

The band started up, and we made our way to the dance floor. JD whirled me around the floor a few times. "You're incredible," he said, smiling down at me.

"I only do what my heart tells me."

"And what is it saying right now?"

"That I'm happy."

He squeezed my hand and smiled at me. "My mother's right, you're special. Very special."

We danced together without stopping for a few more songs and then Dad tapped JD on the shoulder to cut in. "I think I deserve a dance," he said.

"Of course," said JD and nodded at me.

Out on the floor, Dad said, "Big night."

"Yeah," I sighed, "real big." There was silence for a minute then I said, "I should have told you sooner."

"No, no, I suspected but refused to admit it," he said. "So how did JD figure it out?"

"Remember at the Leakey Rodeo, Travis, JD's dog, was hurt. Then Copper got that rope burn," I sighed. "Then when we went on our date and that dog got hit. JD took my hand like you did."

"He put the pieces together," mused Dad. I nodded. "And Candy really did have a crushed skull?"

"I know there was a dent when I picked her up, but there wasn't when Uncle Charlie took her from me," I said.

"And Copper?"

I shrugged. "He did pull something, I felt his pain."

Dad almost stopped dancing. He was shocked. "You feel their pain?"

"Yes, sir. I also feel the drugs that Doc gives them. That's why I got dizzy when Doc gave Custer that shot."

Dad's eyebrows almost disappeared in his hat. "Wow." After a second, he smiled and hugged me to him. Then the song was over. "I think this will take some getting used to."

"I'm not sure I'll ever get used to it," I said as we walked over to the gang. "But let's just keep this to ourselves for now"

"Sure thing," he said and hugged me again.

JD grabbed me before Jared could ask me to dance. "So?" asked JD when we were a few feet away.

"So he's getting it," I said, smiling at JD.

"See, you have nothing to worry about," said JD.

"I have one thing to worry about," I said mischievously.

"What's that?"

"When I'm gonna get my next kiss."

JD threw his head back and laughed. "I thought my sisters were manipulative." When the song ended, Matt claimed me for a dance and JD danced with Celeste.

"So you ready to let him go tomorrow?" asked Matt.

"I've no choice. I have no claim on him."

"He won't be the same."

"Neither will I." I sighed. Matt smiled at me and squeezed my hand.

Then I danced with Jared. "Finally!" he said. "I just wanted to say congratulations."

"Well, thank you," I said.

"Ya know, you really don't have to sacrifice a chicken before you race," he laughed and I slapped his chest.

"Careful, I might work my way up to young men!" He laughed so hard I thought he might stumble. He kept laughing so I started walking off, but he pulled me back and composed himself.

"I'm sorry," he said. "I just can't picture you hurting anything."

"Ask my brothers and they'll tell you different."

Jared laughed again as we finished the song. JD put his arm around me as I walked back to him.

"Come on, your parents, the Martins, and my dad have left. I wanna spend some more time with you, alone."

We walked out along the concession area and over by the fence through some trees. He turned to me and pulled me to him. "You're so very beautiful," he said. He cupped my face in his hands and kissed me lightly. "I know you're young, Sara, but I love you." I looked up at him speechless. "You probably don't know what love is, but I had to tell you how I felt."

"I know what love is," I said. "I feel it each time I heal something. Love is what gives me the power to heal." I took a breath. "Why do you think you're the only human it has worked on?"

"Why?" he asked, pulling me closer to him.

"Because I love you and you love me."

He put his arms around me and kissed me. The warmth flared up inside me, and I let it spread through me knowing JD could handle it.

Last Date

I was standing on a cliff with the wind blowing in my hair. There were dark clouds off to the west that blocked the sun. The lightning struck, and JD was standing behind me pointing over my shoulder. I looked to the east and saw a dark void, but I wasn't afraid. I felt the warmth in my chest and tingles ran down my arms.

The lightning flashed again and the thunder boomed. A light came from the east and it changed into a horse. Wakiza stopped in front of us, JD lifted me to his back, and then he jumped on behind me. We turned and ran into the void.

I woke suddenly as Foxy whined at me. I patted her head and looked around. It was just getting light outside. I smiled as I remembered last night. JD had told me he loved me. My heart sang.

We hadn't gone back into the dance after we spoke. It wasn't long until the dance was over anyway. We spent the rest of the time on the back of his truck. We actually talked about what we thought the next year would hold in store.

I heard someone getting up and sat up. I saw Tad walking out of his room. I whistled softly. He snapped around and came over to my room.

"How long you been up?" he asked.

"Not long," I said. "How'd you sleep?"

"Good." He flopped on my bed. "So think you're off the bad list after helping with the Coulter horse?"

"Maybe," I said. "Did you get a chance to talk to Trish?"

Tad dropped his head to his chest. "Yeah, I did."

"And?"

"She said she couldn't forgive me yet. I told her I didn't blame her."

"Give her time. She'll come around."

We heard Grant getting up. I whistled and he came in.

"Hey, is this a party?"

"Yeah, a sunrise party," I said.

Grant looked at me. "Did you sleep at all last night?"

"Yeah why?" I asked.

"Because I thought you might dream walk all night," said Grant.

"What did JD do to you?" asked Tad.

"Nothing, why?"

"Yeah, nothing," snorted Tad. "I'll bet he told you something, and your heart went pitter-patter."

"So what if he did?"

"Oh man!" said Grant.

"What?" I asked.

"Yeah, she's gone," said Tad. He got up off my bed. "We better prepare for the worst this next week."

Grant got up, too, shaking his head. "I'll be here if you need me."

"What's going on?" I asked.

"It's obvious," said Tad. "You're in love with him, and he's gonna break your heart when he leaves."

"I don't think so."

"Well, let me know how you feel next week," said Tad as he and Grant left.

I patted Foxy. "Are they a little weird or is it just me?"

Foxy whined and I ruffled her fur.

"It's not gonna be like that." She looked at me. "Love isn't something you can just turn off."

She gave me a "raawwll."

"Well, okay, we'll see how it goes, but I'm not gonna cry." She yipped and I laughed.

I got up and dressed. I went into the kitchen and started breakfast. The bacon was almost done, biscuits were in the oven, and I was ready to start frying eggs when the boys came back in.

"All right, breakfast," said Tad. "I'm starved."

I laughed. "Have a seat, brother dear, and I'll get you some eggs."

He and Grant sat down. I put eggs in front of each of them when Mom and Dad came in. "What can I get you?" I asked.

"Why are ya'll up so early on a Sunday?" asked Mom.

"Because we couldn't sleep," said Tad.

Dad laughed and sat down. "I'm gonna enjoy the service. Marcy, sit down and let your daughter fix you some eggs."

I put fried eggs in front of Mom and Dad and they dug in. I made myself some and sat down, too.

We were eating when we heard Joey start barking.

"Kinda early for company," said Dad. He walked out front to see who it was.

We listened but couldn't tell who it was. Dad must have met them at the gate. Grant got up to look.

"It's Mr. Coulter!" he said.

Mom got up and went out. They came back inside, and Mom called us to come to the front room. Mr. Coulter was there, holding his hat.

"There's who I wanted to thank," he said and walked over to me. "I'm so grateful for what you did for Custer last night. I wanted to come by and thank you personally." He looked nervous.

"Won't you sit down, Mr. Coulter?" asked Mom, offering him a seat. "Can I get you something to drink?"

"No, thank you, Mrs. Stillsen, I'm fine. I know it's early, but I wanted to come by first thing and thank you and Sara especially for what ya'll did last night," he said.

"How's Cathy?" I asked.

"She's fine, just a bruise."

"Oh that's good," said Mom.

"And Custer's alright?" I asked.

"He's fine. Doc Henderson says he's gonna be fit in no time. I also understand that you were the one to help calm Midnight at the show and get him in the trailer."

"Yes, sir," I said.

"You have a way with horses it seems," he said. "That's why I think this will show my gratitude." He pulled an envelope out of his pocket and handed it to me.

I took it and opened it. It was a breeder's agreement. It gave me the right to one of Midnight's offspring.

"Mr. Coulter, I can't accept this. It's too much." I tried to hand the papers back to him.

"I won't hear anything of the sort. You saved my baby's horse and helped my best stud."

"I'd have done that for anyone," I said. "I don't need any reward."

"Let me see that," said Dad, taking the papers from me. He read them quickly and looked up at Mr. Coulter. "I agree with Sara that this is too much. We cannot possibly accept this for being a good neighbor." He held out the papers to Mr. Coulter.

Mr. Coulter dropped his head and took the papers. "Would you at least let me replace the shirt you ruined last night?" he asked, looking at me.

"I guess that would be okay."

Mr. Coulter smiled, reached into his pocket, pulled out some bills, and pressed them into my hand. "You go buy yourself something nice." He squeezed my hand and I smiled at him.

"Thank you," I said.

"Oh no, missy, thank you!" He turned for the door. "Thank you all for your help." We watched as he walked down to the gate and got in his truck and drove off.

I looked down at my hand. I unfolded the bills. There were 2 hundred dollar bills. "Whoa," said Tad.

Mom came over. "Oh my."

"Well, guess you can buy a couple of new shirts with that," said Dad.

I nodded my head. I went back and sat at the kitchen table.

"What's with you?" asked Grant. "You in shock?"

"I guess so," I said. "I can't believe he was gonna give me one of Midnight's foals."

"What?" said Tad, Grant, and Mom at the same time.

"Yeah, that's what the papers said," said Dad.

"Do you know how much a foal from Midnight would be worth?" asked Tad.

"A lot!" said Grant.

We all laughed. "Well, at least I don't have an enemy anymore," I said.

We finished breakfast and I went down to the barn to see the horses. I was feeling uneasy and didn't know why. I was in Andrea's stall brushing her when Dad came by. He watched for a few minutes, not saying anything.

"Are you okay?"

"Yeah why?" I said looking up at him.

"You've brushed Andrea twice over."

"Oh," I stopped and stepped back from her. "I guess I have."

"So what's bothering you?"

I shrugged. "I'm just shocked at Mr. Coulter's thank you."

"It was unexpected." We were silent for a minute. "Can you heal more than animals?"

"You mean humans? No, it doesn't seem to work on them," I said. "When I've tried, nothing happens."

I thought to myself that JD didn't count because I didn't try to heal his shoulder.

"How does it feel when you help an animal?"

"I get this really warm feeling in my chest. It spreads down my arms into my hands."

"But you feel their pain?" asked Dad with a concerned look.

"When I touch them I can feel what they feel and where it hurts. I can handle it, at least so far." I looked down then back up at him. "The warmth replaces the pain."

"So you don't know exactly what's wrong, but you can help them?"

"Yeah, that's pretty much it."

He looked at me. "Has it ever not worked?"

"Not worked, as in the animal died? No, not yet."

Dad nodded. We were silent for a minute. "So you're going out with JD tonight right?" I smiled at the change of subject because he was still uncomfortable with all this.

"Yes, sir."

"He's a great guy. I like his father a lot, too. Not so sure about the girls, but the rest are good."

"The girls are harmless," I said. "Tad was just attracted to pretty faces." Dad laughed and we walked out of the barn and back to the house.

I was lying on my bed, trying to read a book, when the phone rang. I jumped up and ran down the hall to answer.

"Hello?"

"Hello sunshine," said JD. I think my feet floated off the floor at the sound of his voice.

"Howdy cowboy," I said.

"I never told you what time I'd pick you up."

"Oh, I hadn't thought about it," I said. "Too much going on."

"Yeah, been a crazy few days," he said. "Would it be okay if I came to get you around four?"

"I don't have a problem with that."

"Good, I'll see you at four then."

"I'll be ready."

"See ya in a little while."

"Bye."

I looked at the clock; it was almost two. I had some time before I needed to get ready.

I wandered back into my room, looked at the book I was reading, and decided I'd give JD my copy of Sherlock Holmes stories. I had recommended it to him on our first date. I was flipping through the pages and had an idea of putting a couple of pictures of me in between them. I walked down the hall into Mom's sewing room to print some pictures.

I was sitting at the computer flipping through pictures when Mom came in. "Whatcha doing?" she asked.

"I thought I'd print a couple of pictures of me to give JD."

"I have some favorites I'd suggest," she said. I let her take over the mouse, and she pulled up one that I hadn't seen yet. I was in my sequined suit in front of our house. I was smiling but hadn't put my hair in a bun yet, and it was flying out behind me as I practiced twirling.

"I think JD would like this one," said Mom.

"I think he would, too," I chuckled. "He kept talking about seeing me in sequins."

"Okay, what size?" she asked.

"Uh, three by five," I said. "What else did you have in mind?"

She showed me one where I was sitting on May Day, smiling down at something. I was leaning forward slightly, and the sun was shining through my hair from behind so it looked as if I was glowing. "This one," said Mom. "If we crop it like this and zoom in a little, see?"

"Wow, that's great," I said. "You really should sell pictures. You take great ones, and you know how to make them look even better. I'm not just being polite."

"I've been thinking about it," she said. I grabbed the pictures that printed out.

"Well, think harder. Thanks for the pictures, Mom."

Back in my bedroom, I put the pictures in the book and laid it on my dresser. I turned to figure out what to wear and had settled on a dark blue shirt when Tad wandered in.

"You sure you wanna wear that one?" he asked.

I turned, holding it. "Why, what's wrong with it?"

"Well, not much, but you have a few that look better on you," he said. "Ya know, that show off your eyes and tan."

"I remember last time you wanted me to wear one of your old flannel shirts," I said laughing.

"Well, that was before," he walked over to my closet. "Now you need to give him a memory he won't soon forget." He held up a silky green shirt.

"You don't think that's too dressy?" I asked. "We're only going to eat and the movie."

"I think it's great," said Tad. "A little flash goes along way."

"Thanks," I took the shirt from him. "Now if you'll excuse me, I need to shower." I hung the shirt on the back of my door and walked across the hall to the bathroom.

Later I was sitting at my dresser drying my hair when there was a knock at my door. "Come in," I yelled over my hair dryer.

Mom came in and sat on my bed. "Need any help?"

"I think I got it," I said, flipping my hair back and looking at her in the mirror.

"Nice choice," she said, pointing at my shirt.

I turned off the dryer and looked at her while I brushed my hair. "Tad picked it out."

"He did?" asked Mom in mild shock.

"Yeah, I know." I chuckled. "Big difference from the flannel one he wanted me to wear the first time."

I picked up the curling iron and Mom took it from me. "Let me," she said. She curled my hair so it fell in waves down my back. "Mrs. Dalton may be right, you should be a model."

"I think I'll just stick with being a teenager. I don't wanna be paraded around."

Mom laughed. "You can model just for me then."

"I can do that," I said.

We heard Joey barking. "That must be JD," said Mom. "I'll go greet him while you finish up."

"Okay, but no pictures!"

"Aww not even one?"

"Not even one," I pointed my finger at her. "Promise!"

"Oh, alright I promise!" she play-pouted as she left.

I looked around for my black slip-ons but only found one. I was looking under the bed when Grant came in.

"You trying to hide?" he asked.

"Nope, just looking for my shoe. Got it." I stood up.

"Wow, you look great!" he said.

"Thanks." I brushed the front of my pants and fluffed my hair a little. I looked at Grant in the mirror. "You still here?"

"Oh yeah, I'm supposed to tell you JD's here."

I smiled picked up the book for JD and walked toward Grant. I patted him on the arm as I walked by. "Come on. You can give him 'the all-seeing eye' as we leave."

He followed me down the hall. I walked into the living room where JD was sitting on the couch. He looked up; I could see his eyes widen slightly and a slow smile spread across his face. He stood up and his blue eyes twinkled. I felt my breath catch in my throat, and my heart skipped a beat.

"Where are you two off to tonight?" asked Dad, getting up from his chair beside me. He put his arm around me, and I tore my eyes from JD to look up at him.

"We're going to dinner and then a movie in Uvalde," said JD. "I'll have her home by eleven."

"Good enough," said Dad. He looked at Mom and she smiled. "JD if I don't see you again before you leave, have a safe trip and give your family my best. We've enjoyed having you around this summer."

"Thank you, sir," said JD. "I'll be sure to pass along the message." He turned to me. "You ready?"

"I am," I said and walked over to him and took his hand.

Grant and Tad were there. They shook JD's hand as we walked out the door. We were almost at the gate when Foxy bounded up. "Hey girl." I rubbed her head. "Wait here for me."

She gave a "rawwll," looked at JD, then bounded off.

JD snickered. "She's something else."

"I think so, too," I said, smiling at him. JD led me to the passenger side of his truck and opened the door. I smiled and got in. As he went around to the other side, I scooted over so I'd be beside him. He got in and we were off.

"So you gonna tell me what the book is for or do I have to guess?" he asked.

"It's something I wanted to give you," I said. I held it up so he could see the title.

"Sherlock Holmes," he said and chuckled. "I'll have to give it a try."

"There's a surprise in here, too," I said. "I'll wait until we stop to show you."

JD smiled. "Why, will it make me crash?"

"Maybe," I teased. "Maybe not."

JD laughed and put his arm around me. "I got a little something for you, too."

"Is it warm with blue eyes?"

"You try me so." He hugged me to him. We crossed the river and he stopped, putting the truck in park. "Now show me this surprise."

I held up the book and he took it. "Just flip through the pages," I said. He did and came to the first picture of me in my twirling outfit. He smiled. "This is a really good shot, almost as good as a dream."

"Just almost?"

"Dreams are in moving pictures," he said. "Thank you."

"There's more," I said.

He flipped through the book again and came to the other picture. He held it up. "Whoa, this is like looking at an angel. Like my very own angel."

He turned and kissed me. My heart fluttered. He started to pull back, but I held him to me. After the warmth started to flow, I let him go. He held my hand to his face and smiled. Then he let my hand go and reached across me to open the glove compartment.

He pulled out a CD and handed it to me, "Kenny Chesney's Greatest Hits."

"Now you can listen to our song whenever you want."

"Thank you," I said and kissed him.

He pulled back and took a breath. "We keep kissing, and we won't make it to town. And don't even ask me to skip going into town because I couldn't look your dad in the eye if I did."

I laughed and nodded. "I know."

We drove on down the road. "So anything exciting happen while we were apart?" he asked.

"Mr. Coulter came by this morning."

"He did? What for?"
"He wanted to say thank you for helping Custer."
"Wow! That was unexpected, wasn't it?"
"Very!" I said. "But not nearly as unexpected as the thank you he tried to give me."
"What was that?"
"One of Midnight Fury's foals."
"Whoa, that's, well, that's worth lots I imagine," said JD. "So you gonna take one?"
"No, it was too much. Besides, I'd have done it for anyone."
JD smiled and patted me on the leg. "Yeah, you would."
"He did offer to replace the shirt I ruined."
"That's nice. So did you accept?"
"I did. I thought it would be a little bit, but he pressed some bills into my hand and I didn't look at them until after he left. He gave me two hundred dollars."
"Wow," said JD. "That's some thank you."
"Yeah, but I feel kinda bad taking it," I said, looking down.
"Why?"
"Because the shirt was only worth twenty."
"So do something good with the rest."
"Like what?"
"I don't know, donate it to charity or something."
"Hmm, that's an idea." I smiled. "You're full of good ideas."
He smiled at me. "Why thank you, ma'am."

We pulled onto the highway and before we knew it, we were in town. JD drove to the movie theatre.
"Why are we here so early?" I asked.
"Thought we would catch an early movie then eat dinner," he said. "I'd like to linger over dinner. Any objections?"
"No, sir," I said with a smile. "As long as I'm with you, I'm happy."
JD smiled but something in his eyes was a little off. "What is it?" I asked.
"We can talk about it later," he said, helping me out of the truck. "I don't wanna spoil our time together."
I put my hands on his chest and looked up at him. "I get the feeling it's about you going back to Houston tomorrow."

He nodded. "Yeah," he sighed. "But let's not think about that right now okay?"

I rolled up on my toes and kissed him lightly. "We'll always have this summer," I said, smiling up at him.

He hugged me to him. "You're the best thing that has ever happened to me." He released me and smiled. "Now, let's go sit in the dark and hold hands for a while." I nodded and he took my hand.

We got our tickets. He bought us a soda, and we found seats toward the back of the theater. There were only a few other people there, so we were almost alone.

The movie started and JD took my hand. It was a suspense thriller. When I jumped at the scary parts, JD would chuckle a little and squeeze my hand. There was the typical damsel in distress, and the hero rescued her. Then they walked away from the wreckage hand in hand down a beach and it was over.

"Not bad," said JD. "But he should have carried her away in the end."

"After all that jumping and running, you think he had the energy to carry her?" I asked.

He laughed. "Always the logical one, aren't you?"

"What fun is it if the hero gets worn out before they get to be alone?"

"Ah, you have a point there. I like your ending better."

"I hope you don't mind the same restaurant again," he said as we drove up to Luigi's.

"Not at all," I said. "I never get tired of Italian food, or just food in general."

"Where do you put all that food you eat?"

"I guess I just burn it off quickly. I better enjoy it while I can because someday I might get fat," I said, sliding out of the truck.

"No way, I wouldn't let you." He pulled me into his arms.

"You gonna chase me around the rest of my life?" I asked, looking up at him and laughing.

"I could," he said and kissed me. My knees went weak as the warmth simmered in my core. I knew I was really going to miss this when he was gone.

He raised his head. "Let's go eat." I smiled and nodded.

He took my hand and we walked into the restaurant. They sat us at a booth in the back. JD sat next to me like last time. The waitress handed us menus and told us about the specials. She took our drink order and left.

"What are you gonna have?" I asked.

"I think I'll try that special with the bowtie pasta," he said. "What would you like?"

"More kisses." I said smiling at him, "but I'll start with the baked ziti."

He gave me a smile that took my breath away. His eyes twinkled, and I started leaning toward him when the waitress showed up with our drinks. JD chuckled and cleared his throat. He gave our order to the waitress and she left again.

"Now, where were we?" he asked, turning his gaze on me and leaning in. He kissed me very softly, and I sighed as he pulled back.

I opened my eyes and he was smiling at me. "That's intoxicating," he said.

I smiled slowly. "You're intoxicating."

"Better than on your birthday?" he asked.

"By far," I said. "I can get up and walk now, or at least I think I can."

He laughed. "Yeah, that was a good night. I got to carry you then."

"Ah, but you didn't get to come with me for real like in your movie ending."

"What do you mean for real?"

"Well, you were with me in my dreams then, but now you're really here."

The waitress brought our salads over. "So tell me where the saying 'our heart is our first teacher' comes from." he said.

"Where did you hear that?"

"From my dad. He said you told him that when you two were talking about breaking my heart."

"It's something Uncle Buck told me. It's one of the clues that helped me understand the source of my gift." I looked into his blue eyes.

JD nodded and looked down at his salad. I took a bite of mine and watched him out of the corner of my eye. I knew he was thinking about something, but I thought it best to let him ask the questions right now.

"I feel like the luckiest guy alive right now," said JD. He turned and smiled at me, a real smile that reached his eyes.

I smiled back at him in relief. "I'm the lucky one here."

"How do you figure?"

"I needed a teacher and I got you."

He laughed. "You make me feel so good in so many ways. What am I going to do without you?"

"It's not like we're never going to see each other again. You'll get along just fine," I said, trying to keep things light.

"See, you always look at the bright side of things. Are you sure you're only fifteen?"

"I feel like I've grown way beyond that this summer." I looked at him. "And you've helped me do that."

He smiled and turned back to his salad. We ate in silence for a moment. Then JD asked, "How much more do you think you need to learn?"

"I'm learning more and more every day. I don't think it will ever end, but I somehow think I've learned the hardest part," I said, smiling at him.

The waitress came with our main dishes, set them down, and disappeared. "What do you think was the hardest?"

"Learning the source wasn't me. It flows through me."

"Why was that hard?"

"I thought it came from within me, but I'm led by it, not the other way around." I looked at JD. "Do you believe in fate?"

"You mean like things happening for a reason?"

"Yeah, like that."

"Isn't that just coincidence?"

"I don't believe in coincidence anymore. I think things happen for a reason. Like being in the right place at the right time." I took a bite and chewed while looking at JD to see what he would say.

He looked at me. "You think you and I met for a reason?"

"Yes, I do."

"Why?"

"Because I needed a teacher, one who could earn the respect of my family and stand up to my overprotective brothers. You needed to be reminded that the challenge is better than the thrill. Besides, now you know there's more to life than just chasing girls."

JD laughed. "You're amazing and you're right. There's more to life than chasing girls." He looked at me. "Catching them is much better."

We laughed and ate. "Let's go park by the river so we can be alone," said JD. I nodded, he paid the bill, and we left.

We listened to the radio on the way. We turned off onto the gravel road to my house. Just before the river, we turned and drove to the rise that overlooked the river and stopped.

JD helped me out. We walked around to the back, and he let down the tailgate. I sat on the tailgate, and he stood in front of me. I wrapped my arms around his neck, and he put his hands on my hips.

He kissed me softly. "Know what my instinct is telling me?" he asked.

"No."

"To kiss you all I can." He kissed me again and I pulled him close. The warmth in me surged, JD moaned, and pulled me closer to him. "Whoa. That's intense." He leaned his forehead against mine.

"Sorry, I can't help myself," I said breathlessly.

"Don't ever apologize for something that feels right."

I smiled, remembering when I had said the same thing to him. Then he kissed me again. Tingles ran up my spine and down my arms. JD took my hand and put it on his chest. I felt his heart pounding in his chest and mine skipped a few beats. I looked into his eyes.

"Oh this is too much," he said, moving around to sit beside me. He took my hand and laced his fingers with mine. "Sara, when I said I love you, I meant it. I don't know how I'll walk away from you."

I got up and moved around in front of JD. I put my hands on his legs and looked up at him. I took a deep breath and smiled.

"JD, one thing I know about love is that it doesn't divide. It multiplies and grows. It grows in me every time I heal an animal; every time I kiss you, it grows. When we kiss, the warmth you feel from me is my love for you. You opened my heart and showed me the way. I'll always have a part of you with me, no matter where I go or what I do."

I took a deep breath. "Houston isn't that far away, but it's far enough that I can't keep any ties on you. I have no right to." I could see he was about to object. I put my fingers on his lips. "I've learned so much from you this summer, and I'm grateful for that."

He took my hand. "It sounds like you're brushing me off." He had a pained look on his face.

I shook my head. "I'm just letting you know that I've no ties on you. It's your senior year. You're too vibrant and full of life not to have fun. You can have your pick of girls in Houston. You can't disappoint them." I smiled weakly at him.

He asked, "What about you?"

"You've seen what my choices are here." We laughed a little.

"I'll call and write you," he said.

"I know you will. Please don't be sad. I knew this day would come, but it isn't an ending. I'm happy for the experience and things you've helped me with. You've been there for me every time I needed you." I pointed to my heart. "You'll be here for me every day."

JD wrapped his hand around my hand that was on my chest. He looked me in the eye and smiled. "I don't think there's any room in my heart for sadness when I'm with you or thinking of you when I'm not."

He pulled me to him. I wrapped my arms around him and we kissed. The warmth within me bloomed and flooded my whole body. Every care in the world fled, and I was only with JD.

I sighed as JD released me. I turned in his arms to lean my back against him. The moon gleamed on the river below. We listened to it flowing and the crickets chirping for minute. He kissed my neck and hugged me to him. "I love you," he whispered in my ear. "Always remember that."

He hugged me again then pushed me forward and got up off the tailgate. He turned me to him and kissed me lightly. "We better go; it's almost eleven."

I nodded and we walked back to the cab of the truck and got in. Neither of us spoke as we drove up to the house.

"Don't forget your CD," he said as we got out. I grabbed it off the dash. Foxy was there by the gate. She came over to JD, jumped up on him, and gave him a "rrrraawl."

JD rubbed her neck. "I'll be back. I'm not going far." Foxy got down and bounded off.

JD scooped me up in his arms, and I laughed as he carried me down the walk to the front door. When we got to the porch, he set me down and I turned to face him. "See this is a much better ending." We laughed. "I never got your address," he said.

"I wrote it on the last page of the book I gave you," I said, smiling up at him.

He smiled at me. "Always thinking ahead." He took a deep breath. "I guess this is it but only for a while. I'll come back when I can."

"I'll be here with all these animals to keep me company. I've had a great summer, and I hope to have many more great days." I put JD's hand on my chest. "You're here with me always, where the warmth of my love comes from. Remember that when you think of me."

He kissed me and hugged me to him. He whispered in my ear. "I do and will always love you." He backed away from me. I watched him get into his truck and drive off. I watched as the taillights dropped below the rise. I heard the bump gate before I turned to go into the house.

When I walked in the front door, Mom and Dad were in their chairs reading. They looked up and I smiled at them.

"Well, you look chipper," said Mom.

"It's been a great summer," I said and plopped down on the couch twirling the CD JD gave me.

"And you said she'd be crying," said Dad to Mom.

"I did not!" said Mom. "You were the one all worried about that."

"I'm not gonna cry," I said. "He didn't break my heart. He didn't die; he's only gonna be a few hundred miles away."

"Well, good for you," said Mom. "What's that you have there?"

"JD gave me a CD," I said. "I think I'll go listen to it now." I got up, said good night, and bounced down the hall to my room.

I passed Tad's room and he looked up from his reading. "Hey!" he said.

I poked my head in and smiled. "What?"

"You're smiling!"

"You sound surprised."

"I am. I thought you'd be sad."

"Nope, no sadness. Just happy to be alive."

"What did you do?"

"What do you mean?"

"Why are you so happy? He left!"

"He didn't die. It's not like he'll never come back. He's only going a few hundred miles away," I said.

"That's a good way to put it."

"Yeah, so, night!"

"Night" he said and I bounced to my room.

Grant stopped by as I was shutting the door. "Can I come in?" he asked.

"Sure, what's up?"

He looked at me closely. "You're okay?"

"I'm fine." I laughed. "Like I told Tad, he didn't die. It's not like he'll never come back. He's only going a few hundred miles away."

Grant laughed and shook his head. "Okay, I'll leave you alone."

"No, you won't," I said. "You'll be here for me no matter what."

"You're right. I will." He winked at me. "Night!" and he started out

the door.
"Grant!" I said. He turned back. "Yeah?"
"Thanks!"
"Don't mention it," he said and closed the door.

Acknowledgments

I would like to give a big thanks to Robyn Larkin who actually read and gave me feedback on this book. You didn't even know me but you gave me great advice and insight.

Thanks to my lunch group who encouraged and listened to my neurotic venting and are continually amazed by my childhood adventures as I am of yours.

A very heartfelt thanks to Kerry Neuberger, my editor, who helped make this a much better story and enjoyable read than it was. Thank you for your tireless efforts and encouragement. You must be a great teacher because I have learned so much from you.

And finally to my family, thank you for your patience when I disappeared into my world and ignored you. I hope this was worth it.

About the Author

Carol Stucki was raised on horseback in southwest Texas along the Nueces River. Carol graduated from Angelo State University, in Texas, with a degree in Computer Science. She has lived in Texas, New Mexico, Florida, Nevada, and now resides with her family in Utah.

Although, she has written books on auditing, computers, and other technical topics, she has a fondness for fantasy and science fiction. An avid reader, she decided to try her hand at writing something for fun and thus, the series Sara's Gift was born. The background and characters in the book are based on some of the experiences Carol had growing up in Nueces Canyon.